The
Poplar Creek
Murders

CHARLES CONNOR
&
BEVERLY CONNOR

Copyright

Published By QBFOX

Quick Brown Fox

Books by the Authors

Charles Connor
The Poplar Creek Murders
Murder In Macon

Beverly Connor
The Poplar Creek Murders
Murder in Macon
Dead Hunt: Gold Edition
One Grave Less
The Night Killer
Dust to Dust
Scattered Graves
Dead Hunt
Dead Past
Dead Secret
Dead Guilty
One Grave Too Many
Airtight Case
Skeleton Crew
Dressed to Die
Questionable Remains
A Rumor of Bones

Table of Contents

Chapter 1
The Sweet Smell of Death

Small red and green lights on the front of the computer flashed urgently and gentle chirping sounds came from within. A greeting from halfway around the globe flowed onto the screen, awaiting a response, but the lifeless fingers never lifted from the keyboard.

THE CRIME RATE in Bartram County, Tennessee was so low it didn't even appear on the charts. It was a quiet little county that still contained healthy remnants of what America used to be. Perched on the edge of yesterday, looking toward tomorrow, some people still didn't lock their doors at night.

Deputy coroner Lee Turner lived in the lovely old cottage she inherited from her grandmother on a quiet street in the little county seat town of Carters Mill just five minutes from her office. All-in-all, a charming place to be and a lifestyle that suited her well. But on this particular September morning Lee Turner awoke before daylight in a state of near panic.

It had been building for two weeks. It was the phone call from Chicago that set it off. She had been back in Carters Mill almost a year. She had gone against the wishes of her father and the advice of friends and had given up a successful university career to come back to the little town of her childhood. Her father's words still rang in her ears.

"Jesus, Lee, the coroner's office? Do you have no pride?" he had said. "You're throwing away your career to move to Carters Mill, Tennessee and work in the coroner's office? I'm very disappointed.

1

"It's an honorable profession, Dad. They need me in Carters Mill. Besides, I'll be teaching part-time at the university."

"A part-time scholar and a part-time coroner, not a full-time anything. This is a giant step backward. I had hoped for better things for you, Lee. You've grown beyond Carters Mill. It's not the same town you remember as a little girl, and you're not that little girl anymore. I think you'll find you can't go back. You'll stagnate. You'll die of boredom in a week."

She hadn't died of boredom. She hadn't been bored at all. It wasn't easy at times. Old Mr. Terry the county coroner could be a pain to work for. And her part-time faculty status kept her out of the mainstream of academic life on campus. The transition from university life to small town life had not been easy and she often questioned whether she had made the right decision. Now here she was facing a deadline on the Chicago job offer, having to decide all over again whether to stay or go.

After tossing and turning the better part of two hours, Lee got out of bed about 5:30 A.M. Her head was pounding with a headache. She slid open the glass door to the patio and stepped onto the deck outside her bedroom. The stars were still shining. There was a whippoorwill calling from the ridge, and another answered in the distance. The buzzing of katydids and the rhythmic song of tree frogs filled the night around her house. She stood breathing in the fresh pre-dawn air, hoping it would clear her head of the pain and of her lingering anxieties.

But Mother Nature wasn't going to ease her pain this morning. So with a cup of hot coffee, two aspirin and a warm Pop Tart, she wrapped herself in a blanket and settled onto a lounge chair on the deck with this week's edition of the county newspaper, the *Bartram County Echo*, waiting for the sun to come up.

The front page news was the continuing story over the proposed regional landfill facing stiff opposition from the residents of Bartram County. But nothing earth shattering had occurred in the county this week, or this year. That in itself was reassuring. She closed her eyes, waiting for the aspirin to take effect.

When she opened her eyes again the sun was shining in her face and the phone was ringing. Her head was still aching. She half stumbled back to her bedroom telephone. The clock on the bedside table said it was 8:45. Her Caller ID showed the number of the radio dispatch desk at the Bartram County Sheriff's Department.

"Lee, honey, I'm sorry to bother you on the weekend." Margy's voice was kind but business-like as usual. "Mr. Terry asked me to call you."

"No problem, Margy. What's going on?" Lee took the aspirin bottle from her nightstand and shook out two more tablets into her hand.

"We just got a call from a woman in Los Verdes, New Mexico who is real concerned that something may have happened to her elderly husband here in Bartram County. His name is Dr. Alexander Hamrick. He lives on Paradise Road. She says she has tried for three days and nights to get in touch with him but can't get him on the phone and she's beside herself with worry. She asked if someone could check on him."

Couldn't they do without her just this one time, she thought to herself. She really didn't feel like doing a home check, unless there was no one else. She made her way back to the patio. "Does Dr. Hamrick live alone?"

"Yes, he does. Mrs. Hamrick says he retired from the CMU faculty several years ago and lives alone. She says there are no other relatives in the area, no close neighbors that she knows, and she doesn't know anyone here to call."

"When's the last time anyone heard from him?" Lee tossed the two aspirin to the back of her tongue and took a drink of the cold coffee. It tasted awful but maybe the combination of caffeine and aspirin would stop the headache.

"Mrs. Hamrick said she talked with her husband about a week ago and Dr. Hamrick was supposed to call back the next day but didn't. She said he had not been feeling well, and she's concerned that he may be ill or in need of help. I'm sorry about this, Lee. The sheriff and deputies are at a big truck wreck out on Highway 95 at the University farms near the Roane County line, and they've got all the paperwork to do on it when they get back to the office. Mr. Terry is over at the courthouse but he says he's tied up with something else and he asked if you might have a chance to go to Dr. Hamrick's house and make sure everything is all right."

Lee was back at her nightstand now, sitting on the edge of her bed–the bed that she really wanted to crawl back into–but her conscience and sense of responsibility won out once again. Someone might really be in need of help.

"Sure, I'll do it. What's the address?"

"The house is 1201 Paradise Road. Do you know where Paradise Road is?"

Lee knew most of the communities in the county and many of the houses by the names of the families who lived in them when she was a girl growing up in Carters Mill. But then again, she had been away for some years. "I don't recognize the address. Do you know where it is exactly?"

"I don't know for sure. The address is not pulling up a GPS location on my computer maps. That happens sometimes when you get out on some of the backroads in the county. I don't have any directions. Mrs. Hamrick says it's a famous old house and it's on a dirt road somewhere near Poplar Creek. And that's about all she could tell me."

"Shouldn't be too hard to find," Lee said. "I'll check it out and get back to you."

"Mr. Terry said take Buddy Ruff along with you, you know, just in case."

"I understand. Have you seen Buddy this morning?"

"No, he hasn't been in today. This time of morning I imagine you might find him at Helen's Diner."

Lee opened her phone book and found the listing for Hamrick, Dr. Alexander on Paradise Road. She dialed and waited as the phone rang but there was no answer. Looks like there is no way around it, she thought to herself. She would have to drive out to Paradise Road. At least the headache was a little better.

She made a quick pass through the bathroom to make herself presentable, changed into the khaki pants and shirt and brown work shoes that had become her unofficial uniform, and headed out the door. Unsure what she might find at the Hamrick house, she drove by her office to pick up her forensics bag and her white lab coat, then set off toward the diner in search of Buddy Ruff.

As she pulled her Land Cruiser to a stop in the diner parking lot, she could see Buddy through the window, sitting at the counter stirring a cup of coffee and flirting with owner Helen Simmons who was standing behind the counter holding a pot of coffee. They were both laughing, probably at one of Buddy's humorous stories or jokes. Buddy saw the Land Cruiser pull up outside. Lee got out and held up her coroner's bag. Buddy said a few words to Helen who smiled and filled two Styrofoam cups with coffee. He slid off the stool and made his way toward the door of the restaurant.

Buddy Ruff had turned out to be a rough cut jewel for Lee. She had been skeptical and a little angry when Mr. Terry assigned Buddy as her "assistant," as Mr. Terry called him. Buddy was a mixture of lay-about, mountain cowboy, and good ole boy. Everybody knew him and he knew just about everybody within driving distance of Carters Mill. He was full of good humor and laughter that often manifested itself in practical jokes. He was a little man, no more than five-seven, quick on his feet, and of a medium muscular build that Lee had heard referred to on more than one occasion as "wiry," which was him—lean, strong and tough—along with a lot of sparkle. He had dark curly hair just beginning to grey that he kept cut short, and a perpetual grin that had produced permanent laugh lines in the corners of his blue eyes. From the stories Lee heard, a number of women in the area had at one time or another found him to be attractive and charming. For the past year or more, Helen Simmons had been the appreciative recipient of his attentions.

Lee discovered within the first week of their association that Buddy had virtues of intellect and character that were easy to miss behind his rustic easygoing manner. Whatever Mr. Terry's intention, Lee and Buddy, as it turned out, made a good working pair.

Buddy opened the passenger door of the Land Cruiser and got in. He handed Lee one of the cups of coffee. "What's up?" he said.

"Thanks," she said, indicating the cup. "Got a house call. You want to come along?"

"Sure thing."

Lee turned out of the diner parking lot, back up the hill past the university and along Ridge Road, the notched mud and snow tires of the four wheel drive Land Cruiser humming almost in harmony. Lee related the information about the missing Dr. Hamrick as Margy had told it to her. Buddy cocked one eyebrow up, squinted the other eye and watched her carefully as she talked.

"I hope you don't mind me sayin' so, Lee, but you don't look your usual self this morning. You feel OK?"

"I'm a little tired and have a headache. This coffee is helping."

"You out late last night?"

Lee smiled at the irony. "No, I didn't enjoy getting this one. I haven't been sleeping very well lately."

Buddy felt for his jacket pocket. "I got a Darvon for that headache if aspirin won't cure it. You want it?"

"Darvon? What are you taking Darvon for?"

"Nerve pain in my leg. Regular painkillers don't do any good. It flairs up sometimes, especially when the humidity changes."

"You've been to a doctor about it, I guess, since Darvon is a prescription drug."

"Oh, yeah. It's for an old injury. I got shot years ago."

"How did that happen?"

"I'll tell you about it sometime over a beer."

"Darvon's strong stuff. You had better be careful with it."

Buddy just smiled at her. As they drove along, Lee's police band radio squawked several messages back and forth between the sheriff, his deputies and the sheriff's office regarding the traffic accident on the highway.

"They've got a mess out there. Did you hear about it?" Buddy asked.

"None of the details. What happened?"

"Word out of the sheriff's office is, this big tractor trailer flipped up on its side at the bridge on Whiteoak Creek just this side of the county line and blocked the road. The driver wasn't hurt. The truck was pulling double trailers that cracked open and spilled their load for a quarter of a mile all over the highway. The funny part is the truck was carrying what looks like a year's supply for the entire southeastern United States of condoms and sexual aids."

"Are you making this up?"

"No. I swear to god. The word got out and half the kids in town went down there and picked up as many free samples as they could get away with. Now, this truck was laying up on its side blocking the highway. Somebody in a car trying to squeeze past the truck, you might say, ran over a case of personal lubricant, which mashed out onto the road. The next car in line slipped in the stuff and run over other cases of it. That started a chain reaction and the first thing you know twelve or fifteen cars piled into each other and the entire surface of the highway is covered in KY jelly."

"You *are* making this up."

"No, I'm not. You can ask anybody at the sheriff's office. It was shift changing time at NRL and traffic is backed up a mile and a half in both directions and they can't figure out how to get the jelly off the road. The volunteer fire department went out there to hose it off the blacktop, but it turned out that one of the cars in the pileup was a government car and the guy driving it just happened to be from the EPA. Well, when the fire department started hosing down the road, the runoff started killing fish in the creek."

"This is ridiculous, Buddy."

"No, they say twenty-pound catfish came floatin' belly up at the very spot the runoff ran into the creek. This EPA guy starts looking into it and discovers the lubricant has got spermicide in it, and he says the spermicide is killing the fish and it's headin' downstream into the Clinch River. He put a stop to the cleanup, and last I heard they're all standing around trying to figure how to get the stuff off the road. They say it's as slick as goose grease."

True or not, Lee couldn't help but laugh at Buddy's yarn. Buddy laughed too.

"Do they know what caused the wreck?"

"The driver claims he swerved to miss a deer in the road. Somebody said he was just driving too fast. Came down off that long winding slope the other side of the creek and got out of control. He might have fell asleep, he'd been driving all night. Probably pumped himself full of pills to stay awake."

"Why do they do that? Don't they know they're putting themselves and everyone else on the road in danger?"

"That rig he was driving with the double trailers probably cost him $250,000. Upkeep, fuel, tires, taxes, insurance–the only way to break even and hope to pay for the rig is to haul as much as he can in the shortest time. A fellow told me they figure every mile they haul is worth $10 to them. I've known some of them around here to take a buddy with them and drive straight through to Texas, swap out their load and drive straight back again without stopping except for fuel. Thirty-two hours straight."

"Jesus, what a life."

"One thing's for sure. Between the lawyers and the insurance companies, it'll keep the county court tied up for the next two years, at least," he said and laughed again. "Speaking of tied up, Mr. Terry is tied up with something, you say?"

"That's what Margy says."

"You know what he's tied up with, don't you?" Buddy grinned until his eyes were almost closed.

Lee looked across at him, smiled and nodded. Everyone around the courthouse knew that Mr. Terry and some of the old fellows held a meeting of the "town fathers" every Saturday morning in a back room of the courthouse to have coffee and donuts, discuss events of the past week, talk a little local politics, and speculate on the course of world affairs.

"I'll bet the hot topic around the coffeepot this morning is the landfill," Buddy said. "Did you see the letters in the *Echo* this week?"

Lee had not read the letters to the editor. She fell asleep before she got that far. She shook her head.

"The whole county's up in arms about the way the regional landfill authority is running over Bartram County. The vote was nine to one by the other counties against Bartram on the last three votes. Ol' Ray Durbin says he was told by somebody on the inside that it's already been decided the landfill is coming to Bartram County."

"That would be a disaster," Lee said. "Why don't the county commissioners vote to pull out of the authority?"

"That's a damn good question. I think some of them have got the idea that a five hundred million dollar landfill will be some kind of goldmine for Bartram County."

The idea of gold mining in a landfill struck a humorous chord in Lee's mind. There was a pause in the conversation just long enough for Buddy to shift topics.

"What do you make of this situation?" He said, nodding his head in the direction of the road ahead.

"Your guess is as good as mine."

"A little bit strange. Parents are always calling, looking for some student who's not where they're supposed to be. And that's where we usually find them—where they're not supposed to be. You know, young love. Sometimes, too, some of 'em will just get a wild notion to go somewhere and do somethin' and a bunch of 'em will just take off without telling anybody where they're going. They always turn up. It is a little different for somebody to call up looking for their husband though. Retired faculty, you say?"

"That's what Margy says."

"Hell, he probably just fell in love with some twenty-year-old and they went to Myrtle Beach for the weekend. It happens. Mr. and Mrs. Hamrick are not living together, I take it, him here and her in New Mexico?"

"Margy didn't say about that."

They drove along Ridge Road until it ran off the end of the ridge and dead ended into Popular Creek Road. They had long ago driven past the city limits of Carters Mill and the street numbers had been replaced by rural mailboxes, many of them unnumbered.

"You see anything that looks like Paradise Road?" Lee asked as she drove slowly past a cluster of mailboxes next to a dirt road.

"I don't see anything that looks like *anything*," Buddy

said. "I'm thinking it must be somewhere between Sugar Grove and the National Forest. Can't you look it up on your phone or something?"

"Margy said it doesn't show up on her computer maps. Maybe I should double check on my phone."

Lee pulled to the side of the road and entered the address of the Hamrick house into her Maps app. No luck.

"Nope. Address not found. We'll have to find somebody to ask."

"I ain't seen anybody for the last couple of miles. Mrs. Hamrick couldn't narrow it down any?"

"She just said it was somewhere off of Poplar Creek," Lee said.

"It must be close to twenty miles from one end of Poplar Creek Road to the other. That's about a hundred little hollows and ridges on both sides of the valley, and every hollow and ridge has got its own road. We could be out here looking until this time next year."

Another few minutes down the road and they came to the small community of Sugar Grove. Sugar Grove was one of those remnants of a town where a town used to be. There were perhaps a dozen houses scattered along either side of the main highway and the half-dozen cross streets. Three white wooden churches—one Baptist, one Methodist, and one Presbyterian—with their adjacent cemeteries sat in a row along the main street.

To the left of the highway was a small unpainted building, the remnant of the depot for the railroad spur that branched off of the main L&N line at Sugar Grove and ran south to the site on the Oak Ridge reservation where the K-25 nuclear plant once stood. The train tracks of the siding were grown up with weeds, their crossties cracked open from dry rot. Sitting on the old loading dock of the building was a straw man dressed as a hillbilly. A hand painted sign read "Genuwine Mountain Crafts."

Facing the highway on the right was a brown stained wooden building with a couple of gas pumps out front. A man of sixty or so years sat on the porch of what the faded lettering on the face of the building said was Rebecca's Antiques and Crafts.

Lee stopped in front of the building, rolled down her window and waved a greeting to the man on the porch. The man nodded.

"Can you tell us where Paradise Road is?" she asked.

The man sat for a minute looking blankly at them, not speaking, as if he may not have understood the question.

"We're looking for Dr. Hamrick's house," Lee said, "on Paradise Road."

"Hamrick?" The man said and stood up from his chair. "Paradise Road?" He rubbed his beard stubble with the fingers of one hand for a few seconds, apparently searching his memory. "I know just about everbody in the valley, but I don't know any Hamrick's," he said. "No Paradise Road here either." He pointed off toward the south. "If I ain't mistaken there is a Paradise Road the other side of Black Oak Ridge on East Fork Poplar Creek. This is Poplar Creek. You're in the wrong valley for Paradise Road."

"Can you tell me the best way to get to Paradise Road from here?"

"Well, you can't really get there from here. You'll have to go back down yonder the way you came and turn right on Blair Road. They's two or three side roads you can take off to the left and head on up towards Oak Ridge. It ain't too far. Somebody up that way ought to be able to tell you."

Lee thanked him and pulled back onto the highway, headed in the direction from which they had come. She looked over at Buddy.

"The wrong Poplar Creek. Do you have any idea where he was talking about?"

Buddy chuckled. "I got the part about going up the road here and turning right on Blair Road. After that I'm a little fuzzy. I know a little about East Fork Poplar Creek. When I was a kid me and some of the other kids used to camp out down there, fish in it and catch frogs. The usual kind of things for kids. It's about as long as Popular Creek. We could still be out here driving around for the next six months if we don't find somebody who knows him."

Lee turned right on Blair Road. The highway ran due south between the railroad spur on the right and Poplar Creek on the left. After ten minutes or so of watching for anything that might be what they were looking for, Lee braked at an intersection where a sign pointed left to East Fork Popular Road.

"What do you think?" she asked Buddy.

"I think that's the way we want to go," he said.

Lee turned left off the main highway and drove over a bridge that crossed the creek. The unpaved road ahead was well maintained but it had washboard ribs worn in its surface from frequent traffic. Lee increased her speed slightly so the shocks of the Land Cruiser absorbed some of the bumping from the rough surface. She looked in her rearview mirror and groaned.

"What is it?" Buddy asked, as he turned to look out the back window.

"I just washed my truck yesterday."

The dust billowing behind them was so thick that it was impossible to see through it.

"That little rain shower we had yesterday evening didn't do much to settle the dust, did it?" He said.

"We would need about a week of steady rain to settle this road."

They came around a bend in the road and Lee slammed hard on the brakes. The vehicle slid sideways on the gravel surface and came to a stop as the road disappeared in front of them at its intersection with a crossroad. As Lee sat trying to decide which way to turn, the cloud of dust behind them caught up with them and engulfed the Land Cruiser. For several seconds they couldn't see the road in any direction. Lee looked out through the windshield now covered with enough brownish-yellow dust that it was forming little wavy lines as it slid down the glass.

"Which way here? Right?" She asked.

"Left, I think."

"You sure?"

"I think so."

After that they drove through so many intersections and past so many turnoffs that Lee was sure they were lost and had crossed into Roane County. The road curved and just ahead was a narrow bridge spanning a creek. Off to the side of the road was an old faded red pickup truck. A small family was scattered along the creek bank fishing.

"Stop up ahead," Buddy said. "I know this fella."

Lee slowed her speed until there was no dust cloud behind them, then pulled to a stop where the shoulder widened just before the bridge. An old rusted and beat up sign bolted to the end of the bridge said East Fork Poplar

Creek. A man, probably in his thirties, unshaven and she soon discovered, unwashed, arose from his fishing spot and approached the Land Cruiser as Buddy nodded and spoke to him.

"How you doing, Luther?"

Lee noticed Buddy had fallen into his best good-ole-boy dialect. The man looked in through the open window.

"Purty good, I reckon." He spoke with a strong mountain dialect. "I know you, don't I?"

"Yeah. Buddy Ruff. I used to work with your cousin JoNell over in Oak Ridge."

"At's right," Luther said, nodding his head. He spit out the remains of a well used chew of tobacco. "Thought that was you. What you doing out this way?"

"We're looking for a fella. You know where Paradise Road is?"

"Keep on going about two or three miles and you'll run right into it," he said.

Lee asked him, "Can you tell us where Dr. Hamrick lives? His address is 1201 Paradise Road."

The man grinned a stain-toothed, friendly smile across at Lee. "Ain't no doctors I know of out this way. Wish they was."

"You ain't heard of a Dr. Hamrick lives around here any-where?" Buddy asked again.

The man turned toward the others on the creek bank and yelled to the woman with an infant on her lap did she know a Dr. Hamrick lived around here. The woman shook her head.

"Ask Grandma does she know him."

The woman repeated the question to an elderly woman

sitting behind her in a wooden straight chair in the shade of a tree reading her Bible. Then the younger woman shook her head and yelled back, "We don't know him."

Lee took her cellphone off its dashboard mount and keyed in Margy's number. "I don't know if I can get a signal out here," she said.

After broken conversation back and forth over the phone made difficult by the weak signal and the scratchy static, inquiries around the sheriff's office revealed that 1201 Paradise Road was what was known on the old county maps as Howard's Hotel.

"Howard's Hotel?" Luther grinned again, laughed, and shook his head. "You're lookin' for Roadkill Man. At's where he lives, at Howard's Hotel. But he ain't no doctor that I ever heard."

"Roadkill Man?" Lee repeated, not sure she had understood the man's dialect.

"That's what they call him around here. Roadkill Man."

"Why they call him that?" Buddy asked.

"Well, 'cause he buys animals, dead animals, sometimes."

"Do you mean animals killed on the road?" Lee was beginning to hope this was one of Buddy's practical jokes.

"Sometimes."

"What does he do with them?" Buddy asked.

"Don't rightly know. Eats 'em, for all I know."

"You think so?"

"Don't rightly know. Some folks do, you know. Ain't nuthin' wrong with a fresh killed turkey or deer whether it's shot by a bullet or hit by a car."

"You ever sold him anything?" Buddy asked.

"Once't or twice't. Don't pay much. Five dollars, maybe. Sometimes more. Sometimes he won't buy it a'tall. Says it has to be fresh killed. Kids around here take him things sometimes fer a little money. If I find a good fresh roadkill I can get more for the skin than what he pays for the whole thing. A good clean fox hide'll bring fifty or seventy-five dollars, you know. A raccoon pelt is worth thirty dollars any day. I cut a little wood fer him. Do some hauling now and ag'in. He give me a pig once't."

Buddy looked past the man toward the creek. "You caught anything today?" He asked.

The man turned and called to the little girl. "Show him what you caught, Bonnie."

The little girl was about five years old, with long brown hair pulled back from her face and held by a yellow ribbon, wearing a blue playsuit with red and yellow animal designs. She reached into the edge of the water and pulled out a string of fish that was so heavy she could hardly lift it. But she held them up proudly and smiled at Buddy.

"Pretty good string of fish," Buddy yelled to her. "You want to sell them?" and winked at the man. She shook her head and lowered them back into the water.

"You be careful with them fish, Bonnie. They's your supper," Luther yelled. Then he said, "They'll be mighty fine with some cornbread and hushpuppies and some raw onion. Maybe some turnip greens."

"It does sound good," Buddy agreed.

"We could use some more rain," Luther said. "Fishin' is always better after h'it rains."

"Can you tell us where Dr. Hamrick's house is?" Lee

asked.

The man laughed again, leaned against the door of the Land Cruiser, and pointed down the road. The strong odor of stale perspiration filled the cab of the vehicle. "Go on down this road and you'll come to the Oak Ridge highway," he said. "Keep going on across the highway and about a mile or two after that this here road will run right into Paradise Road. Turn left on Paradise Road and go three or four more miles and his place'll be on the righthand side. His driveway's got a rock wall and a big black mailbox next to the road. They's an old barn out in the field." Then he added, with another chuckle, "Doctor Hamrick. That's a new one fer me. Might'a been a doctor one time. He ain't nothin' now but an old coot."

They thanked him and drove in the direction Luther had told them. Buddy didn't roll up his window for a while, until the man's aura was no longer present.

"He was a blast from the past, wasn't he?" Lee said, fanning the air in front of her face. "Strong fellow."

"Part of a dying breed," Buddy replied. "Still hunts, fishes and traps. Living off the land the way his folks have in these mountains for over two hundred years."

"Is that how he makes his living?" Lee asked.

"Part of it. He does odd jobs and he's got a little place with a few pigs and some chickens. Not much of a farm but he keeps a milk goat, grows his own vegetables. Still grinds his own cornmeal, from what I hear." Buddy shook his head and chuckled, "Roadkill Man. You think he's got Hamrick mixed up with somebody else?"

"What is this Howard's Hotel? There couldn't be a hotel

out here, could there? You know where he's talking about?"

Buddy smiled and wiped his handkerchief across his face. "It's kind of a local landmark. It never was a real hotel. When I was a kid growing up it was an old moonshiner's house. They tell me that years ago folks traveling here to get their corn ground at the old grist mill that used to be on Mill Branch would sometimes stay in a room on the back porch of the old house. They say the room was always open and whoever needed it would just stopover the night there. Next morning they'd pay for the room by choppin' a little firewood, or by leaving some cornmeal or whatever they might have. The house was owned at that time by a man by the last name of Howard, and that's how it got its name. I didn't know the old place is still standing. Thought it went to ruin long ago."

"I worry about Luther and his family eating the fish they caught," Lee said. "East Fork Poplar Creek is contaminated with mercury from Y-12."

"Yeah, I've heard Ray Durbin go on a rant about it. And I've seen the warning signs posted on the creek bank where it runs through Oak Ridge. But I thought what little bit of mercury that's still there is not supposed to be anything to worry about. You're a biologist. Do you think it's dangerous?"

"I've read some of the environmental reports. The good news, as they say, is that the mercury is at a low level outside the reservation. The official line is that all the mercury that's left in the creek has sunk to the bottom into the deep crevices. The only wildlife that's contaminated, they say, is bottom feeders, like catfish and suckers, because some of the things they feed on are contaminated. So, you're supposed to be OK as long as you don't eat the bottom feeders. As nearly as I could tell from the string of fish I saw, Luther and his family are catching bream and trout, which are surface feeders and should be safe to eat."

"Just don't eat the bottom feeders, eh?"

"To be safe, I wouldn't eat any of them," Lee said. "Mother Nature is not always so clean cut, tidy, and predictable."

Buddy shook his head. "Don't drink the water and don't eat the fish. I guess I'll just have to stick to RC Colas and Moon Pies from now on."

They passed an old barn, and ahead in the distance was a driveway with ivy covered stone walls on either side.

"1201. That's it, Lee," Buddy said, as they approached the entrance. "Looks like no one is home all right, from the number of newspapers on the ground."

"Let's walk up from here," Lee said, as she pulled the Land Cruiser over to the side of the driveway.

The black metal mailbox mounted in the stone gatepost had items of mail extending just out of its partly opened lid. Half-a-dozen or so newspapers lay in the driveway.

"Somebody's been in or out in the last few days," Lee said, "judging from the tire tracks over those papers. Let's see if we can figure out when the vehicle passed through here."

"How're you going to do that, Lee?"

"Hand me that newspaper, please," she said, pointing to one of the newspapers lying on the gravel driveway.

Buddy picked up the paper and handed it to her. Lee inspected the plastic wrapper, pulled out the newspaper and shook it open.

"Now let me look here in the classifieds. Ah, ha! What good luck. An expensive German automobile came through here sometime after 6 P.M. yesterday," she said.

"How in the hell do you know that from the classified ads?" Buddy said.

"Well, my good man, this is yesterday's paper, delivered sometime yesterday morning. The vehicle drove over the paper after it was delivered. The tire tracks were made when the road was wet. And it rained yesterday afternoon late at about six o'clock."

"What makes you think it was a German car?"

Lee looked up the winding driveway through the dense growth in the direction of the house. She held up the plastic wrapper. "You can see from the tread mark that it probably was not a truck tire. This Hamrick is some kind of retired doctor. Doctors always drive Mercedes or BMWs. BMWs are more yuppie automobiles. By recent accounts, Dr. Hamrick is not a yuppie. I'd say he drives a five to ten year old Mercedes. Of course, I'm just guessing about the type of automobile. It's all a matter of probabilities."

"Pretty damn slick."

"Elementary, Watson."

Buddy chuckled as they walked up the drive, knowing he had been had. "Counting the number of newspapers," he said, "and the fact that a car was here last night, I'd say Hamrick was off somewhere for about a week and just came home last night. That's why his wife couldn't get him on the telephone. He's probably just sleepin' in this morning."

"Makes sense."

"Fits in with my Myrtle Beach theory," Buddy said. "Old

goat."

The house was a large two story ivy-covered stone and stucco structure with an open porch across the front. The whole thing was almost hidden by huge hundred-year-old magnolia trees. Though the yard was no longer well kept, it had brick walkways and remnants of landscaped gardens. The shrubbery and lawn were overgrown, and what remained of the flowerbeds displayed an array of weeds gone to seed. Off to one side was a closed wooden two car garage.

"Looks like an old country doctor's house," Lee remarked. "Perhaps a little overdue for some yard work, but it's had lots of restoration."

"I don't want to worry you, Sherlock," Buddy said, the smile gone from his face, "but I think I smell something."

"Go back and get the bag out of the truck," Lee said, "and bring my lab coat."

The seriousness of the situation settled over their mood. Instinctively, Lee's eyes began watching for items of possible forensic significance. She walked across the front porch of the large old house. There were no signs of life except for a dog barking somewhere. Lee knocked on the front door. No response.

Buddy came up the steps and across the porch with the bag. He snorted. "Something's dead, sure enough. Something big, by the smell of it."

Chapter 2
The Doctor Will See You Now

"GET US BOTH a pair of latex gloves out of the bag and see if there's not a skeleton key on your keyring that will open this door," Lee said as she put on her lab coat.

"That's called a betty," Buddy said, without breaking his motion.

"What's a betty?"

"A skeleton key. Smokey Brown—you know Smokey, down at the jail? Smokey has considerable experience with locks and keys. He calls a skeleton key a betty."

Lee slipped on the gloves and turned the door knob. "Well, never mind," she said. "The door's not locked." She pushed open the door slightly and yelled, "Hello, is anybody home? Dr. Hamrick?"

Again, there was no response.

"Let's go in."

"God all mighty, what a stench!" Buddy grabbed his nose between his fingers.

"We're going to need masks," Lee said.

They stepped back onto the front porch. Lee took a plastic container of oil of camphor from her bag. "You want some of this?"

Buddy nodded his head and they each smeared a coating of it above their upper lips beneath their noses to reduce the smell of decay. Lee took a filtration mask from the bag and pulled it over her nose and mouth. When Buddy had done the same they opened the door and started in.

"It's freezing in here," Buddy said, as they stepped into

the darkened entranceway. "I wonder why the air conditioning is turned down so cold?"

The interior of the house was dark except for a faint glow coming from what appeared to be the living room. They crossed the entranceway into the room ahead, the two of them looking strangely anachronistic, walking across the polished wood floors of the high-ceiling house, wearing little surgeon's masks and gloves. They could see that on one side of the room in an office alcove was a brightly lit computer screen. In front of the computer was a chair with a large wretched bundle in it.

"He's over here in this chair," Lee said.

"Jeez, look at that. I guess he didn't run off with a twenty-year-old after all. Or maybe he did and this is what happened to him. Too much excitement. How long do you figure he's been dead? It is a *he*, ain't it?"

"His wife talked with him sometime last week, assuming this is Hamrick." Lee turned on a floor lamp next to the desk.

"Dead only a week? Look how much of the flesh is gone," Buddy said.

"I've never seen this much tissue decay in such a short period," Lee said. "Looks like he was nothing but skin and bones when he died. He must have been sick, or starved."

"I guess a diet of roadkill didn't agree with him," Buddy said. "He smells older than a week."

"Yes, he does. Looks like he died working at his computer."

"Think about that." Buddy shook his head. "The computer sitting there running for a week, waiting for him to type or something, and him dead and rotting away."

Lee turned away and scanned the room for anything relevant to the death while Buddy continued to look toward the computer screen. As he watched, small red and green lights on the front of the computer blinked on and off and faint chirping sounds could be heard from inside it. A square window appeared on the screen and a stream of dates, names and numbers began scrolling down the screen faster than the eye could follow.

"Look here." He motioned toward the computer. "There's something on the screen. It's all gibberish. Doesn't make any sense to me."

Lee turned to look, but just as fast as it had appeared, it was gone. She watched for a moment but there was no further activity.

"Probably just an automatic timed backup," she said, pointing to a tape cassette sticking out of the front of the computer.

"Looks like he was writing a hell of a lot about something," Buddy said, lifting the corners of several pages of computer printouts. There were piles of papers and books scattered about the desk and on surrounding tables and chairs. "What do you think all these books and papers are about?"

"Hmm, I don't know. There are a lot of books on scientific topics."

"This is really spooky." Buddy made an exaggerated shiver. "Look at him, all wrapped up in that blanket, sitting in front of the computer with nothing but his rotting head and hands sticking out. It gives me the willies."

"It's strange all right. There are some peculiar things about the condition of the body." Lee moved to the other side of the corpse and looked closely at the exposed teeth. "It should not be in this advanced state of decay this soon, particularly in this temperature."

"Damn, it's cold all right." Buddy rubbed his arms with his gloved hands. "Maybe he died of frostbite. Or do you think maybe it's not Hamrick?"

"I don't know. There's no way to tell from his appearance," Lee said. "Even if I knew what he looked like."

"Look at this." Buddy pointed to the wall next to the computer. "He's got a map here with pins stuck all in it and numbers and dates wrote all over it. I knew a fellow once, did something like this. He had a map of the entire United States with a little dot and a date next to every city he had been to. He was real proud of that. You go see him and stay very long and he'd start telling you every place he'd been, and when he was there, and something that he remembered about every place. Had shoe boxes full of post cards and stuff from places he had been. Most folks thought he was crazy. I guess he was."

"You check the rooms down that hallway," Lee indicated a dark hallway leading off to one side. "I'll check this side of the house. Be careful not to disturb any more than you have to."

"Okay."

Buddy turned toward the door to the hallway and Lee started for a door leading to the kitchen. Just as their backs were turned to the grizzly apparition, a loud high pitched pulsating screaming sound came from the direction of the corpse.

"Jeeezus Christ! What's that!" Buddy spun around.

Lee's heart was pounding in her chest. Then she realized

the sound that had frightened her was mechanical.

"His computer is printing out something," she said.

"How can that be? The guy's been dead a week."

"I don't know." Lee glanced over the computer printout. "There's a whole list of messages here. They must be coming in automatically. This last one looks like a note from somebody inquiring about his health."

"I don't think he's going to answer," Buddy chuckled.

"He must have the computer connected to the Internet." Lee looked behind the computer and lifted several cables. "Yep, he's got some type of Internet connection," she said. "Probably a satellite dish. I don't think there's any cable service out here."

"Well it scared the hell out of me. He's a pretty popular guy for a corpse. That's some mighty fancy computer equipment."

Lee moved toward the adjacent room. "Let's check out the rest of the house."

In a few minutes they met back in the living room.

"Nothing down the hall," Buddy nodded, "but some of the doors are locked and I don't have a key that'll open them. We'll have to get a locksmith over here. I can hear a dog barking behind one of the doors. Sounds like it's in the basement."

"Yes, I hear the dog," Lee said. "Nothing on this side either. The kitchen door was unlocked. I locked it with the dead bolt. Let's leave the computer and everything else just as it is and get out of here. We can get back to these things after the body has been removed."

"What about him? Are we going to bag him?" Buddy grimaced behind his mask.

"No. I'll call for an autopsy and we'll let the medical examiner remove the body. The cold air will help keep the body stable until the M.E. gets here."

"Suits the hell out of me," Buddy said, turning toward the door. "I hate to carry rotting corpses."

"Take the bag and let's go out the same way we came in. We don't want to cover up anything or disturb anything that might be here."

"You mean microscopic like?" Buddy said. "That's what I told Grady Tillman. He was giving me a hard time. He thought you make me wear the rubber gloves. I told him, hell no, I wear them because I want to. I told him there's all kinds of little microscopic things you can get from a dead body, things you can't see. More that you can't see than you can."

Back on the front porch, Lee closed the door to the house and Buddy locked it with his skeleton key. They pulled the filtration masks from their faces and both took deep breaths of fresh air, trying to flush the stench of death from their airways as they walked down the driveway toward the road.

"Look," Lee motioned toward the front gate, "there's the paper carrier now. You tell the kid to hang around for a little while. I need to ask her a few questions. Try not to scare her."

Ahead of them at the entrance to the drive a girl of eleven or twelve dressed in jeans, a short sleeve summer shirt and Reebok shoes, stood with her bicycle. A bag of newspapers hung across the handlebars. Lee waved to her and smiled.

"Let's get the tape out of the truck and cordon off the

whole place—yard, garage, everything," Lee said.

"I'll tell you," Buddy said, "There's something about the smell of a corpse. It's like, when you breathe that stench in, it gets right in your throat and lungs and up your nose. And you just can't hardly get rid of it. Sometimes I think I smell it on me, or in me, a week after we pick up one like this one here."

"All *right*, Buddy. I get the picture."

"Sometimes I think I can even smell it in my pee," Buddy continued undeterred. "Like onions or penicillin, you know. The last one was so bad I burned my clothes. Wasn't anything wrong with them. I mean, no blood stains or anything. And they had a lot of wear left in them. I just didn't want to put them on me again. I guess that's why you wear that lab coat—to keep the smell of death off of you."

"It doesn't work. Now, will you please talk about something else? I tell you what, you get the tape and mark off the place," Lee said. "I'll talk to the kid."

"How far do you want me to string the tape?" Buddy asked.

"Block off the drive from where it first comes into the yard. And pull the tape around the edge of the yard. We want to keep everybody out."

"You want me to get the driveway too?"

"Yes, it looks as if a car or truck has been out here and there might be some evidence in the drive or in the yard."

"Yeah, I see what you mean," Buddy said.

The dog was still barking.

"But check the basement first. See about that dog," she said.

By this time, they were approaching the front entrance where the girl had parked her bicycle and was collecting the old newspapers from the driveway.

"Hey, honey, don't mess with anything in the driveway," Buddy yelled to her.

"You go ahead, Buddy. I'll talk to the girl. And bring back a two liter specimen bag from the truck with you."

The girl had her lips and eyes formed into a little bit of a sullen pout.

"What did he mean, 'Don't mess with anything'? I wasn't messing with anything. I was just picking up the old papers."

"I know. He didn't mean it like that." Lee tried to use a soothing tone. "There has been a death here. We just want to leave everything as it is until some people can come and look it over."

"I didn't mean to bother anything," the girl said.

"It's all right," Lee said. "Tell me, when was the last time you saw anyone home here?"

"Last Saturday when I came by to collect for the paper." The girl twisted her bicycle grip, her eyes downcast.

"Did you see the man who lives here last Saturday?"

"Mr. Hamrick? Yes, but I didn't collect. He didn't pay. He said I would have to come back today and he would pay me this week."

"Did he seem okay when you saw him last week?"

"I guess so. I don't know exactly. Is he okay now?" The girl glanced past Lee toward Hamrick's house. "Was it Mr. Hamrick that died?"

Lee noticed a visible tremble pass over the young girl. "It's okay. You don't need to be afraid. I thought maybe if he had been sick, you might know about it and could tell me. Did he look all right when you saw him? Did he come outside?"

The girl remained cautious. "I don't know if he was sick. He didn't come outside. I didn't see him very much. I thought he wasn't here at first. But after I knocked on the door I heard him moving around inside and he came to the door and opened it just a little bit and talked to me from inside."

"Do you remember what he said?"

"He said he hadn't been out to get any money and I would have to come back this week. I told him okay and I would appreciate it if he could pay me next time because I needed the fifteen dollars he owed me."

"How long have you been delivering the paper to him?"

"Since last summer. Nobody around here knows much about him. He's creepy."

"How was he creepy?"

"Just creepy. I don't know. He looked funny. And he never talked to anybody much. And his house always stinks."

"Do you know if he lived by himself? Did you see anyone else here?"

"Sometimes I saw another man here. I don't think he lived here, though. He just visited sometimes."

"Do you know the other man's name?"

"I heard Mr. Hamrick call him Eddie."

"Can you tell me what Eddie looked like?"

"He was tall, and had blond hair, and wasn't too old."

"Was he as old as the man with me?"

"No."

"Was he as old as me?"

"I think so."

"Tell me about last Saturday. Did Mr. Hamrick seem normal to you? I mean, did he look normal and sound normal?"

"I couldn't see too much of him because, like I told you, he kind of stayed behind the door. I told you, he was creepy. He was real skinny, you know, and kind of dirty, you know, greasy looking. And he hadn't shaved in a long time. And he smelled bad. That's all I know. I just came to collect for the paper. And I didn't bother anything," the girl said with finality.

"I know you didn't."

"Can I go now? I've got to finish delivering my papers and my mom will be expecting me."

"Yes. Thank you for your help. I'm sorry you had to find out about this. But you have been a big help to me."

"Okay, you're welcome. I've got to go now. My mom will come looking for me if I don't get home. She might not like me being here."

"Here, take her this card. It has my name and telephone number on it if she wants to talk with me."

"Lee Turner. Is that you—Lee?"

"Yes."

"Deputy Cor...ner. Are you a deputy? You work for the sheriff? My Mom's not going to believe that old Mr. Hamrick is dead and I talked to the police and all."

"I'm a deputy coroner. I work for the coroner's office."

"What is a deputy coroner?"

"Well, we sort of check out dead people."

"Gee whiz." Putting the business card in her front jeans pocket, the girl hopped on her bicycle and peddled off down the road, repeating the business card to herself. "Lee Turner, deputy corner. Lee Turner, deputy corner. Deputy cor-o-ner."

Buddy returned from behind the house, stringing the barricade tape along the way.

"There is a door to the basement in back but it's bolted or somethin' from the inside. I couldn't get in," he said. "The dog is in the basement. Did the girl know anything?"

"According to what she told me, Hamrick was definitely alive last Saturday. She said there's another man, named Eddie, who stays here sometimes." Lee held out her hand to Buddy. "Let me have that specimen bag. I need to empty the mailbox."

"Is that what you wanted the bag for?" Buddy said with relief. "I was afraid we were going to take some kind of, you know, specimen."

"No. We need to check the mailbox for valuables and anything that might help in the investigation."

Lee took a large handful of accumulated mail out of the mailbox and began sorting through it. She stopped and looked at one item.

"What's that?" Buddy asked.

"This is a newsletter from the credit union at the National Research Laboratories at Oak Ridge."

"What kind of doctor do you think he might be?"

"I'll be interested to find out."

"This don't add up for me." Buddy pushed his cap back on his head. "Unless Luther Morris was talking about somebody besides Dr. Hamrick."

"How's that?"

"We know he was a doctor of some sort, and according to you he probably drove a Mercedes." Lee started to protest, but Buddy held up his hand. "And didn't you say he was a faculty member or something on campus?"

"That's what the wife seemed to indicate when she talked to Margy. What's your point, Buddy?"

"I'll admit, you can't tell much from the appearance of a man in the condition he's in. But I have a hard time picturing this Dr. Hamrick, a Carters Mill University faculty member who drives a Mercedes, buying roadkill from Luther Morris."

"Your friend Luther didn't seem to think we had the right man. Maybe he was right."

"Some mighty damn fancy computer equipment in there." Buddy shook his head. "Not the kind of house a road bum would keep. It just don't add up."

Lee put the contents of the mailbox in the specimen bag, zipped it shut and headed for her Land Cruiser. "I've got to drive back to the office. The medical examiner won't respond without an official request on our office letterhead. I'll have to fill out a form and use the office fax. It's still early. They'll probably be coming from Knoxville. They should be able to get here before dark. I'll radio the sheriff's office for some security here, but you'll have to stay until the sheriff can send somebody to relieve you."

"Yeah, just what I was looking forward to, babysitting a

rotting corpse."

"You can wait down here by the gate. Just be sure nobody comes inside the cordoned off area." Lee said.

Lee called the sheriff's office on her radio.

"Margy, this is Lee. You copy?"

"10-4, Lee. Go ahead."

"I'm at the Hamrick house on Paradise Road. I've got a 10-55 here with no positive ID"

"Say again, please."

"There is a 10-55 here with no positive ID I need an officer to secure this location until the medical examiner gets here."

"10-4. Let me notify the sheriff."

At that moment the sheriff's voice broke over the radio.

"This is Sheriff Eberhard. I copy, Margy. Anybody there with you now, Lee?"

"Buddy Ruff is here."

"10-4. What is your location?"

"Twelve zero one Paradise Road. It's a private dwelling. An old place that is listed as Howard's Hotel on the old county maps."

"10-4. I'll cut Billy loose from here. ETA about 20 minutes. Is your 10-55 secure?"

"Yes. In the house and cordoned off. Buddy will remain here until the officer arrives."

"10-4. Need any further assistance?"

"Negative. Thanks."

"10-4 and out."

Lee checked her watch.

"It's 11:00 now," she said to Buddy, "I'll be back as soon as I can get back or I'll send someone out to get you."

"Don't hurry on my account." Buddy complained. "I can probably get a ride back with Billy Longtree."

"You may have some company, Buddy. No telling who overheard the radio report. Just keep any curious visitors clear of the area."

"Sure thing. I'll threaten them with my betty."

"You keep that thing in your pocket . . ."

At that moment a distinct bang sound came from behind them, followed by other, weaker sounds.

"What was that noise?" Buddy looked back toward the house.

"We better go back up and have a look," Lee said.

"You think somebody was hiding in the house? With that dead body in there? Jeez!"

"I don't know."

"You think we better wait for Billy?"

Lee shook her head. "We can't wait. The deputy can't get here for another twenty minutes and we have to protect the integrity of body."

"I wish I had more than my skeleton key with me." Buddy groaned. "I don't like the feel of this."

Chapter 3
Where Have All the Flowers Gone

LEE AND BUDDY walked briskly, half trotting back up the driveway to the house. They took the front steps two at a time and stopped outside the front door while Buddy fumbled for his skeleton key. They were both breathing hard.

"You hear anything?" Lee asked.

Buddy shook his head and whispered a quick "No," as he put the key into the lock.

"Okay, now, Buddy, let's go in quiet and easy. Whatever it is, we still have to be careful not to disturb anything."

"You let me go first," he said.

"No, we'll go together." Lee held up a finger to her lips.

There were more bumping sounds coming from somewhere inside the house.

"I definitely hear something going on in there." Buddy tried the key impatiently. "I can't get this damn skeleton key to work."

The lock turned. He opened the door and they started across the threshold, both of them breathing in short shallow breaths.

"Easy now." Lee spoke almost under her breath. "You see anything?"

"No," Buddy whispered.

They crept slowly and silently like two spies engaged in espionage across the entranceway and into the living room. Lee did not at first trust what she thought she saw in the low light inside the house.

"The body is gone," she said, quietly.

"Gone? How can it be gone?"

In the office alcove, the chair in which the body had been sitting was turned on its back on the floor, empty. There were more sounds from somewhere. Daylight was coming through the darkened kitchen.

"The kitchen door is open," Lee said.

"Didn't you deadbolt it?"

"Yes."

They moved quietly to the kitchen. The door to the outside was standing open, its wood frame splintered where someone had kicked in the door. Buddy at her back, Lee crossed the kitchen and emerged into the rear yard of the house. Still there was no sign of anyone.

More sounds came from the direction of a concrete block building that might have been an old dairy barn about a hundred feet off diagonally from the back of the house. They crossed the distance at a trot. A side door to the building was standing ajar. They stepped through the narrow opening into a darkened hallway.

"Shh, I hear something," Lee said.

"Down the hallway," Buddy said. "I see a light."

They moved quietly through the darkness, their backs to the wall. The hallway turned a corner and ahead was a brightly lit open doorway. As they neared the doorway they could hear sounds of clinking glass and a spraying or fizzing sound almost like bacon frying. The odor of chemicals was in the air. They hesitated for a moment next to the lighted opening. Lee motioned to Buddy and with a swift movement they both stepped quickly into the open doorway.

Inside was a laboratory-looking room. A large-built man dressed in a hooded protective suit and wearing a gas mask was standing in the middle of the room next to a large vat, his side toward them. He was pouring a clear liquid from a half-full five liter glass jug into the stainless steel vat. The frying sound was coming from the vat. Extending over the edge of the vat hung the feet of the corpse.

"Hold it, fella. What do you think you're doing with that body?" Buddy yelled.

The figure jerked around toward them.

"Who are you?"

"Who the hell are you?"

The figure gestured with his arm and yelled, his voice muffled by his mask. "Get out of here! Get out! Do you know what this is?" He raised the half-empty glass jug.

"Sulfuric acid," Lee answered.

"That's right, it *is* sulfuric acid. Now get out of here."

Buddy spoke in an almost kind voice. "Just put it down, fella. I can't let you go on with what you're doing. Put down the acid and come out of here."

"Do what he says." Lee spoke firmly but calmly. "We're from the coroner's office. The sheriff is on the way. You cannot escape. Put the acid down."

The man was agitated, almost hysterical. He moved with quick jerky motions. "I'm not trying to escape. Get out of here."

"We'll all go out together. Are you Eddie?" Lee asked.

"How do you know . . ."

"Eddie, you'll have to come out with us," she said.

After a moment's hesitation, the figure made an exasperated wave with his arm.

"All right, all right. It's all over now anyway. Get out. Hurry. I'll come with you."

As the man lifted the jug of acid to a nearby table, he

made a sudden move toward Lee and Buddy, his arms raised from his sides.

"Look out, Lee."

Buddy threw himself toward the oncoming man, his shoulder hitting the man low, near the waist. The man was stopped by the charge and stumbled backward toward the table, Buddy still attached to him.

"Buddy, watch out for the acid!"

Buddy raised up to look and the large man pushed him toward the door. There was the sickening sound of bone and muscle hitting the wood door frame and a cry of pain as the struggling men's bodies rammed against the door. Buddy dropped to the floor in the hallway, the masked man on top of him. The hooded figure got up quickly, rushed back into the laboratory, slammed and locked the door, leaving Lee and Buddy in the dark hallway. Buddy lay on the concrete floor.

"Oh, damn," he moaned.

"Buddy, are you hurt?"

"Damn. I hit my head. The crazy bastard."

Lee bent down to inspect Buddy's head in the dim light filtering through the long hallway. Her eyes had not adjusted to the darkness but she could feel a wet stickiness on the right side of his head.

"We need to get out of here to where I can see you. You're bleeding. Can you walk?" Lee put an arm under Buddy's arm to help him up.

"Whoa! Shit! Wait a minute," Buddy said. "My left ankle hurts like hell."

"Push yourself with your good leg," Lee said.

Buddy slid across the floor a few feet, leaving a smear of blood behind him. Lee found the wall switch and flipped it but the hallway light didn't work. She could now see in the dim light that Buddy's hair on the right side of his head was wet with fresh blood still gushing out of his wound with each heartbeat.

"You got a handkerchief?" she asked.

"In my back pocket."

Lee found the folded bandanna in Buddy's pants pocket.

"You get any friendlier and you're gonna have to marry me," he said.

"Hold this tight against your head," she told him. "I don't think it's bad, but we have to stop the bleeding." She felt his ankle. "Can you move your foot?"

Buddy moved his left foot slowly back and forth, his face grimaced in pain. "I can move it, but I can't walk on it. Not right now. Give me a couple of minutes and I can probably get up." He looked at Lee with a half grin. "I've been hurt worse. It's been a while, though. Did he lock himself in there with the corpse?"

"Yes."

"You go on out and get on the radio to the sheriff. I can make it out on my own in a minute. Go on. I'll be right behind you."

"You sure?"

"Yes. Go on."

Lee didn't want to leave Buddy but she knew they had to have help. And Buddy needed medical attention. She ran down the hallway, through the open door, across the yard, around the side of the house, and down the long driveway. She was out of breath when she reached her Land Cruiser. She quickly opened the door, jumped in and grabbed the handset of the radio. Looking back toward the house she did not see Buddy coming.

"Margy, this is Lee, you copy?

"10-4. Go ahead, Lee."

"Code 20. Code 20. Man down. I need help. I need police officers and ambulance at 1201 Paradise Road at Howard's Hotel. You copy?"

Margy's voice was crisp and efficient. "10-4. You have a code 20 alert and request assistance at 1201 Paradise Road."

"Send an ambulance. Buddy is hurt."

"10-4. 10-23. Standby."

Lee took in air in deep gulps, trying to catch her breath and stop her heart from pounding as she listened to the radio traffic.

"Car 14." Margy's voice.

Deputy Billy Longtree responded, "10-4, Margy. I'm already on the way. ETA about 10 minutes."

The sheriff broke in. "Billy, you wait there for me."

"10-4, Sheriff." The deputy responded.

Then the call was back to her.

"Lee?"

"I'm here, Margy."

"How many injured?"

"One at this time."

"10-4. Officers and ambulance are en route. ETA 10 minutes."

"Lee, this is Sheriff Eberhard."

"I'm here, Sheriff," she responded.

"Are you hurt?"

"No, I'm okay. Buddy is inside a farm building. We were jumped."

"You stay back. Let us handle it. We're on the way."

"10-4. Hurry."

Lee got out of the Land Cruiser and looked back up the driveway. Buddy still was not in sight. She ran over the possibilities in her head. If Buddy was unable to walk and the man came out of the laboratory, Buddy could be in real danger. The man was large and strong and desperate. Lee knew that without some way to neutralize his size and strength she was no physical match for him. But she couldn't just stand around and leave Buddy in there. She needed a weapon.

She looked behind the seats in the Land Cruiser. Nothing. If she could get the lug wrench out of the spare tire well, she thought, that would do. If she had to she could break a bone or knock him unconscious with that. She opened the rear door of the Land Cruiser. The lug wrench was under the spare tire which was held tight by a screw clamp. This is going to take too long, she thought to herself.

She turned around at the sound of a vehicle coming down the road. It was the red pickup truck of Luther Morris and his family. She ran into the middle of the road and waved her hands above her head. The truck came to a stop in the road and Luther stepped out.

"Ma'am, do you need help?"

"Do you have a weapon?"

Luther stared at her with a look of confusion.

"Do you have a gun?" she yelled.

"Yes, ma'am. I do."

"May I have it, please?" Lee walked across the space separating them. "I'm Deputy Coroner Lee Turner, and I am requesting your assistance in a matter of possible life and death. Here is my identification."

Lee held up her official identification with her picture and her coroner's office badge. That was the first time she noticed that her hands and white coat sleeves were red with Buddy's blood.

"Yes, Ma'am."

Luther reached behind the seat of his pickup and pulled out a double barreled shotgun. From inside the truck the voice of Luther's wife could be heard saying, "What is it, Luther? What's going on?"

"This lady needs some help." He reached again behind the seat and came up with two shotgun shells in his hand. With a series of quick efficient motions he flipped the lever that unlocked the barrels, the shotgun fell open, he dropped the shells into the two empty barrels and snapped the gun closed. The whole process took no more than three or four seconds. He handed the shotgun to Lee.

"You ever used one of these?"

Lee looked at the gun. "Yes."

"Hold it good and tight when you shoot, it's got a hard kick."

"I hope I don't have to use it. Buddy is hurt and I'm going back in for him."

"You want me to come?" Luther said, following her as she ran back toward her vehicle.

"No. Stay here by the gate. The sheriff's deputy will be here in less than ten minutes. You tell him Buddy is inside a concrete block building behind the house and I went in to get him. You understand?"

"Yes, ma'am. I know where that is."

"Tell him there are two of us and at least one suspect in the building." As she talked she took a roll of gauze and adhesive tape and a pair of scissors from her forensic bag and shoved them into the pocket of her lab coat.

"Yes, ma'am, I understand."

Lee ran back past the house, across the rear yard to the block building. She paused at the side door long enough to inhale and exhale two long breaths. Standing tall, with her back to the wall she slipped quickly around the opening of the door. She paused for a moment inside the hallway to listen, the shotgun pressed against the front of her body.

"Buddy, are you there?"

Nothing. She walked quickly down the dark hallway to the point where it turned and said, without stepping around the corner, "Buddy, are you there?"

Buddy responded in a low voice. "Yeah, Lee, I'm here."

He had pulled himself a few feet farther along from where she left him. She moved quickly to him and knelt to one knee, not looking entirely away from the closed laboratory door.

"Are you okay? I thought you were coming out."

"Looks like I broke my ankle."

"Let me see. Here, hold this." She handed Buddy the shotgun.

"Damn, what a cannon. You keep this in your truck?"

"No. Luther Morris."

"Well, good ole Luther. You going to blow the door off its hinges?"

"No. I just brought that in case I need to protect you." Lee felt his ankle.

"Ouch!"

"I can't tell if it's broken. It's not an open fracture anyway. Have you heard anything out of the lunatic?" she said as she examined his head.

"Sounds like he turned on a fan or some kind of motor, and there are a lot of chemical smells. There was banging around, but it's stopped. What in the hell's going on in there?"

"I'm going to get you out of here. You'll have to help me with your good leg. Ready?"

"Yeah, let's go."

Lee helped Buddy stand on his good leg. He placed the butt of the shotgun under his left arm and used the gun as a crutch. Just about the time they reached the open door they heard a sudden loud bang like a door slamming shut somewhere behind them, followed by automobile motor sounds. In a few seconds they could hear the sound of a car engine whining at high rpm coming around the building, shifting gears.

Luther Morris stood in the middle of the driveway wide-eyed as a dark blue automobile swerved sharply out from behind the concrete building then raced toward him, running off the edge of the driveway and smashing shrubbery, its engine screaming and its brake lights flashing as it careened down the winding drive. It was clear to Lee the driver was barely in control of the speeding vehicle.

Luther turned to look at his wife and children standing in the driveway entrance next to his truck. He yelled and waved to them to get clear of the danger as the car showed no signs of slowing. Luther jumped over the waist-high stone wall next to the driveway, shook his fist in the air and yelled at the driver as the auto slid past him. He watched helplessly as his wife, infant in arms, dragged his young daughter toward safety behind the rock entranceway. The car broke through the crime scene tape, hit the rear fender of his red pickup, tearing it half off the truck, slid onto the roadway, and sped off into the distance.

Luther yelled to his wife, "You all right, Jenny?"

She stepped from behind the corner of the wall and yelled back, "We're OK, Hon."

"Is Grandma all right?" he said.

It was then Lee noticed the old woman was still sitting in the cab of the truck. Luther's wife Jenny, carrying the infant in her arms, and the little girl Bonnie holding onto her skirt tail, hurried to the truck and looked in. After a moment's conversation, she turned toward Luther and yelled, "We're all OK, Hon."

Luther came up the driveway toward Lee and Buddy, stopping dead in his tracks when he saw them.

"Oh, God A'mighty," he said.

Buddy's face had blood streamed down one side and the whole front side of his shirt was wet with it, looking a lot worse in the daylight than he had in the darkened hallway. Lee had blood on her hands and face and caked on her lab coat from helping him. She could see the alarm in Luther's eyes.

"It's not as bad as it looks," she said. "Can you find some clean water for me to wash some of the blood off Buddy?"

Luther found a bucket and a faucet at the side of the house and brought water. Lee wet a wad of gauze and washed the blood from Buddy's face. They were sitting on the edge of the porch when Deputy Billy Longtree arrived a few minutes later in his patrol car, siren screaming.

He yelled to them as he ran up the brick walkway, concern showing in his face, "Lee, are you hurt?"

"I'm okay. We're okay."

"What happened? Is anybody else hurt? Anyone inside?"

"He got away," Luther said, pointing in the direction the car had disappeared. "Bout five minutes ago. Drivin' a dark blue Pontiac like a bat outta hell. Headin' down the road toward the state highway."

"Damn!" Billy barked the word. "I must have just missed him. You hurt bad, Buddy?"

"Nah," Buddy said through swollen lips. "Just ran into a door." He tried to laugh but he grimaced and grunted instead.

"His ankle may be broken, and he has a cut on his head," Lee said, as she removed the bloody bandanna and replaced it with clean gauze.

Two sirens could be heard winding their way up Paradise Road signaling the approach of the sheriff and the ambulance.

"You'll be all right, Buddy." Lee looked in the direction of the approaching ambulance. "The medics will take you to the hospital."

"I sure want to get a look at the lunatic that busted me up," Buddy said.

The sheriff got out of his car along with deputy Faust and waved to the EMTs to bring their stretcher. The two technicians came in a synchronized trot, the stretcher swaying between them. After some examination they attached an inflatable splint to Buddy's left ankle.

"Flush his bare skin as soon as you can," Lee told them. "He's been exposed to sulfuric acid fumes."

The technicians strapped Buddy to the stretcher and rolled him off in the direction of the ambulance.

Deputy Longtree had put out an APB to all area law enforcement to watch for the blue Pontiac with a damaged left front fender. Lee went to the water faucet next to the house and washed Buddy's blood from her hands and face.

"You want to tell me what happened here, Lee?" Sheriff Eberhard asked.

Lee recounted the events that had taken place since they first arrived.

"This is damn bizarre," he said, taking off his hat and wiping his neck with his handkerchief. "You say you got a good look at him, Luther?"

"I reckon I'd know him if I seen him agin. He could have killed my wife and children and Grandma. An' he's got to answer fer my truck."

"He's got a lot to answer for," the sheriff said, looking toward the rear of the house. "Billy, you better check out the inside to see if there are any other surprises. Don't touch anything you don't have to. Deputy Faust, you watch the back to see that there are no surprises around there." The sheriff turned back to Lee. "Where's the body now?"

"As far as I know it's still in the building out back. The last we saw, the door was closed and locked from the inside. We didn't see the way the man went out, so there must be a back door."

"Luther, you go on down to the road and take care of your family," the sheriff said. "Wait for me there. I'll be down in a little bit."

Luther Morris headed back down the driveway, shaking his head and talking to himself.

The sheriff turned back to Lee. "Was the suspect hiding in the house the first time you and Buddy came in?"

"He must have been out back in the other building. I deadbolt locked the kitchen door from inside before we left, and it was kicked in from the outside when we came back to the house."

"This is damn weird. How long do you say Hamrick has been dead?"

"Less than a week, according to witnesses," Lee said. "But I'm not certain about that, and I don't have a positive ID on the body."

Deputies Longtree and Faust came walking around from the rear of the house. "Nobody dead or alive inside the house, Sheriff," Billy said. "There's a dog in the basement. It seems to be OK."

"Then I guess we better take a look out back."

Lee and the sheriff stopped outside the door to the concrete building where she and Buddy had entered. The two deputies scouted around the outside of the building and reported over the radio that a door at the far end was standing partly open.

"You go on in and work your way through to us," the sheriff radioed back. He drew his Glock 9mm and motioned for Lee to get behind him. They stood close to the outside wall of the building away and to one side of the doorway, listening for the sounds of the deputies' progress. In less than five minutes they heard footsteps and voices approaching the door they stood guarding.

"Nobody in here." Billy said. "Judging from the open door on the other end and the tire tracks, I'd say the suspect had a vehicle out of sight behind the building. I'm sure that's the one you saw, Lee. You better come in here and take a look at this."

Lee and the sheriff followed Billy through the doorway, back down the dark hallway to the laboratory. They hesitated outside the door to the lab.

"You better let me go first," Lee said. "The fumes from the chemicals could still be dangerous." She took a filtration mask from the pocket of her lab coat and placed it over her nose and mouth and pushed the door open.

The bright lights of the laboratory were a sharp contrast to the dark hallway. Her eardrums crackled from the pulsating pressure of the air caused by the too loud sound of the blower running in the fume hood over the vat. The sharp smell of chemicals was still in the air but not as pungent as before. Lee stepped to the side of the vat and looked in. She saw a bubbling bloody broth of human hair, tissue and bone in a liquid chemical. She stepped back from the edge, removed her mask and spoke to the sheriff and deputies.

"I think it's safe to come in, but if you experience any burning of the eyes, nose or skin, shortness of breath, or dizziness, get out immediately."

The lawmen stepped cautiously over broken glass past overturned furniture, and moved across the room toward the vat.

"Good Lord," the sheriff said, as they stood watching the rolling, bubbling agitation of the acid. "It's hard to see through that mess, but it looks like there's nothing much left of the body but teeth and bones."

"It's pretty well gone," Lee agreed. "Don't stand too near the vat. In fact, I think it best if we keep our distance from these fumes."

The four of them stepped back into the hallway.

"I've seen some crazy and gruesome things," the sheriff

said, looking back through the open doorway. "But what kind of guy would kill a person and then wait a week before coming back to get the body and dissolve it in acid? It doesn't make much sense."

"I've never heard of anything quite like it," Lee said. "In his state of mind I'm not sure there is a rational explanation."

The sheriff motioned toward the assorted lab equipment and the many vials and bottles of chemicals. "What kind of place is this? Is it a meth lab or some kind of drug factory? Can you tell?"

"I don't know what it is," Lee said. "It doesn't smell like meth and I don't see any of the chemicals and lab equipment that are used in a meth lab. Whatever it is, it looks like it's been her a while."

"You don't suppose somebody has been usin' that vat to dispose of bodies, do you?" The sheriff's voice echoed his incredulity as he shook his head slowly. "How in the hell did they get into our county?"

Lee had no answer. "I'll have to call for the TBI crime scene unit and we'll need special help with the body. We don't dare try to retrieve what's left of it until we know for sure what it's soaking in."

They closed the doors to the laboratory and strung more crime scene tape to await the arrival of the TBI forensics unit. Lee and deputy Billy Longtree walked back down the driveway to the entrance where Lee's Land Cruiser was parked.

"I have some cold drinks, Billy. Do you want one?"

"I believe I do." Billy stepped to the rear of the Land

Cruiser. She took two drinks out of the cooler and handed one to the deputy.

Billy Longtree was a head taller and perhaps seventy-five pounds heavier than Lee. He took the drink from her hand and looked down at the ground and then looked up a little self-consciously.

"I want you to know, Lee, I think that was a brave thing you did, going in there for Buddy. I don't know many men who would've gone back in that dark place knowing there was a crazy murderer in there. Especially one that just got the best of Buddy Ruff."

Lee was embarrassed. "I wasn't so brave. I had Luther's shotgun. I could sink a battleship with that."

Billy laughed. She laughed too. As she drove back toward town her hands were shaking, but her headache was gone.

Chapter 4
Reporting to Mr. Terry

LEE DROVE STRAIGHT to her office. She knew she would need Mr. Terry's authorization to request the assistance of the TBI crime scene forensics unit. She hoped he would be there when she arrived. He wasn't. Surely, if he was at the courthouse he had been notified. She looked in his office just to make sure. There was no sign he had been there today. There was no note on her office door or on her desk. She checked the message light on her answering machine. No messages. Not surprising. Mr. Terry expressed on more than one occasion his distaste for "electronic secretaries," as he called them.

She went to the bathroom to scrub her hands and face and to straighten her hair. She felt strange, guilty that the blood stains she was washing from her skin had come from Buddy's injury. Guilty because, even though she had just felt some of the greatest fear of her life, she had also felt an exhilarating excitement, an exuberance of emotions. It was almost as if her exhilaration had come at the expense of Buddy's injury. Now she felt shaky and very alone in the solitude of the quiet office.

In the refrigerator in the kitchen she found orange juice and poured a glass. She suddenly found herself ravenous for it. She drank the entire glassful without stopping, and then a second glass. Her hands were still shaking. She became sick to her stomach, hot and sweaty. She thought she was going to faint. She leaned over the sink and splashed her face with cold water. After a few minutes, she didn't know how long, the nausea passed and she no longer felt flushed. Her hands were shaking less. She dried her face, walked on unsure legs back to her office and sat down at her desk.

She looked at the computer sitting lifeless on her desk, turned it on and waited for it to boot up. Finally after moments of hesitation, grinding of disk drives and several loud beeps, the home screen appeared. Lee clicked on the icon for her word processing program. Her head still spinning from the near faint, she filled out a blank Certificate of Death on screen, listing the identity of the deceased as unknown and the cause and manner of death as pending. Still no word from Mr. Terry. Lee dialed the County Clerk's office.

"Cybil, is Mr. Terry still at the courthouse?"

"No, Lee. He went out to where that man's body was found to see you. Where are you now?"

"I'm back at my office."

"He must have just missed you," Cybil said, and added in a conspiratorial whisper, "He stormed out of here all red-faced. I thought his eyes were going to pop out." Then she laughed.

"OK, thanks," Lee said. "I'll catch up with him."

"Are you OK? You sound a little shaky."

"I am a little shaky, but I'm all right."

"I can send someone over if you need me to."

"No, thanks, Cybil, I'll be OK."

She slumped in her chair, her eyes closed, her head in her hands. In a few minutes she heard the distinctive sounds of Mr. Terry's old blue Ford as it came to a stop outside. The engine made a rattling noise as if it needed tuning, and the motor continued to run on bumpily for several seconds after he turned it off.

The door to the outer office opened. The first thing Lee

saw was Mr. Terry's little dog, always with him. She heard it first, its little nails clicking on the wood floor. It stopped midway in front of Lee's open doorway and looked in with a blank stare, its two eyes appearing to look in different directions at once.

The dog was of indeterminate breed. It was larger than a chihuahua but smaller than a dachshund, and it was old and over-weight, the result of too many table scraps. It was not an attractive dog and looked as if it never had been. Its once tan color was now more grey than tan, particularly around its mouth and its eyes which bulged as if they had outgrown their sockets. The combination of the dog and Mr. Terry together reminded Lee of those humorous photographs in which dogs and their owners look alike. The old dog turned and started into Mr. Terry's office toward a box that lay under his desk but changed its mind and walked toward the kitchen.

Mr. Terry came in from the outside. Lee could see him through her open door. He crossed the outer office and followed the old dog in the direction of the kitchen. His face was red and he was breathing heavily. He mopped sweat from his balding head with his handkerchief as he disappeared down the hallway. The sounds of him pouring himself a glass of cold water echoed up from the back and she could hear the little dog lapping from a dish of water.

After what seemed like a long time Mr. Terry came into her office. He looked at her for several moments through the thick lenses of his old fashioned wire rimmed glasses before he spoke. His old eyes were perpetually red and moist. From his blank, hard stare Lee couldn't judge his mood.

"Quite a ruckus this morning," he said finally. His voice sounded choked.

"Yes, it was." Her voice had a little bit of uncontrollable shaking.

"They tell me you had a gun."

"Yes." Lee cleared her throat to steady it. She held her hands together in her lap. "We discovered a man in the act of disposing of the body. Buddy and I were attacked and Buddy was hurt. I borrowed a gun from a local citizen and went back in to get Buddy out."

"This is the coroner's office. We are not law enforcement. You should have left that sort of thing to the sheriff. Didn't the sheriff tell you to wait and let him handle it?"

"Buddy was in immediate danger."

"You might have gotten both of you killed."

Lee could feel her blood rise in her face. But she didn't respond to his scolding. She was a little afraid of what she might say.

"What's this about acid?" he asked.

She wanted to yell at him but she spoke clearly and evenly, if a little shakily, telling him what had happened.

Mr. Terry seemed to speak to himself. "In all my years as coroner. . ."

"I'll need your authorization to call in the TBI crime scene unit."

"Yes," he said with resignation. "There's nothing else to do. You know, before you came here less than a year ago, I never once in almost forty years as coroner had to call in state officials to help me do my job. Now this will be the second time this year." He added sardonically, "I wonder how we got along all those years without them?"

Then, with his voice drifting off into the distance of time, he turned and took a step toward the door, "Of course, nothing is the way it used to be." He paused a moment. "You'll have to meet them out there, you know."

"Yes."

"This Hamrick have any family?"

"In Los Verdes, New Mexico. I'll see that they are notified," Lee said.

"Mmm. You going to wait for positive identification?"

"We'll need their help in locating records. I'll make it clear we have no positive ID."

His back still turned to Lee, he stopped at the doorway. "You seen Buddy?"

"I'm going to check on him as soon as I make a couple of phone calls."

Another moment's pause. "You were not hurt, were you?"

"I'm fine." She lied.

Without acknowledging her or turning around, Mr. Terry made his way toward the front door. The old dog, responding to the sounds of movement, had walked out of Mr. Terry's office and was sitting, half-heartedly scratching in the general direction of its side, making a thump, thump, thump, thump sound as its hind leg hit the floor. As part of a mandatory ritual, Mr. Terry grunted a "Come-on, dog" to the animal, which had stopped as if waiting for the command. The dog followed behind Mr. Terry, the door closed, and in a minute Lee heard the rattling of the engine as the old Ford pulled out into the street and drove off in the direction of the courthouse.

She put in the call to the TBI crime scene unit, explained the situation to them and received assurance that a forensics team would be dispatched to Bartram County that afternoon. She typed out the request on office stationary and faxed the letter to the TBI regional office in Knoxville to confirm the request.

Lee got on the Internet and looked up the number of the Los Verdes, New Mexico coroner's office. She dialed the number. After a couple of transfers and some explaining, she was connected to Fred in forensics.

"How can I help you?" Fred said.

Lee explained the situation to him. "I have not notified Mrs. Hamrick. I was hoping that someone in the coroner's office in Los Verdes might make a visit to notify her in person."

"Yes, send us the paperwork and I'll see that it's taken care of. Do you need anything else from us?"

"We're hoping the family can help us locate medical or dental records to aid in making a positive identification."

"I'll do what I can."

"Thanks for your help."

Lee hung up the phone, turned to her computer, typed and printed a letter of request to the Los Verdes coroner's office, punched the phone number into the fax machine and waited for the connection. The line was busy so she put the machine on automatic redial. She looked at her watch. It was almost 2:00 P.M. She would like nothing better than to lie down and close her eyes. But there were still things that had to be done. The fax made connection with Los Verdes. She watched as the letter fed through. The little window on the fax machine signaled RECEIVED OK, and the fax machine printed out a log sheet of the call. Lee filed the log in her record of telephone calls. Documentation for Mr. Terry.

She needed to see about Buddy. She closed up her office and headed out the door. As she walked toward her vehicle in the parking lot, the sheriff's car pulled up alongside her and stopped. The sheriff rolled down his window, smiled and nodded to her.

"You got any idea what this mess is all about, Lee?"

"No, Sheriff. I don't know any more than what we found at the scene."

"It's about the damnedest thing I've ever seen. If I had to say right now I'd say the guy killed Hamrick, got to thinking about it, and came back to destroy any evidence. His bad luck that you and Buddy caught him at the scene of the crime."

"Maybe the TBI lab will come up with prints or something we can use."

"I hope it's not drugs or some kind of cult thing," the sheriff said.

"I'm not familiar with all the different drug manufacturing processes, but it didn't look like a drug-making operation to me."

Lee hesitated a moment. She felt as though she still owed the sheriff an explanation. "I know I went against your instructions, Sheriff, not waiting for you and the deputies."

The sheriff held up his hand in a motion meant to stop what Lee was saying.

"You used your best judgement in the situation you faced, Lee. You protected Buddy. I would have done the same thing if I had been in your shoes. Think no more about it."

Lee made a small nod. "Thank you."

"You'll keep me informed of anything I need to know, won't you?"

"Yes, I will," Lee said.

"You get some food into you and get some rest," he said. "You've been through an ordeal." The sheriff nodded his head to her, tipped his finger to the brim of his hat, and drove off.

The sheriff was right, she needed to eat. Buddy was still at the hospital and probably hadn't eaten anything either. She drove to the hospital.

Chapter 5
Collecting Buddy

WHEN LEE WALKED through the doorway of the emergency room the first thing she heard was laughter coming from somewhere. She asked the receptionist at the front desk where she might find Buddy Ruff, and the receptionist, with a grin and a nod, motioned toward the treatment area. As Lee walked down the row of white curtained rooms she heard the tones of Buddy's voice. He was retelling the story of their massacre at the house of the mad doctor and his giant assistant to a group of EMTs, nurses and doctors.

Dr. Peter Raymond stepped out of the treatment room just as Lee approached, shaking his head and smiling. He stopped in the passageway, a different, more personal smile forming on his lips as his eyes met Lee. Peter Raymond was in his early forties, slim, athletic, about an inch taller than Lee, attractive and divorced.

"Hello, Peter," she said. "You working emergency this afternoon?"

"No," he said, motioning toward the treatment room. "I heard reports about the trouble you had and the ambulance coming in. I came down to see if I could be of help."

"How is Buddy?"

"A couple of stitches in his scalp. His ankle has a bad sprain and some bruised cartilage, but the x-ray didn't show a break. He'll need a crutch for a couple of weeks. He's ready to go. Just try to get him to slow down for a while. How about you? You OK?"

"I'm fine."

"You sure?" He took her hand in his and examined her

fingers. He pressed and released her fingernails gently, one by one, watching their color response. "I could give you a thorough examination if you have an hour or two," he said, looking into her eyes and bringing her fingers to his lips.

Lee smiled, pulled her fingers away and slapped his hand. "Thanks for the thought, but I have work to do. I'm too busy to let you play doctor."

"Well then, how about dinner?"

"Sorry, I'll be tied up all evening with the Hamrick case. The TBI crime scene unit is on the way."

"How about a raincheck then?"

"Give me a call one day next week," she said as she headed toward the sound of Buddy's voice.

Buddy was sitting on a large chair that looked as if it belonged in a barber shop. His hair had been cleaned and someone had supplied him with a change of green surgical scrubs to replace his bloodied clothes. He had his left pants leg pulled up midway to the knee and a wide elastic bandage wrapped around his left foot and ankle. Everyone had pink-red faces from laughing at Buddy's story. The little crowd of well-wishers were returning to their duties as a nurse helped him ease to the floor with his good right leg. He hobbled toward the door on his crutch. Lee took a bag containing Buddy's clothes and shoes from the nurse.

"You look better," Lee said. "Are you in any pain?"

"Nah. They gave me something."

Peter Raymond looked up from his clipboard from behind the nurses' station and winked at Lee as they passed. Lee held the door for Buddy and the two of them walked together out into the sunshine.

"Hey, listen," he said. "If you've still got that headache,

I've got some really good stuff here. After one of these little pills you won't feel pain anywhere in your body."

Lee smiled but shook her head. "My headache disappeared at Hamrick's somewhere near the first rush of adrenalin."

She opened the door of the Land Cruiser for him. After a couple of false starts Buddy raised himself into the passenger seat.

"How about dropping me off at Helen's?" he said. "She probably wants to have a look at me to make sure I'm not missing any parts."

"You want to stop by your place for a change of clothes?"

"I've got some clothes at Helen's." Buddy tilted his head back toward the hospital. "Is he the reason you've been losing sleep?"

"Who?" Lee said. "Peter Raymond? No, he was just flirting."

"I don't know, Lee. He's good looking. He's young enough. He's a doctor. Of course, he doesn't have as much money as he used to. His ex-wife cleaned his clock, I heard."

"A nasty divorce?"

"Took everything he had. He was almost bankrupt a couple of years ago. Got real bad in debt. Lost his practice. He seems to be doing better now. Borrowed some money from his family, I think. Hell, he's a doctor, he'll recover from it. Seems like a real nice guy. You sure it's not him?"

Lee shook her head and smiled. "No, it's not a man."

"It's not a woman, is it?"

Lee laughed. "No. It's nothing like that."

She hesitated, not sure whether to tell Buddy what was

on her mind. But Buddy had been a good friend and companion and she felt she owed it to him.

"I got a university job offer."

"At Carters Mill?"

"The University of Chicago."

Buddy whistled. "That's pretty impressive. Are you going to take it?"

"Some people will say I'm a fool if I don't."

"Haven't made up your mind?"

Lee shook her head. "I have to let them know by the end of the month."

"Sounds like it could be a good opportunity. Chicago would let you pick up what you left behind when you came here, I guess."

"Yes, more or less. I would be back teaching and doing research in my field. And the money would be a whole lot more than my salary here."

"What made you decide to come back here?"

"I wasn't happy doing what I was doing and going where I was headed. This looked like a good place for me to come."

"You been happy here?"

"Mostly. I have the peace of mind that I needed. I like most of the people here. The University is close by. I like the job I'm doing. I think it's important. And as long as the people I do it for appreciate the work I do . . ." Lee waved her hand.

"Old man Terry hasn't been giving you the kind of respect you're used to, has he? Bartram County's not exactly making your head swim with excitement either."

"Today was pretty exciting."

"No argument there." Buddy stared out the windshield. "You've been here what, about a year?"

"A year next month," Lee said.

"Might not get too many good chances to go back."

Lee didn't say anything.

"I'd hate like hell to see you go."

It was well after the lunch hour rush when they arrived at Helen's Diner. The place was almost empty. Helen stood looking at Buddy's swollen and bruised face and his bandaged foot. Her fingers were touching her lips and tears were in her eyes. She made a small involuntary sob under her breath as Buddy put an arm around her and whispered something to her. She smiled, laughed quietly, whispered something to him, kissed him and wiped her eyes.

"I'm hungry as hell," Buddy said, turning around. "All I've had since breakfast was a package of cheese crackers. You want something to eat, Lee?"

She did. Lee could feel her strength returning as they ate, drank and laughed at Buddy's stories about how big the guy in the laboratory suit was and how big Luther's shotgun was, and how strong the guy was, and how bad the corpse smelled, and about the acid vat. Each time he told it the story got a little funnier and Lee could see an epic tale taking shape.

"To tell you the truth, Lee, I was scared to death lying in the dark in that hallway. I could hear that crazy bastard on the other side of the door bumping around, running motors. I could just see him pouring acid into that vat from those big glass jugs. I didn't know if he was going to come out of there or stay in. And me just laying there helpless. I've never been so glad to see anyone as I was to see you coming down that dark hallway holding that big old shotgun of Luther's."

"If we hadn't run across Luther and his family we might still be driving around those backroads trying to find our way to Hamrick's house," Lee said. "I can't believe we went all the way to Sugar Grove."

"You went all the way down to Sugar Grove?" Helen laughed. "You went in the wrong direction for Howard's Hotel."

"We didn't know we were looking for Howard's Hotel at first," Buddy said. "Hell, by the time we found out that's what we were looking for, we'd drove ten or fifteen miles out of the way."

Buddy laughed again. "Did you ever get a look in Hamrick's garage, Lee?"

"Yes, I did."

"What kind of car did he drive?"

"An old yellow Buick."

They both laughed again. It felt good to Lee.

"I said it was only a probability that it was an expensive German automobile."

"Oh, don't make me laugh any more," Buddy said. "It's making my head hurt too much. You talked to Mr. Terry yet?" Buddy grinned.

"I saw him at the office a little while ago."

"His usual goodnatured self?"

"He was not very complimentary about our morning's work."

"I can imagine." Buddy shook his head. "I don't know why the old fellow doesn't just retire and turn the coroner's office over to you. I think he's losing touch. You do all the work anyway."

"I don't mind so much. It's the deputy coroner's job to do the dirty work. The coroner has to deal with the mayor and council. I'm glad he's around to do that part. Besides, I'm still the new kid on the block."

"I'm sure he's glad you're around to do the work, but he could show his appreciation by being a little easier to get along with."

"It must be hard for him, don't you think?" Lee said. "How long has he been coroner?"

"God, I don't know. Since the beginning of time. His father was coroner before him, you know." Buddy laughed. "I remember when I was a kid Mr. Terry had a Model A Ford panel truck he drove. A black one. Of course they were all black. The truck belonged to his father when his father was the coroner. Had the words CORONER, Bartram County, Tennessee painted on the sides in big white letters. Us kids used to tell each other scary stories about dead bodies in that truck. We used to dare each other to go up and open the back doors and look in it when we found it parked on the street. No one ever did. We were always too scared. Model A Fords make a kind of clucking sound out the exhaust when they run. Sometimes at night when some of us kids would be camped out in the woods, for fun you know, we would hear that clucking sound of a Model A going by and we would say, 'There goes the death wagon.' And we would get chills all over and wonder who had died." Buddy laughed again at the thought of it. "Mr. Terry was a young man then."

"Things are so much different these days," Lee said. "It must be difficult for him to keep up with all the new things in forensic science and laboratory procedures. He probably feels threatened by the changes. He probably feels threatened by me. Maybe that's why he's such a grump."

"Nah, that's just the way he is," Buddy said. "He's always been a grumpy man. As I recall, his father was a grumpy man too. I think he likes you."

"Likes me? He surely never lets on that he likes me. I don't think I've ever seen him smile."

"He may not always act happy about it, but he has actually been known to brag a little about you. And that's saying more than you might think. Not everyone of the older generation around here thinks a woman should be working with the dead naked bodies of their friends and family. And he knows he's not able to keep up with the day to day legwork. You can take my word for it, he's happy to have you making him look good."

"I'll try to be more generous in my feelings toward him the next time he snaps my head off."

Buddy smiled and shook his head. "I was just thinking," he said. "The car Mr. Terry drives now makes a rattling sound that's a little bit like that old Model A Ford hearse. Maybe his car's being haunted by the spirits of all them dead people he carted around for years and years." Buddy made a ghost-like "Oooo" sound.

"And I thought all this time it was just the cheap gas he uses," Lee said.

Their conversation was interrupted by a pleasant looking lady who came over from one of the cafe tables.

"Dr. Turner, I'm Madeleine Brown, from the University library. I heard you talking about the death out on Paradise Road."

Madeleine was neat and prim in a flowered dress and she spoke with a quiet voice.

"I know you said you didn't want to say who it might be, but I know Dr. Hamrick who lives on Paradise Road. I was worried that it might be him. He normally comes in the library every few days, but I haven't seen him in over two weeks."

"Thank you for telling me, Miss Brown. I can say that it was Dr. Hamrick's house where the dead man was found. It may be Dr. Hamrick or it may be someone else."

"Oh, goodness. Well, I'll tell you the truth. Dr. Hamrick did not look well recently. He was so thin. But he worked very long hours on his research in the library and I thought perhaps he was just working too hard."

"Was Dr. Hamrick a faculty member?" Lee asked.

"Emeritus," Miss Brown said. "He retired from Carters Mill University quite a number of years ago, moved off somewhere out west, and just returned here a short while ago. I understand he was quite a famous man in his time."

"What kind of research was he doing?"

"Goodness, I don't know. He retired from the Department of Agriculture, as it was called then. It's called the Department of Agri-Sciences now. We have a book in our archives on the history of agriculture in this area that was written by him. It's a rather old book. I remember I asked him about it one time after I first met him about a year ago. I recognized his name on his library card. He said the book was long overdue for a revision. He may have been working on that. I don't know for sure what he was doing. He was a very eccentric kind of person—a real workaholic."

"Did you ever meet anyone named Eddie with Dr. Hamrick?"

"Tall and blond, and quite a few years younger than Dr. Hamrick? Yes. That would be Dr. Wilkinson. They came in several times together. I don't know much about him. Dr. Hamrick did ask if Dr. Wilkinson could have library privileges on Dr. Hamrick's card. I told Dr. Hamrick that Dr. Wilkinson would need his own card, that it is a violation of university policy to give or lend one's library card to anyone else. Goodness, I hope nothing happens to the library's books and journals Dr. Hamrick has checked out. Do you think they could be returned to the library?"

"I'll try to see that they are."

"Well, thank you. If you will come by the library sometime, I'll show you the materials Dr. Hamrick was working with."

"Thank you. I may do that later on."

"Yes, of course, I guess you must have some very pressing matters to take care of with everything that's happened. Poor Dr. Hamrick. It's so sad to think of him dying under such circumstances." Madeleine smiled and returned to her table.

After Lee left the diner, people were talking about that awful business out on Paradise Road. Somebody said he heard it might be a homicidal maniac loose in the county. Someone else said someone had told her there was a drug ring operating out of the house. A man said his preacher told him devil worshipers were using the old house. Helen told them it was just rumors and nobody knew anything yet. Helen said the only thing they knew for sure was that Lee was one brave woman. Somebody else said mountain women have always been brave and strong, from way back when.

Lee started to go back to her office but she felt grubby

and wanted to clean up. It was only 3:30. The TBI crime scene unit was due by 6:00. She should have plenty of time. She drove home for a shower and a change of clothes.

She didn't realize until she stood under the warm shower how tense she had been and how much her energy had been drained. She got out feeling calmer and more relaxed. She drank a glass of milk and lay down on her sofa for a few minutes while her hair dried. She laid her iPod on her stomach, put on her headphones, closed her eyes and listened to the recorded sounds of birds singing and gurgling mountain brooks as her mind wandered.

Lee opened her eyes. She had fallen asleep. She felt her hair. It was dry. Her music had stopped. She heard the sound of her phone alert coming from the bedroom. When she picked it up the display indicated two calls had come in twenty minutes apart, both from the sheriff's radio dispatcher. The first call had been drowned out by the music player when she was asleep. She called Margy's number.

"Lee, the TBI people just left here with the sheriff on the way out to the Hamrick house."

"Thanks, Margy. Radio ahead, please, that I'm on my way."

Chapter 6
The Crime Scene Unit Arrives

THE ROADWAY IN front of Hamrick's house was lined with vehicles when Lee arrived. A small group of men and women stood in the driveway talking. Deputy Billy Longtree was directing traffic and trying to clear back a cluster of curious local citizens. Two white vans with the logo Crime Scene Unit, Tennessee Bureau of Investigation were stopped in front of the entrance to the driveway. Lee parked her Land Cruiser just across the road and walked past the two vans where the members of the unit were unloading. One of the men standing at the entranceway wearing a TBI Crime Scene Unit jacket waved to her. It was Tom Davis. She had worked with him on the MacDonald drowning case the past spring.

"Hello, Lee, good to see you."

"Good to see you, Tom. Got a strange one this time."

"I brought along extra help," Tom said, "To deal with the chemical situation."

"Glad you could make it on such short notice. Maybe we can wrap it up quickly and get you back home before too late."

"Late hours are all part of the job," Tom said. "The Grim Reaper doesn't punch a time clock. We better get started, to take advantage of the daylight we have left."

Three members of Tom's team began a meticulous search of the driveway, starting at the entrance where the fender from Luther's damaged truck and other debris from the collision were scattered. Wherever they found a piece of possible evidence they stuck a small numbered flag in the ground at the spot, photographed it, measured its location with a tape measure, bagged it, and recorded the information on an evidence log and a map of the scene.

Tom brought out a large pad of paper. Following Lee's instructions he drew a rough floor plan of the house, marking and labeling the office area where the body was first discovered. On another sheet of paper he sketched out the floor plan of the concrete block building containing the laboratory.

"As I see it," Tom said, "we have two crime scenes. The first one is in the house where the body was found–the probable location of death. The second crime scene is the laboratory where the attempted disposal of the body and the assault on you and Buddy took place. As far as you know, the only persons on the premises other than the suspect were you, Buddy Ruff, Sheriff Eberhard, Deputy Faust and Deputy Longtree?"

"As far as I know."

"I'll need to have the shoes and clothes that each of you were wearing when you entered the crime scene, your fingerprints, and a sample of your hair. I'll give you some large plastic evidence bags. Seal up everyone's things separately."

* * *

"He wants my shoes and my clothes?" Billy asked when Lee told him of the instructions from Tom Davis.

"Plus your fingerprints and a sample of your hair. So he can eliminate our effects from the crime scene. The logic is that any prints or fibers that weren't left at the crime scene by us were left by one or more persons of possible interest."

In no more than thirty minutes the lab team had searched a clear path up to the house and around to the laboratory. They brought back several bags containing possible evidence. Then the vans were driven up the driveway closer to the crime scenes, one near the front of the house and one near the entrance to the laboratory. Tom briefed his crew on the situation inside each structure, went over the floor plans with them and assigned each of them their responsibilities.

After setting up floodlights to illuminate the outside work areas around the house and the laboratory building, the team unloaded cases and satchels containing their equipment. The technicians slipped Tyvek boots over their shoes. The five members of the crime team, carrying various sizes and shapes of equipment and containers, disappeared one by one into the dark buildings. Three technicians went directly to the laboratory to try to neutralize the action in the acid vat.

Back at the house, one technician took canisters and specialized lighting equipment from an insulated metal case and began a sweep of the foyer of the house, spraying a fine mist before him as he proceeded very slowly, shining a laser light over the surface as he went. Footprints and other shapes appeared on the surface of the floor as the light passed over them. Another technician with a camera followed closely, taking photographs at several spots as they worked their way across the living room toward Hamrick's computer.

Lee started back toward her vehicle. She watched the windows of the house light up from inside as the team went about their work. She called ahead before driving back to Carters Mill to leave word for Buddy and the sheriff that she was on her way to pick up their shoes and clothes.

She went first to her house to retrieve her soiled clothes and to get another pair of shoes to wear. Then she drove back to her office where she got the bloodied lab coat and put it in the evidence bag with her clothes and shoes. While she was there she also got evidence bags and stickers, and her camera, along with several memory cards and batteries for it. Buddy was still at Helen's Diner when Lee arrived there.

"He's in the office lying down," Helen said. "He's been dozing for a couple of hours. He wasn't feeling too good."

Lee quietly opened the door to Helen's office. Buddy was lying on her sofa. He cracked one eye open and grinned.

"How you doing, tough guy?" She asked.

"Well, besides the fact that my head is hurting like hell and I got pains shooting up from my ankle, I feel pretty good. Something up?"

She told him about Tom Davis' request.

"Easy enough for me. My stuff's still in the bag from the hospital. Hold up just a minute if you can. Let me put on some clothes. I want to go back out there with you."

"I don't think you're in any shape to be going back out tonight."

"Now, Lee, you be careful or you'll hurt my manly pride."

"Buddy, I'm serious. I think that lick on your head did more damage than we thought."

"This ain't nothin, Lee. Let me get up and have a cup of Helen's coffee and take some pain pills for my ankle. I'll be good as new. You might need me."

Lee humored him only because she thought that after he sat up for a few minutes and moved about, he would come to his senses and realize he needed time to recuperate. They sat at a quiet table, drank black coffee and each ate a slice of apple pie as she filled Buddy in on the events at Hamrick's.

Their conversation was interrupted by the low drone of heavy motors. Everyone in the restaurant stopped talking as the drone grew louder and louder and was joined by a whop, whop, whop sound.

"Helicopters," Buddy said. His face had turned a pale gray.

Dishes rattled as the sound grew nearer and louder until finally the deep rumble of big motors and the whop of chopper blades sounded as if they were right on top of the little diner. People went to the windows and the doors of the restaurant to look out, holding their hands over their ears.

Lee turned to look at Buddy and he was gone. He was already halfway to the front door, half pushing and half dragging his crutch as he ran to the door and out of the restaurant.

Two large helicopters, their running lights blinking in the night sky, hovered above the parking lot, then turned slowly and headed south, their bright floodlights shining in their path.

Buddy was standing in the parking lot looking up at the source of the noise and light, the look of fear on his face.

"Who do you suppose that is?" Lee shouted.

"They're headed toward Hamrick's place." Buddy shouted back.

"How do you know that?"

"Where else?"

"I better get out there," Lee yelled.

"I'm going with you," Buddy yelled back.

"No, you're not." Lee shook her head emphatically.

"I'm going." Buddy said. "Do I go with you, or do I beg a

ride with somebody?"

"Oh, all right!" she said. "I don't think you're up to it, but I don't have time to stand here and argue."

By the time they were inside Lee's Land Cruiser there was already traffic about the helicopters on the police radio. Lee told Buddy to buckle up. She pulled into the street, accelerating rapidly. They were still ten minutes away when she heard a call from the deputy at the Hamrick house reporting the landing of two helicopters in a meadow adjoining the house. He was asking for instructions from the sheriff. The evening dispatcher radioed back that he would try to locate the sheriff who had left the Hamrick house and was off duty. Lee radioed in.

"HQ this is Lee Turner. You copy?"

"10-4, Lee."

"I'm on my way to the Hamrick house. ETA, ten minutes. Tell everyone to hold tight until I get there."

Chapter 7
The Federal Connection

THEY SPED ALONG the streets through campus, out on to Ridge Road toward Paradise Road, Lee trying to make sense out of what was happening.

"Who could possibly have this kind of interest in Hamrick?" Lee asked.

"And where the hell did they come from?" Buddy said.

When they arrived at the Hamrick house the driveway was blocked by a collection of vehicles of spectators and by sheriff's department patrol cars trying to get through. Blue lights flashed on all sides and flashlights waved in the darkness in seemingly nonsensical movements. Deputy Billy Longtree was still there directing traffic. Lee stopped several cars short of the driveway. Billy came over to her window.

"Any chance I can get up the drive, Billy?"

"Not right away, Lee. Half the county's come out to see what's going on."

"Is Sheriff Eberhard here?"

"No. We're trying to get in touch with him."

"How about getting in with us, Billy. I want you at the house with me."

Billy opened the door and got in the back seat. Lee told them, "Hold on," as she flipped the vehicle into four wheel drive and turned off the shoulder of the road. She drove across the drainage ditch and through the tall grass and scrub trees in the direction of the house. Limbs and leaves and tall weeds quivered and shook in the headlights of the Land Cruiser and disappeared under the front of the vehicle as she plowed forward.

When she pulled out of the undergrowth into the yard near the house she could see the bright lights from the helicopters sitting in the adjoining field. Two groups of people were facing each other at the front of the house in the floodlights. Tom Davis and his TBI forensics crew were standing at the gate to the front yard of the house, a sheriff's deputy with them. The group facing them was composed of perhaps a half-dozen men dressed in military camouflage. Two other uniformed men were moving through the lights of the helicopters, driving a small dolly loaded with metal containers in the direction of the crime scene van which was blocking the driveway. The leader of the uniformed men was talking to Tom Davis and Tom was shaking his head from side to side. Tom made a remark to the leader and pointed toward Lee's vehicle.

"What in the hell?" Buddy said.

Lee and Billy got out followed by Buddy and walked toward the two men. Tom nodded and spoke to her.

"Lee, this is Major Cates. He says he has some interest in your crime scene."

There was no mistaking that Major Cates was a military officer. An officer of what branch of the military Lee couldn't tell by his uniform. His lean muscular fitness belied the age indicated by his short graying hair. He had an arrogance about him that smacked of military rank.

Lee introduced herself. "I'm Dr. Turner," she said, extending her hand. "I'm in charge of the crime scene. What can I do for you?"

The Major did not nod, offer a greeting, or a handshake. He remained a little too erect, and what might have been a tight smile turned at the corners into a just barely noticeable smirk.

"Major Harold Cates, Director of Security at the National Research Laboratories at Oak Ridge, operating under the authority of the National Security Agency."

"What brings you to our little county, Major Cates?" Lee said, smiling as casually as she could manage under the uncertainty of the circumstances. "Do we have a national security situation here?" Lee's gentle attempt at humor was lost on the Major.

"At the time of his death, Dr. Alexander Hamrick was the object of a federal investigation. I'm here under orders to secure this location and the body of Dr. Hamrick and to preserve certain items of federal property and evidence germane to the federal investigation."

Cates produced papers and Lee studied the documents for several moments in the glare from the floodlights. They were written on letterhead from the National Research Laboratories at Oak Ridge, addressed to Major Harold Cates, Director of Security at NRLOR, and signed by the Director of NRLOR.

"You have walked into the middle of an ongoing crime scene investigation involving a wrongful death, Major Cates. The location is under the control of the Bartram County Coroner's Office, and secured by the Bartram County Sheriff's Department. We already have a Tennessee Bureau of Investigation Crime Scene Unit in the process of gathering and securing evidence.

"We prefer that all evidence remain undisturbed. We have our own forensics team on the way."

"Undisturbed?" Lee said in disbelief. "You make it sound as if Tom and the TBI crew are stumbling about the crime scene, smudging fingerprints and stepping on bloodstains. No one here is disturbing evidence, Major Cates. These papers indicate the object of your investigation to be Alexander Hamrick. We have not yet confirmed the body to be that of Alexander Hamrick."

"We have the ability to make that determination," Cates said.

"Do you? And when will your forensics people arrive?"

"By morning."

"Morning?" Lee could not contain a small snicker. "I don't think they will find any distinguishing characteristics on the body. The remains are being dissolved in acid even as we stand here and discuss it. When your forensics people get here tomorrow there won't be anything left to identify unless we can get on with our work."

Cates was shaken by that last information, evidenced by a visible twitch of his jaw and a small quick sideways jerk of his head.

"Look," Lee said, "it's not just Hamrick. There is a fugitive from the scene that we're trying to apprehend. We're searching for evidence of his identity and anything that might lead to his location. We have a very competent crime scene investigative unit who are patiently waiting to get about finishing their collection of evidence. Under most other conditions I would be willing to wait to sort this out. But we cannot afford to wait. I have no alternative but to exercise my duty and proceed with this investigation as expeditiously as possible." She turned to Tom Davis to instruct him to continue processing the crime scene, but was interrupted by Major Cates.

"I'm sure you are aware that federal interests supersede local government interests in this matter."

Cates' arrogance and his aggressiveness were beginning

to make Lee's blood boil.

"I don't think so." She said emphatically. "Not in this county at this crime scene."

"Dr. Turner, these orders authorize me to assume control of the crime scene. Are you refusing to allow us to proceed with the federal investigation? You are aware, I'm sure, that such a course of action could subject you to charges of interfering with a federal officer and obstruction of justice."

"Major Cates, you cannot just walk in here and take this investigation away from our lawful jurisdiction. Under Tennessee State law I have full authority over the crime scene. There is nothing in your orders that changes that. Those documents are not addressed to me or any official of Bartram County. They are addressed to you. They do not authorize me to relinquish the responsibilities of the Coroner of Bartram County to you. Without positive identification of the body as that of Dr. Hamrick, you have only property repossession claims. Those do not take precedence over a wrongful death investigation. But in any event, any claims you have must be reviewed by our County Attorney before I could consider turning the investigation over to you."

Cates took a step toward Lee. He looked as if he might explode. "I can have a federal court order here in a matter of hours. Is that what you want?"

"Do whatever makes you happy," Lee said. "Right now I want you and your men off the crime scene."

Cates glared at Lee for several moments. Blood vessels were swollen in his neck and temples. Billy Longtree moved up behind and to one side of Lee. He looked ready to tackle Cates. Lee thought for a moment that Cates might order his men forward, but he suddenly turned full around on his heels and walked straight back toward the helicopters. As he passed by his uniformed squad he said in short sharp tones, "You men, come with me."

Cates issued some unheard orders to his men, climbed into the side door of one of the helicopters, and within a few seconds its engines cranked over and roared into life. Leaves, grass and dust blew about as the helicopter lifted into the dark sky, its running lights blinking red and green and white, and its spotlight sweeping the house and meadow as it turned away, whined and roared off into the darkness. The remainder of Cates' men stayed near the silent second helicopter, some of them looking toward the house, some of them sitting and talking idly among themselves.

Tom Davis and his crew gathered around Lee. "We're through with most of the house now. The laboratory will take a little longer, maybe an hour."

"I need to get to Hamrick's computer," Lee said.

"That part of the house has been processed. You can go in."

"All right, Tom. Get photographs and lists of everything, particularly of the laboratory. If he gets back here with a court order, we won't be able to remove anything from the crime scene."

Tom took his crews back into the house and the lab, giving them their instructions.

Buddy hobbled over to Lee.

"I thought for a few minutes there we were about to have the shootout at OK Corral all over again. Why do you think Hamrick is so important to the feds?"

"It beats the hell out of me," Lee said.

"What did the papers say that he showed you?"

"His orders are to secure all documents, files, materials

and equipment, and to retrieve and hold the body of Alexander Hamrick for postmortem analysis. It looks like they're about to take this investigation away from us."

"You think he'll be back tonight?" Billy asked.

"If he can get the court order he wants," she said. Her mind was racing. "Buddy, stay outside and give me a yell if Cates or his men start back this way. I'm going inside."

Inside the house Lee went to the office alcove off the main living room area. She used her camera to photograph the scene of death from all sides and made shots of the items lying near the computer workstation.

The printouts had been removed from the printer, checked for fingerprints and placed in a stack. Lee browsed through them. There was a lot of email with a number of people, and printouts from library searches. But there was no single focus to the items. One thing was clear. Hamrick was still actively conducting research in his field of agriculture before he died. The computer probably held answers to many of the questions about this whole investigation.

The power to the computer was turned off. Lee flipped on the switch of the power strip. After what seemed like too long, the computer began the boot-up process and Lee stared at the words on the screen.

Enter Password:

"Damn," she said aloud. She hurried out through the kitchen door to the laboratory. Tom sent his most computer-literate technician back with her to the house. For the next half hour the technician tried without success to find a way around the password.

"I'm sorry," he told her finally, "You're going to need a computer guru and some specialized software to get around that password security. There may be a way to do it, but it's beyond my ability."

Lee checked her watch. She didn't know when Cates might be back. Tom had come in the house to tell her she could come inside the laboratory. As they passed through the kitchen there was a whining on the other side of a closed door. Lee reached for the door knob.

"Be careful when you open that door," Tom cautioned. "There's a big dog in the basement. I don't think he bites, though."

Lee turned the knob very tentatively. When the door was open no more than four inches, a tiny white short-haired dog with brown spots streaked out of the opening, ran quickly in circles around Lee, barked twice and stood at her feet, looking up appealingly, wagging its bobbed tail.

"Big dog," Lee said.

"Jack Russell Terrier," Tom said. "She had food and water in the basement. We found instructions on the refrigerator for feeding Henrietta. That must be her. She likes you."

Lee reached down and patted the dog who took great delight in it and whined again when Lee stood up. Lee crossed her arms unconsciously and looked down at the dog. Suddenly, the dog sprang straight up to Lee's chest. Caught by surprise, Lee reached reflexively and the dog landed in her arms. Tom and Lee both laughed.

"Cute trick," Tom said.

Lee tried to put the dog down, but each time she set her on the floor, the dog sprang up to her again. Lee cuddled the dog in her arms. "Lonely little Henrietta, aren't you?" The small terrier rested its chin in the crook of Lee's arm and wiggled its ears attentively as Lee talked. After a moment she set the dog on the stair landing and closed the door.

Tom led Lee out back to a storage room next to the laboratory. In it were cases and shelves containing unopened bottles of acid and other chemicals. A dozen or more laboratory animal cages in various sizes, all of them empty, stood on racks.

"These cages look as if they have been used," Lee said.

"Take a look at this." Tom directed Lee to a large chest freezer of the type used to store frozen meats and vegetables. He lifted the lid. Inside were dozens of bags containing what appeared to be frozen animal carcasses. Tom picked up a bag with a label that said *Peromyscus* along with a code number and date.

"A common mouse." Lee inspected several other bags. "These don't appear to be varieties of animals normally used in laboratory work. They look more like local indigenous varieties."

"I think they have a connection with the vat in the laboratory," Tom said.

Lee turned toward the laboratory door. "Let's take a look."

The crime team had their oxygen tanks and hoods off and were busy making an inventory of the items in the lab.

"We removed the body remains from the vat," Tom said. "When you get some medicals or dentals, we'll attempt an identification. It's a good thing you and Buddy came along when you did. According to the list of printed instructions we found taped to the wall, if the fellow you interrupted had finished the job, there wouldn't be anything left to identify."

"What condition are the remains in?"

"There's not much left. There is very little flesh. Enough for a DNA test maybe, but it's probably been compromised by the chemical bath. The teeth are pretty much still there, but the fillings and other dental work are badly eroded by the acid. The bottom teeth are disconnected from what's left of the mandible. Some of the upper teeth are still attached to the remains of the skull. Pieces of the larger bones are undissolved. If all the steps in the procedure had been followed to completion, everything that could be dissolved would have been."

Tom directed Lee's attention to cabinet shelves lined with sealed glass bottles, most of them no more than two inches tall, containing small amounts of powdery substances.

"Take a look at these," he said.

"What is it?"

"I'm not exactly sure at this point what it is. Minerals, chemicals, maybe. My best guess is that it's what's left of those animals in the freezer chest once they go through this vat. Laboratory analysis can tell us."

Tom took a vial from the cabinet. The vial was labeled *Rattus norvegicus*. Lee picked up another one labeled *Vulpes canis*.

"The same labeling as the frozen remains in the freezer. Mice, rats, fox, birds. Hamrick is reported to have bought roadkill from local citizens. I wonder if that ties in to what we're seeing here?"

"I couldn't say at this point. It's not like anything I've ever seen before. We found this checklist." Tom picked up a plastic coated sheet of instructions and handed it to Lee.

Lee looked at the checklist. "There's something familiar about this procedure. I've seen something like this before." She turned one of the vials in her fingers for a few moments, looking at it, hoping the thought eluding her would reveal itself. "Maybe it will come to me. Someone in the biology or chemistry department on campus may be able to help us figure it out."

"The liquid from the vat passes through filters connected to these drain tubes," Tom said. "The solids are filtered out. Judging from the other equipment here—centrifuge, oven, microscopes—it looks as if the filtrate was separated, dried in the oven and stored in these glass vials."

"Are there any logs, research notes or reports that describe the purpose of the process?"

"The file cabinets contain folders full of completed analysis sheets but the categories of data are all in shorthand or code. I can't tell you what they mean. Maybe we'll know more after we have a chance to analyze everything we've collected. Look at this." Tom indicated a metal door on one wall.

The door had a glass viewing window, two round holes covered with rubber flaps, and numerous switches, knobs and dials. Lee looked through the window.

"It's a cleanroom," she said. "What was he doing that he needed a cleanroom?"

"You got me," Tom said. "That's one of the mysteries I'll have to leave for you to solve. In any case, we're about finished up here."

"You and your team have done a great job, Tom. I don't know exactly where this is all leading, but maybe the evidence will shed some light on what all this means. Take a few of those vials with you to the crime lab, if you will, and let's have some analysis run on them."

"I already have samples. We also have prints, fiber and hair from the lab and from the house. We should be able to get something useful from that. If you don't have any further job for us, we're about ready to pack up our equipment and pull out."

"The only other thing I would like to do is get a look at his computer files." Lee said.

"Wish we could help you," Tom said, and shrugged.

Tom and his team began to carry their equipment, their bags of evidence and the case containing the remains of the corpse out to the TBI vans. As they filed around the front of the house carrying their cargo, Buddy came toward Lee at a rapid hobble on his crutch and his one good leg.

"Lee, something's up. It was all quiet until Tom and his people started loading up. But something is going on now. I think we're in for some trouble."

They looked over toward the remaining helicopter sitting in the dark. There were a dozen uniformed men coming across the yard, some of them carrying military rifles.

Lee walked out toward them.

"What can I do for you men?" She asked.

The members of the squad were tense and looked straight ahead, not making eye contact with Lee or members of the crime scene unit. The one who appeared to be in charge of the operation in Cates's absence spoke in a slightly too loud voice.

"We have orders from Major Cates that nothing is to be taken from this location without his expressed permission. He has instructed us to secure these premises if any attempt is made to remove anything before he gets back."

"May I ask your name?" Lee gave the young man a sweet smile as she looked pleasantly into his eyes.

"I'm Lieutenant Stewart, Ma'am."

"Lieutenant Stewart, I'm Dr. Turner. I represent the coroner for this county. The members of the Tennessee Bureau of Investigation Crime Scene Unit are just preparing to take the crime scene evidence they have collected and their equipment and leave."

"I have my orders, Ma'am. They can take their equipment, but Major Cates gave specific orders that the body and all evidence are not to be removed except with his approval."

"You have your orders from Major Cates, Lieutenant, and I have my duty as an officer of the court under the constitution and laws of the State of Tennessee. What are we to do?"

She waited, hoping for a reasonable response from the lieutenant, but all he could manage was, "I have my orders, Ma'am."

Lee could see the danger of precipitous action by Cates' men, having no other option available to them but to follow the orders left by their commander.

"All right," she said. "We're all tired. I need some rest. The deputies need some rest. We won't be able to finish up until tomorrow anyway. All evidence will be kept under refrigeration in the laboratory building."

Lee turned to Tom Davis, who had walked up next to her and the lieutenant some moments before. "OK, Tom. Have your people seal the evidence in the freezer. Lieutenant Stewart and his men will be responsible for its security. I'll settle up with Major Cates later. You all get packed up and go on home and get some rest."

As she and Tom walked back to the house, she said in a lower voice, "These people will not be reasoned with, Tom. I don't want to put anyone in danger, but I don't want to turn the evidence you've collected over to them either."

"I'm not of a mind to give them the state's evidence," Tom said. "They can ask for it through proper channels, but they're not taking it by force. Like you said, we have our duty."

"What do you suggest?" Lee asked.

"Leave it to us," Tom said.

Tom and his team continued with the normal process of packing equipment, bagging their protective lab suits, and generally preparing to abandon the scene. In the laboratory building they placed evidence seals on the freezer chest containing the frozen animal specimens and wrapped crime scene tape through the handle and across the lid of the freezer. They closed and sealed the doors to the laboratory with crime scene tape and stickers.

Lee went into the house. In the kitchen she opened the basement door and let the dog out. When they passed by the living room she turned and went to Hamrick's computer again. It was her guess that the computer files held the key to what had been going on in the laboratory, and perhaps clues to Hamrick's death and how he was connected to the feds. She pulled the backup tape from the slot in the front of the computer. Printed on the label on the side of the cartridge was the word 'Monday'.

"Monday," Lee said to herself. She opened the lid on a flip-top box on the desk. Inside were six additional tape cartridges, one labeled for each of the other days of the week. Hamrick was on a seven-day backup cycle. The tape hadn't been changed since Monday. He must have died sometime Monday or Monday night. Lee dropped the Monday tape in an evidence bag and slipped it into her pocket. She took the cartridge labeled 'Tuesday' from the box and clicked it into the backup tape drive.

As she and Henrietta came down the front steps, Lieutenant Stewart was there to inspect. He looked at the dog, seemingly unsure whether it fell into the category of evidence.

"She's my dog," Lee said. "She's trained to locate concealed evidence." Lee patted her chest, called "Henrietta," and the little dog jumped into her arms. "This is Henrietta. Henrietta, can you speak to the Lieutenant?" she said. And to her surprise, the dog barked at Lieutenant Stewart. "I'm leaving the crime scene in your custody, Lieutenant. I trust you will keep it secure." Lieutenant Stewart did not answer.

Lee and Buddy got in Lee's Land Cruiser and pulled down the driveway. They were hardly back out on the road when Buddy began to laugh.

"I'd like to be there when Major Cates looks in that freezer full of frozen roadkill. Tom left him a little surprise in the laboratory too."

"What?" Lee asked.

"A couple of specimens that should be well thawed out by morning. Ought to smell bad enough to gag a maggot."

He laughed under his breath and stroked Henrietta's head. "My teeth almost fell out when you pulled that stunt with the dog. You'll have to tell me sometime how you did that. By the way, why do we have the dog?"

"I like the dog." Lee said.

"Sure."

Lee didn't know why she had taken the dog. Partly she felt sorry for her. Partly she wanted a small personal victory over Cates and the feds. And partly she just liked the dog and wanted it for whatever reason humans are attracted to dogs and dogs are attracted to humans. Buddy's voice interrupted her thoughts.

"What do you think the feds are investigating Hamrick for? Transporting roadkill across state lines?"

"I don't know. But I'm sure as hell going to find out."

Chapter 8
Stranger in a Strange Land

BUDDY CLEARED HIS throat several times as they drove along. He turned the air vent on himself and rolled his window partway down.

"You OK, Buddy? You're not running a fever, are you?" Lee reached over, trying to feel the temperature of his skin.

"I'm OK. It's been a long day. My tank's just running low. That's all."

"Of course. I should never have let you go back to Hamrick's. You must be dead on your feet. I'll get you home."

"Nah," he said, clearing his throat again. "How about dropping me by the Blue Eagle. I need a beer and a hamburger."

"You sure? What about the pain medication you're taking?"

"I'm supposed to take it on a full stomach."

"No, I mean can you drink alcohol while you're taking it?"

Buddy's lips curled into an amused smile and he wrinkled his eyebrows. "Damn, Lee. You need to lighten up. It's Saturday night. It takes more than a little bouncing around to put me out of action. Why don't you come along with me? It'll do you good. You need something to eat too. You can look after me if you're worried about me."

Buddy was partly right. Lee was starved. But there was the matter of what to do with the dog. Lee didn't want to leave Henrietta alone in the truck. Her house was only five minutes out of their way.

They arrived at Lee's house and she took Henrietta inside and left her in the kitchen with a bowl of water and some leftover tuna from the refrigerator. Henrietta made short work of the tuna then lay down, spraddled out with her chin flat on the floor, looking pitiful. She whined when Lee turned out the light.

"Oh, don't be such a baby. I'll be back in a little while."

She couldn't be carousing at the Blue Eagle with crime scene evidence in her truck. She drove by her office and placed the backup tape from Hamrick's computer and the memory cards from her camera in her office safe with the other items she had put there earlier. She wanted to know what was on the backup tape but she would need help with that. It would have to wait until Monday when the shops opened.

The Blue Eagle Tavern was just across the county line on Warehouse Road in Oak Ridge. It was a favorite Saturday night hangout for locals and the university community. Every weekend there was a live band. The food was good and it was the only nearby place open that time of night.

Lee pulled to a stop in the small parking lot. A fog was rolling in off Melton Hill Lake with the cool night air. The neon sign on the roof of the building was a blue eagle in motion, flapping its wings. Blue neon lettering underneath the image spelled out the words *Blue Eagle*.

Buddy opened the door of the Land Cruiser. Muffled music drifted from inside the night spot. "Come on," he said. "You need a little fun. This will recharge your batteries."

"You're too old for this kind of late night nonsense, Buddy," she said, as she got out of the Land Cruiser.

"Old?" He laughed. "I ain't old. Mr. Terry, he's old. I'm just in my prime."

The volume of cars, trucks and motorcycles in the parking lot reflected the crowd inside swelled by CMU students returning to town for fall semester. As the doors closed behind them the lively, loud, Saturday night good-time atmosphere of the place—the smell of grilled onions and hamburger, laughing voices, low lights, the band playing rock and roll, cold beer and companionship—all those elements tried and tested by innkeepers throughout the centuries to salve the tired and wounded psyche, to submerge and drown their patrons' worries, had their effect on Lee.

One glass of cold beer in a frosted mug on an empty stomach and Lee quit worrying about Buddy. After a hamburger steak smothered in onions and mushroom gravy and two more frosted mugs, Lee was content and quit worrying about anything.

Ralph West, editor of the *Bartram Echo*, showed up about mid-evening. He, like everyone else in Bartram County, had heard about Hamrick's death and the helicopters. He wanted to know all about it. Lee gave him the bare essentials but declined to discuss any of the details. Buddy and Deputy Faust, who had arrived after them, were less restrained and, off the record, gave the newspaper editor a blow by blow description. West was clearly delighted with his evening's work and left sometime after midnight with a satisfied smile.

A couple of acquaintances of Lee's and a couple of Buddy's joined them at their table, and several other friends of friends floated in and out until Lee found herself sitting across the table from a gorgeous hunk of man of about her age. He had black wavy hair and was dressed in blue jeans, a t-shirt and black leather jacket. He could have come straight from a poster of Brad Pitt in his leather jacket and sunglasses riding his big red motorcycle. He was introduced as Jack Sheridan, a new CMU faculty member in linguistics or language or something. He kept looking at Lee and smiling in a very inviting way. After the first pitcher of beer when she asked him to dance, she discovered he had very strong arms and wore a wonderful cologne that made her think of sex. Everything about him made her think of sex—his smell, his lips, the way he pressed her gently to him when they danced, the way his hands carefully caressed her, his baritone voice that resonated in his chest.

Somewhere in the middle of a slow and beautiful tune with violins and saxophones they were dancing close when the sound of a helicopter could be heard passing overhead. They both stopped for a moment and looked up.

"I don't even want to know," she said, and they kept on dancing.

After the third pitcher of beer Lee realized she could not drive home. It didn't seem to matter much at the time. She certainly wasn't worried about it. In fact, it occurred to her that the situation was pleasant enough.

She remembered the band packing up. And she remembered that in the late night hours the fog had become thick and white and the letters of the neon sign on the building looked out of focus through the mist. She remembered Buddy had made some objection to her driving in the condition she was in and someone took her car keys. All she remembered about getting home was that Jack Sheridan brought her and that it is great fun to ride in a Jeep with the top off when you're slightly drunk.

She had enough presence of mind to know she was going to feel terrible in the morning so she drank as much water as she could stand and took two aspirin before she climbed into her bed, alone. She remembered looking at the clock just before she turned out the light. It was 2:30 a.m.

* * *

The dog was whining. Lee opened her eyes. The dog whined again and woofed. Lee looked at the clock. It was 8:30 A.M. Why had she gotten a dog?

"OK, Henrietta. I know, you need to go outside. I'm coming."

The sun was shining through the window. She tried to get up. Her mouth was dry and her head pounded. The dog barked again.

"OK, Henrietta, I'm coming."

She thought there was a tapping coming from somewhere. She tried to wake up. Her brain wasn't cooperating. She wasn't sure she had heard it.

There it was again. Tapping.

She fell off the side of the bed and headed toward the front door, glancing at herself in the mirror as she passed. Death warmed over. She grabbed a brush and pulled it through her long hair as she made her way toward the noise that had awakened her.

Henrietta was standing at the door wagging what would have been her tail if she had one. Lee opened the door without looking. It was Jack Sheridan. He looked clean and fresh, tall, broad-shouldered, and handsome. He was smiling that same sexy smile and holding the keys to her Land Cruiser.

"Hi," was all she could manage to say as she opened the screen door and took the keys from him. She knew she must be blushing.

"Hello," he said in that wonderful voice. "I apologize if I came too early. I found your car keys in my jacket pocket when I got home last night . . . I thought you might need your things, so I brought your . . ." He motioned toward her Land Cruiser now sitting in her driveway.

"Yes, thank you. I'm sorry you had to come out so early. I appreciate you bringing me . . . last night, I mean." She was stuttering. "I'm so embarrassed."

"I had a good time. I thought perhaps we might . . ."

Lee glanced at the keys in her hand and a sudden panicked thought came into her mind. She interrupted whatever it was Jack was about to say.

"Forgive me, Jack. Do you know what happened to Buddy Ruff last night? He was the man with the crutch sitting at my table. I was supposed to take him home."

"Buddy? The last I saw of him he was leaving with a woman. I heard her name, but . . ."

"Was it Helen?"

"Yes, I think so. Someone he called, I think."

"Thank goodness. I feel so guilty forgetting about him."

"He seemed to be having a good time. He told you to go on without him."

Lee felt relief and was embarrassed again. "I'm sorry, Jack. I'm not usually so scatterbrained. What were you saying?"

"I thought we might have breakfast, if you don't have any plans. Maybe you would be willing to show the new guy in town around a little. See some local sites?"

Lee had forgotten her house shoes in her hurry to answer the door and was suddenly aware of her bare feet on the cold hardwood floor. She glanced down quickly to make sure she hadn't forgotten anything else. Thank goodness her pajamas weren't unbuttoned. Or worse.

Talk about your approach-avoidance conflict. Here she was in her pajamas at arm's length from the sexiest man she had met in years and she was hung over so badly she could hardly smile. She was having alternate visions of being made love to in those strong arms, and throwing up on him.

"I would love to, Jack, but . . . I'm really in no condition right now to . . . I have a terrible hangover, and I'm dying from lack of sleep. Maybe later, after I've had time to recover?"

God, she sounded like a wimp. This was all her fault. If she hadn't behaved like a freshman last night, drinking until she couldn't see straight. She twisted her keys nervously in her hand.

Her keys? How dumb could she be? He couldn't come back later. He couldn't go anywhere unless she took him. He had come in her Land Cruiser.

She could call him a taxi. No, that was preposterous. Bartram County didn't have any taxis. She could call someone...

She looked from the keys up to his eyes. He was still smiling and seemed to be following her very thoughts and was waiting for her to change her mind. She smiled back at him. He had looked after her . . . done her a big favor, for heaven's sake.

"How about some coffee?" he said. "You'll need something to eat."

It was clear that whatever universal forces were at work, they had conspired to put her and Jack Sheridan together at this spot at this moment and there was no way they were going to turn him away from her door. There was no point in resisting further. Her heart wasn't really in it anyway. She could only pray for a rapid rejuvenation. She opened the door to him.

"If you don't mind waiting until I return from the dead," she said.

"Death never looked more lovely on anyone."

His deep voice was so seductive. She was feeling better already. Hormones can be wonderfully soothing.

"If you care to," she said, "you can take Henrietta for her morning walk. Give me a chance to freshen up."

At the sound of her name Henrietta jumped up and down. She obviously new the meaning of the word *walk*. She was at the door and ready. Lee watched the two of them as they crossed the front yard toward the sidewalk. Jack was tossing a stick and Henrietta was running back and forth chasing it, yipping.

She took two aspirin to try to ease her headache and drank a glass of water and bicarbonate of soda to settle her queasy stomach. She brushed her teeth and gargled with mouthwash twice.

About halfway through her warm shower she began to feel better. She could smell the aroma of fresh coffee. When she got out of the shower to dry off she found a cup of hot black coffee Jack had left for her on the counter. She pulled on her jeans and a sweater and went to the kitchen in her bare feet, her hair still wet.

Jack was in the kitchen and he was whistling. *Whistling,* she thought. She was dying from a hangover and he was whistling. He must take vitamins. He was spreading peanut butter on hot toast fresh from the toaster. It smelled delicious.

"You look great," he told her when he saw her standing

in the doorway. "I have here a sure cure for hangovers."

"Peanut butter?" She was skeptical.

"Not just peanut butter. Warm peanut butter on toast. Guaranteed to go straight into your bloodstream to replenish your sagging blood sugar level. And there is hot coffee and chilled tomato juice."

"Sounds terrible." She made a face as if she had just eaten a bitter green persimmon.

He took two small glasses of chilled tomato juice out of her refrigerator and set them on the breakfast table.

Lee set her cup of hot coffee on the table, opened the door of her refrigerator and took out a jar of locally made blackberry jelly. "I've got something here I think you'll like," she told him, and held it up for him to see.

Jack was standing right next to her. His eyes never made it to her hand. When they were face to face he reached an arm ever so gently around her and told her, "I'm sure I will," and they kissed.

It was a calm and rational kiss. A serious kiss, not an urgent and unthinking one. They stood in the embrace for a long minute, both of them very aware of the other's body. Jack smiled a gentle smile. "If the jelly is nearly as sweet as your lips, I'm sure I'll love it."

"Something is about to get too hot," Lee said, smiling back at him. "I think it's the toast."

Two more pieces of hot toast popped up from the toaster. "Just right," he said.

Later, after Lee had eaten the last piece of blackberry jelly-and-peanut-butter-covered toast, she said, "I'll have to admit, I do feel much better. Do you make breakfast every day, or just on Sundays?"

"Whenever you will let me."

"Can you cook anything besides toast?" She teased.

"I'll have to show you sometime soon."

"I asked Henrietta what she thought about you. She says I should watch out for city boys."

"Tell Henrietta I grew up in the suburbs."

Henrietta was lying under the kitchen table between Lee and Jack's feet. Every time her name was mentioned she perked her ears a little and wagged her stub of a tail.

"How about our deal, then?" Jack asked.

"What deal is that?"

"Breakfast and a tour of local attractions?"

"Are you sure you want my company?"

"Absolutely."

"Where would you like to go? What would you like to see?"

"I don't know. Just some of the local sites. Why don't you take me someplace you would like to go?"

"OK, but I warn you, you'll have to be easy with me. I about wrecked myself last night."

"I can be easy," he said.

Why was it everything he said sounded so sexual? "I'll have to check my office answering machine before we leave, to make sure nobody died overnight," she said. Jack grimaced. Lee laughed. "Just a bit of grave humor."

There were messages from news services and reporters looking for information and an official statement on the Hamrick death.

"Nothing that can't wait until tomorrow," she said. "I've already worked one day of my weekend."

When the front door was opened, Henrietta ran out ahead of them and waited expectantly next to the Land

Cruiser. Lee picked her up and kissed her on top of the head.

"You don't mind if my dog comes along, do you? I don't want to leave her alone right now."

Jack smiled and put a finger up to Henrietta's mouth, which Henrietta obliged with a lick. That was the first time Lee noticed the bruises on the knuckles and fingers of Jack's left hand.

"What happened?" She said, nodding toward his hand.

Jack looked at the back of his hand. He seemed a little embarrassed. "It's nothing," he said. "Just a little accident."

"When did you do that?" The scene of her and Buddy's encounter with the hooded man the day before leapt into her thoughts.

"In the fog last night, trying to put the top on my Jeep after I dropped you off. No serious damage."

As she drove out into the street it occurred to Lee that she knew little or nothing about the charming man riding in her passenger seat, aside from the obvious. Maybe she needed to slow down. On the other hand, maybe she was becoming too jaded and suspicious. She had been vulnerable and he had taken care of her. He could have taken advantage of her, but he didn't. All her instincts said he was a good man. *Relax and enjoy the day*, she told herself. *Get normal.*

"So tell me, Jack, how did you come to join the Carters Mill faculty?"

"I heard you were here and I wanted to meet you."

"I may be an easy drunk, Jack, but I'm not completely naive and gullible."

"Carters Mill had a faculty position open in Linguistics

and I was looking for something in this region. I thought this would be a good place to do some firsthand field research on Appalachian dialects."

"Your specialty is in dialects?"

"My specialty is really computer speech recognition. I just have a personal interest in southern dialects."

"Computer speech recognition, eh? Sounds impressive. Are you a computer nerd? You don't look like a computer nerd."

"I wouldn't want to brag, but I'm pretty good at what I do."

"I got that impression." *Shut your mouth,* she said to herself, *you're being naughty.* "I didn't know that CMU is a hotbed of activity in computer speech recognition."

"OK, to be perfectly honest, I have a temporary appointment to fill a last minute vacant position for a regular professor who's on leave. I was lucky to get it. I don't have any previous university teaching experience."

"I may be a short-timer myself. What were you doing previously?"

"I taught English and literature in the American schools overseas for three years. In Europe, mostly."

"Really? I thought once that I might like to teach overseas. Did you go to a lot of exotic locales?" Lee asked.

"More than I care to remember. But I got to do a lot of touring around Europe, the Mediterranean, and North Africa. That was good."

Lee watched him as he talked. He had a nice smile. Everything about him was attractive.

"I left teaching two years ago to go back to graduate

school at Georgetown University. I completed my Masters last year and stayed on as a research technician for a year until I heard about the opening here."

"So here you are."

"Here I am."

"It all sounds very romantic to me."

"It had its moments. What about you?"

"There's nothing to me. I grew up in Carters Mill, went away to college, taught at a university for awhile, became homesick, and moved back to Carters Mill. End of story."

"You don't really believe that. There's much more to you than that."

"How do you know?"

"Instinct and trained observation."

"You can tell a lot from my southern dialect, can you?"

"You'd be surprised. But tell me, what is there about this little town that brings you back and keeps you here?"

"I grew up here. I know the people and the places. It feels good and wholesome to me. When I'm away from here for very long, I don't know, I feel disjointed, like a stranger . . ."

"In a strange land?" Jack completed her sentence.

"Yes, like a stranger in a strange land. I feel like this is the place I need to be."

"Is your family here?"

"My mom died when I was young. My dad works for a company in Virginia."

"Any brothers or sisters?"

"No."

"You like what you do?" Jack asked.

"What do you mean?"

"A woman as educated and talented as you are, it just seems strange to find you here."

"There's that word again."

"What word?"

"Strange. What's strange about it?"

"Isn't it?"

"No. Everyone has to be somewhere. Most people don't make a conscious decision, they just wake up one day and find themselves somewhere, and that's where they are."

"Wherever you go, there you are." Jack chuckled.

"Exactly. I looked around at where I was, where I had been, and where I was going, and I decided this is where I want to be. The rest of the world has grown strange. This is normal here. A little quirky maybe, but normal."

"Not a backwater?" Jack asked. "This area has a reputation for being... "

Lee watched him carefully as they talked. He didn't seem critical, just curious.

"Hillbilly heaven?" she said. "That's what my dad calls it. That's the view of east Tennessee portrayed in Hollywood and New York City where they think *Deliverance* was a documentary and everyone in the south has a cousin named Bubba."

"Don't they?"

"Only in the movies. These are good people here. They have a sense of community. They know each other and help each other. That's what makes it special. There are still people here who don't lock their doors at night."

"Are you one of them?"

"No. I've lived in the big city. I have a basic fear inside me now that I'm unable to overcome and forget."

"I have that feeling myself sometimes. But if you feel that way, doesn't your job make it worse?"

Lee shook her head. "No. The death I deal with almost always comes from old age, illness, accident, or bad judgment. It's always sad and sometimes untimely, but it rarely results from meanness or violence. You might say it's a natural part of life. There hasn't been a murder in Carters Mill in forty years."

"That's amazing. What about the case you had yesterday?"

"The Hamrick case? Now, *that's* a strange one. I don't know what's going on with it."

"What was the business with the helicopters? Buddy said federal troops from the National Research Labs were involved."

"I'm going to have to speak to Buddy." She smiled.

"It definitely seems to fall outside any definition of normal."

"It is worrisome."

"Buddy told me about the vat of acid."

"I am definitely going to have to talk to Buddy."

Jack laughed and shook his head.

"What is it?" Lee said.

"I was just thinking about Buddy. He is a character."

"He's a good man."

They rode along in silence for a few moments.

"I'm looking for a place to stay," Jack said. "You know of anything?"

"Not happy with where you are?"

"Not for the long run. I'm sleeping in my office."

"You are not!"

"It's true. I got the job offer on short notice. By the time I got to town, there wasn't a single decent apartment to be had for less than a one-year lease. Being completely new to town, not knowing anyone, and not knowing the area, I wanted time to look around before I made a decision about where to live."

"In your office?"

"My office is quiet, private, and there are lots of public showers and such on campus. So I said, why not? I figured I would find something to my liking within a week or so."

"How long has it been?"

"Three months."

"Three months!"

"It's actually been fun. I'm a regular at the campus P.E. center every morning for a workout and a shower. The staff there think I'm a dedicated athlete in training. The faculty find it amusing, and the students think I'm cool."

"I find it weird. Kind of romantic, but weird."

"It's all a matter of perspective. Many places I've lived and taught, my current accommodations would be considered a luxury. In the future when I'm a renowned linguist, this will be looked back on as my bohemian days."

"I can see how that could be true. Are you looking for a house, apartment, or what, Mr. Kerouac?"

"Something furnished. Nothing big. No noisy neighbors.

Something sort of comfortable and quiet with privacy and atmosphere. Maybe something in one of the old houses or a cottage."

"I may know of something."

Lee drove them through town and turned at the courthouse onto Gilmer Street. One block south she pulled to a stop in the driveway of a large white two story Georgian style house with porches on three sides.

"Does it come furnished?" Jack asked. "I said nothing big."

"Come on in."

They were met at the door by Mrs. Garrison, the great, great granddaughter of George Jefferson Cunningham, the original owner and builder of the house.

After introductions, Lee asked, "Is your guest house still available?"

Mrs. Garrison looked Jack over and gave him a wink. "Sure is, honey. Take him out back and give him the tour."

The guest house was originally a detached freestanding two story kitchen that now was connected to the main house on the back by a veranda. It was over a hundred years old but it was newly renovated and everything was clean and shiny with central heat and air. The rooms above ground had polished wood floors, open beam ceilings, and were furnished in high Victorian style. Down a flight of stairs with a polished wooden handrail was the old basement, converted to a beautiful and comfortable den with slate stone floors and granite masonry walls. The back of the basement was above ground and opened onto a landscaped walled garden containing flowers, shrubs, and a fish pond.

"I love it," Jack said.

Lee took his arm. "I thought you might."

Jack wrote a check for the first month's rent and became the new tenant of the Cunningham guest house.

"When will you be moving in?" asked Mrs. Garrison.

"The next day or two," Jack said. "I don't have too much to move—just a computer and stereo, clothes, and books—a few odds and ends."

"Humph, you need to find a place and settle down," Mrs. Garrison offered.

Jack looked out the back window as they drove away.

"That's a great place," he said. "I'm going to like it here."

Lee's phone sounded a chime and she took it out of her pocket and looked at the display. It was a text from the dispatcher at the sheriff's office. "A Major Cates is here looking for you. He has papers."

Lee pulled to the curb and texted back. "Not available. Thanks."

Jack looked over at her. "You don't look happy. Anything wrong?"

"Just office stuff," Lee said. "Nothing important." She tried to put on a smile.

"You know what I think?" Jack put his hand on hers.

"What?"

"I think your job is getting to you. I think you see too much of the darker side of life. You're becoming much too somber."

"You think so?" Lee watched Jack's lips. They were playing with a smile.

"I think you need more fun in your life."

"Do you?"

"Yes."

"And what do you suggest I do to put more fun in my life? It wouldn't involve you, would it?"

"Yes, it does."

"I'm beginning to see the picture."

"I suggest you help me find some good barbecue."

She couldn't help but smile. "Barbecue? I thought you were being serious."

"I am being serious. I was out of the country for three years. And then I was at Georgetown for two years. I don't really know my way around this area. Do you know how long it's been since I've had really good Southern barbecue?"

Lee laughed. "You may have come to the right place." She looked up at the sun and down at her watch. "It's about lunch time. Let me take you someplace I know."

"I'm your willing slave."

Lee drove them to a very unassuming building off the main street in Carters Mill. There was a cluster of vehicles out front. Inside was crowded with people eating at the few tables and a steady stream of customers with takeout orders coming and going. Following Lee's suggestion, they ordered their food to go and Lee drove them fifteen minutes out to Carters Mill Covered Bridge State Park. They sat on the grass on the shaded bank of the creek and ate their fresh barbecue plate lunches.

"Good food," Jack said. "Paul's Barbecue. Strange little place. I almost didn't see the sign. He could do a lot more business if he had better visibility. How long has he been in business?"

Lee laughed. "Oh, two or three generations. They may have advertised once, many years ago. Now they're a tradition. They cook their barbecue on Friday and Saturday, open on Saturday and Sunday for a few hours, then they close until next weekend. Practically everyone within thirty miles knows about them. Consider yourself lucky. We got there before they sold out of barbecue."

"Strange . . . but good."

The creek was calm and they could see the occasional swirl of water caused by fish swimming near the surface. Two wild geese swam by. Henrietta divided her attention between Lee and Jack and the many attractions of the creek bank.

Lee looked up from her thoughts to find Jack looking at her and smiling.

"What is it?" She asked.

"You're a beautiful woman. I was just admiring you and thinking how curious the circumstances are that brought us here."

"That's a good line," she said.

"It's more than a line."

Lee took Jack's hand and led him into the long, dark, covered bridge. She could feel the muscles of Jack's chest against her shoulder and his thigh against her leg as they stood at a window overlooking the waterfall and the creek cascading down the rock outcrops below. She felt a soft press of his lips on her temple and she turned to face him in the deep shadows. She stepped into his arms and was suspended in a kiss that she would have been satisfied to have last all afternoon. But they were interrupted by the clapping sound of the wood floorboards as a carload of sightseers drove through the narrow one-lane passage inside the bridge. Lee patted her chest and Henrietta jumped into her arms. She stood close against Jack to one side and heard the giggles of young girls through an open window as the car passed.

"You're trying to seduce me, aren't you?" Jack smiled into Lee's eyes.

"Seduce you? I thought you were volunteering."

"Well, what do we do now?" he said.

"You said you want to see some stuff. I'm going to show you some stuff."

"Oh yeah?"

"It's a short drive. It'll be worth it."

Lee drove them east through Oak Ridge, passing through the little city of Clinton.

"So, where are we going?" Jack asked.

"Into the past," Lee said. "Through a time warp."

They left the main highway and within a couple of minutes turned under a picturesque sign that said Museum of Appalachia. The entranceway was a long, shaded drive overhung by thick trees and bordered by very old split-rail fences of weathered silver-gray wood. Behind the fences were green pastures with small groups of cattle, horses, sheep, and goats grazing. Small clusters of ducks, geese, turkeys, and chickens scratched and pecked about in the leaves under the trees and in the grass.

As they neared the center of the complex, on all sides were weathered log cabins, barns, museums, and meeting houses connected by brick walkways and gravel paths.

"Is this where Maw and Paw Kettle live?" Jack said, indicating the rustic log houses and nearby antique farm machinery and implements. "Or the Beverly Hillbillies?"

"You're not far wrong," Lee said.

"What is this place?"

"It's a kind of living museum," Lee said. "Where the last surviving artifacts of Appalachian frontier and pioneer life are brought for safekeeping and preservation. It's part of the Smithsonian Institution."

For the remainder of the afternoon Lee led Jack through buildings and rooms filled with items from everyday life among the Appalachian mountain people dating back to the seventeen hundreds. There were thousands of tools and items of handmade clothing, bedding, guns, knives, cookware, furniture, glassware, farm implements, unfamiliar machines, clocks and timepieces, jewelry, shoes, boots, hats, toys and gadgets. There were hand hewn wooden boats, cook pots, wash pots, and watering troughs.

They visited the preserved log cabins of Daniel Boone and Mark Twain, smoke houses, outhouses, a one-room log school house, a one-room log church, a frontier two-story log farmhouse where the farm family and their hired hands had lived. They saw a grist mill, a cane press powered by a mule, frontier barns, and a frontier general store. There were wagons, plows, and ancient harvesters.

At one point late in the day they stopped in front of a crude and horrific looking one-room jail made of weathered iron plates, iron bars, chains, and coarse wood timbers. Jack was shaking his head, looking into the dark interior.

"Not a place anyone would ever want to be," he said. "It looks like something out of the old west."

"It's older than the old west," Lee said. "Settlers hadn't yet settled the west when this jail was in use in some little town back in these mountains and valleys."

Jack shook his head again. "It gives me the willies just thinking about it. Like some kind of medieval torture chamber."

A few yards further along the path they came to a tiny one-room unpainted wood house with a tin roof and a small stoop front porch. There was one small window with no glass and a wooden shutter. The handmade door was hung on leather hinges and was locked by means of a wooden latch operated from outside by a string that ran through a small hole in the door. Inside was a sleeping cot, a single straight backed wooden chair, and an oil lamp. A blackened iron skillet sat atop a small pot bellied wood-burning iron stove. The entire living area was no more than eight by eight feet.

"Now, this I know about," Jack said.

"Do you?" Lee said.

"Yes, I've seen similar cabins in Virginia when I was growing up."

"Where in Virginia was that?" Lee asked.

"I grew up just outside Norfolk. But I've seen cabins like this standing in fields and along dirt roads in the countryside. They looked just like this. The inside walls were often lined with cardboard and newspapers to keep the wind from coming through the cracks in the walls. No electricity and no running water."

"Who lived in them?" Lee asked.

"Often just one person. Could be black or white, man or woman. More than once I have seen small families living in them. This was when I was a boy. They're all gone now. I used to visit with an old fellow who lived alone in one. Whenever I went by and talked with him for a while he would give me a piece of hard candy or chewing gum from a jar. He was a kind old fellow. His tiny house always fascinated me. It was like, if things in the world all go to hell, I could always build a little one room house in the woods beside a freshwater stream and live a good life."

Inside the museum gift shop Jack browsed among the bins of items and asked the clerk, a middle-aged man with gray hair and a beard, to explain the operation of a handmade whirly-gig and several of the other hillbilly toys and mountain crafts.

While Jack was entertaining himself browsing among the novelty items, Lee's attention was drawn to a glass display case containing items of jewelry made from sterling silver, gold nuggets and sparkling gemstones native to the area. She asked the clerk to show her a necklace of three pure pink cut amethyst crystals linked on a silver chain and was holding it up to her neck, looking at herself in the mirror when Jack moved up beside her.

"It's beautiful," Jack said.

"Yes, it is," Lee replied. She looked at the price tag. "But it's too rich for my blood. I would be afraid I would break it or lose it. I think I'll stick with the synthetic diamonds. They're beautiful and no one can tell they're not the real thing."

"Kind of like some people I've known," Jack said.

Back on the road as Lee drove them in the direction of Carters Mill, Jack examined the sackful of items he had bought and wrote in a small black notebook he took from his pocket.

"Whatcha doing?" Lee asked.

"Making notes about that fellow's dialect," Jack said. "While it's still fresh in my mind. I heard traces of vocabulary and pronunciation in his speech that sounded like they might have come straight out of the fifteenth century British Isles. I've read about some of these rarer mountain dialects reflecting their Middle English origins, but to hear it first hand was absolutely fascinating."

"You think that was fascinating, I'll have to take you back up in the mountains to some of the communities that are really isolated. I can hardly understand some of them myself."

"Could you do that? That would be great," Jack said.

"What do you find so fascinating about dialects?"

"Dialect tells so much about a person. It reflects your experience and history and the history of your family and community. There is a lot of social history that has been lost that still shows up in dialect. Linguists solve puzzles about things like origin and migration of families and populations—where they lived, who they came in contact with."

"You mean like the clerk back there with the Middle English?"

"Yes, exactly. At the individual level, every life experience you have and many of your personal and psychological characteristics show up in your speech. A skilled linguist can sometimes tell you surprising things not even you know about yourself."

"OK, Mr. Linguist, tell me what you know about me from my dialect."

"What do you want to know?"

"Whatever my dialect tells you."

"All right, but first I need a structured sample of your speech. Say your vowels for me."

"What, you mean a, e, i, o, u?"

"Yes." Jack turned and watched her lips very carefully. "But say them more slowly."

Lee repeated the vowels slowly.

"OK, now count from one to ten, slowly."

Lee counted slowly with growing self consciousness. "I feel so silly," she said.

"No, no. Just a couple more short things. Say the word for the slick substance in quart containers that you pour into your engine for lubrication."

"Oil," Lee said.

"OK. Now, one last thing. What is the name of the masonry structure that sits atop a fireplace and carries smoke from the fire out of the house."

"Chimney," Lee said.

Jack wrinkled his brow. "It's made a little more tricky because you've lived in other parts of the country."

"Where else have I lived?"

"You have a little of the sound of the Great Lakes region. Not much, just a little of that. But I'm pretty sure you spent a longer period of time in California. Am I close on that?"

"Very good," Lee said, with honest admiration. "I taught at Michigan for a year, and you're right about California. I was there for five years. That was good. Anything else?"

"You are probably not the only professional in your family. I'd say, maybe your mother or your father?"

"Yes, my father. How can you tell that?"

"Your pronunciation of certain numbers and diphthongs," Jack said. "I'll go out on a limb and say also, from your pronunciation and inflection, that you attended a private prestigious university. If I had to guess, I would say Vanderbilt."

"That's incredible, Jack. Is this how palm readers work,

do you think? I mean, they learn voice patterns and dialects?"

"Hmm. I never thought of it. Could be. I'll have to make a note to look into it."

"This is great. What else can you tell about me?"

"OK, give me one more sample. Say the first two lines of *Mary Had a Little Lamb*. Slowly, please."

"Mary had a little lamb. It's fleece was white as snow."

Jack motioned for her to continue.

"And everywhere that Mary went, the lamb was sure to go."

"OK, that's good. I missed that the first time. You've recently been under a great deal of stress, probably at the office, and your boss is not understanding."

"My god, does that show up in my speech? What else?"

"You engender a great deal of loyalty in your subordinates."

"That would be Buddy, but I wouldn't call him my subordinate. He's more of a sidekick. But that's cheating, you met Buddy last night. What else?"

"You have a great deal of curiosity and want to get to the bottom of every puzzle."

"That's certainly true. My father used to warn me that curiosity killed the cat. What else?"

"You have great natural instincts and ability to judge people. Those abilities are enhanced by your Cherokee Indian heritage."

"Ah ha." Lee shook her head. "Your first obvious error. I don't have any Indian ancestry."

"You don't?" Jack asked.

"Nope."

"I could have sworn Buddy said you do."

Lee laughed and slapped Jack on the shoulder. "You idiot," she said. "I knew you've been stringing me along. Buddy told you all those things about me, didn't he?"

"But only after a great deal of prying on my part."

"Why were you asking him about me?"

"Because you're a beautiful and fascinating woman and I was instantly attracted to you."

"I can't tell if you're sincere or just giving me another line."

"Really? Such cynicism for a small town girl."

"I learned that in the city. What makes you think I have Cherokee blood? Is it my dialect?" Lee taunted him.

"Your eyes and your cheekbones. Also your general features and proportions. They seem almost unmistakeable. You're really not part Indian?"

Lee looked at herself in the rearview mirror, trying to see what it was Jack saw in her face.

"I would be delighted if I were part Indian. I always wanted to be an Indian when I was a little girl. It would add some romance to my otherwise mundane genealogy. Nevertheless, I'm going to have a talk with Buddy. He can't be telling my life story to strange men."

"Buddy is a good man. He's very loyal to you."

"He is a good man."

They stopped at a fish house on the Broad River and had a dinner of fried catfish and hush puppies. By the time they headed back to Carters Mill it was late Sunday evening.

They were both quiet. Jack held Lee's hand in his during the drive. It was well after dark when they pulled into the parking lot of the Blue Eagle where Jack had left his Jeep. They sat in the Land Cruiser several minutes in the dark, talking small talk interspersed with a lot of silence.

"It's still early," Lee said, "Would you like to come by for a cup of coffee or something?"

In her headlights Lee watched Jack in his Jeep riding through the night and she kept thinking of the feel of his touch.

They sat on Lee's sofa drinking hot cocoa and talking for a long while.

"I've been talking all day," she said. "You have to be bored to death with me by now."

"Not in the least. I love listening to you talk."

"But I've been doing all the talking. You know every-thing about me, and I know almost nothing about you. Why have you let me run on so long?"

"I want to know everything about you, and you need someone to talk to."

"What makes you think I need someone to talk to? I talk with people all day long every day," Lee said.

"What kind of people?"

"Business contacts, friends, neighbors, acquaintances."

"Close friends? Intimate friends?"

Lee did not answer.

"What kinds of things do you talk about?"

"All kinds of things. Regular things."

"The kinds of things we've been talking about?"

Lee did not answer again. She found herself looking at Jack through misty eyes. He had touched her where she needed to be touched, and his touch had been gentle and soft. Jack couldn't seem to take his eyes off her. She noticed it and felt a growing attraction to him. She wanted his arms around her. She leaned across and kissed his lips.

Jack moved closer to her and was about to say something when there was a sound on the front porch, a heavy bump that shook the door, like something falling against the wall.

Lee went to the front door, pulled the curtain back from the window and looked out. "There's someone lying on the floor," she said.

Jack opened the door and they stepped out onto the porch. Buddy was lying on his face in the dark. The smell of alcohol left no mistake.

"He's drunk," Jack said.

"Help me get him inside."

They each took him under an arm and tried to lift him up.

"Buddy, it's Lee. Help us get you to your feet. Come on, let's go inside."

"Lee?" Buddy said, looking at Jack.

"No, I'm Jack. That's Lee."

Buddy looked to the other side. "Lee?"

"Yes, it's Lee, Buddy. Come on in my house."

"OK."

Buddy couldn't stand on his hurt ankle. They supported him and helped him into the living room where they managed to get him over to the sofa.

Buddy looked at Lee through bloodshot, unfocused eyes and said in a slurred voice, "You stay right here, Lee. It's going to be OK."

"All right, Buddy. I'm right here. You lie down on my sofa and take a nap. I'll stay right here with you."

Buddy slumped onto the sofa. They turned him around, pulled off his shoes, and lay him down. He passed out. Henrietta came out from behind the sofa and tiptoed up to Buddy's face. She sniffed his mouth and nose and sneezed, then she licked his face a couple of times and lay down under the table. Jack chuckled to himself and shook his head, but Lee was worried.

"I've never seen him like this, Jack. I've seen him drink, yes, but this is something else . . . and on Sunday night. I'm going to call Helen Simmons. She knows Buddy better than just about anybody."

Lee dialed Helen's number.

"Helen? This is Lee. I apologize for calling you so late. Listen, Buddy is over here."

"He's at your place?"

"Yes..."

"Thank goodness. I didn't know where he went. I guess I should have known. He was saying he had to go see about you."

"What's this all about, Helen? I've never seen Buddy like this."

"Buddy's an alcoholic, Lee. Once he gets on a drunk, nobody can do anything with him. God only knows when he will stop drinking and sober up. Sometimes it's a day, and sometimes it's a week or more."

"I've seen him drink before, but I've never seen him drunk like this."

"It's those helicopters and the soldiers last night that set him off. He's having flashbacks to when he was in Iraq, Lee. He just kept drinking after I brought him home last night. He talked on and on about helicopters with spotlights at night, and soldiers with guns. He was shot bad at night in battle and they had a hard time getting him out. Lots of his friends were killed. He's got the past all mixed up with the present."

"I didn't know about that." The Darvon, Lee thought to herself, for his pain.

"He was saying all last night that he had to go and see about Lee. I left him at his place early this morning when I went to work. I thought he would sleep it off. But when I went by to check on him after lunch he was gone. I found empty bottles where he had been drinking again. I've been worried sick about him. He doesn't even have his crutch with him. I've been afraid he was out in the dark someplace and would pass out and die from exposure."

"Don't you worry. He's here with me and Jack Sheridan. Do you want us to keep him here or bring him over there?"

"What condition is he in?"

"Passed out on my sofa right now. He just appeared on my front porch five minutes ago. I don't know how he got here."

"He ought not be left alone, Lee. When he's lost in his nightmares about the past, he doesn't even know where he is. I would be happy for him to come and stay with me but I have my sister's children with me, and I don't think it would be a good thing for them to see him like he is. Let me try to get Billy or one of the deputies to come and get him. Maybe one of them can take care of him. I'll call you back."

Jack saw the worry in Lee's face when she hung up the

phone. She told him what Helen had said.

"He thought I was in danger and came over here to protect me."

"Poor guy. Still fighting battles from the past."

"Helen is looking for someone to take him home and stay with him until he sobers up."

"I'll take him. Tell me how to find his place."

"Are you sure about this? He can stay here with me. You hardly even know him."

"He's a friend of yours. I'll take care of him. I've had a little experience at this. Besides, I feel partly responsible. I was buying him drinks last night. Tell me how to get to his place."

Lee called Helen and told her that Jack was taking care of Buddy. About the time they got Buddy in the front seat of Jack's Jeep and closed the door, Buddy came to and looked around. He smiled an inebriated version of his typical grin and said, "I love this Jeep," and passed out again.

Jack drove off down the dark street in the direction of Buddy's house. Lee went back inside and closed the door. She shuffled around the kitchen putting dishes in the dishwasher and whiling away the time until Jack called and said he had Buddy at home and in bed.

She lay awake a long time thinking about all that had happened, about the emotions the day's trip had brought up in her. She thought about Jack. The thought of him was suddenly a constant companion to her. It was unsettling. He was not the kind of man she needed to get involved with. He was accustomed to getting his way by using his good looks, his wit and his smooth talk. The average woman probably found his charm irresistible. She could still smell the faint fragrance of his cologne on her skin, and the touch of his lips. Why lie to herself? He was exactly the kind of man she needed to get involved with.

Chapter 9
Ghosts of thePast

WHEN LEE LOOKED out her window the next morning her Land Cruiser was sitting in her driveway as it should be. She wished Jack were there again, bringing her keys to her. While she was waiting for Henrietta to do her morning duties, in the flower bed this time, the phone rang. It was Jack.

"Hello, beautiful."

"Hello, handsome."

"I'm about to take Buddy to breakfast at the diner. Will you join us?"

"Sure. How is he this morning?"

"More buoyant and good natured than he has a right to be, considering."

"He always is. Did you stay with him last night?"

"Most of the night. Helen showed up this morning to check on him and I ran over to my place for a shower and a change of clothes."

"Did Buddy say anything about last night?"

"Not much. I don't think he remembers much."

"I appreciate everything you did for him, Jack."

When she arrived at the diner, Buddy was at the table with Helen and Jack, waving his hands about. They were laughing at something he had said. Jack watched her as she came to their table. Buddy and Helen made little knowing winks at each other. Buddy grinned real big and winked at Jack.

"Lee, Jack tells me the two of you were out dancing all

night Saturday and didn't come in 'till the rooster crowed."

"Buddy, that's not exactly what I said."

"Why, sure it is, Jack. Lee, I woke up this morning and found Jack asleep on my sofa. I guess he dragged himself in there in the middle of the night. And he had this silly little grin on his face. He was asleep, you understand, and dreaming and he had this silly little grin on his face, and he was talking in his sleep. I never could understand exactly what he was saying but he was kind of sighing, and I thought he said 'Lee' two or three times."

Jack looked embarrassed for a moment, then he laughed, and they all laughed.

Helen offered Lee a copy of the morning *Knoxville News Sentinel*. The headline read Mystery Death in Carters Mill, and there were front page pictures of the helicopters at Hamrick's house from Saturday night and of members of Tom Davis' lab team dressed in full protective suits looking like astronauts. The article said the pictures were taken by Katie Horne, a journalism graduate student at Carters Mill University.

"I forgot about all the floodlights, it must have been lit up like a movie set," Lee said.

"There are more pictures on the inside," Helen said, turning the pages. "Look. Here you are."

A picture of half a dozen people standing together in front of Hamrick's house clearly showed Lee, Tom Davis, Billy Longtree and Major Cates. There were short quotes from the sheriff's office and from the coroner's office saying that there was no information to report at this time, but confirmation from the sheriff's office that a suspect was being sought.

The door to the restaurant opened and Sheriff Eberhard

came across the room to where they were sitting. Lee introduced Jack Sheridan to him and they shook hands. The leather of the sheriff's gun holster and wide belt squeaked as he pulled up a chair and sat down at the corner of their table.

Helen poured him a cup of coffee. The sheriff glanced at the newspaper lying on the table and turned to Lee with a grin and one cocked eyebrow.

"Well, Lee, the deputies tell me you all had quite a time with the federal troops Saturday night. Down at the station they're calling you Natasha."

Lee wrinkled her brow at him. "Who?"

"Natasha Romanoff, the Black Widow," Buddy said, grinning.

"The black widow?"

"Yeah," Buddy said. "The Avengers — Thor, Ironman, Captain American. Black Widow kicks ass and takes no prisoners. I swear, Lee, you need to get out more. You're going to embarrass me one of these days."

Everybody at the table laughed. The sheriff continued, "It makes me damn mad, them coming in here the way they did. We would've been happy to cooperate with 'em, but to come flying in helicopters unannounced in the middle of the night . . . that just about tops all the arrogant high-handed things I ever heard of. What do you think is so important about the Hamrick case?"

"I don't have an answer for that," Lee said.

"How did they even know about Hamrick's death?" The sheriff asked. "Have you thought about that?"

"I just assume that someone at NRL picked up on our radio traffic and passed the information along." Lee thought for a moment, searching her memory. "I called the Los Verdes coroner's office Saturday afternoon and asked them to notify Hamrick's family. It could be that NRL somehow found out about the death through their connections with the Los Verdes Labs or from Hamrick's family."

"They sure as hell got here in a hurry," the sheriff said. "I never knew of any federal agency to respond that fast. Must be important to them. I guess you heard, Cates showed up yesterday with some kind of federal order for the feds to take control of the case. My people gave him county attorney Goodman's phone number."

"I was notified by dispatch, but I wasn't in town."

"Just as well. Let Goodman handle it. He's good at it."

"Natasha, eh?" asked Buddy. He nudged Jack with his elbow. "Natasha. I like it. You should've seen her, Sheriff. That damned Major Cates came in here trying to steamroll over us and Lee took the steam right out of him."

"I think I'm glad I didn't see him," Sheriff Eberhard said. "Were you able to get enough evidence from the scene to carry forward your investigation, Lee."

"I believe so."

"Good. If Major Cates ever comes back into my county, I want to be the one to personally kick his butt. But I imagine we've seen the last of him. My deputies tell me the feds loaded everything up and cleared out."

"Any word on Igor?" Buddy asked.

"Igor?" The sheriff raised one eyebrow.

"Yeah, you know, Dr. Frankenstein's lab assistant. The guy who supplied the body parts," Buddy said.

Lee interrupted. "He means the guy in Hamrick's lab

who jumped us."

"The fugitive in the blue Pontiac." The sheriff shook his head. "No luck so far in locating him or the car. I've got people checking body shops and insurance companies now."

The sheriff looked at his watch and rose from his chair. "I've got to get rolling. I just came in to get a thermos of coffee. By the way, Lee, you seen Mr. Terry this morning?"

"No, not yet."

"Umph," the sheriff grunted. "Watch yourself. He's in a foul mood."

When Sheriff Eberhard had gone out the door, Buddy turned to Lee, an amused look on his face. "Well, Natasha, now that the feds have probably stripped all the evidence from Hamrick's place, where does that leave us?"

"That leaves us with our job still to do," Lee said. "We have an unsolved suspicious death in the county. If we can, we need to established the identify of the deceased and the cause of death. Our obligations don't end just because federal agencies are involved. And if you're going to help me with it..." Lee handed him a napkin. "You had better wipe that silly grin off your face."

As they were talking, local insurance broker Lonnie Chapman came in along with local businessman Bill Miller, and retired county commissioner Larry Bryan. It was clear even to the casual observer that the three of them had just come off the golf course. They were discussing with a great deal of animation their score sheets. Lonnie approached the table where Lee was seated. In his early forties, Lonnie had an even, dark tan and the physique of an athlete.

"Hello, Lee," Lonnie said, with a large cheerful smile and a firm handshake. "Buddy, Helen." He held out his hand to

Jack. "Lonnie Chapman. Chapman Insurance."

"This is Jack Sheridan," Lee said. "He's a new faculty member in town."

"Glad to have you here, Jack. You look like you might be a golfer. We can always use another player if you're interested."

"Thanks," Jack said, "I'm more of a fisherman."

"Fishing is good," Lonnie said. "There's lots of good places around here to fish. Just let me know if you need a good place or want somebody to show you around. I've been trying to get Lee here to join our golf club. Haven't had any luck yet with her, but I'm not giving up."

"Lonnie holds the record for the most golf games played in a single week," Buddy said. "How many was it, Lonnie?"

"Twenty-one," Lonnie said. "Of course that was an unusual week. I normally play five or six. My early mornings are almost always free so it's a good time to get out on the links."

Lonnie squatted down next to Lee and spoke in a lower tone. "Don't mean to disturb your breakfast, Lee. I just wanted to ask if the dead man out on Paradise Road has been confirmed to be Alexander Hamrick."

"We've not made a positive ID yet, Lonnie. Is Hamrick one of your policyholders? The reason I ask, I'm trying to get as much information as I can about Hamrick."

"Yes, Dr. Hamrick is . . . or was, whichever . . . one of my policyholders. My dad sold him his original policy close to twenty years ago, before I was even in the business. If it was Hamrick who died, or any one of my policyholders, I always like to start the paperwork as soon as the certificate of death is filed. You have any idea when you might have a positive identification?"

"In this case, that's a tough one, Lonnie. Without going into the details, I can tell you that DNA is about our only hope of a positive ID."

"Oh, my goodness. There's going to be family members and lawyers knocking on my door. I can see it coming. Well, I guess we can only do what we can do. You want to drop by my office, I'll be happy to show you everything I have in my records about Dr. Hamrick."

"Thanks, Lonnie. I may be around in a day or two, depending on what else is happening."

Lonnie Chapman gave his usual cheerful smile and a wave to everyone as he stood to leave.

"Lonnie, how many hole-in-ones have you made?" Buddy asked.

"Five altogether. Two this year. Mostly just lucky, I guess," he said, with a boyish shrug. "Jack, if you change your mind about the golf, give me a call. We play just about every morning."

"Thanks, Lonnie," Jack said. "I may take you up on that."

As Lonnie returned to the table to rejoin his golf threesome, Buddy said, "Lonnie could sell insurance to a pumpkin if it could sign the policy."

"He would find a co-signer if it couldn't," Helen said.

"You can be sure that every one of his golf buddies is a client of Chapman Insurance." Buddy chuckled.

Outside the restaurant, Jack took Lee's hand and pulled her gently aside, out of earshot of Buddy and said, "If you can, I'd like to have lunch with you today."

The touch of his hand seemed warm and personal to her. The only warm and personal thing in her life lately, she thought, if you don't count the dog. And it turned her thoughts away from the Hamrick affair toward more pleasant and happy feelings.

"If you can take a break from work, I mean," Jack was saying.

"Yes," she said, "I think I can manage that. How about meeting me at the campus grill around noon?"

"OK. I'll be wearing a rose," Jack said, kissing her hand.

At that moment, Lee would have gladly spent the entire day letting Jack kiss her hand if she hadn't had a job that was calling.

Actually, it was Buddy who was calling. He was saying, "Lee, do you want me with you this morning? If not, I have a few things I could do." He was standing next to Lonnie Chapman's new black Cadillac.

"You go ahead, Buddy. I'll call you if anything comes up."

Buddy grinned and waved to her, got in with Lonnie and they drove out of sight in the direction of Oak Ridge.

It looked as if Mr. Terry had already been in the office when Lee got there. That was unusual. Lee usually got in around eight-thirty. Mr. Terry usually came in around ten.

The sheriff's question had resonated with her own thoughts and stuck in her mind. What was it about the Hamrick case that was so important to the feds? Was Hamrick involved in secret NRL research? One thing she did know, Hamrick was retired from Carters Mill University. So she would start there. She turned on her computer and called up her Internet browser, found her bookmark for the CMU Library and signed in to the online card catalog. She searched under authors for the name *Hamrick*. There were two listings.

Hamrick, Alexander M. *A Comprehensive History of Agriculture in Tennessee*, 1988. Academic Press, First Edition, 868 pages.

Hamrick, A. M., and Campbell, G. *Techniques to Control Post-Harvest Crop Loss*, University Press, 1994, 223 pages.

Nothing suspicious about that. She went to the web homepage for the CMU Department of Agri-Sciences and searched again for *Hamrick*. The search engine found three items.

Hamrick, Alexander M., Ph.D. Professor emeritus. Department of Agriculture. B-4 Garland Hall.

Dr. Gerald Campbell was appointed Department Head in 1995 when the position was left vacant upon the retirement of Dr. Alexander Hamrick, who had served . . .

Since its founding in 1978 by Professor Alexander Hamrick, The Agri-Sciences Research Laboratory has become a nationally recognized center . . .

Department history, Lee thought to herself. Nothing secretive about that. She went back to the library main menu options and clicked on the connection to the Library of Congress. She searched for authors named *Hamrick, A*. After several seconds, the LOC search engine responded with 158 items. Either there were several A. Hamrick's, or Dr. Hamrick had been very prolific. She narrowed the search to include only the years 1990 to present. 22 Items. She asked to see the first 10 items from the search results. All were government documents published by the National Research Laboratories at Oak Ridge. She requested the text of the first item and received the message:

Not available to this work station

She tried each of the NRL document references in turn, with the same result. One item on the second screen was not an NRL document, and it held an unexpected surprise.

D'Ambrosio, Paulo, Hamrick, Alexander, and Wilkinson, Edward. *World Food Supply and the Promise of Science: Some Cautionary Notes.* Report to the Committee on Agriculture and Technology. UNESCO, 2010. 225 pages.

Wilkinson, Edward. Eddie Wilkinson. No doubt the same Dr. Wilkinson who had accompanied Hamrick to the CMU library. And the same Eddie reported by the paper carrier to be a sometime guest at Hamrick's house. She printed the publication references from her screen and shut down her computer, then dialed the sheriff's office and found Sheriff Eberhard still there.

"On the fugitive from Hamrick's," she said, "you might be looking for a Dr. Edward Wilkinson. He's a professional colleague of Hamrick."

"You wouldn't have an address for him, would you?"

"No. Only the name at this point."

"Thanks, Lee. I'll add him to the APB to pick up for questioning."

Lee opened her safe and took out the bag of evidence from Hamrick's. Among the items from his mailbox was what appeared to be a bank statement. She would have to ask the county attorney if she had the legal right to open and inspect that. The newsletter from the credit union at the National Research Laboratories at Oak Ridge was not sealed and contained no personal or confidential information. Another connection to NRL. She glanced through it and found nothing but the usual. There was one item of interest. An article assuring the credit union stockholders that downsizing of some federal programs and the resulting reduction in membership were not affecting credit union profitability or dividends on credit union shares.

She took Hamrick's computer backup tape out of its evidence bag, turned it over in her fingers and looked at it as if she might somehow see its contents if she concentrated her thoughts. She sealed the tape back in its bag and dropped it into her pocket. She looked at her watch. It was almost nine o'clock. The local computer shop would be opening about the time she got there if she left now.

Butch Hubbard was the closest thing to a computer genius Carters Mill could lay claim to. Lee had discovered him when she first arrived on her new job in Carters Mill and found that the only computer in the coroner's office was in need of the coroner's services itself—it was dead. Or so she thought. All the graduate students she asked said Butch was the person to see for any computer problem. She looked him up in his shop, a converted service station just off campus.

Once you met him, Butch was easy to remember. He had bright colored tropical rainforest theme tattoos over ninety percent of the visible area of his body. Once you got past the tattoos, Butch's genius for computers was unmistakable. On that first visit he had pronounced Lee's office computer to be not dead but merely comatose. After an investment of forty-nine dollars, and forty-five minutes work, he brought the old derelict back to life, unclogged its arteries, and had it beeping and chirping as well as a computer of its vintage could.

On this morning he had just opened up his shop when

Lee got there.

"Hi, Lee," he said, with a wave of his newspaper. "I was just reading about Dr. Hamrick's death. Sounds like *Tales From the Crypt*. Weird stuff. They find the guy who got away?"

"Not yet."

"I knew Dr. Hamrick, you know."

"No. How did you know him?"

"He called me out to his place last spring. He was having electrical power interruptions every time a thunderstorm passed through. Normal stuff for around here but he wanted something done about it. I put a backup power supply and surge protectors on his computer and his phone line. He seemed like a nice enough sort of fellow to me. A little eccentric, but aren't we all?" This coming from a man who could be a carnival sideshow tattoo exhibit. "He had some pretty impressive computing power. A little old, but impressive."

"That's what I came by to talk with you about. I need some help in finding out what's on this tape." She handed the evidence bag containing the computer tape to Butch.

"Hmm, high capacity digital," he said.

"Can you read it?"

"Not with the equipment I have here. This come from Hamrick's?"

"Let's just say it's critical to an ongoing confidential investigation."

"Yeah, I thought I remembered a tape drive on Hamrick's computer. If it's important I can get a drive and software to read it."

"How long will that take?"

"If I don't have something in my storage room—two or three days. If I have to order something I should be able to get it by overnight or second day air. You plan on running this on that old bucket of bolts down at your office?"

"What will it take to run it?"

"I can do it here on some of my equipment. You have a USB port on your personal computer at home, don't you?"

"Yes."

"When I get the tape drive set up, why don't I make you a copy and put it on a high capacity USB drive? That will be a lot easier to work with than this clunky tape. Depending on what's on the tape, you may need some hard disk space to restore the data."

"How much, do you think?"

"This tape can hold 64 gigs. It's probably compressed, and may be encrypted. But we don't know how much is actually recorded on it. Let me have a look and I'll let you know."

"I knew you would be able to help."

"Don't count your chickens just yet."

"If anyone asks about this tape, you never saw it." Lee said as she had Butch sign a receipt for the evidence bag.

"What tape is that, Lee?"

Chapter 10
Swine and Roses

LEE FOUND THE nearest empty parking space on campus and walked the two blocks to the Agri-Sciences Department. Students were standing in lines backed out through both doors of the office waiting for their packets of registration materials. The two clerks were obviously overburdened at the moment and probably would be for the rest of the morning.

When Lee was able to get the attention of Estelle Warren, the department secretary, and introduce herself, Estelle said, "You're here in connection with the death of poor old Dr. Hamrick, aren't you?"

"Yes. I'm trying to get background information." Lee looked around at the sound of a student complaining about some problem with his registration schedule. "I guess I caught you at a bad time, didn't I?"

"The absolute worst." Estelle laughed. "I don't know why they always wait until the last minute to register, but that's just students, isn't it?"

The sign on one door read, *Dr. Gerald Campbell, Department Head.* "Is Dr. Campbell in?" Lee asked.

"No, and I don't know where you might find him at the moment. He went over to late registration at Memorial Hall earlier. It's a madhouse over there. You might try the research lab first. I know he said he was going by there." She looked around nervously at the crowd of students in the office. "I apologize for the confusion here. We have several staff members out sick with the flu that's going around. It

143

looks like a bad flu year."

As if to confirm the truth of Estelle's assertion, her statements were punctuated by students in line coughing, sneezing and blowing their noses.

"Would it be possible for me to see Dr. Hamrick's office?" Lee asked, wanting more than anything else to distance herself from the concentration of sniffling, sneezing, coughing students.

"Yes, of course." Estelle turned and retrieved a key from her desk. "It's room B-4 in the basement. Please don't forget to bring the key back. It's my master key and I would be lost without it."

The old elevator moaned and bumped as it descended, and sat so long before its doors finally opened, slowly and uncertainly, that Lee thought that it, like her old computer, might be on the brink of death.

The basement definitely was not a high prestige office complex. The walls were of painted cement block and the floors were bare concrete. Lighting was your basic fluorescent.

It does have its advantages, Lee thought to herself. It would be hard for anyone to sneak up on you, the way footsteps echo off the hard surfaces. And it would be a safe place in the event of a tornado or a nuclear attack. It would also be ideal for anyone with eyes sensitive to sunlight. Lots of advantages.

The office doors were unevenly numbered and seemingly illogically sequenced. She searched for a probable location for room B-4. Finally she gave up in favor of looking for someone to ask. She found her way to an open doorway at the end of a winding hall by following the chugging sound of a coffee maker and the aroma of herbal tea.

There was a graduate student sitting with her feet

propped up on a beat up wooden desk, a sucker in her mouth, plaiting her long brown hair into a braid, an open book in her lap. The walls around her desk were decorated with posters of rockstars and movies, the most impressive one being a life size image of Darth Vader glaring menacingly from the wall at the end of the room. The caption read:

DON'T BE TOO PROUD OF THIS TECHNOLOGICAL TERROR YOU HAVE CREATED

The rest of the office was obviously that of a much older person. There was an old executive style desk next to an antique floor lamp and an ancient stuffed chair. Faded framed certificates and newspaper articles hung on the wall above an old bookcase filled with age-cracked volumes.

The student sneezed and dabbed a tissue to her red nose before she looked up and saw Lee standing in the doorway.

"Hi," she said, and sneezed again. "Sorry."

"I'm looking for room B-4?"

The student shrugged.

"Do you happen to know where Dr. Hamrick's office is?"

"Oh, yeah, sorry. Dr. Hamrick. That's here. He and I share this office." She said, motioning toward the unoccupied desk. "I mean, this was his office. B-4? Is it called B-4? Everybody down here in the dungeon just calls it Hamrick's office or Judy's office. That's me, I'm Judy Vining."

"I'm Dr. Turner, from the coroner's office."

"Oh, gross! Sorry, I didn't mean gross *you*. I mean, I heard how Dr. Hamrick died. Triple gross."

"I'm doing a follow-up background investigation."

"Yeah, I see. Suspicious circumstances and all that, huh?"

145

"I just have to tie up a few loose ends. Was this his desk?"

"Yeah. And those are his books," Judy said, pointing in the direction of the old bookcase, "And those were his," indicating two faded army green metal filing cabinets. "He was a nice old man—kind of weird, you know—but he was always nice to me." Judy blew her nose into a tissue.

"Have you shared the office with Dr. Hamrick long?"

"Over a year. I was lucky to get it. Office space is scarce. But Dr. Hamrick offered to share with me because I need the space for my research stuff and because he wasn't in the office all that much."

"Are you an Agri-Sciences major?"

"Yeah."

"What kind of research are you doing?"

"Gathering specimens. You know, plants and animals. My research project is on agricultural ecosystems." Judy pointed to clusters of colored pins on a map of the tri-county area that covered most of a wall. "I'm surveying the flora and fauna in three different crop ecosystems. I'm following up on a study done by the Agri-Sciences Research Center ten years ago."

"Interesting," Lee said. It was the same kind of map she had seen at Hamrick's house. "Did you work on the project with Dr. Hamrick?"

"No. Dr. Campbell is my advisor. Old Dr. Hamrick was retired. He spent most of his time in the library or at home."

Lee opened the drawers of Hamrick's desk but found nothing noteworthy, just paper clips, pens, notepads, scattered pieces of candy and chewing gum. The kinds of odds and ends that collect in a desk over time.

"I've been out doing field work for two weeks," Judy said. "I only heard about Dr. Hamrick yesterday. It's still hard to believe."

"Was he working on any current projects?"

"His memoirs, maybe. He was pretty famous in Agri-Science research in his day. One of the pioneers, according to Dr. Campbell. Dr. Hamrick used to tell me stories about the university and the department and stuff, about when he was younger. Ancient history. You know how old people are. But as I said, he was always nice to me, asking about my project and reading my field notes. He gave me some good ideas."

"Did Dr. Hamrick keep a journal or a notebook?"

"He had notebooks and papers in the briefcase he carried with him. I know he kept a journal. He used to tell me that every good scientist keeps a daily log of all his work and his observations. He showed me how to keep one and I've been pretty good about doing it."

Lee tried the filing cabinets. They were locked. Judy shrugged. "I don't know where you might find a key. Probably nothing in them but cobwebs. There were some books here that he used, some of the newer stuff. But they're gone now. Someone took them. You know how people can be, hanging around like vultures every time someone leaves, waiting to pick over their things. I know someone got his desk lamp and his chair. They shouldn't have done that. They should have more respect."

Judy suddenly had tears in her eyes. She pulled a tissue from the box on her desk. "I don't know why I'm crying," she said. "He was a kind old man. I probably should have been nicer to him."

"It's a normal reaction." It was painful to see Judy Vining in distress, but Lee didn't know exactly what to say to her. "I'm sure he enjoyed your company." Lee put one of her business cards on the corner of Judy's desk. "Would you give me a call if his journal turns up?"

Judy nodded as she dabbed her eyes.

Lee headed back to the Agri-Sciences Department office to return the key. She had taken note of the map on Judy Vining's office wall. It looked remarkably like the one on the wall in Hamrick's study. Judy was collecting plant and animal specimens. Hamrick was collecting animal specimens. Judy didn't know about Hamrick's current research. He must have been keeping the knowledge from her. Why? Were the points on his map the same as the points on her map? Did they stand for the same things? Was it a coincidence that Hamrick offered office space to Judy Vining? What was going on? Could there be any connection to what happened to Hamrick?

Lee wanted a look in Hamrick's journal. "Where could that briefcase be?" she said aloud to herself as she walked along the narrow basement hallway.

"Wherever you had it last." A familiar voice said in response.

The sound of another human voice startled Lee. She jerked out of her thoughts and found herself looking into the face of Jack Sheridan.

"Jack? What are you doing here?"

"My office is here. What are you doing here walking the halls and talking to yourself?"

"I was just thinking out loud. Your office is here? I didn't know Linguistics faculty have offices here."

"But I'm not real faculty so I don't get a real office. I'm just a lowly temporary instructor, cast down into this catacomb to suffer penance until I can achieve the rank of assistant professor. Or, more likely, until my time is up and my office space is given to the next unworthy person on the waiting list. These dark hallways are lined with offices filled with academic untouchables, social outcasts, and various forms of slaves, serfs, hags and crones. We're a community who joyously share our inequality. What are you doing in these depths? You know someone else down here, or are you casting lots among the lepers?"

"Dr. Hamrick's office is just around the corner."

"Hamrick? The late deceased Dr. Hamrick?"

"Yes. You never met him?"

"In the three months I've been here I don't guess I ever saw him."

"His office was with Judy Vining."

"I've met Judy. She's a nice kid. She gives me tea and cookies sometimes. I think she feels sorry for me. I haven't seen her in several days. Dr. Hamrick was her officemate?"

Lee nodded her head. "She's in her office now. I just met her. Did she ever mention to you what kind of research she is doing?"

"Nothing specific that I remember. Something outdoors. Isn't she in biology, or ecology, or something?"

"Agri-Sciences."

"Hmph. How is Hamrick's death affecting her?"

"She was crying when I left her."

"Poor kid." Jack looked at his watch. "Uh, oh. Got to run.

Got a department faculty meeting. Is lunch still on?"

"Sure. See you at the campus grill at twelve?"

Jack gave her a nod, a quick wink and a smile and headed up the nearby stairwell, taking the steps two at a time.

Lee returned the key to the Agri-Sciences Department office. The student rush had not abated.

"Dr. Campbell is in now," Estelle Warren said. "He may be able to see you if you care to have a seat."

Lee sat on one of a row of chairs that lined the wall in the department office. Students came and went, struggled with their schedule of classes, laughed, complained and whined until Lee began to feel that she was having one of those bizarre dreams common to students that it's the last day of the semester and she had forgotten to attend any of the classes.

The department secretary went into Campbell's office several times with papers and messages, and Lee several times heard Campbell's raised voice. Lee was watching the time. She had waited forty minutes. Finally the secretary stepped out and asked her to come in.

Campbell was on the telephone when Lee entered the room. He continued his conversation, giving her a nod and a summons to come in, by means of a quick motion of the fingers of one hand. Lee stood before his desk waiting while Campbell stood with his back to her, looking out his office window and speaking quietly into his telephone. At some point the telephone conversation stopped and he turned around to face Lee, his head raised so that he was looking down his nose at her.

"Dr. Campbell?" Lee said.

"Yes, and you are . . . ?"

Lee was irritated already by his lack of courtesy and his

condescension. "Dr. Lee Turner, from the Bartram County Coroner's Office."

"Yes, the Hamrick death, I presume," he said, not bothering to hide his impatience. "You've come at a devil of a time."

"The devil came at his own time, Dr. Campbell. I'm just following in the aftermath, trying to sort out the circumstances of Dr. Hamrick's death. This is no better time for me than it is for you, and certainly no better time for Dr. Hamrick."

Lee surprised herself at her own aggressiveness. She must have surprised Campbell too because he changed to a more polite demeanor.

"Of course. How may I help you?"

"Can you tell me Dr. Hamrick's status in the department?"

"He was Professor Emeritus, retired a full professor some dozen years ago."

"Was he actively working in any capacity for the University at the time of his death?"

"Yes, he was commissioned by the president's office to write a section of *The History of Carters Mill University*. Dr. Hamrick was one of the few people with living memory of events in the University's development over the past fifty years. We supplied him with an office and clerical support for his work. So many people just drop out of professional life after they retire, but Dr. Hamrick stayed active, tried to keep in touch with the place where he was so much a part of its history."

"I met his office mate, Judy Vining."

"Miss Vining is one of our outstanding graduate students. She won last year's graduate research award for her work at the Agri-Sciences research lab. Dr. Hamrick was one of the judges of her award winning project. He had great expectations for Judy. He served as a mentor to her. He was a very generous man with his time and his knowledge."

"So far as you know, was the history project the extent of the work he was doing at the time of his death?"

"That's all he was doing for the University, to my knowledge, but I know he was working privately on a modernization of his text on the history of Tennessee agriculture, of which he was the original author some twenty years ago. But, if you don't mind, I must honestly say I don't see how this relates in any way to his death or to the coroner's office."

Campbell's reversion to his original condescending tone indicated to Lee that he had decided there was no need to be deferential to her and that she had taken enough of his time.

"The coroner's office has the responsibility by law," Lee said, "to determine the cause and manner of Dr. Hamrick's death. I'm simply trying to identify all contributing factors."

"Dr. Hamrick was a very elderly and infirm man. His death was tragic, as death always is, but it was no real surprise. I'm told that he suffered from his pancreas and his prostate, either of which can be deadly at his age."

"Because of the circumstances of his death, Dr. Campbell, we have to be sure that his pancreas and his prostate didn't have any help."

"Surely, you don't suspect any connection between his

death and the University? That's absurd."

"I don't suspect anything or anyone. It's my job to gather the facts and to identify the agent of his death, whether it was accident, disease, old age, or foul play."

"I should think that a competent autopsy would answer that question for you."

"It might, if we had a body to autopsy."

"Oh," he said.

Lee could see his mind turning that one over.

He didn't pursue the obvious question. Instead, he said, "I apologize for the haste, but I have a stack of appointments waiting." By some hidden signal the door opened and his secretary stood waiting. "Mrs. Warren, will you supply whatever additional information Dr. Turner may require from us, and show my next appointment in please."

Campbell reminded Lee of what she hated about academia. He was the worst administrative type—a pompous, arrogant, condescending, officious son of a bitch.

As she walked along the shaded brick path toward the campus grill, she wondered what it was about Campbell that had gotten under her skin so badly. He was probably just an overworked, dedicated department chair, short on hospitality from trying hard to meet heavy obligations with scarce resources. Or, he could just be a son of a bitch.

Lee had made herself smile by the time she reached the cafe patio of the campus grill. It was just before noon and inside was packed. She looked around for Jack without seeing him, decided that she was early, and sat down at an outside table with a glass of ice water to wait.

Her thoughts drifted back to their chance meeting in the hallway. She was gazing off into space thinking about Jack when she looked up and he was sitting down at her table with two trays of food, the exact contents concealed by Styrofoam containers. He had a red rose showing from the pocket of his shirt.

He looked as if he belonged there among the students. He seemed uncontaminated by any of the diseases of academia. He smiled and looked at her with those dark eyes.

"What are you smiling at?" He said.

"Nothing in particular," she lied. "Just enjoying the break. Do you have lunch for two, I hope?"

"I do, but I had a hard time deciding. They had so many delicious and healthful looking things—turkey flavored tofu, fresh bean sprouts, ginseng tea. You know, I think it's wonderful that young people are so concerned about nutrition and good health."

None of those choices sounded very appetizing to Lee. "What did you decide on?"

"I decided on a balanced meal—hot dogs with chili, a salad and iced tea."

"I'm glad you decided against the tofu," she said.

They were eating and laughing when an attractive female student approached their table. She had a camera around her neck and was holding a drink and a bag of potato chips.

"Hello, Dr. Turner. You don't know me. I'm Katie Horne."

"You're the reporter who wrote the newspaper articles and took the photographs," Lee said. "Are you with anyone? Sit down and have lunch with us."

Katie smiled at Jack as she sat down across from him. Lee introduced him to her.

"Oh, you teach linguistics," Katie said. "Is that something a journalist could use, do you think?"

"If you plan to travel much I think it could improve your insight and make it easier to converse. Of course, I think everyone should take linguistics."

Lee watched with growing irritation as Katie flirted with Jack. She was so young, Lee thought, and healthy. Her skin was rosy and smooth, her eyes sparkled, and her beautiful long dark hair shone in the sunshine. She was dressed in sandals and jeans that fit her trim body just a little too well. Around her neck she wore a silver and gold arrowhead on a thin gold chain. The arrowhead rested in the vee formed by the front of her blouse, open to the third button.

She had a way of flipping her hair back over her shoulder, and she leaned forward casually to gently rub an ankle with her fingertips. As she did, the shiny arrowhead swung down, naturally attracting one's eye to it. One might think from her seemingly innocent, flawless face that she was unaware that her position and movement and the dangling arrowhead presented Jack with a focused view of her bare breasts.

It was unclear whether Jack deliberately watched or whether he was unable to keep his eyes from following the show, but it was clear that he was enjoying Katie's efforts.

"Those were great photographs in the newspaper," Lee said, hoping that it sounded natural.

"Thanks. I owe it all to my point-and-shoot," Katie said, holding up about two thousand dollars worth of digital camera. "I have dozens of shots besides the ones that were published in the paper."

"So, how long have you been a reporter?" Jack asked.

"About ten years," Katie said.

Jack laughed. "You must have been twelve when you started. Were you a child prodigy?"

Katie seemed accustomed to jokes about her age. "I was thirteen when I sold my first news story. I kind of got hooked on it."

"Don't let him kid you," Lee said. "He's just feeling old by comparison."

"He's not so old," Katie said, smiling at Jack.

Oh, please, Lee thought to herself, enough is enough. Your face is going to break out if you don't get your hormones under control.

An unmistakable electronic signal sounded. Lee and Katie simultaneously reached for their phones.

"It's mine," Katie said. "It's the newspaper. They're probably calling to see if I'm going to meet my deadline. I've got to run but I just wanted to stop and introduce myself and ask if there are any new developments in the Hamrick death."

"Nothing I can give you right now. All evidence is sealed until the coroner's verdict is released."

"Any idea when that might be?"

"No, I'm sorry," Lee said. "I honestly don't know."

"What about the federal court order? Has that put a stop to your investigation?"

"No. My job still has to be done."

"What is that exactly? I mean, what still has to be done?"

"Identify the deceased. Determine the cause of death."

"Why do the federal people think they should have control?"

"Good question. I'd like to hear the answer to that."

Katie was busily writing notes on her pad. Her phone alert sounded again. "All right!" she said with exasperation.

"Must be important," Jack said.

"No, not really. It's a rinky-dink assignment to cover complaints about cockroaches in the dormitories. It's a big letdown after the Hamrick story. I've been trying to think of some angle to make it interesting, like maybe doing it from the point of view of a cockroach. What do you think?"

"I read your newspaper articles," Jack said. "They were really good."

"Thanks," Katie said, smiling at him again with a flash of her white teeth. She stood to go, straightening her clothes and tossing her hair in such a way that she was able to show, without seeming to do so, that she had what Jack should want if he was half the man he appeared to be. She wrote something on the corner of her note pad and tore it off.

"I'm going to be out running around a lot. Here's my phone number," she said, laying it on the table in front of Jack. "I would really appreciate a chance at the Hamrick story. It would mean a lot to me right now. You can call me day or night," Katie said, flashing that beauty queen smile again, punctuating it with a wink at Jack. Then she hurried off through the crowd of students, reviewing her notes as she went.

Lee looked at her watch. "I've got to run. My life has gotten nonstop lately. I've got to find some time to get some rest."

"Rest?" Jack said. "I have some exciting things planned for the two of us."

"Hold that thought, and call me this evening."

As Lee walked back to the parking lot she was angry at Jack, or Katie Horne, or herself, or somebody. Why was she getting upset? What did she care if Jack Sheridan looked down the blouse of some gorgeous twenty-three year-old student with perfect skin, a tight little butt, glossy hair and a beauty-queen smile?

She saw her own reflection in the window of the campus bookstore. Her khaki outfit wasn't exactly Ralph Lauren, but she had to admit there was a certain mystique about her appearance. And she certainly wasn't half bad looking. No, in fact, she was about half good looking. She almost threw the rose away, but its fragrance was sweet and it was beautiful. Jack did give it to *her*, after all, and not to little miss tight butt.

Lee's phone alert sounded again. This time it was Margy at the sheriff's office.

"Hey, Margy. What's up?"

"Dr. Turner, you have a visitor here in my office who would like to see you. Will you be available this afternoon?"

"Who is it?"

"It's Mrs. Alexander Hamrick."

Dr. Hamrick's widow, Lee thought to herself. I guess I had better regain my professional composure and think about business. What am I going to tell her?

Chapter 11
Off the Case

THE WOMAN STANDING before Lee in her office was not what she expected. The deceased Dr. Hamrick was something past seventy years of age. This woman was hardly more than half that. Only a little older than Lee herself.

"Dr. Turner," she said, "I'm Barbara Hamrick. Alexander Hamrick is . . . that is . . . was . . . my husband."

"Mrs. Hamrick, please accept my condolences."

"Thank you," she said, in a voice heavy with grief. "I want to express my appreciation to you for looking after my husband's . . ." She trailed off, then tried again. "I wanted to tell you I appreciate your helping to straighten things out here."

"You're welcome for anything I might have been able to do, Mrs. Hamrick."

"My husband and I haven't lived together for almost two years. But still it came as a great shock to me. And there is our son Douglas, of course. He's taking his father's death very hard. My husband was the kind of man who became absorbed in his work, but Douglas was always close to him. And it came so suddenly. No one had time to adjust to the idea that Alex might not be with us much longer. But I guess that's the way these things are sometimes. Alex never even told me he was suffering from heart trouble. He kept so much to himself, especially in recent years. But anyway, Dr. Turner, there are a couple of things I wanted to ask you about."

Heart trouble? Lee thought to herself. But she said, "I'll

be happy to answer whatever I can."

"Alex had a little dog and I don't know what has happened to it."

Oh, no, Lee thought, she's come for Henrietta. I should have expected it. "Henrietta has been staying with me, Mrs. Hamrick. She's happy and healthy."

"Well, that's good. I felt some obligation about it, but I have no place in Los Verdes for a dog. And Douglas is at the university and he couldn't have it. And it really was Alex's dog. Is there someone here, do you think, who would like to have it and would take care of it?"

"Don't be concerned at all about that, Mrs. Hamrick. I'll see that Henrietta is well cared for and has a happy home."

"Well, thank you, Dr. Turner. The other thing is, and I don't know how to say this, but there is some problem about the insurance."

"Dr. Hamrick's insurance?"

"His life insurance. There is some problem with them about the certificate of death or something. I don't understand. We're going to need the money." She said it as if she were ashamed to be talking about anything so mercenary at such a time.

"The only thing I can tell you now, Mrs. Hamrick, is that we do not know the cause of death and we don't have a positive identification of the deceased as being Dr. Hamrick."

"I don't understand. I can identify the body. And as to the cause, I thought Alex died of a heart attack."

Oh, God, Lee thought to herself, how can I tell this poor woman?

"When we found the body he had been dead for some

time. It was not in a condition that it could be identified."

Mrs. Hamrick looked as if she might faint.

"I'm sorry, Mrs. Hamrick, I know this is difficult for you."

"What is there to do then about the identification and the cause of death?"

"We have to wait until all laboratory results are in before we can make a final determination." That wasn't much of a white lie.

Barbara Hamrick was silent for a long moment.

"Do you know when that might be?"

"Normally all results are returned to us between ten days and three weeks."

"That's such a long time to not have closure."

"Yes, I know it is, and I'm sorry. If I had any way to do it sooner, I would. I have to wait for results from the state laboratory. I'm not permitted by law to do it any other way." That still wasn't much of a lie.

"Will you let me know, when..." Mrs. Hamrick didn't finish the sentence.

"Yes, I will."

"Thank you," she said, in a low voice that was almost a whisper.

While they were talking, Buddy had come in through the front door and stopped just inside Lee's office, behind Barbara Hamrick. He was listening with some concentration to their conversation. Lee looked over Mrs. Hamrick's shoulder at him. He was staring at the back of Barbara Hamrick's head and had the queerest look on his face. As she turned to go, she came face to face with Buddy. She was obviously shaken by the sight of him.

"Hello, Buddy," she said, after a moment. "How have you been?"

Buddy made a pretty good job of putting on a smile as he looked into her eyes.

"Hello, Barb. It's been a long time. I don't think you've changed a bit since the last time I saw you."

"Everything has changed, I'm afraid," she said, and walked past him and out the front door. Lee thought she heard a muffled sob from her.

Buddy sat down on the edge of the sofa in Lee's office and stretched his injured leg out onto its cushions. His face was uncharacteristically blank. He seemed to be looking into his own thoughts.

"You know Mrs. Hamrick?" Lee asked.

"Yeah," he said. "She and I knew each other a long time ago."

"You didn't know she was Hamrick's wife?"

"No. I lost touch with her. I was in the service and when I came back here she was gone. Nobody ever said anything to me about her marrying anybody. I don't guess anybody knew. None of her family live in these parts anymore."

"How well did you know her? I mean, did you go to school together, or what?"

"I knew her real well. Me and her was engaged at one time."

"Jesus, Buddy, it must have been a shock to see her."

Buddy looked up at Lee from his thoughts. "It sure as hell was. What was that business about a heart attack? Who told her that, I wonder? Nobody could know that, could they, Lee?"

"Not unless they were there when he died. They certainly couldn't have made that determination from the remains I saw."

Buddy screwed up his eyebrows in a look of skepticism. "You think maybe they were just being kind to her and the kid? You know, didn't want to tell them the truth about how he died?"

"Perhaps. Maybe he had a medical history of heart trouble."

"How old is her son, do you know?" Buddy asked.

"She said he's in college. If he's undergraduate, somewhere between eighteen and twenty-two, I would guess. Why?"

Buddy came back out of his own thoughts again. "Nothing. I was just wondering."

"How long has it been since you saw her last?"

"About that long."

Lee suddenly wished she hadn't asked that last question. The implications of Buddy's answer were more than she was prepared to contemplate.

"Poor woman," she said. "She has no idea what's going on here."

"She's not the only one," Buddy said quietly.

Their conversation was interrupted by the characteristic sounds of Mr. Terry's car coming to a stop out front. At the sound of the front door opening and closing, Buddy gave a wink at Lee and began rummaging through papers on her desk. Mr. Terry appeared in her doorway, a scowl on his face.

"May I see you in my office, Lee," he said as a statement

and not as a question. He turned without waiting for a response and walked to his office. Lee followed, a few steps behind him.

Mr. Terry's dog walked ahead of them at a little faster pace than usual, its tail between its legs, glancing back with a worried look as it hurried to the safety of its box under Mr. Terry's desk. Inside the office Mr. Terry sat behind his desk facing Lee, an intense look in his eyes that Lee was not able to decipher.

"You are to discontinue your investigation into the Hamrick matter," he said. "It's out of our hands now."

Lee had a sudden flash of emotions that she fought to control.

"Discontinue? I have responsibilities in this case," she said. "We, the coroner's office, have responsibilities."

Instructing Mr. Terry as to his responsibilities was, of course, the wrong move. His look quickly clarified into anger. He rose with a struggle to his feet and leaned forward across his desk.

"You are not to tell me my responsibilities. I successfully performed the responsibilities of this office for thirty-nine years before you came here. And the way things are going right now, I may still be performing them after you are gone. If anyone here needs to be informed of her responsibilities, it is you." He was red-faced now. "These last few days I have tried desperately to give you the benefit of mounting doubts, but I can only conclude that you have completely lost your judgement."

Lee's shock showed on her face. Mr. Terry ignored her reaction, he was looking inward to his own emotions now. He continued, gesturing in the air with one hand and bracing himself against the desk with a supporting arm.

"First, you take upon yourself the duties of the sheriff's office and try to apprehend a suspect, resulting in the injury of a member of our staff, and narrowly evade a catastrophe involving a local citizen and his family, including two children. Then you deliberately provoke a confrontation and interfere with the duties of an officer of the federal government. Now I am informed that you have accused a respected member of the Carters Mill University administration of complicity in Dr. Hamrick's death. Just what do you think you are doing?"

Lee was stunned by his words and was instantly filled with hurt and resentment. "Mr. Terry, you are being extremely unfair about this."

"Unfair? Fairness is not the question. Your judgement as an official of the coroner's office is the question. Did you or did you not remove evidence from the jurisdiction of a federal investigation?"

"There was no federal jurisdiction at Hamrick's house. All I saw there was a bunch of arrogant tough guys claiming federal authority. I did what I thought was appropriate. I was doing my duty. I know that *I* had authority there."

"Well, you don't any more." Mr. Terry was almost spitting with anger as he talked. "I have been in meetings half the day with the county attorney, the mayor, and the county commissioners over this matter. Mr. Goodman, our county attorney, in addition to having been served papers by U.S. Federal Marshals, received a call this morning from the Tennessee Attorney General's office informing him that the governor has responded to a request from the U.S. Department of Justice. The Governor has instructed the Tennessee Bureau of Investigation to make available to federal investigators all evidence relating to the Hamrick death. The State

Attorney General has asked for our cooperation and we are going to cooperate with that investigation. When federal investigators arrive here tomorrow, I want you to turn over to them copies of your records and all evidence related to the Hamrick death. We are the coroner's office, not the police department, and not the county attorney's office. I will certify the cause of Dr. Hamrick's death when there is sufficient evidence, if ever, to reach a determination. I want you to abandon this matter and go on to other duties. As I said, this is out of our hands now."

Mr. Terry's last statement was one of finality. He dismissed Lee with a wave of his hand.

"I have to go now and meet with the president of Carters Mill University. God only knows how you managed to step on so many toes in such a short period of time." He took a walking cane from his coat rack and shuffled with some difficulty through the door of his office and out to his automobile, followed by the old dog, which was trying to stay out of his way.

Lee was hurt and she was furious. Buddy stood aside as she came back into her office.

"What was all the shouting about?" He asked, treading tenderly.

"Mr. Terry ordered me off the Hamrick case. On orders from the governor's office. It is now a federal investigation."

"No. You've got to be kidding. He's rolling over? Just like that?"

"Do I look like I'm kidding?"

"No, I guess you're not. The governor's office? Why would the governor be so quick to turn this over to the feds?"

"Good question. It's got to be political. CMU is mixed up in it somehow too."

Buddy handed her several sheets of paper. "These faxes came in for you a couple of minutes ago."

"They're from the Los Verdes coroner's office," Lee said, inspecting the pages. "Dental charts and medical records on Hamrick."

"Too bad we don't have a body," Buddy said.

"These may still come in handy. We, or rather, Mr. Terry still has to officially identify the dead man. There may be enough teeth left to make an ID from these records."

Lee looked over the faxes from Hamrick's family doctor in Los Verdes. "There is no mention in his medical records of heart disease or any potentially life threatening condition. Why am I not surprised?"

"What will you do about the investigation, Lee?"

She thought for a long time but she did not answer.

Chapter 12
A Big Decision

THE REST OF the day dragged on and on. Lee's thoughts wouldn't stay away from her meeting with Mr. Terry. She had to fight the anger and frustration that kept bubbling up in her unexpectedly and uncontrollably. She tried to be rational about the situation but her feelings of betrayal and embarrassment overwhelmed her reason. It was during this period of emotional volatility when she was least able to deal with the issue that Ira Aaron from Chicago called her about the job offer.

"So, Dr. Turner, can we expect you to be joining us in January?"

"It does sound attractive, Ira. I hope you understand, I must have the full time I asked for to consider your offer."

"Oh, I do, Lee. But in the meantime I hope you will not be too angry if I try to sweeten the offer to entice you here."

"Of course not, but I would hope that you made me your best offer."

"At the time, yes, we did. One of the reasons I called is to let you know that we have been able to obtain a little something extra. The president's office has agreed, contingent upon your acceptance of our offer, to give priority to your request to establish a forensics research and training center. I cannot promise anything, of course, but they have agreed to consider the proposal."

"You don't have any indication of what the final decision might be?"

"The president will assign the matter to his staff and they will make a recommendation to him."

"I wish there were something a little more concrete."

"Well, we all do. I just thought you would appreciate the fact that the matter has been presented to the president."

"Yes, I do. Thank you, Ira. I will still need some time to consider. I'll let you know as soon as I know."

As Lee put the phone back on the hook, she thought to herself, *Academia americana,* same old same old. She was rescued from her thoughts by a call from Jack.

"How about dinner this evening? May I pick you up about eight?"

"Sounds great."

It was nice to have something pleasant to think about. That evening after work her thoughts lingered on Jack as she stood under her warm shower. Looking back now, her anger over Katie Horne's flirtations seemed silly.

He arrived just before eight with a kiss and flowers. He looked great. He smelled great. He tasted great. And he felt great to her as she stood with his arms around her.

"Anyplace in particular you would like to go?" He asked.

"Someplace where I won't think about work."

"We can stay here and I think I can make you forget about work."

"You already have, but I need something to eat."

When Lee returned with a jacket from her bedroom, Jack was standing looking at her computer and holding Henrietta, scratching her head. He looked up when she came in the room.

"Nice computer," he said. "Where did you get it? I mean, is there a computer store in town?"

"I brought it with me when I came from California. But we do have an excellent computer guru that I go to with difficult problems. Are you in the market for a new computer?"

Jack smiled. "No, but you never know when I may need the services of a guru. My problems never turn out to be simple ones." He winked at her and took her hand.

They decided on the Blue Eagle. It was close, the food was good, and it would be quiet on a weeknight. When they arrived there the place was dark.

"This is unusual," Lee said. "This place always has a respectable evening crowd."

Jack turned in the parking lot. There were three cars out front and a half dozen people standing near the door to the restaurant. He pulled in beside them.

"It's closed," someone yelled out.

Someone else said in a loud voice, "Only the roaches are eating tonight."

Lee recognized George Gardner the owner standing beside the front door. She waved to him. He walked toward Jack's car. George was a tall thin middle-aged man. Normally on week nights he dressed in a western suit with a string tie and a cowboy hat. Tonight he was wearing work coveralls.

"What's going on, George?" Lee asked.

"Hey, Lee. I come in to open up this morning and the whole place was covered in roaches. I ain't talking about a few roaches. I'm talking thousands, maybe millions. I'm fumigating now. I hope I can open up by tomorrow night. I can't afford to miss the business. But I don't know. I never saw nothing like it. I don't know where they come from. We've always tried to run a clean place. This is something else."

"When did you start fumigating?" Lee asked.

"About three-thirty. Just as quick as I could get somebody over here to do it. It's terrible."

"How soon before you can go back inside?"

"The man from the pest control company said to give it four or five hours." He looked at his watch. "It's been five hours right now."

"Do you mind if I take a look inside?" Lee asked as she got out of the Jeep and motioned Jack to come with her.

"No, ma'am, I don't mind if you don't. I just hope you ain't squeamish about roaches. I might have to open the windows and doors and air it out a little to get rid of the fumes."

George unlocked the front door and pushed the handle. The door seemed to be stuck.

"That ain't right," George said. "Something's got the door jammed. It must be the carpet."

Jack gave him a hand and they shoved the door open. It was dark inside. The smell of pesticide fumes was strong. George went in ahead to turn on the lights.

As he walked through the dark they could hear him say, "Oh, this is awful, just awful." And there was a buzzing sound.

The lights came on inside. Except for a clear semicircle where the door had opened, the floor of the entrance foyer was piled to a depth of three or four inches with roaches. They were a very large dark brown variety, about an inch and a quarter long and broad across the back. They were not all dead. Most of them were still wiggling their legs, unable to walk upright because of the effects of the insecticide. The surface of the entire mass appeared to roll and bubble like the surface of boiling water. Some were buzzing their wings in a futile attempt to fly. And the air was punctuated by the uncontrolled erratic flight of those that were still able to get themselves airborne for a last blind effort at escape from the poison.

"Watch your step if you come in," George yelled back to them. "They're slick as glass."

Lee and Jack stayed at the door. Lee could see across the restaurant to the other side of the building. The floor was not visible at any spot through the layer of wriggling roaches.

"You weren't exaggerating about the number," Jack said.

"I don't guess we gave the fumigation quite long enough. Or, maybe he didn't use enough for this many bugs. Did j'ever see anything like this before?" George asked, brushing away several of the insects that were clinging to his clothes and swatting with his cap at one that was caught in his hair.

"Never." Lee said. "When did you first notice a problem with roaches?"

"That's just it," George said, "We ain't had no unusual problems. The first I know'd of it was this morning when I opened up."

"When was the last time you were here before today?" Lee asked.

"Last night. I cleaned the whole place and locked up about 1:00 A.M. I didn't see nuthin' wrong then. They's something bad wrong here now. This ain't normal."

George stood looking across the half-ton or more of roaches, shaking his head and rubbing his chin.

"I'll have to hire a crew in here the first thing in the morning if I expect to open up tomorrow night. It'll take shovels and garbage cans to get this lot out of here. I ought to just set a match to the whole thing and be done with it."

"I would like to take a bag of these with me," Lee said.

George looked at her as if she had just said, "I love roach sandwiches. May I have some?" He said, "Sure, take all you want. Let me get you a bag or something. How many do you want? A bushel?"

"A gallon size freezer bag will be plenty."

He walked across the room to the kitchen to get a plastic bag and a broom, his shoes making crunching sounds with each step. As he walked back across the thick brown layer he kept saying, "This is awful."

Lee held the mouth of the bag open at the edge of the clean spot made where the door had opened. George swept dead and nearly dead roaches into the open bag. When it was about full, Lee told him that was enough. She sealed the bag shut.

"You going to make brownies or something?" George asked her, disbelieving that she was actually going to take a bag of roaches with her.

Lee laughed. "No, I'm going to have an entomologist look at these to see if there is anything unusual about them."

"Entomologist?" George asked.

"A bug man," Lee said.

"I'll make him a special deal if he wants the whole bunch," George said, with a grin and a good natured chuckle. "Forty cents a pound, or three pounds for a dollar. I don't know why I'm laughing about this. This is awful," He reached inside his collar to retrieve a buzzing roach that had flown headlong into him and fallen inside his shirt. "I'll be here all night I guess, with this mess."

Back in Jack's Jeep, Lee dug through her handbag and found the small slip of paper with Katie Horne's number on it. Using her cell phone she left a message on Katie's voice mail. Katie returned the call almost immediately.

"Katie," Lee said, "How did your cockroach caper turn out?"

"You're a biologist, aren't you? You should be interested in this. Dresswell Hall, one of the girls' dorms, couldn't be opened for fall quarter. It had millions of great huge ugly cockroaches in every room. They were falling off the ceiling and everything. It was awful and creepy. They called the exterminators but about ninety students still don't have any place on campus to stay. The University is putting them up in the Holiday Inn. A bunch of parents showed up and are threatening to sue the University. I got pictures. You wouldn't believe it unless you saw it."

"I've got another one for you. You know where the Blue Eagle Tavern is?"

"Sure."

"Same situation as the dormitory. You might want to get the story."

"Roaches?"

"Millions of them. Tons of them. It's like a horror movie."

"What's the deal with roaches all of a sudden?" Katie said. "What am I, the cockroach queen?"

"It's a good news story if nothing else. It's the kind of thing the news services might pick up."

"Yeah, you're right about that. Thanks. I'll get right out

there."

Jack was the one who started laughing, but once he started, Lee started too and couldn't stop.

"What are you going to do with your bag of goodies?" He asked, indicating the freezer bag.

"I don't know just yet. Put them in cold storage for the time being."

"What do you think might account for these weird explosions in the roach population? That's two occurrences within ten miles of each other in the same week."

"I don't know. I'm on pretty good speaking terms with someone in the ecology department at the CMU who might be able to help out with this. I'll give him a call tomorrow."

"I've got some wonderful fried chicken in my refrigerator that Mrs. Garrison brought over to me, and some really good imported beer. We could pick up some potato salad. Would you like to just go back to my place and eat?"

It was cool enough to have a fire in the fireplace in the basement room of Jack's apartment. They lay on a thick rug in front of the fire and sipped beer.

"I want to give you something," Jack said as he kissed her on the neck just below her earlobe.

"What?"

He took a small white box from the pocket of his jacket hanging over a chair.

"Open it," he said.

Lee removed the cover from the box and inside on a bed of white cotton was the silver amethyst necklace she had admired that day at the Museum of Appalachia gift shop. The three gems sparkled in the light from the fireplace.

"Jack, it's beautiful. But it's much too expensive. You

shouldn't have. You don't know me well enough to . . ."

Jack lifted the necklace from the box and put it around her neck.

"I wanted it for you the first time I saw you holding it," he said. "It looks beautiful on you. You've got to accept it. I'll be heartbroken if you don't."

* * *

It was six A.M. when Lee finally got home. She hadn't meant to do it. Maybe it was the beer. Maybe it was Jack's sweetness, the necklace, the attention after the bad things that had happened to her lately. Maybe she and Jack were just a matched pair. Whatever it was that had made her do it, she wasn't sorry. They had spent the entire night in each other's arms making love, and she had loved every moment of it.

She had not planned to become sexually involved with Jack or anyone. But now as she thought about it, it seemed that it was inevitable. When she was close to him and alone with him, her mind and her body wouldn't let her think of anything else.

It was even better than she had thought it would be. Now as she made herself get ready for work, the thought of him, the feel of him, the smell of him was still with her.

Chapter 13
Judy Vining

LEE TRIED TO act normal that morning. She also tried to wake herself from the dream-like state she was in. But her fingers kept finding the new necklace around her neck, and her mind kept returning to Jack and the night before. It was hard to motivate herself to get back into normal routine, made all the more difficult by the fatigue resulting from her lack of sleep. Her muscles were aching. What she wanted more than anything else was to sleep for about ten hours. She drank three times her usual amount of caffeine and doubled up on protein and carbohydrates at breakfast, hoping that would compensate for lack of rest.

Buddy didn't seem to notice anything different about her, but Helen kept glancing at her. Finally when Buddy was away from the table Helen asked, "How are you and Jack getting along, Lee, honey?"

Lee had been caught a little off guard in a daydream thinking of Jack, her fingers tracing the gemstones on the necklace. She smiled at Helen but didn't know what to say.

Helen smiled back. "I know that look. I think you may be in love."

Lee was sure she felt herself blushing. "I think I may be."

"That's what I thought. It looks good on you. I've thought for a long time you needed a good man. I sure can't blame you. He's a mighty handsome one."

Then Helen saw the necklace beneath Lee's fingers. "Oh, that's beautiful, honey. Let me see that. Did he give you that? Mmm, it's more serious than I thought."

Buddy was coming back toward the table. Helen leaned

close to Lee's ear.

"You might want to cover that whisker burn on your cheek with a little makeup. If Buddy sees it he'll kid you about it for the next six months."

Lee reflexively touched her fingers to the warm spot on her left cheek. This time she was sure she blushed. Helen just gave her a very small discreet smile and winked.

Lee didn't normally wear much makeup but she could see in the mirror in the ladies' room that Helen was right. She had the unmistakable tell-tale mark of whisker burn on her cheek and neck. This hadn't happened to her since she was twenty. She borrowed a tube of makeup base from Helen and applied just enough to hide the discoloration. With her hair down long, the place was hardly visible. She smiled again at the thought of how she had gotten it.

As she unlocked her office and began her morning routine, Lee tried to forget about the feds. But it was something that wouldn't just go away. She knew they would be coming this morning and she would be required to turn over all her evidence and records relating to the Hamrick death. She made copies of all documents and reports for herself.

She was headed out the door to retrieve the backup tape from Butch's computer shop when she received a call from Dr. Peter Raymond requesting the services of the coroner's office. Mrs. Jamie Anderson, an elderly lifelong resident of Bartram County, had passed away during the night. It was a short drive to the picturesque farm.

Mrs. Anderson had lived alone and self-sufficiently until the day of her death. She had called her son Herschel, age 71, the day before to ask him to come around and check on her.

"I got here around 2:30 yesterday afternoon," Herschel

said. "I knew right away she must be feeling pretty bad, be-cause she always got up with the chickens and went to bed with the chickens–up before daylight and to bed by dark. I can count the times on the fingers of one hand that she slept past 7:00 A.M. during the past fifty years."

"What did she say was wrong yesterday?" Lee asked.

"Said she just didn't have any strength and her head was swimming. I was concerned she might not be eating or drinking, but she said she had a bowl of cereal, her fruit juice and a cup of coffee in the morning. Said she just didn't feel well enough to stay up and went back to bed. I got her a glass of buttermilk and some cornbread late yesterday. She took a bite or two but she said she just didn't have any ap-petite for it."

"Any aches or pains or any irregularity of any kind?"

"Nothing but what I told you. She was hardly sick a day in her life. She didn't take drugs of any kind except an occa-sional aspirin. Just lived here on the farm all her life, ate good food and did her daily chores. She used to joke that her only vice was a sweet tooth." The son picked up a small sampler box of chocolate candy from the nightstand, looked at it and smiled. "We should all have so few vices."

"What time did you leave her last night?"

"I stayed until about eight-thirty. She was sleeping when I left. I came back this morning about eight o'clock and she had passed away during the night. She was still lying in the same spot. Didn't look like she had moved since I left her last night."

A single tear ran from the corner of the man's eye down the side of his cheek. Lee put a hand gently on his shoulder and turned to Dr. Peter Raymond who had returned from placing the body in the ambulance. They stepped into the front room, leaving the son alone in the bedroom.

"No unusual signs of any kind," Peter said. "All indications are she died peacefully in her sleep. Primarily due to old age, I would say. She was ninety-one."

It was a routine natural death and a routine death certificate. Death at age ninety-one is sad, but it is normal.

Mrs. Anderson had been just a few years younger than Lee's grandmother. She had seen the beginning of the twentieth century, the invention of the automobile, the airplane, the atomic bomb, the first and second world wars, the great depression, Korea, Vietnam, Iraq, space exploration, the building and fall of the Berlin wall, and all the other ups and downs, achievements and foibles of mankind for almost a century. From age 22 until age 60, Mrs. Anderson had been a school teacher. But for most of her life she simply had lived.

It seemed such a contrast, Lee thought, while much of mankind had been bustling about, making themselves rich and making themselves poor, preening themselves, or killing each other and destroying a good part of nature, Mrs. Anderson had lived a natural existence, trying to live her own life and ride out the ripples and waves that flowed into this rural countryside from time to time as the result of activities of some tyrant, politician, or economic kingpin or other.

Lee left Mrs. Anderson's farm a little after 11:00 A.M. and headed to Butch's computer shop.

Butch looked up and waved when Lee came through the door.

"Hey, Lee. I got the tape copied. Had a used tape drive back in the warehouse that I was able to jumpstart."

Lee didn't have the heart to tell Butch it was all for nothing. She just smiled and said, "I knew if anyone could manage it, you could." She could see he appreciated the compliment.

"Don't hesitate to bring me any problem you might have. It's the little challenges that keep my skills honed to a fine edge." He laughed at himself. He handed her a USB memory stick. "Fortunately, the tape was not filled to capacity. The files fit on the USB drive with room to spare."

Lee gave him a receipt for the tape, sealed it in its evidence bag, and headed back to her office. As she pulled out of her parking space she opened her glove compartment and dropped the USB drive in.

She had thought seriously about ignoring Mr. Terry's order to abandon the case. But today it just didn't seem so important that she personally stay involved. The TBI had evidence from the crime scene. She could wait for their findings.

Two federal marshals accompanied by the sheriff and watched over by Mr. Terry showed up at the coroner's office right after Lee returned there. She turned over to them the bag of evidence from her safe, copies of all faxes and reports that had been generated, copies of her notes, and the computer backup tape. She had them sign a receipt for the items, and that was that. End of case.

Three days passed and that might have been the end of it. It was dark and raining that morning. It had been raining since midnight and the ground was saturated. Water was standing in puddles, and sheets of it covered the streets.

In her line of work it was not unusual for Lee to encounter grief. And perhaps it was Lee's own state of mind that had left her a little unsteady. But when she heard the woman's voice on the phone it was as if the dark clouds covering the town were of something other than rain. The voice sounded tired. The speech was slow and halting.

"Dr. Turner, this is Anita Vining. I'm Judy Vining's mother. I believe you may have met my daughter."

Judy Vining. Alexander Hamrick's officemate, Lee thought to herself. "Yes, I talked with her for a few minutes several days ago in her office."

"I'm at the hospital here in Carters Mill. Judy has been admitted. She's unconscious."

"My gosh, what happened to her?"

"The doctors don't know what is wrong with her. But they say she is in very serious condition."

"I'm terribly sorry to hear about Judy. Is there anything you can tell me about what happened to her?"

Anita Vining's sniffle and her irregular breathing told Lee she had been crying.

"Some of her student friends found her last night unconscious in her dormitory room. No one had seen her for two days. The doctors think she may have been lying there unconscious for twenty-four hours or more."

Anita Vining began crying again. After a few moments she regained herself enough to talk.

"She didn't come home for the break between semesters. She stayed here so she could work straight through at the university to make some extra money. Dr. Turner, they tell me the retired faculty member Judy shared an office with died mysteriously just last week. And no one seems able to tell me what is going on. A student news reporter, a young woman named Katie Horne, said I should talk with you. She said you have been investigating Dr. Hamrick's death?"

Lee could hear the desperation in Anita Vining's voice.

"Who is the doctor in charge of Judy's care?"

"Dr. Peter Raymond is her main doctor."

"I'll consult with Dr. Raymond right away. He's a good man. Let me talk with him and see what I can find out."

"Thank you, Dr. Turner."

"Try not to worry."

Lee briefed Buddy on the conversation as she called the hospital. She asked to speak with Dr. Peter Raymond. After a short wait she got him.

"I'm glad you called, Lee. This is a bad situation. The girl is comatose. She had a temperature of 105 when they brought her in. She has fluid on the brain which we're preparing to relieve. We think it may be meningitis but the diagnosis is unconfirmed. We're keeping her quarantined until we know for sure what we're dealing with."

"I can tell you Judy has been working for the past year on a research project in which she collected animal field specimens. That could certainly be a possible source of bacterial or viral exposure."

"Mrs. Vining mentioned that her daughter was working on campus."

"Peter, she shared an office with Alexander Hamrick."

"Who is in charge of the research she was working on?"

"Her major professor is Gerald Campbell, the head of the Agri-Sciences department."

"You think Campbell could have information that might help in diagnosing her illness?"

"I just don't know. If he does, he would be more likely to give it directly to you. I don't think he would tell me anything."

"By God, he'll talk to me."

"Peter, how critical is Judy?"

"It's very serious. We won't give up on her. We always try to have hope."

Lee gave Dr. Raymond three numbers where Gerald Campbell could be reached, and hung up the phone.

"Hamrick's officemate. And she was ill when I talked with her. I thought it was the flu." Lee put her face in her hands.

"Jesus, Lee," Buddy said. "You had no way of knowing. Half the kids on campus have the flu."

"I should have been more suspicious. But she said she hadn't seen Hamrick in a couple of weeks. I just didn't think."

She picked up the phone and dialed the Agri-Sciences department at the university. The department secretary answered.

"Estelle, this is Lee Turner at the coroner's office. I have rather an urgent situation. Do you know a student named Judy Vining who works at the Agri-Sciences research lab?"

"Yes, of course. We heard about her hospitalization. You aren't calling because, I mean, she hasn't died, has she?"

"No. Her condition is very serious but she is alive. The hospital is waiting for lab results. They're concerned that Judy may have contracted an infectious disease such as meningitis or encephalitis, but it may be something else. Have you had any other students or faculty reported seriously ill?"

"No, we haven't, Dr. Turner, not through this office. Lots of cases of the flu, of course, but no serious illness reported that I know of. Can you hold the phone just a minute, Dr. Turner, my other line is ringing."

Lee waited for what seemed like a long time before Estelle came back on the line.

"I'm sorry to keep you on hold so long, Dr. Turner. That was Dr. Peter Raymond at the hospital on the other line, trying to get in touch with Dr. Campbell. I don't know when Dr. Campbell will be back in the office."

"Estelle, we need to locate everyone who might have been in contact with Judy Vining who could have possible information about her illness or who might have become ill themselves. Could you fax me a list of all the faculty and students who work at the research lab, and we'll call that list."

"I would be happy to, Dr. Turner. I'll have to get the names from the personnel records. I guess you want telephone numbers too, don't you?"

"Yes, and local address, in case we need to pay them a visit. Home phone numbers also, if you have them."

"How far back do you want me to go?"

"Can you give me a list of those employed anytime from June 1st to now? I think Judy said she has been working in the field with people all summer."

"That will be quite a long list. They hire lots of student workers during the summer. Are you at your office?"

"Yes, I am."

"It shouldn't take more than thirty minutes."

"Thank you, Estelle."

"Will you need any help with the calling? I would be glad to help."

"Thanks, Estelle. Let me see how it goes. If we need help I'll give you a call."

In about twenty minutes Lee's fax signaled an incoming transmission. It was the list of Agri-Sciences research lab summer employees, divided into faculty and students.

"Buddy, I want you to start with the list of students and work your way down. You can use the phone in Mr. Terry's office. I'll start at the top of the faculty list. When I finish the faculty list, I'll work my way up from the bottom of the student list."

"What are we looking for?" Buddy asked. "What do I tell them?"

"We want to find out if anyone else has been ill, or if any of them was aware of anything out of the ordinary with Judy before she became ill. Right now we don't know what might be important, so be sure and ask about any illness whatsoever during the past six months. Make a list of everyone you call and the results of each call. Then we'll look over our lists and see if anything important shows up. Of course, if you find anyone with a serious illness, tell me immediately. OK?"

"What should I say is the reason I'm calling and asking these questions?"

"Tell them the truth," Lee said. "But only as much as is necessary. We don't want to scare anyone unnecessarily. Tell them Judy is in the hospital and we're trying to locate anyone who might have possible information about her illness, or who might have been ill themselves. We're particularly interested in identifying people who worked closely with Judy or who might have seen her recently."

Buddy took the first page of the list of names and went to Mr. Terry's office and began calling.

After eight calls Lee was able to get just three faculty members on the phone, and none of them knew anything.

Almost an hour had passed when Buddy came into her office and handed Lee a slip of paper with names and telephone numbers on it.

"This student, Robert Drummond, didn't come back to campus for registration. I called his home. He's sick—too sick to come back to school."

"Were you able to find out what's wrong with him?"

"He's in the hospital in Terre Haute, Indiana. His parents say the doctors don't know what's wrong with him but he has severe flu-type symptoms and is dehydrated. He was running a high fever and complaining of headaches and stomach cramps when they took him to the hospital."

"When was this?"

"Two days ago. He's been in the hospital two days."

"Do his parents know if he worked with Judy Vining on the research project?"

"No, they don't know. They said they will try to find out from him and call me back."

"You've done very well, Buddy. Keep calling. I'll get this information to Peter Raymond."

Lee keyed the details of Buddy's finding into her computer and faxed the information to Peter Raymond at the hospital. She then continued to call the names on the list of faculty. None of the faculty had any symptoms of illness. Neither had they worked closely with the field crew containing Judy Vining.

By the time they had called all the names on the two

187

lists, they had identified three more students on Judy Vining's field crew who were ill with flu-like symptoms. None were as sick as Judy, but two were in their doctor's care. Lee called the Agri-Sciences department and left a message asking that Gerald Campbell call her. She sat looking over their phone notes about the ill students.

"There are a variety of symptoms — nausea, vomiting, stomach cramps, diarrhea, fever, headaches, dizziness, lethargy, disorientation, dehydration, loss of strength."

"It sounds a lot like a bad case of the flu," Buddy said.

"Yes, it does, but there are many infectious diseases that produce flu-like symptoms. So can food poisoning and chemical contamination. At least we have something to start with now."

The phone rang and Buddy answered it. He took a short message and hung up.

"That was Estelle in the Agri-Sciences department on campus. She called to let you know Dr. Campbell is on his way over here."

In a little under twenty minutes a black Mercedes SUV pulled rather too quickly into the driveway of the coroner's office, causing a spray of gravel. Two men were in the vehicle. From her office window Lee couldn't see through the dark tinted windows of the SUV who they were. The driver's side door opened and a red faced Gerald Campbell got out and walked toward the door of her office.

They heard the front door open and close followed by hard footsteps and Campbell appeared in her doorway. When he approached, Lee attempted an introduction.

"Gerald, have you met Buddy Ruff?"

Campbell cut her short. "What's this newest uproar all

about, Lee?"

"Have you heard about Judy Vining?"

"Yes, I and half the campus have heard about her. Your calling all over and the hospital making inquiries are creating an atmosphere of unnecessary anxiety and concern bordering on near panic in certain quarters. With all the sensationalism that has been in the news, uninformed people are drawing unwarranted conclusions about a connection between Miss Vining's illness and her work in our department. I would urge you to exercise some judgement and restraint until we can get the straight facts in this unfortunate situation."

"Getting the straight facts is exactly what I have been attempting to do. Do you know about Robert Drummond and the other members of the field crew who have been working with Judy Vining?"

"Yes, I just talked with Miss Vining's doctor. I told him there is absolutely nothing in the research duties Miss Vining and the other students have been performing that could in any way result in the type of illness they are displaying."

"Are you certain of that?"

"I would not have said it were I not certain. Do you seriously think that if there were a danger I would attempt to hide it or cover it up? I was hoping to talk some reason into you. This field crew of students were working and living closely together all summer. Miss Vining is showing classic symptoms of meningitis. It is a very contagious disease. This time of year it is not uncommon to have outbreaks of it spread by mosquitoes."

"There are no reported cases of meningitis in East Tennessee or surrounding areas."

"Whether it is meningitis or something else, I'm sure when we have the opportunity to sort it all out, we will find they were all exposed to some external source during their stay together. Until that time we must be calm and methodical about our approach and avoid the kind of sensationalism you have been instigating."

Campbell's hostility was burning Lee, but she remained matter of fact. "The occurrence of illness in the field crew is undeniable. What remains is to determine whether they are all displaying symptoms of the same illness, and if so, to identify the source of the illness. I was about to ask you to lend the resources of the Agri-Sciences department in helping to narrow down the possibilities."

"You are much too premature in that request. Miss Vining's doctors have not had time to make a definite diagnosis. We must allow normal procedures to take their course. In the meantime, your sounding of alarm bells is of no benefit to anyone, and your insinuations that the Agri-Sciences department and the University are somehow connected to her illness are harmful to us . . . and to you, I might point out."

"I have made no such insinuations, Gerald. That sounded awfully close to a threat. I am doing my duty as I see it, and I will continue to do it so long as any possible danger to the community is present. Judy's mother and doctor asked for my help. I intend to respond to their requests in any way I can. I suggest you reinspect the connection between the illness of the field crew and the work they were doing on your research project."

Campbell's neck was bulging over his collar again, his lips were pursed, and his nose was making those characteristic little pointings into the air that it made when he was beside himself.

"You must realize what is at stake here. Dedicated people's careers and reputations can be destroyed by careless, ill-considered words and irresponsible actions," Campbell said.

"Then I suggest you consider carefully before speaking or acting." Lee said.

Campbell turned two shades redder. "This is getting us nowhere. I give you fair warning. Be very sure of your facts before you allege or insinuate that the University has played any role that would place the student body, the faculty, or the community in danger."

"Are you speaking for the University now, Gerald? If it should turn out that I have to choose between revealing all of my findings in order to protect the community or withholding some of those findings in order to protect your interests, let me assure you that my duty lies with the protection of the community."

Campbell actually seemed to explode as he spat out an exasperated gasp.

"You had better give careful consideration to the effect of your actions on your own career and interests," he said. "And make no further requests of my staff unless you come through me first."

He turned without further conversation and walked back to his car. Inside the car he talked animatedly with his passenger for a few brief seconds before backing out of the driveway and accelerating down the street in the direction of CMU.

"You sure have a calming influence on him," Buddy said. "Who was that in the car with him?"

"I couldn't see." She paused for a moment, trying to digest what had just happened. "I wish we had Campbell's cooperation, but we have to go ahead with or without his help."

"What do we do next?" Buddy asked.

Their conversation was interrupted by the ringing of Lee's phone. It was Sheriff Eberhard.

"We got a break," he said. "We turned up the blue Pontiac."

"Where did you find it?" Lee asked.

"Car rental place at the Knoxville airport. One of their cars came back with serious damage to the left front and side, the same day as the incident at Hamrick's."

"Who was the driver?"

"The car was rented to an Edward Wilkinson of Los Verdes, New Mexico. That's the name of Hamrick's associate you gave me earlier."

"Hamrick moved here from Los Verdes," Lee said.

"I sent a request to the Los Verdes authorities to locate and hold Wilkinson for questioning. I've also requested a photo of him. Thought we might have Luther Morris have a look at the photo. Maybe Luther can ID him as the driver of the getaway car at Hamrick's."

"If this Edward Wilkinson is the mysterious masked man, maybe we can begin to get some idea what happened out there," Lee said.

"If Los Verdes cooperates, we might have a photograph shortly."

"Have you had any report back from Tom Davis at the TBI crime lab?"

"Not a word. I assume the Attorney General ordered an end to that investigation when it was turned over to the feds."

"Thanks for the update, Sheriff."

"I'll let you know as soon as we have anything."

Lee filled Buddy in and dialed Tom Davis' number at the TBI lab in Knoxville. His voicemail message said he was not in the office. Lee left a message telling him briefly about the rental car and asked him to call her regarding the forensics report on the Hamrick investigation.

"You had better not let old man Terry hear you asking about the Hamrick investigation," Buddy told her.

"This is now a possible public health issue relating to the Vining situation," Lee said.

"Sure it is." Buddy grinned at her. "Listen, Lee. I need to see a man about a dog. You mind if I make myself scarce?"

"No, Buddy, you go ahead. I'll beep you if anything important comes up."

Nothing did, and about 4:30 Lee phoned Jack's office.

"Hey, handsome. You interested in dinner?"

"Sure. What did you have in mind?"

"I'll grill some steaks. Want to come over around seven?"

"You've got a date."

Lee stopped by the grocery to pick up a few things. On her way back to her SUV she ran into Lonnie Chapman in the parking lot.

"Hey, Lee."

"Lonnie." She returned the greeting.

"Some folks tell me you've been taking a whipping over the Hamrick business. You holding up OK? Anything I can do to help?"

"Thanks for asking, Lonnie. I appreciate the offer. I've been wanting to come talk with you about Hamrick but things have taken another turn lately."

"Still no word on his cause of death, I guess."

"No word back from the feds, and I have not received a report from the TBI lab. I'm waiting for a return call from them now."

"I got the death certificate on Mrs. Anderson."

"Was she one of your customers too?"

Lonnie chuckled pleasantly. "No, not one of mine. She pre-dated me by about fifty years. She was one of my dad's old original clients from when he first went into the insurance business. She was a fine lady. Taught school to my dad and lots of the folks of his generation around here. I've known her all my life. I used to drop by and talk with her from time to time. I hated to see her go. But, she lived a long and happy life. Well," he said as he waved to her, "Yell if you need me. When you see that boyfriend of yours, tell him we're still looking for a partner to make our golf threesome into a foursome. The offer still stands for you too, as always."

"I'll tell him." *Boyfriend,* Lee thought. So, people think I have a boyfriend. I kind of like the way that feels.

* * *

At two o'clock in the morning the phone rang. It was Peter Raymond at the hospital.

"I apologize for waking you Lee. I thought you would want to know. Judy Vining died an hour ago."

At first Lee didn't say anything. Her sleep had been

troubled. She had been having recurring bad dreams. She felt as though she were waking from a nightmare and this call was part of the nightmare.

"We still do not have a certain diagnosis for her illness."

Peter Raymond's voice helped Lee's mind to clear.

"Be sure and take samples of organ tissue, Peter. I want to have analyses run to check for the presence of bacteria and fungi."

"Already done."

"Did you save samples of the brain fluid?"

"Yes."

"One other thing, Peter. Keep the body under constant refrigeration and do not release it until all post mortem analysis is complete. I don't want to sound overly dramatic, but it could present a danger."

"You don't have to convince me. We're treating this as a case of lethal infectious disease until we know something different. I have been in contact with the medical team in charge of Robert Drummond in Terre Haute. So far they are no more enlightened about him than we are about Miss Vining."

"Thanks for calling, Peter."

"Tough business."

She had met Judy Vining only once, but as Lee lay in Jack's arms, she cried over Judy's death.

Chapter 14
Betrayal

LEE AWOKE TO the smell of fresh coffee. She could hear Jack talking but she couldn't hear the words, just the sound of his voice. He laughed occasionally in a very pleasant tone. Then she heard some movement and Jack's voice again.

"Go get Lee," she heard him say. "Go wake up your mommy."

Lee pulled the covers over her head just as Jack and Henrietta came through the bedroom door. Henrietta bounced over to the side of the bed and stood on her hind legs, pushing her nose under the covers looking for Lee.

"Is this your dog?" she asked.

"She told me she's your dog." Jack said, reaching under the sheet and tickling Lee.

"Can't a person sleep in this house?" she said, holding onto Jack's hand.

"Sure, sleep as long as you want. I'll just put breakfast in the refrigerator."

"You made breakfast?" she asked, peeking from under the covers.

"Coffee is ready now and breakfast will be ready in about twenty minutes. The biscuits are ready to go in the oven."

"It sounds wonderful," Lee said. "I didn't know you knew how to make biscuits."

"I read the instructions on the bag."

"I'm glad I brought you home with me."

"You are?"

"Yes, I am."

"I'm glad you did, too."

It was wonderful having breakfast with Jack. But Lee was restless. Her mind kept returning to her meeting with Judy Vining in Judy's office. Several times Lee dried tears from her eyes.

"What is it, Lee?"

"Judy Vining. I can't shake the image of that innocent young girl plaiting her hair and sucking on a Tootsie Pop. It's hard for me to think of her as dead. Whatever Hamrick may or may not have been mixed up in, Judy Vining was an innocent child."

"You think Hamrick somehow caused her death?"

"Oh, I don't know. I don't know what I think."

Jack kissed her on the temple and on the lips.

"You're very sweet," she said.

"I think you're knocking yourself out for no reason. What could you possibly have done to save her?"

"I should have listened to the little voice in the back of head."

Jack tried to lightened the atmosphere. "You're hearing voices?"

"Something was bothering me from the time I left her office the day I met her. My subconscious was trying to tell me. It was the map."

"What map?"

"The map on her office wall. It had little pins sticking in it. Hamrick had one like it on the wall of his office at home. Not only was Judy's similar to the one at Hamrick's, I think they may have been identical."

"Well, what do you make of it?"

"I think Hamrick was working secretly on the same project Judy was working on. She said he was always asking her questions about her work, reading her field notes, and making suggestions. I'm sorry, Jack. I've got to run."

"It's still early," he said, looking at his watch.

"I know. But I keep thinking about what happened in the Hamrick case. I've got to get to Judy Vining's office and her dorm room."

"Why? What are you looking for?"

"Answers," Lee said. "I've got to have some answers."

Lee found Buddy at Helen's Diner having his breakfast. Buddy could tell from Lee's manner that she was agitated. She didn't sit down but stood close to Buddy and spoke in a low voice.

"I may need your help, Buddy. It's kind of urgent."

Buddy stood up, facing Lee. "Sure, what is it?"

"Judy Vining died last night. We need to have a close look inside her office and her dorm room before anyone else gets there ahead of us. Bring your keys."

They went straight to Judy Vining's office in the basement of Garland Hall, bypassing the Agri-Sciences department. Judy's office was closed and locked.

"Do you have a key that will open it?"

Buddy bent over and took a close look at the door lock. Without a word he used his pocket knife and within ten seconds had the door open.

"How did you do that?" Lee asked.

"Look here and I'll show you."

Buddy closed the door back and showed Lee how the

bolt could be pried back a little at a time with the point of the knife blade, holding it back by pulling the bolt against the door frame.

"What are we looking for?" Buddy asked.

"I want to know about the project Judy was working on, and anything else that might provide a link with her illness. Keep your eyes open for anything that might tie Judy Vining to Alexander Hamrick."

"This map looks pretty much the way I remember the one in Hamrick's house," Buddy said, indicating the map on the wall.

"I want to take that with us when we leave. We'll compare it with the one in Hamrick's house, but take some good clear photographs of it before you take it off the wall."

"I guess that mean's we're going back to Hamrick's place."

"Yes."

Buddy photographed the map, removed it from the wall, folded it and placed it in Lee's briefcase as Lee removed files and papers from Judy's filing cabinet and her desk. When she had finished with Judy's desk, Lee searched Hamrick's desk a second time.

They were interrupted by a knock at the door and looked up to see two campus policemen standing in the doorway.

"Ma'am?" One of the policemen said with a question on his face.

Lee smiled and took out her identification badge.

"Coroner's office," she said.

There was a slight change, a relaxing of the policeman's posture. "Yeah, I heard about the two of them dying. Is it something contagious? There's lots of rumors flying around."

"No medical connection has been discovered. That's why we're here, following up all the possibilities. Right now Miss Vining is the only case of its type on campus that we know about."

"It sounds pretty bad," he said. He backed from the doorway. "We'll get out of your way. Lock the door behind you when you leave, would you, please? We've had a rash of computer thefts lately."

"Yes, we will," Lee said.

When the two policemen were gone, Buddy said, "You're pretty cool, Lee. I thought for a minute we were on the way to the clink."

The policeman's mention of computer thefts spurred a thought in Lee's mind. She went to Judy Vining's bookcase and removed a small clear flip-top box. Inside the box were three USB memory sticks. The labelling on them indicated they probably contained computer files relating to Judy's research. Lee dropped them into an evidence bag and stored the bag in her briefcase.

Just then there were footsteps and voices echoing down the hollow hallway from the direction of the elevator.

"Let's get out of here," Lee said.

They quickly gathered up their things, closed and locked the door quietly behind them and hurried around the back hallway to the stairs, avoiding whoever was approaching from the direction of the elevator.

"Sorry about the stairs." Lee said to Buddy as he hopped up the flight with his one good leg.

"Never a dull moment," he said. "Chicago could not possibly compare with this."

They were too late at Judy Vining's dorm room. It was in the process of being stripped and sterilized. Whatever might have been there had already been removed.

As they drove back to Lee's office, Lee cautioned Buddy.

"You and I are the only ones who need to know what we have in this briefcase and how we got it," she said.

Buddy shook his head and grinned. "This is a whole new side of you I've never seen before."

"I didn't have time to write a letter of request," she said.

Mr. Terry was not yet at the office when Lee and Buddy arrived there.

"You have a message on your phone," Buddy said. The red light on the phone set was blinking. Lee played the message back. The voice sounded like gravel rattling in a bass note played by a trombone.

"This is Frank Hayes at the Rocky Mountain Bonding Company in Los Verdes, New Mexico. I am calling in reference to a Dr. Edward Wilkinson. Call me anytime."

Lee took the number from the message and phoned the Rocky Mountain Bonding Company where a too cheerful gruff voice answered.

"Rocky Mountain Bonding, where it's always spring time. How can we help you?"

"This is Dr. Lee Turner with the coroner's office in Bartram County, Tennessee."

"Yes, ma'am. You must be calling about Dr. Wilkinson," the deep gravelly voice said in a more serious tone.

"Yes, I am."

"I understand you would like to locate Dr. Wilkinson for questioning."

"Yes, we would. Can you be of help to us?"

"No, ma'am, not at the moment. Dr. Wilkinson is being a bad boy. He was due to appear before a federal judge yesterday afternoon and failed to show. We have some people inquiring. We'll find him. I *have* to find him, I guaranteed his return to the tune of $100,000. I don't suppose you've seen him in Bartram County, have you?"

"The last anyone saw of him in Tennessee was at the Knoxville airport on his way back to Los Verdes. Was he being held on charges?"

"Yes, ma'am he was. Several counts of theft of federal property and flight to avoid prosecution, among others."

"I want to suggest that you have your people check the hospitals. There is the possibility that Dr. Wilkinson is seriously ill someplace. He may be being held in an isolation ward."

"Well, that is bad news for him, but it may be good for me. If he is seriously ill and unable to appear in court, I may be relieved of having to pay over the bond. Thank you for the tip. I'll work on that. I suppose you would like to know if and when we locate him?"

"Yes, it is important that we know."

"If this lead works out, you'll know as soon as we find him."

"Thank you."

"Thank you, ma'am."

Lee hung up the phone.

"I don't think I would want the man with that voice looking for me," she said.

"They can be a rough bunch," Buddy said. "But they can

be real clever too at tracking somebody down."

The phone rang and Lee answered.

"Coroner's office, this is Dr. Turner."

A very gravelly voice said, "Dr. Turner, this is Frank Hayes at Rocky Mountain Bonding. Did you just call me in regard to Dr. Wilkinson?"

"Yes, I did."

"Thank you, ma'am. I was just verifying that you are who you said you were. We can't be too trusting in this business, you know. You wouldn't believe the wild goose chases people have tried to send me on."

"Yes, I understand."

"In relation to this illness that Dr. Wilkinson may be suffering from, do my people need to take any particular precautions when they locate him?"

"If he is ill I would not advise direct physical contact with him. If he is in medical care I would like to put the medical people here in touch with his doctors."

"If he's that ill we won't need to touch him. I'm off the hook if his medical condition prevents him from appearing. As I said, I appreciate this information and if I find him sick or well, you'll know about it."

"Mr. Hayes, do you have a photograph of Wilkinson? No one here knows what he looks like."

"Yes, ma'am I do. Give me your fax number and I'll send it to you. Do you have a connection to the Internet?"

"Yes, I do."

"If you go to my website, you will find a picture that is of better quality than the fax can transmit. My web address is RockyMountainBonding.com. You will be asked for a password. Your password will be *peach*."

And with that, the gravelly Mr. Hayes was gone. Lee placed the receiver back on the phone. The call had aroused the interest of Buddy who waited for an explanation.

"Rocky Mountain Bonding," she said, "Verifying their source of information."

"A serious business," Buddy said. "I wouldn't want those guys looking for me."

Within a couple of minutes Lee had received the facsimile of a photograph of Edward Wilkinson along with his physical description, last known address and phone number in Los Verdes, New Mexico. Buddy looked over the image.

"Not the best quality in the world for making a positive ID."

It took Lee only a minute or two to call up her internet browser and locate the website for Rocky Mountain Bonding. She went to the section labeled "Missing and Wanted" and found the name *Edward Wilkinson* next to a thumbnail photo of him. She clicked on an item labeled *Download Info* and was asked for a password. She typed in the word *peach* and clicked on the Start Download button.

It took less than a minute for the eight by ten inch color image and the accompanying report to transfer across the internet from Los Verdes to Bartram County and another thirty seconds for the high resolution color image to print. She printed a second copy for the sheriff's office. Lee and Buddy headed back toward the sheriff's office with the photo.

"We know several things about Wilkinson from the evidence we have," Lee said. "He flew to Knoxville from Los Verdes, rented a car in his name at the Knoxville airport, and returned the car with damage matching what we saw happen at Hamrick's. We don't know if he was the driver we saw. We do know that he was a colleague of Hamrick's and shared professional interests with him."

"I'll bet money it was him we saw at Hamrick's disposing of the body. Look at his description. Six feet-two inches and two hundred and ten pounds, muscular build. By my estimate, that's about the size of the man I wrestled with. And he's thirty-eight years old. That would be the right age to be as strong as he was." He grinned at Lee. "And I'm not just saying that because he whipped me, either."

"I agree," Lee said. "I think it was probably Wilkinson we encountered. I wonder what he was doing there. I wonder what he knows about this whole situation. I wonder why he ran."

"He probably ran because he killed Hamrick."

"Maybe we'll find out when they catch him."

"Jumped bail, eh?" Sheriff Eberhard said. "We'll make copies of this notice and circulate it among the law enforcement agencies in the area. I think we should have Luther Morris take a look at the photograph. He's the only one who can give us a positive ID on Wilkinson. And maybe Luther's wife. She said she got a look at him. I'll have Billy take it out to Luther's place."

Mr. Terry was in the office when Lee and Buddy returned.

"You and Buddy seem to be awfully busy," he said. "What are you working on?"

"The Judy Vining death," Lee said.

"Judy Vining? What's your interest in her?"

"Dr. Peter Raymond asked me to consult with him because of my knowledge of infectious diseases."

Mr. Terry seemed to consider that as he looked at Lee's face through his thick glasses.

"We're always happy to lend assistance," he said as he shuffled toward the front door. "But don't let it take too much of your time."

"No, I won't."

Buddy wagged his finger at Lee, rolled his eyes back and shook his head.

The morning's mail contained the beginnings of what Lee knew would be a steady flow of queries and forms surrounding the Hamrick case. There was a form from the Social Security office, one from Hamrick's mortgage insurance company, one from the Millennium Viatical Insurance Benefits company, and one from the Commercial Bank of Oak Ridge, all requesting certification of Hamrick's death. She took them to Mr. Terry's office and filed them in Hamrick's folder. They'll have to stand in line with the rest of us, she said to herself.

The phone rang as Lee was returning to her office. It was Tom Davis.

"Lee, sorry I didn't get back to you on the Hamrick case. It got put on hold here and I was pulled off to the mountains along the state line with North Carolina to work with the FBI on a terrorist fugitive man hunt they've got going over there."

"Any luck there?"

"Oh, we found a little evidence left for us. I personally don't think the guy is there. My personal opinion is that he has relocated to some entirely different area like Atlanta or

Dallas where there is no really concentrated search for him. Or he may be hiding out with some of his militia buddies out in Montana or someplace. I think he left a false trail in the mountains to draw our attention there, and that's what the feds are following. All I've got to show for my efforts is about a thousand mosquito bites. Anyhow, I don't guess you want to hear my problems. I hear you've had another death locally."

"Yes. It's a sad case. I'm looking for a connection. Has the lab been able to process any of the Hamrick evidence?"

"All the major stuff like DNA analysis is on hold. I had already sent the vials from Hamrick's lab for analysis. I got the results back on them. Not much help, I'm afraid. Each of the vials contains a mixture of chemicals and minerals that would result from the chemical reduction of the animals. There were also some organic substances, such as spores, that were not broken down by the reduction process."

"What kind of spores?" Lee asked.

"Plant spores, fungal spores, bacterial spores. An assortment."

Lee had a sudden insight. "Spores. That's what the checklist was about in Hamrick's lab. I knew I had seen that procedure somewhere before. I've seen it used to isolate and recover pollen spores. That chemical procedure dissolves everything but spores. They're practically indestructible. Hamrick was doing some kind of research on spores. Maybe he was studying the diets of local animals. I don't know. Perhaps his records will shed some light on it, if we ever get access to his records."

207

"I was able to run the fingerprint evidence through the scanner and got some matches on that. I'll fax the results to you."

"Anything interesting in the prints?"

"That's why I called. We found several sets of prints all over the house and lab. One set was of Mr. Edward Wilkinson of Los Verdes, New Mexico, who you already called me about."

"So, he was in Hamrick's house?"

"House, lab, guest bedroom and bathroom, kitchen, office, everywhere."

"He's apparently skipped bond on federal charges in Los Verdes."

"Interesting. Another set of prints belongs to one of your local citizens, a Ray Durbin," Tom said.

"I know Ray Durbin," Lee said. "He's pretty active and outspoken in the county, but I don't know what his connection is to Hamrick. What file did you find his prints in?"

"He was arrested once several years ago for trespassing on state property. Doesn't look like a serious offense. Judging by the number of his prints in the place, he was there more than once. We found another set of prints in the main part of the house belonging to another local named Leonard Chapman."

"Lonnie Chapman. He's Hamrick's insurance agent. Were the prints anywhere they shouldn't have been?"

"We found them in the study and the kitchen—the kinds of places you might expect an insurance agent to go. The fourth set we've been able to identify belong to, now get this, an FBI agent. Apparently he got there before we did.

The prints seemed very fresh."

"Not too surprising, I guess," Lee said. "We know there was an ongoing federal investigation of Hamrick. Is it a local agent?"

"No. Someone out of Washington D.C. His name is Sheridan, special agent Jack Sheridan."

Lee didn't hear the rest of what Tom said. What she did hear was her own voice saying, "Forgive me, Tom. I have to go. Can you fax that information to the sheriff's office, please?"

"Sure thing, Lee."

Lee had her finger between her teeth, biting to keep from sobbing aloud. She tried to make it to the bathroom but she felt the sour taste of vomit in her throat before she took three steps. She covered her mouth with her hand but she gagged and coughed and the sticky putrid mess was suddenly on her hand, her clothes and on the floor.

Buddy was coming toward her saying, "Jesus, Lee. What's the matter? Do you need help?"

Lee held out a hand to stop him as she ran down the hallway into the bathroom and shut the door behind her. She sat on the edge of the old tub in the bathroom, bent over the bowl of the toilet crying, nausea gripping her and her head pounding. She felt the uncontrollable spasm of her stomach, followed by the gagging and the awful sensation of sour vomit coming up her throat into her mouth and she coughed and spat into the toilet. Her stomach cramped and heaved until there was nothing left in her to come up and she was left weak and trembling. Her sinuses were swollen and hurting from the crying, her nose was running, her eyes were swollen. She wanted to die. She looked at herself in the mirror. Her eyes were swollen almost beyond recognition and she was so pale she didn't seem to have any blood in her cheeks.

How stupid could you be, she said to herself. *The son of a bitch lied to you. He lied to you from the beginning and you fell for him. Everything was a lie. You fell into bed with him. He was playing with you and you fell for it–I fell for it. I hate the son of a bitch. I made a perfect fool of myself. All the time he could have told me. He watched me and knew things I didn't and he didn't tell me. I hate him. I hate myself.*

Lee sat alone in the bathroom unable to move, unable to get up, unable to do anything. Her mind kept going back to all the times she and Jack were together, all the things he had said and she had said. She didn't want to believe it was all a lie based on a lie. But what else was there to think?

She splashed her swollen face with cool water, trying to take away some of the swelling in her eyes and return her color to normal. It was no use. She drank a glass of water and took aspirin to ease the pain. She wanted to go home and not see anyone. Buddy was in the office and she had to face him. What must he be thinking of her right now?

She weaved and stumbled as she left the bathroom. It was hard to keep her eyes focused. She walked unsteadily back to her office to get her car keys. Buddy had mopped the floor and was waiting for her to come back.

"What's the matter, Lee? Do I need to get you to the hospital?"

Lee couldn't answer except to shake her head. She took her keys from her desk and left her office without another word. She knew what she had to do.

She was almost unaware of the drive. She arrived at Jack's apartment. The apartment that she had arranged for him because he was sleeping in his office. What a lie.

He wasn't there. She let herself in. She had an almost irresistible desire to break everything that was his. She searched his drawers. Nothing incriminating.

She went to his clothes closet and found his suitcase. Inside it in a side pocket was a single unused envelope from the Federal Bureau of Investigation, Washington, D.C. She put the envelope in her pocket.

She searched through his clothes in his closet. On a rack inside a suit hanging in the closet she found a leather shoulder holster for a pistol.

It was true.

She drove to his office on campus. The door was locked. She used her pocket knife and gouged at the lock bolt. It took her longer than ten seconds but she worked the bolt back and opened the door.

There was nothing in his desk linking him to the FBI or to anything but his classes. There was nothing incriminating in his filing cabinet that she could find. She turned to leave the office. It was then she saw the corner of an old brown leather briefcase showing from behind his sofa. She had little doubt what it was. She slid it from its hiding place. Engraved on the side of the briefcase below the handle in time-worn lettering was the name A. M. Hamrick. She opened it.

Inside were assorted odds and ends belonging to Alexander Hamrick. The one important item not present was Hamrick's daily journal. Judy Vining said he always carried it with him in his briefcase.

It was no coincidence Jack's office was around the corner from Hamrick's. It had been arranged. He said he didn't know Hamrick. Another lie. His questions about the Hamrick case—he had been grilling her to find out what she knew. He knew more about Hamrick than she did. That was obvious. He had Hamrick's journal. He must know what Hamrick was working on in his lab. He knew about Wilkinson and about Ray Durbin. He must know all about the federal investigation. She hated him.

Lee was having recurring bouts of dizziness and trembling. She thought she might pass out. She had to keep going. She wanted to find Jack Sheridan. She wanted to scream at him and hit him with her fists. She wanted to hear an explanation that could change the reality she was now living.

She left his office in a daze. Her head was spinning and she couldn't think straight. The one thing that kept coming into her mind again and again was the feeling of betrayal. She headed her Land Cruiser toward home. If he wasn't there waiting for her, she was at a loss as to where else to look.

What was she going to say to him anyway? All she really felt like doing was crying. She sure as hell wasn't going to cry in front of him. Not again. She had let him get too close to her too fast. He was a son of a bitch and she didn't see it coming. He was too smooth, too charming, too good looking. She had seen that in the beginning. Why hadn't she listened to herself? Because she had been lonely for love. She hadn't told anyone. Hadn't even admitted it to herself. But he had seen it. He had played her like a familiar old song, and she had fallen right into his lying arms. *What a stupid bitch I am.*

The sound of her phone brought her out of her spiraling self-pity as she drove along the familiar road from CMU toward home, not even aware of where she was. *What now?* she thought. She picked up her cell phone. She missed the call. It was the sheriff's office. She pushed the autodial key.

"Margy, it's Lee."

"Lee, hold on, I need to connect you with Deputy Longtree."

In a moment she heard Billy answer.

"Billy, it's Lee. What's up?"

"Lee, I'm out at Luther Morris's place. We have a situation."

Billy's voice sounded strange. Probably a weak signal.

"What is it, Billy? I've got something here of my own."

"It's Luther and his family."

"What about them?"

"I can't get close enough to tell. Nobody will go near it. It looks like Hamrick all over again. I think it may be the whole family, Lee. You need to get out here."

Chapter 15
Luther Morris

"DON'T GO NEAR them, Billy. Don't let anyone near them. I've got to get some gear. Give me directions and I'll be there as soon as I can get there."

Lee dialed radio dispatch at the sheriff's office.

"Margy," she said, "this is Lee. Please notify Emergency Rescue that I need two complete hazmat suits available to me as soon as possible out at the Luther Morris place. Tell them I'm on my way to the Morris place and will meet them there."

Lee called her office hoping to catch Buddy still there. No answer. She headed back into town, toward Helen's Diner. Please be there, Buddy, she said to herself as she called Helen's number.

"Helen's Diner."

"Helen, is Buddy there?"

"Just walked out the door, honey."

"Catch him, please, don't let him get away, I'm on my way there."

"Hold on a second, let me see if he's gone."

Lee was driving too fast, she knew. Her eyes darted left and right and to the rearview mirror as she passed cars and trucks on the two lane road. She could hear the background noise in Helen's Diner as she waited for someone to pick up the phone again. The phone rattled and she heard Buddy's voice.

"Lee, what is it?"

"Stay there, Buddy. I'll be there in ten minutes to pick

you up. Something's happened to Luther Morris."

"Luther? Where is he?"

"At his home. Don't say anything to anyone. I'll be there. When I pick you up I want a quart of milk and half a dozen doughnuts or a couple of candy bars."

"OK, Lee. Whatever."

When Lee pulled to a stop in front of the diner, Helen and Buddy both came out to meet her. Helen was carrying the sack of items Lee had requested. Buddy opened the door to the Land Cruiser and got in. Helen handed in the bag of food. She looked worried. Lee thanked her and pulled back onto the street, headed in the direction of the Morris place.

"Damn, Lee," Buddy said, "You don't look too good. You're not weirding out on me, are you? What's going on?"

"I feel worse than I look. You got the milk?"

"Yeh. What is this, some new health diet?"

"I threw up my breakfast, I couldn't eat any lunch, and my hands are shaking uncontrollably. The milk contains lactose sugar to give me energy, calcium to calm me down, and protein for strength. The doughnuts are pure carbohydrates–more energy."

"Well, I sure hope it all works."

"Me too. I hope I can keep the milk on my stomach."

"Let me know if you feel like you're not going to be able to. I want to get out first."

"Don't make me start laughing."

"I wish you would. I've never seen you upset like this before."

"I don't think I ever have been."

"You want to tell me what's happened to you?"

"Give me a little time."

"OK. What's happened out at Luther's?"

"Billy went out to show him the photo of Wilkinson. From what Billy says, it looks as if the whole family may be dead. I've got hazmat suits on the way. You and I have to go in."

"Do you think maybe we ought to let someone else handle this situation? You're a basket case and I'm a cripple. Put us both together and you still got just half a person."

"No, Buddy. For more than one reason this is something you and I have to do. Whatever is going on, we're going to find out. My chain has been jerked one time too many. You and I are not mushrooms to be kept in the dark and fed crap."

"Well, I for one know that I have been kept in the dark and fed doo-doo many times. You sure you don't want to tell me what's happened? If it's personal I can understand."

"I can't talk about it right now, Buddy, please."

"All right. You know I'm just trying to help. I'll do whatever you tell me to do."

"I've been thrown for a loop, Buddy. I can hardly think right now. I need someone thinking straight and talking straight. You've always done that and that's what I want you to do now. I can't do this by myself."

"It's hard for me to imagine anything you couldn't do if you set your mind to it, Lee."

Lee's voice caught in her throat for a moment.

"You have a higher opinion of me than I have of myself

right now."

"Lee, I ain't never pretended to be anything but what I am. And I'm not pretending now to have any ancient wisdom. But I have got a few years on you, and some of those years were hard ones. I've had lots of ups and downs in my life. What I'm saying is, whatever this is, you'll get through it. It won't be any time at all until you'll look back and this point in time will be just a little blip on your radar screen of life. You and me'll be as happy as two little kids, riding down the road in your truck laughing and scratching."

"Thanks, Buddy," she said, and she smiled for the first time since morning. Buddy's mention of kids made Lee's thoughts turn to Luther Morris's children.

"Just supposing for a minute that what Billy says about Luther and his family is true," Buddy said. "What do you think is going on here?"

"Everything seems to go back to Hamrick. His lab presents more possibilities than I care to even think about. We know his work involved handling dead animals. That opens up a spectrum of possible diseases from bacteria, viruses, parasites, maybe even chemicals."

"Parasites?" Buddy said. "That sounds like *Aliens* or *Invasion of the Body Snatchers*."

Lee ignored him and continued. "I suppose it's possible he infected himself with something from his lab or the dead animals. Perhaps he then passed it on to his officemate, Judy Vining. Luther told us he has done odd jobs for Hamrick. Luther might have become infected and carried it home to his family. But that's just guessing. There are too many unknowns. I just don't know how the pieces all fit together."

"I talked with Barb some about her and Hamrick."

"What's the story with them?"

"Barb says the old man got irrational. Paranoid. Suspicious of everybody around him. She says he kept talking about people stealing his ideas and money that should have been his. She says he wanted to move back here from Los Verdes and start up his research laboratory again. He had these ideas about some new patents he wanted to register."

"She didn't have confidence he knew what he was doing?"

"No. She said he's been putting good money after bad into expensive lab equipment and such. She's afraid he spent the kid's inheritance."

"Was the separation her idea?"

"Hers and his too, according to her. He was hiding stuff from her and she was afraid to move back here with him. She says they had a nice place in Los Verdes. And the kid in school. She didn't want to move back here to some old house on a dirt road in the middle of nowhere, not with him changed the way he was."

"When did she tell you all this?"

"I was with her last night."

"Is there any future in that?"

"Probably not. We all change."

Lee wanted to ask him a dozen other questions but their conversation was cut short by their arrival at the turnoff to the Morris place.

The EMT rescue unit was there ahead of them, pulled to one side. Billy's patrol car sat blocking the narrow road. A pickup truck and a couple of automobiles were parked to the side. Word had already leaked out. Lee and Buddy got out of the Land Cruiser and walked to where Billy Longtree was standing.

"What have we got here?" Lee asked.

Billy motioned for them to follow him up the road away from the cluster of people. They walked about a hundred feet and the deputy stopped.

"Do you notice anything?" He asked.

They stopped and looked and listened. They were still a good quarter mile from the Morris house.

"I see them," Buddy said.

"What?" Lee asked.

Just at that moment something blocked out the sun and a clearly defined shadow passed on the ground in front of them. They looked up. A large vulture was gliding easily, almost in slow motion over them just above the tree tops. It was so large and so close it was startling. Without a visible motion of its four-foot wingspan it sailed in a straight line toward the Morris house. As they followed its course, the solitary figure rose into the sky and joined a revolving constellation of members of its tribe circling over the house. In the trees near the house, large black birds, too large to be crows, appearing to be almost too large for the limbs on which they perched, sat motionless.

"Has anyone been up to the house?" Lee asked.

Billy said, "I was on my way to Luther's place to show him the photograph when I was flagged down on the highway by Luther's brother Itch. He's the one that found them. Itch said he went up to the house and saw the buzzards. He looked in the kitchen door where he saw Luther dead. He said he yelled, but there was no sign of human life. He was too scared to go inside. He left to get help and that's when he ran into me and I called you."

"I can smell something from here," Buddy said.

"Itch said the smell at the house is suffocating."

"Let's get the hazmat suits and get started," Lee said.

They walked back to where the rescue van was parked. Lee pulled the EMT technicians to one side.

"Here's the situation," Lee said. "We know the bodies could contain something contagious. Buddy and I are going up to take a look. We'll be protected by the hazmat suits as long as we're careful. When we come out we need to have a 50-50 solution of tincture of iodine ready to spray us down. That will kill just about any fungus or bacteria on the surface."

"Let's suit up, Buddy" she said, without taking her eyes off the sinister flock circling the house.

She and Buddy pulled the hazmat suits over their clothes, slipped their sock feet into the rubber boots, and zipped themselves up. Each of the suits was fitted with a radio and a small headset with an ear speaker and a microphone. An EMT technician took two oxygen packs from his van and helped Lee and Buddy into their harnesses. They pulled their face masks on, verified the oxygen supply, pulled the hoods of their suits over their heads and sealed the face masks. They pulled thick latex coated gloves over their hands. All external seams were then sealed with plastic tape.

"You there, Buddy?" Lee said over her radio.

Buddy answered. "I hear you. You read me?"

"Loud and clear."

"We can hear you over our radios here," the technician said, "but you will be out of our range by the time you get to the house."

"Watch for us," Lee said, "If anything happens, we'll signal to you."

They waved an OK to everyone and started on the road toward Luther's house.

As they drew nearer the house, the vultures in the trees, one after the other, flapped their huge wings and flew away from their approach. At the edge of the barnyard a small flock of the scavengers flapped and rose suddenly from just in front of them, startling both Lee and Buddy.

"Damn! They're big ugly sons of bitches, ain't they?" Buddy said.

On the ground where the vultures had been was the carcass of what appeared to be a small dog.

"The dog too?" Buddy said, "Why would the dog be dead?"

To one side of the barnyard was a barn, and beside that was a livestock pen. There were vultures inside it eating at several large carcasses.

"Hog pen," Buddy said. "Everything is dead. What could kill everything? Gas? Poison? Disease?"

"Any of those and more," Lee said.

Connected to one side of the barn was a chicken pen enclosed with wire running the width of the barn. On the floor of the enclosed area and in the laying boxes were the decomposing bodies of three or four dozen chickens.

"We have a disaster on our hands," Lee said.

"How bad do you think it is?"

"As bad as anything I have ever seen."

Buddy said, "On a scale of one to ten, ten being total global destruction, where would you rate this situation?"

"Whatever caused this appears to kill both mammals and fowl. That would seem to point to a poison and not a disease. If it is a disease that has jumped species, we should all be afraid. But at this point, I don't know what it is."

They walked past the corner of the barn. Luther's pickup truck was parked in front of the small unpainted house. There was a large gathering of vultures in the yard of the house. They were actively interested in something on the ground. Buddy turned and looked at Lee who had stopped and was looking toward him. But the glare on Lee's face visor hid the fact that she was looking past him to the scene over his shoulder. Lee raised her arm to point and Buddy turned to look behind him.

Buddy's voice came over the radio in two long and one short syllable, "Holy shit."

They walked in silence across the open drive toward a black gathering. There was no sound over their radios except the sound of their heavy breathing.

The vultures were crowded together, their sooty black forms merging into an undulating mass as they bobbed forward, down, and back up again in random order, feeding on something on the ground.

"I hope it's a dog," Buddy said.

As the two orange suited figures approached the feeding flock of scavengers, a repeating ritual played itself out. At some undefined distance known only to each bird, some invisible threshold was crossed by the approaching humans, and the vultures, sometimes individually, and sometimes in groups of two or three, squatted for a moment on bent legs, gave themselves a push upward with a heavy hop, and raised their large dark bodies into the air with the deep beating of strong wings. What was left on the ground when they were gone was almost unrecognizable.

Lee's voice came over the radio first.

"It's a child," she said. "The little girl."

"Oh, Jesus, no," Buddy said.

But there was no mistaking the soiled remnants of the small blue playsuit with red and yellow animal designs and the yellow shred of material that had been the ribbon in little Bonnie Morris' hair.

Lee stood for a moment, unable to move, transfixed by the horror. She hoped this was a nightmare.

"Breathe, Lee," Buddy's voice came over her headset. "Breathe or you'll pass out."

Lee pulled in a slow, full breath of oxygen.

There was a sheet of black plastic in the back of Luther's pickup truck. Lee covered the remains of the small body with it and weighted down the plastic with old bricks from the yard to protect the body from the return of the vultures.

"Let's take a look inside the house."

The screen door to the house was closed but the front door behind it was standing half open. In the front room on an old sofa lay the badly decomposed body of a woman with white hair wearing an old fashioned black dress. There was a Bible on the table next to the sofa.

"Grandma," Lee said.

Slumped in his chair and lying face down on the kitchen table was the decomposing body of Luther Morris, judging from the clothes. Dishes containing remnants of moldy food stood on the table. Pots and pans of moldy food lay open on the stove and counter top. On the floor next to a table was an open tin container of corn with a corn grinder clamped to it.

"Look at what they were eating, Lee." Buddy pointed to a plate piled with fish bones. "You think the fish poisoned them?"

"Don't jump to any conclusions, Buddy. There are too many possibilities."

While Buddy was talking, Lee's eyes came to rest on the door of the refrigerator. There under a refrigerator magnet next to a picture colored by Bonnie Morris was a business card. The name on the business card said Edward Wilkinson, PhD, Desert Flats National Laboratories, Los Verdes, New Mexico. Lee couldn't pick up the business card through the thick gloves of the hazmat suit. She tapped it with her finger.

Buddy looked at it and looked at Lee.

"God all mighty, Lee. Would Wilkinson kill Hamrick, then come out here and kill the whole Morris family and then leave his calling card? That don't make sense to me."

They walked to the open doorway of the parents' bedroom. In the bed was a mass of bedclothes, decomposed tissue and human hair.

"The mother and baby," Lee said.

"I'm going to be sick, Lee. I need to get out of this face mask."

"No. You stay in the suit. Breathe easy and let yourself calm down. Let's get outside away from this."

The two of them walked back out into the sunlight. Buddy's breathing over the radio sounded labored. They walked to one end of the porch. Buddy sat down next to an old stone well.

"Are you OK now?" Lee asked.

"I will be," Buddy said. "I never saw anything like that before. What was the little girl doing out in the yard?"

"She must have been the last to die," Lee said. "The

mother and infant were bedridden. Luther and Grandma must have been caring for them until they both died. The little girl, with no one to watch after her, wandered into the front yard and died. It must have all happened quickly or Luther would have gone for help."

"What killed them?"

"I don't know."

"What about the animals?"

"The hogs may have died from lack of water."

"What about the dog?"

"A dog can usually find food and water out here in the country like this. Something must have caused its death."

"I never saw anything like that before," Buddy said again.

"We better get back and tell the others. We need to have the TBI crime lab and the state epidemiologist come in here."

Buddy got up and they stepped off the porch and started across the yard. Lee stopped. She thought she heard something – something like the cry of a bird.

"Wait a minute, Buddy. Listen."

"What?"

"Listen."

They both stood still, listening.

"Hold your breath, Buddy, to stop the noise in the earphone." She did the same.

They listened.

Nothing.

"I can't hold my breath any longer, Lee. I don't hear anything."

Lee had a prickly sensation all over. She wondered if she

were passing out. Then she heard it again. Then Buddy's voice was in her ear.

"I heard it," he said. "What was it?"

Lee turned and headed for the front door of the house.

"It's the baby. Look in the truck. It's here somewhere."

She heard the sound of Buddy opening the door of the pickup truck as the screen door of the house slammed behind her.

"Nothing here," his voice said in her earphone.

Lee searched room to room in the house. A small room connected to the parents' bedroom served as the children's bedroom. In it was Bonnie's bed, and at the foot of Bonnie's bed was a baby bed. In the bed was a small, barely conscious baby.

"She's here, Buddy."

But Buddy had already found them.

"How in the name of God is she still alive?" Buddy said. "She must be immune to it."

Within seconds Lee had the baby in her arms wrapped in a blanket and she was headed out the front door.

"See if Luther's truck will crank," she directed Buddy.

The key was in the ignition. Buddy got behind the wheel and Lee climbed in the passenger seat, holding the baby. The engine started on the first try.

The look of surprise on the faces of Billy Longtree and the others was evident as Lee and Buddy approached them in the old truck. A sizable crowd of onlookers had gathered, including Katie Horne and other members of the press.

Buddy stopped the truck and Lee got out with the baby. At first no one knew what to do—whether to take the baby from Lee or to stay clear from them for fear of contamination.

"Bring a clean blanket," Lee said into the radio mouthpiece.

As the emergency technician approached with a blanket, Lee handed the bundled baby to Buddy. She then took off her protective gloves, her helmet and her face mask.

"Someone has to touch the baby," Lee said. "Give me a pair of latex gloves."

The EMT handed her a fresh pair of gloves and stood holding a clean blanket. Lee pulled the latex gloves on her hands. She took the bundled baby from Buddy and laid the baby and blanket on the ground. She removed the baby's soiled clothes and placed the naked baby in the clean blanket in the arms of the EMT technician.

"Get her straight to the hospital," Lee said. "She has been without liquids or nourishment for three days or more."

Before Lee had finished her instructions, the EMT ran back to a waiting ambulance with the baby in arms and a doctor was on the radio from the hospital giving emergency instructions.

Lee and Buddy were both wet with sweat and relieved when they were finally able to get out of the hazmat suits following decontamination. Deputy Longtree approached them, accompanied by a tired, sad looking, middle aged man.

"Dr. Turner," Billy Longtree said, "this is Itch Morris. He's Luther's brother. Itch is the one who first discovered the bodies."

"Was there nobody else alive, Ma'am?" Itch said, the answer already showing on his face.

"No, Mr. Morris. I'm sorry. Just the little girl."

"Elizabeth," he said. "The baby's name is Elizabeth.

Grandma?" He asked.

"No, I'm sorry."

"Can you tell what happened to them? Was it murder or what?"

"I saw no signs of violence and nothing was disturbed, Mr. Morris. There is no way for us to tell right now. We'll get some experts in here today. We'll know more when we can have autopsy and lab results."

"I knowed I should have come yesterday when Luther didn't show up." Itch offered in explanation, "Yesterday was our regular day to do some hauling over at the University farms. Luther was supposed to come by and pick me up yesterday morning, like always. I just figured his old truck wouldn't start or somethin' come up. I never figured nothin' like this."

"Try not to worry, Mr. Morris. I have hopes the baby will recover. And don't blame yourself. The others were all dead before yesterday. There is nothing you could have done to save them."

"It's too hard to think about." He ran his hand through his hair.

"Mr. Morris, Billy was on his way out here to ask Luther to identify a man from a photograph. Would you mind looking at it?"

"Why, no Ma'am, I wouldn't mind."

Lee nodded to Billy and he got the photograph of Edward Wilkinson from his police cruiser. Billy showed the photo to Itch.

"No, Ma'am, I don't know that I've ever seen this man. Should I know him?"

"No, there was just a chance you might. Thank you."

"Well, I best get my wife and go see to the baby. Poor little thing. She's got nobody but us now."

"I'm sorry for your loss," Lee said.

"Ain't no way I can ever repay you for what you did." He extended his hand to Lee and Buddy in turn.

Lee was holding back tears. She put in the call to the TBI from her cell phone to request the crime scene unit. Then she called Dr. Peter Raymond at the hospital to brief him on the situation and asked him to request the state epidemiologist to send a team to the site.

As she sat in her Land Cruiser eating a candy bar and drinking a bottle of Gatorade the EMTs had given her, Ray Durbin tapped on her window. She rolled the window down enough to talk to him.

"Can I talk to you, Ma'am?"

"What's it about, Ray? I'm completely exhausted and just about too tired to talk."

"It's about Dr. Hamrick and everything that's gone on here. I know some things."

"Get in," she said.

Chapter 16
Ray Durbin's Story

LEE DIDN'T KNOW Ray Durbin well but she knew who he was. She had seen him at public hearings speaking in opposition to the proposed landfill and in the audience at meetings of the county commission. He was the author of a long string of controversial letters to the county newspaper. His position on most matters seemed to be filtered through a weird brand of libertarianism influenced by a generous dose of paranoia.

He was in his early forties and looked fit. He was dressed in his trademark U.S. Army surplus camouflage fatigues and jungle boots. He got in the passenger side of Lee's Land Cruiser and closed the door. He sat for a moment without saying anything, adjusting his army camouflage cap on his head as if considering where to start.

"The FBI came to pay me a visit yesterday," he said. "They said they found my fingerprints at Hamrick's place. Which is not surprising, since I've been there many times. They wanted to know what I know about how and why Hamrick died. I didn't tell them a damn thing."

He turned and looked Lee in the eyes. "But I want to tell you some things."

His eyes bore an intensity that was uncomfortable for Lee. She wasn't sure she would trust anything he said. But she wanted to hear what he had to say.

"Would you mind if I ask Buddy Ruff to hear this with me?"

Durbin shook his head. "I ain't got anything against Buddy. He's a good man. But I won't talk in front of anybody but you."

"Why me?"

"I've got my reasons."

"Do you know something about Dr. Hamrick's death?"

"Oh, yeah. I know just about everything about it."

Lee could feel her ears burning. She hoped he did know something.

"Tell me what you know and how you know it."

As Durbin began to tell his story, Lee's eyes looked past him and she saw Buddy Ruff and Billy Longtree watching from a distance. She relaxed a little.

"Have you ever heard of the Sons of Freedom?" Durbin asked.

"No," Lee said.

"We're a private organization of patriots. We have a network all across the country. We believe in protecting freedom and the rights of the individual from encroachment by the government or big business or by any organized force."

"Are you militia?"

"Some of us are. Some are not. But that's not what's important here. What's important here is that the Sons of Freedom make it their business to keep track of certain types of government projects."

Lee didn't know what to say so she didn't say anything. She listened.

"Many of us have been in the military and worked in all kinds of military operations. When all this business here in Bartram County first started I knew almost nothing about the National Research Labs at Oak Ridge, had never heard of Desert Flats National Laboratories, and had no idea about biological warfare."

"Biological warfare?" Lee asked. She was doubting that this interview with Durbin was going anywhere but to *Believe It or Not.*

"Desert Flats National Laboratories was set up by the U.S. Government in 1962 as a secret installation to develop biological and chemical weapons."

"You're saying that's what Hamrick was working with?"

"Just a minute. Don't get ahead of me. I'll get to that. As I said, in the beginning I didn't know anything about Desert Flats. I first met Dr. Hamrick at a public hearing to stop the plans to develop that damned mega-landfill in Bartram County. Did you ever hear such a crazy-assed idea as that?"

"You were at the public hearing. You heard my opposition to the landfill development," Lee said.

"Yes, I did. The whole landfill thing is a scheme to relocate toxic waste out of the Oak Ridge national research reservation and dump it in poor little ignorant backwoods Bartram County. The company that's supposed to manage the landfill – the so-called Eco-Safety Waste Disposal Company – is just a cover. It's a New Jersey outfit owned by the mafia. The Sons of Freedom have got a file on them two miles long. Eco-Safety Waste Disposal operates cess pools masquerading as landfills all over the country–wherever they've been able to hoodwink the public and control the government. They almost had our county commission in their pocket, promising them millions in revenues, and under the table. But I'll tell you right now, they never would have opened their gates for business in Bartram County. The Sons of Freedom would have seen to that."

"What about Dr. Hamrick?" Lee tried to steer Durbin back on track.

"I heard Dr. Hamrick speak against the landfill. He seemed to have a lot of scientific knowledge and knew what he was talking about. I struck up a conversation with him afterwards and discovered him and me shared some of the same ideas. I was impressed with a lot of what he said. I would tell him my ideas and he would tell me the scientific facts. I could see right away he would be a good person to know. So I used to drop by and talk with him. He was an older man, you know, and I was able to help him out with things he couldn't do himself."

"What kind of things?"

"Oh, his car battery went dead one time and I took him into town to get a new one and put it in for him. And I crawled under his house and repaired a drain pipe for him. Things like that. He seemed to appreciate what I did for him and he started to trust me a little and to talk to me about himself. He told me about his career in agriculture in Tennessee, about the research laboratory he started at CMU and all the discoveries they made. He told me about being hired by the National Labs at Oak Ridge to do research for them. But he never would say exactly what that research was. He did say that most of it was top secret. I didn't know at the time whether he was telling the truth or not. I found out later, he was.

"One thing was clear from the time he started to tell me about NRL – he was truly pissed at them. He said NRL and CMU both took his projects away from him and cut him out of his share in patents after he had put years of work and millions of dollars into the research and after he had made the important discoveries. You might say he was obsessed over it. But he kept saying he was going to make it all up. Said he was developing new patents that would make him a multi-millionaire. He was convinced there were spies in key places trying to find out what he was doing and steal his ideas again. He said he was in a race with NRL to develop the patents, but he said he thought NRL didn't really know what they were doing. He said they stole his research and turned it over to a bunch of fools and incompetents. He said they're playing with dangerous materials they don't understand."

"What does all this have to do with his death?" Lee asked.

"It turns out he was right. You see, I told some other members of the Sons of Freedom on the Internet about Dr. Hamrick and the National Research Labs at Oak Ridge, and it was like sirens and whistles suddenly went off. They knew all about the secret biological and chemical weapons development at NRL. They had copies of dozens of articles and research reports written by Dr. Hamrick and his buddies."

"So, Hamrick was involved in weapons development?"

"No, Hamrick worked in a part of the Oak Ridge labs where they focused on developing commercial peacetime uses out of the national lab research. A spears-into-plowshares kind of deal. For years it was a nothing operation. But then came 1990 and the fall of the Evil Empire. No more superpower threat. Federal money for military weapons development started drying up. All the national labs – Oak Ridge, Los Alamos, Hanford, Desert Flats, Savannah River – all of them suddenly had to look for some new reason to exist.

"Hamrick's little nothing unit at NRL overnight became one of the bright hopes for corporate partners and new streams of revenues. The work Hamrick and his team at NRL did was suddenly a valuable commodity. Then Hamrick became a victim of downsizing. You know what downsizing is, don't you? It's when the more powerful squeeze out the less powerful, when the big asses take over operations they know nothing about and become dumb asses, when experts are replaced by incompetent buddies of the big shots."

"So, Hamrick was bumped out of his work with NRL. Is that when he moved to Los Verdes, New Mexico?"

"That's right. Some of his buddies was at Desert Flats. He moved out there so he could work with them after NRL cut him out of his projects here. It was kind of like corporate raiding. Desert Flats wanted to take some of the researchers from NRL for themselves."

"Why did Dr. Hamrick come back to Carters Mill?"

"It was about time for him to retire for real. So he was kind of winding down at Los Verdes. But about that time he learned over the grapevine that Desert Flats was teaming up with the Oak Ridge lab to move into field trials with some of the swords-to-plowshares stuff they had developed from his research."

"What, in particular, were they going to test?"

"He never would say. I know it had something to do with agriculture. Plants, animals, seeds – something about DNA and genetics. I don't understand any of that technical stuff and he wouldn't talk about it. His patents, you understand. But he showed me a bunch of stuff in his laboratory he said was so dangerous that a jigger full could wipe out the entire population of Bartram County. Scary stuff. He said Oak Ridge and Desert Flats have no idea how dangerous the stuff is they're dealing with, that they're about to unleash a catastrophe."

"Do you know Edward Wilkinson?"

"I met him a couple of times. He started out as one of Dr. Hamrick's students. Him and Dr. Hamrick worked on research projects together for years before Hamrick moved out to Desert Flats. Wilkinson still works there and was feeding information of some kind to Hamrick back here. That's how Hamrick kept up with what Desert Flats is doing."

"How does all this tie back to Dr. Hamrick's death?"

"They killed him."

"Who? Desert Flats?"

"Desert Flats or Oak Ridge or both. He knew what they're doing in Bartram County. And not just here but at a hundred research sites around the world. Hamrick threatened to blow the whistle on them to put a stop to their multimillion dollar projects. He told them he would expose them, and they killed him. Him and Luther and Luther's family and the Vining girl. They'll kill Wilkinson too. They'd kill me if they knew what I know."

"Why Luther? What does he have to do with any of it?"

"Luther knew something – something that I know too. I don't think Luther knew that he knew, but he saw some things and they had to get rid of him."

"But why Luther's family?"

"They probably used poison, something quick and untraceable. Luther's family just happened to get in the way. And they won't stop there. They'll kill everybody who knows anything. And they'll destroy all the evidence that would connect them. And when it's all over, they'll be rich, we'll be dead, and the world will go on. Unless we stop them. Just like we stopped the landfill. You can't ever let your guard down."

Ray Durbin sounded as if he was sinking deeper and deeper into a paranoia with heavy delusions of persecution. Lee didn't want to be on the wrong side of his paranoia, at least not until she got out of her truck.

"Do you have anything I can use as evidence? I can't do anything without some kind of proof."

That's when Durbin's face took on a very scary smile.

"That's why I'm telling you all this. I'm going to have proof positive. And I want you to be there. People will listen to you. I want you to see the proof for yourself and I want you to let the people around here know."

"What? When?"

"Soon, but not yet. I'll let you know where and when. If you're clever enough you may be able to figure out the *what* without me telling you. When the time comes, if you haven't figured it out, I'll send word. But don't call me. And I won't call you. Your phone has a tap on it."

"My phone is tapped?" Lee asked. She was incredulous.

"Your home phone, your office phone, your cell phone."

"Who has it tapped?"

"NSA, FBI, NRL, Desert Flats. Take your pick."

"How do you know?"

"I can't tell you that. But I know."

A chill passed over Lee as Ray Durbin opened the door and got out.

"You can do what you think is right with the information I gave you. I'm trusting you to," he said.

Durbin got into his military surplus Jeep and drove away. Buddy came over and climbed into Lee's passenger seat.

"What was that all about?" He asked.

"Either I just listened to the most unbelievable paranoid drivel, or we're all in really big trouble."

"You know, you can suffer brain damage just sitting next to Ray Durbin for too long. The guy should carry a warning label with him wherever he goes. At the risk of regretting the words I'm about to say, what did he tell you?"

Lee told Buddy the whole tale as best she could remember it.

"Holy shit, Lee. Do you believe any of it?"

"That's the thing about tales of paranoia and conspiracy, there's just enough truth in them to keep the lines blurred between reality and delusion. The trick is to be able to separate out the truth, if there is any, and discard the rest."

"Well, to be honest, some of the things he told you about Hamrick sound a lot like what Barb told me. Looks like the old guy definitely thought Oak Ridge labs and Desert Flats were up to no good."

They were interrupted by the bright lights of a small convoy of trucks and vans. It was the TBI crime scene unit accompanied by a mobile laboratory from the Communicable Disease Center of the Tennessee Department of Health, and two Knoxville TV news teams.

Lee briefed the TBI and CDC personnel on what she and Buddy had found at Luther's farmhouse and then turned the scene over to them. Though the news teams were persistent, Lee declined to give them an on-camera interview, but she did give them a brief summary of the situation. She motioned Buddy to her vehicle and they left the scene behind them as dark began to overtake them.

"I'm hungry enough to eat a mule," Buddy said.

"Wait just a little on that," Lee said. "I want you to go on an errand with me."

"Where to?"

"To Hamrick's."

"Hamrick's? Jesus, Lee. Can't it wait an hour? My stomach's eating its way through to my backbone."

"How about a Moon Pie? That will hold us for an hour."

"Man shall not live by Moon Pie alone."

"That's why there's RC Cola." Lee laughed.

"Sugar and caffeine. All you've had to eat today is milk and candy, Lee. You've got to stop and have some food. You told me to talk straight, and now you're not listening."

"One hour, Buddy, and I promise to sit down and eat a real meal."

"Yeah, if we don't have total nuclear annihilation or something between now and then. Then we'd have to face that on an empty stomach. I'll bet Ray Durbin has got some emergency rations at his place that he would share. Why are we going to Hamrick's?"

"Something Ray Durbin said."

"You're not believing any of that craziness, are you?"

"You know what they say about paranoia, don't you?"

"No, what?" Buddy said.

"If it's true, is it still paranoia?"

"Come on, Lee. You can't be taking Ray Durbin seriously. Why *are* we going to Hamrick's?"

"Durbin reminded me that I have half of a piece of a puzzle, and I want to get the other half."

"What's that?"

"I want the map off of Hamrick's wall."

Lee turned onto Gilmer Street in the middle of Carters Mill and drove the one block to Jack's apartment.

"This ain't the way to Hamrick's," Buddy said.

"I'll just be a second."

No lights were on. Jack still wasn't home. Lee took her briefcase and walked to Jack's front door. She retrieved the envelope with the FBI return address from her briefcase. On the front of the envelope she wrote "Special Agent Jack Sheridan," took the amethyst necklace from her pocket, dropped it into the envelope, sealed the envelope and slid it under the door.

She made a two minute stop at the Quick Stop for Moon Pies and drinks and headed toward Hamrick's. After five minutes Lee broke the silence.

"I can't get the images of the Morris place out of my mind."

"Me either," Buddy said.

Ten minutes later they arrived at the Hamrick house. As they stepped onto the front porch Lee experienced a flushed feeling and a ringing in her ears. She stopped and braced herself by holding onto one of the poles supporting the porch roof.

"What's the matter, Lee? You OK?"

"I don't know. I think so." Her head cleared a little. "Yes, I was just a little flushed for a second."

"I knew I shouldn't have let you come out here."

"Nonsense. I'll be fine."

Buddy opened the front door and turned on the lights. They walked across the entranceway to Hamrick's living room office. The map was gone from the wall.

"Well, hell," Buddy said. "This trip was for nothing."

He turned to look at Lee and his eyes widened.

Lee saw the look on his face and said, "What is it?"

But before the words were past her lips she was falling to the floor. She tried to talk again but her tongue wouldn't work right. She tried to reach toward Buddy but she couldn't make her arm lift. She was hot and flushed and nauseated.

Buddy was saying, "Don't pass out here, Lee. Try to make it back to the truck. I don't know if I can carry you."

But it was no use. Nothing would work right. Her heart was pounding and she felt very warm. Then she closed her eyes.

Chapter 17
The Mermaid Dream

LEE HAD A vague awareness of being handled, lifted, and moved. She could feel someone next to her. Then she was lying flat on her back and there was the sensation of flying. No, it was rolling, it was bumpy. Each time she tried to open her eyes she seemed to be in a different place. But always people's voices. Some of them familiar and some of them not. Reassuring voices telling her she was all right, everything will be all right now, you can go to sleep now, you are OK. She tried to awaken. She had a terrible throbbing pain in her head and unbearable nausea. Something bright in her eyes. Hands on her. A voice saying, "I'll take her. I'll take her." She was naked. Cold things and wet things touched her. She shivered. There was pain.

Now she was wrapped in warm blankets tucked under her arms, and voices were telling her she could sleep and rest now, everything is OK, she is safe. You can go to sleep now, you are OK. She felt someone's hand holding hers.

"Jack?"

A voice responded, "This is Helen. You sleep now."

It was quiet, a pillow, she was in bed. She tried to move her hand and found she had something dangling from it. She opened her eyes just long enough to see the plastic bag of clear liquid hanging next to her bed. And something else, she had an uncomfortable pressure in her groin, and something attached to her leg.

She saw Buddy looking at her and smiling. "Why are you smiling?" She tried to say. But the words were only in her mind. She tried to smile back at him, but her face would not smile. She slept an unconscious sleep. A nurse kept waking her saying, "Dr. Turner, I need to take your temperature now," and she felt the cold little thermometer under her tongue. She tried to cooperate by staying awake but couldn't. And she kept trying to ask what had happened, but couldn't.

There followed a confusing succession of dreams, of sounds and voices, of strange looking people looking at her. She heard a familiar voice saying, "Is she going to be all right?" Lee tried to wake up out of the crazy dreams but she was too sleepy. She tried to open her eyes whenever she heard voices but she couldn't concentrate. She realized after a while that she wasn't dreaming and she couldn't remember where she was.

The impression when she next opened her eyes was that she was underwater. Lights were on and she could see things moving but nothing was clear. She thought she was a mermaid in a tank of water and people were standing around the tank looking in at her, talking about her. She wondered how she could breathe. There was white all around her. Maybe she was an angel in heaven. She was sure she was floating. Then she closed her eyes again. It must be a dream.

There was a sound, a movement, and Lee heard a familiar voice. It was Peter Raymond. She opened her eyes. Peter was turning back a large piece of clear plastic from over her.

"No, she's not contagious," he was saying.

He was smiling at her.

"You gave us quite a scare, young lady."

Lee licked her dry lips.

"Don't try to talk. Your mouth is dry because of the sedative I gave you."

He was reading her chart.

"You've been in hypoglycemic shock bordering on coma. Scared the natives. They thought you were carrying the Black Death."

He put a gentle hand on her shoulder.

It was a struggle to keep her eyes open at first but she managed to squeak out a faint, "How long have I been asleep?"

"Not long enough," Dr. Raymond said. "You were exhausted and dehydrated. We're going to get some liquids and nourishment into you and then you're going to sleep some more."

Lee felt a panic that was uncontrollable. "I don't remember," she said.

"That's perfectly normal," Dr. Raymond said. "You suffered a collapse yesterday evening. Buddy brought you to us. The worst is over now. You rest."

Lee couldn't remember. It must have been a car accident. Yes, she remembered driving too fast. She remembered last night she was with Jack and they were at her house. No, that's not right. They were making love in front of a fireplace. Where was that? The answer just eluded her.

Dr. Raymond must have seen the confusion and fear in her eyes.

"It's the medication," he said. "And the trauma. Just try to relax. It will all come back to you in a little while. Everything is fine now. You're safe and in good hands. You will be your old self in no time."

Lee had the feeling of being a stranger to herself. Her mind wouldn't cooperate. She couldn't remember. She knew she trusted Peter Raymond. She knew he cared for her. He would tell her the truth. But somehow she was afraid to ask him. It would tell too much and make her seem too badly hurt. She had to remember. And she knew she had to get out of here.

Dr. Raymond looked into her eyes and nose and ears, and examined her face, and lifted her gown and explored her ribs with his fingers. He pressed on the right side of her abdomen and then the left side. He put his cold shiny stethoscope under her left breast and listened, and on her upper chest and listened, and on her back and listened, and had her breathe in and out, and listened, and thumped her with his finger tips on her back, and listened. He shined a light in her eyes. The light hurt. He said, "Follow this light with your eyes." Then he said, "Extend your arm outward and touch the tip of your nose with your finger."

Her arm was shaky as she lifted it, but she managed to touch her nose.

"Now the other arm." He said. And she did.

"How do you feel this morning?" He asked.

Lee answered through a dry mouth. "Not very well."

She tried to reach for the water pitcher and a glass on the table beside her bed. The nurse poured a glass of water and handed it to her. Lee tried to smile a thank you. The nurse had a worried look on her face. Lee sipped the cool water as the doctor talked.

"That's perfectly normal under the circumstances. Are you experiencing any dizziness, disorientation, or blurred vision?"

Lee had to make an effort to speak without mumbling. "Disoriented. I've got about the worst headache you can imagine . . . and just about everything else about me hurts."

"We took x-rays and an MRI of your head and torso. Everything looks normal. I want you to stay in bed the rest of the day. I'm going to leave the IV in, but I'll remove the catheter because I want you on your feet and going to the bathroom."

On my feet? Lee thought. I can't even see straight. I can't think. I can't remember anything. I can't get on my feet.

Lee made an effort to eat the lunch they brought her. She at least drank all the liquids. With some awkwardness, rolling the IV along with her, she did make her way to the bathroom and back to bed.

The nurse pushed a hypodermic needle into a connection on the IV and injected something into the stream of clear liquid making its way through the plastic tubing to the back of Lee's hand.

"That's a sedative. You'll go to sleep in just a minute," she said.

Suddenly the room was spinning and she was overcome by a pleasant feeling. She closed her eyes.

The rest of that day was made up of sleeping, eating, having her blood pressure, temperature and pulse checked and her blood sampled every hour. Peter Raymond came by after the evening meal.

"You've been pushing yourself too hard. Even Super Woman has to eat and get her rest. I'll let you out of here in the morning after we've gotten you re-hydrated and your blood sugar back in balance and stabilized."

Sometime late that evening she remembered what had happened the day before. She remembered about the phone call from Tom Davis and about Jack and the FBI, and about Luther Morris and his family. She was sorry she remembered. She cried herself to sleep.

Chapter 18
Home Work

AT NINE O'CLOCK in the morning Lee was sitting on the edge of her hospital bed dressed and waiting to be released. Peter Raymond came into her room and sat down opposite her.

"Feeling better?" He asked.

"Yes, I am."

"Did you know that you are hypoglycemic?"

"No. I had no idea."

"Have you noticed yourself having peaks and valleys of energy, frequent headaches, shaky hands, a feeling of dizziness, nausea, periods of ravenous appetite, stuttered speech perhaps?"

As Peter ticked off the list, Lee recognized the symptoms in herself. She nodded her head. "Yes, all of that."

He smiled and patted her on the hand.

"Might not ever have amounted to anything if you hadn't been under such stress lately. You'll have to watch your diet. From what Buddy told me, you consumed fewer than 1,000 calories the day you came in here. With all the things that happened, I estimate you expended perhaps five times that amount. It doesn't take a genius to subtract those numbers and see what the consequence will be."

He picked up a booklet and gave it to her.

"This is the diabetic diet. It's also good for your condition. I want you to follow it. You have nothing to worry about as long as you take care of yourself."

"Can I go back to work today?" Lee asked.

Peter's face turned into a frown. "Absolutely not. Stay out of the office. I want you to have at least two more days of complete rest and recuperation. Sleep, eat nourishing foods and drink lots of water. Stay away from caffeine and sugar. They are your enemy. Your body will regain its natural balance if you give it time and rest. I'll come by to see you tomorrow, and if you're not following my instructions, I'll spank you.

"In fact," he said, putting her hand to his lips, "I may come by and spank you anyway." He winked at her and helped her to her feet.

When Lee stood up she suddenly felt lightheaded. She wavered for a moment and Peter quickly put an arm gently around her to steady her. She held onto his hand as she leaned against him. At that moment, whether it was because of her weakened condition or the medication or something deeper, she realized what a good man Peter Raymond was and what a fool she had been.

"And you thought you could go in to work," he said, and smiled at her.

"Peter," she said, and hesitated. She wasn't sure what she wanted to say. She looked into his eyes and what she said was, "Thank you for being the one to take care of me."

An orderly came in at that moment with a wheelchair. Buddy was waiting to drive her home when they rolled her out to the sidewalk after her release. He was more quiet than usual.

"Thanks for the other night," she said when they were on the road home.

"Glad to," he said. And with devilment in his eye, "You, know, Lee, if I'm going to be lifting and carrying you around, you're going to have to lose a few pounds."

"Buddy Ruff, I am not fat."

"I never said fat. Did I?"

"You're going to have to take steroids and muscle up."

"What did the doctor say?"

"Too much candy and caffeine and not enough red meat."

"Uh huh. I'm not saying I told you so. Where am I taking you?"

"Home. Two days of R and R. No office work."

"You want to go by Helen's for a bite to eat and get your dog? Helen's niece has been taking care of her while you were in the hospital."

"I don't think I'm up to the lunch hour hustle and bustle just yet. I'll eat something at home where it's quiet. But I really would like to get Henrietta."

Henrietta. What was it about that little dog that filled Lee with such happiness? It made her smile.

Henrietta was as happy to see Lee as Lee was to have her back. As soon as she heard Lee's voice outside the front door of Helen's house she began barking and whining for Lee, ran straight to her as soon as the door was opened, her little stub of a tail wagging, jumped into Lee's arms, snuggled against Lee's chest and licked her under the chin.

"I think she's glad to see you," Buddy said. "Listen, I'm a little worried about you gettin' enough to eat. Why don't I call Helen and have her put some sandwiches in a takeout for you so you'll have something to eat at home?"

"OK," Lee said. "That sounds good."

Buddy called ahead and they drove by the diner. The parking lot was full. Buddy went in and came back shortly with a bag containing a box of food Helen had prepared for Lee.

"You were right," he said. "It's busy in there. Helen says this is only good stuff and you're to eat all of it."

Buddy was just turning onto Lee's street when they met deputy Billy Longtree in his patrol car heading in the direction they had just come. Buddy flagged him down. Billy pulled alongside them and rolled his window down.

"Hey, Buddy. What's up? Hey, Lee. You feeling better? Everybody's been asking about you."

"I'm much better, Billy. Got to stay home a couple of days. Doctor's orders. But I'm OK."

"I'm just taking her home," Buddy said. "Could you give me a ride? I've got to get some lunch and get back to the office."

"Sure," Billy said. "I was just on my way to Helen's to have lunch myself."

They all drove the few blocks to Lee's house. Buddy gave Lee the bag of food and the keys to her Land Cruiser. He smiled at her with a look of concern still showing on his face.

"You sure you're OK to be alone, Lee," he said.

"Yes, I feel fine. I'm going to take it easy."

"OK," Buddy said. "You call me if you need anything. Otherwise, I'll see you tomorrow."

"If you should see Jack," she said, "Please tell him I don't want to see him." Lee turned and walked to her door as Buddy rode off with Billy Longtree.

Lee had good intentions of following the doctor's orders. She selected an egg salad sandwich from the items Helen had prepared, poured herself a glass of milk and curled up on her sofa with Henrietta to rest and recuperate just as the doctor had ordered. The trouble was, her brain wouldn't relax. Her head was too full of unanswered questions. There was too much at stake to just withdraw and relax. OK, she would just be calm about it and go slowly, not get excited. She wouldn't leave the house. She would just think about what she knew and what she didn't know. She started making a list and during periods of alertness intermixed with drowsiness and a short nap, arrived at the following logic.

To begin with, she had six deaths. She didn't know the means of death for any of them. There were no toxicology results for any of the victims. There were no witnesses who could testify to any physical attack, any poisoning, or any other direct act that might have resulted in the death of any of the victims. There was no direct evidence of any disease or means of contamination or disease transmission.

If a toxic substance was involved, how could all of the victims have been exposed to it? All the victims had some relationship to Hamrick.

Judy Vining shared an office with him. They were members of the same profession and seemed to be working on similar types of research. None of Judy's fellow students had died. Did any of them have the same illness as Judy? Don't know.

Luther Morris did odd jobs for Hamrick at Hamrick's home. Luther sometimes supplied Hamrick with animal carcasses that Hamrick used in his research. But that's going the wrong way–if a contaminated animal was involved, Luther would have been exposed first and then Hamrick would have been exposed after Luther delivered the animal to him. But Hamrick died first.

Hamrick died, then Judy Vining died two weeks later.

Luther Morris and his family died after Judy Vining. No, wait. The Morris family was *found* dead after Judy Vining, but evidence indicates they actually died before Judy Vining.

And what about the baby? Why didn't baby Elizabeth Morris die along with the rest of her family? The very old and the very young are usually the most vulnerable. Grandma Morris died. Five year old Bonnie Morris died. Luther and his wife, both in the prime of life, died. But even after lying without food or water for days, baby Elizabeth didn't die.

Then there were the farm animals. What would kill the dog and the livestock? The water? Was the water poisoned or contaminated? That might explain the dog and the livestock. Maybe the baby was drinking bottled formula, or . . . or what? Lee made a note to check on the baby's diet and the water supply for the Morris farm.

Henrietta had lain quietly next to Lee on the sofa through Lee's twisting, squirming, writing and muttering to herself. Now she pushed her nose up under Lee's hand, asking for attention. Lee looked at her and smiled, rubbing Henrietta behind the ears. Then Lee made another note. Why did the Morris' dog die, but Henrietta didn't? Henrietta lived in the house with Hamrick, drank the same water and probably ate Hamrick's food scraps, yet she was unaffected.

"I'm glad you didn't die, sweetheart," Lee said to the little dog now lying on its back with its paws spread eagle, enjoying a tummy rub.

There was another connecting factor. Edward Wilkinson. Wilkinson was at Hamrick's when the body was discovered, but was he there previously, at a time when he could have been involved in the cause of death? Don't know. What was Wilkinson's real involvement with Hamrick? Don't know. What was the nature of the federal charges against Wilkinson? Don't know. How did Wilkinson's business card get on the Morris' refrigerator? Don't know.

What was the focus of the federal investigation of Hamrick? Don't know. What evidence and stolen property were the feds looking for at Hamrick's? Don't know. What was Hamrick working on in his backyard laboratory? Don't know.

What about Ray Durbin and his crazy story about Desert Flats National Laboratories and Oak Ridge Labs, secret research, conspiracies and mass murder? Don't know. Don't know. Don't know.

I don't know anything, Lee said to herself.

Lee's torturous contemplations were interrupted by the ringing of her phone. She reached for it and looked at the Caller ID. It was Jack Sheridan. She turned off the ringer on the phone and didn't answer it. She realized that her heart was pounding again.

I'm not going to get upset, she said to herself.

She went to the kitchen and made herself a cup of hot Sleepytime herbal tea and sat down at the kitchen table with her notepad.

OK, what do I have to work with and what do I need?

<u>Hamrick</u>
(   ) Forensics report — Waiting on TBI
(   ) Hamrick's research journal — Where is it? FBI?
(**X**) Hamrick's computer files – got it
(**X**) Research map — photos – got it

(*X*) Photos from crime scene – got it
(   ) Hamrick's research lab
  — What was he doing?
  — Finances – Bank accounts? Loans? Savings?
  — Animal carcasses ???
(   ) Desert Flats National Labs ??

Judy Vining
(   ) Autopsy & toxicology — Call Peter Raymond
(*X*) Research notes – got it
(*X*) Research map – got it
(*X*) Computer files – got it
(   ) Journal — Where is it? FBI?
(   ) Fellow students ill — Check with Terre Haute

Morris family
(   ) Autopsy & toxicology — Waiting for lab results
(   ) Forensics report — Waiting for TBI
(   ) Water ??
(   ) Health — Check for medical records
(   ) Contact with Hamrick ??

She had the map from Judy Vining's office wall, USB memory sticks she hoped contained Judy's research files, and a set of project folders she took from Judy's filing cabinet. She had pictures of the Hamrick crime scene but she couldn't find the USB memory stick Butch had prepared for her from Hamrick's computer backup tape. Had she left it at her office? She didn't remember having it there. But she couldn't remember much of anything that had happened the last few days.

She searched the pockets of the jacket she had been wearing. Not there either. She went outside to her Land Cruiser. As soon as she opened the glove compartment she remembered dropping the memory stick into it. She was relieved to find it but was shocked that she had not been able to remember. It was a sign to her of the toll the stress had taken on her.

OK, OK, I'll follow the doctor's orders. Give me a break.

She sat at the kitchen table and looked over the list and the items. Forensic and toxicology reports would be the best evidence. They might provide an answer to the most fundamental question of how they all died. She would at least know then if it was disease, a toxic substance, or something more sinister, like murder. Unfortunately, there might not have been enough of Hamrick left to perform a toxicological analysis. His final bath in the chemical vat would have obliterated traces of virtually all foreign substances.

She logged on to her office email from her home computer. No messages about post mortem or lab results. Nothing helpful in her email at all.

She couldn't call Peter Raymond for lab results on Judy Vining. He would become very cross if he knew she wasn't resting in la la land. There was no rushing the TBI or the state epidemiologist about the Morris investigation. She would just have to wait on the lab results and hope they showed something definitive.

Lee opened the file folders from Judy Vining's office. An examination of the reports and notes confirmed just what Judy had said. Her research appeared to be a straightforward ecological time lapse inventory of plants and animals in the area around Carters Mill. Three of her sample sites were in Bartram County – two on University farms and one on a private farming operation. The purpose of the study was to compare ecological profiles of the area now with a similar survey conducted ten years earlier by the CMU

Agri-Sciences Research Center.

The tables and graphs showing midpoint results of the study revealed just the type of shifts in the echo system that one might expect as a result of changes in agriculture, industry and the expanding human population in the area. Nothing really earth shaking or controversial. Just good solid environmental data.

She unfolded Judy's research map on the kitchen table. It was too big. She moved to the living room floor. What did she hope to find here? There were markings on the map–numbers and dates where each pin had been–just like Hamrick's map.

Hamrick's map. She didn't have it but she had the photos she and Buddy had taken of Hamrick's office. She looked in her file folders for the memory cards from her camera but they weren't there. She looked in the box of items from her office. Not there either. What could she have done with them? She would have to locate them later. But what did she have now? Anything? She had the memory stick containing the backup files from Hamrick's computer that Butch had prepared for her.

Lee plugged the USB memory stick into her computer. She sat at the keyboard unsure what to do. She could see directory names, dozens of directories, and directories inside directories on the memory stick. She looked for something that made sense. It appeared that the files Hamrick used were not readable by her programs.

Now what? She didn't know what kind of files were on the memory stick. Were they data files? Word processing? What could she use to read them? She picked up the phone and called Butch's computer shop.

"I'm out of my depth, Butch. I don't know what kind of

files I have here or what I need to read them. I don't know if they're compressed or encrypted or what. Could I ask for your help?"

"Always glad to help with an investigation, Lee. You want to bring them over?"

"The doctor has me homebound, Butch. I'm not to leave the house. I hate to ask you, but is there any way you could come over here?"

"Would this evening be OK? We've got some rush jobs here and I can't get away until 5:00."

"I'm sorry, Butch, I don't want to put you to all that trouble."

"Trouble? No trouble. If you'll supply the pizza and beer, I'll be happy to work 'till I drop. You know that. I'll do anything I can to help you out."

"You bring the beer and I'll pay for it," Lee said. "I can't get out to pick it up. We can have pizza delivered."

"You've got a deal."

Buddy called from the office in the late afternoon to see how Lee was feeling and if she needed anything.

"You want me to bring you some supper?" He said.

"Butch is coming over after work to take a look at my computer. We're having pizza and beer. You want to come by?" As soon as she said it, Lee regretted it. She didn't want any part of encouraging Buddy to drink alcohol, but she had said it without thinking.

"I might come by and have some pizza. But don't get your feelings hurt if I don't."

"Come by if you want to. I'll be here. Is there anything at the office I need to know about?"

"Oh, there's lot's of stuff came in, but just about all of it is junk. You got half a dozen offers for pre-approved credit cards with special introductory interest rates of 3.9% and credit limits up to $100,000."

"You can put those in the round file next to my desk."

"I wouldn't be too hasty about rejecting these offers, Lee. It appears to me that you got a total credit line here of about a half-million dollars. And that's just this week alone. We ought to be able to take a sum like that and invest it in some high growth mutual funds and make a lot more than 3.9% in return. I read that Apple stock is set to double in value. Maybe we ought to get in now. Buy low, sell high."

"What's this *we* business, white man?"

"I could be your financial counselor."

"Have you been going to an investment seminar, or watching those get rich quick infomercials on TV?"

Buddy chuckled. "Nah. I was listening to Hardy Cook and Lonnie and them talking over at the diner. They got an investment club going and they were talking about a mutual fund they've got money in that increased 31% in value last year and the year before that."

"Is that where you're putting your money?"

"I wish. My money is in a big glass jar at home. You might say I'm investing in coins. I've got a jar full of pocket change."

"Anything else in the mail?"

"You got an offer for some life insurance. No, wait, this is something called a viagra."

"Viagra is for you, Buddy. So you can be like the Ever Ready bunny."

"It's not a viagra. I must have had that on my mind. It's something called a viatical, 'to let you put your life insurance policy to work for you now, when you need the income.' How do they know all this stuff about you, Lee?"

"The trash can, Buddy. Any faxes or any lab reports?"

"Not a thing."

"Come on over this evening if you want to."

"Thanks, Lee."

It was almost 7:00 P.M. when Lee heard Butch drive up and the sound of cheerful voices. By that time she had already had a tuna sandwich, a glass of milk, an apple and a Pop Tart so that she wouldn't get too hungry. She opened the front door and there stood Butch with a silver keg on his shoulder. Next to him was a very interesting looking girl.

Chapter 19
Secret Revelations

"HEY, I DIDN'T want to run out," Butch said, motioning toward the keg of beer on his shoulder and laughing. "Have you met my friend Denise?"

It's hard to believe anyone could be as distinctive in appearance as Butch, but Denise did him one better. She had spiked black hair, black eye makeup, red lips, dangly silver earrings, a black leather vest opening to a black leather bra, black leather shorts over black mesh stockings, and high heel black leather boots. She had a tattoo in the design of a band of interwoven lightning bolts that circled her left biceps. Her fingers were lined with silver and turquoise rings and there was a silver thingy through her tongue that looked painful to Lee. She might well have been on the way to a celebration of some holiday falling between Halloween, New Year's in New Orleans, St. Patrick's Day in Savannah, and national Harley Davidson day. She was carrying a black leather case hung across her shoulder that Lee guessed to contain a laptop computer.

"Hi," she said, with bright eyes and a friendly smile that seemed remarkably innocent and unpretentious in comparison with her appearance.

"Come on in," Lee said.

Henrietta was unaffected by the appearance of either of them. In fact, she seemed particularly happy to have them as guests. She sprang into the air, hopped about, brought her ball to play with, and generally anticipated a good time.

"What a cute dog," Denise said, placing her fingers to her chest. She had no way of knowing the gesture was a signal to Henrietta who immediately dropped her ball and sprang up to Denise's arms. This was the critical moment of friendship or rejection. Denise caught Henrietta, laughed and snuggled her against her bosom.

"If Henrietta likes you, you must be OK," Lee said.

Butch set up the keg in the kitchen and brought three glasses of beer to the living room. They ordered two large loaded pizzas and settled into easy conversation, laughing and playing with the dog.

"I've been hearing about all the things going on," Butch said. "Kind of scary."

"Yeah." Denise's eyes got big. "That whole family dying is like the apocalypse or something. I've been thinking about stocking my cellar full of provisions for, you know, like the end of the world or something. Except for one thing." She laughed. "I don't have a cellar."

"Yeah, Lee," Butch asked, "What killed all those people? I've heard all kinds of things. I mean, what could kill a whole family like that?"

"We don't know yet. It could be something as simple as food poisoning."

"But what about the old guy and the student?" Denise said. "Did they eat at the same restaurant or something?"

"There are a thousand possibilities," Lee said. "We just have to wait for the laboratory results and hope they give us something to work from."

"What do *you* think, Lee?" Butch asked.

"That's why I'm looking through all these computer files and documents. I know that Dr. Hamrick and Judy Vining were working on similar research projects. I'm looking for anything in their work that might connect their two deaths. I know pretty well what Judy was doing, but I don't have much information on what Hamrick was doing. He was a scientist. He is supposed to have kept complete records. I'm hoping you can help me get into his computer files and I can find some answers."

"He didn't have any written records?" Butch asked.

"Those are all in the hands of federal investigators. And they aren't sharing."

"Well, *that* makes no sense," Denise said.

"No it doesn't. But most of the world makes little sense to me sometimes."

"You and me, too." Denise said. "If you'll get the memory stick for me, I'll get started on it." She took the laptop from its bag and opened it up on the coffee table in front of Lee's sofa.

Lee glanced at Butch with a question in her eyes.

"She's the brains of this operation," he said. "I do the grunt work. When it comes to the tricky stuff, Denise is a hottie. She carries her workshop around in that laptop. If she doesn't have the tool to do it, it probably can't be done."

"Quit. You're embarrassing me." Denise smiled and waved a hand at Butch.

Denise plugged the memory stick into a USB slot on the side of her laptop and Lee watched as Denise's fingers flew in a blur over the keyboard. She talked under her breath to herself and occasionally made a comment to Butch or asked him a question, all of which were mostly in a foreign language to Lee.

The pizza came and they all moved to the kitchen table.

"Butch, do you know Ray Durbin?" Lee asked.

"Crazy Ray? Yeah, I know him. Or I should say, I know *about* him. It's like a rattlesnake. You know enough about it to stay away from it. You don't get to know it personally. He and his buddies are bad news."

"His militia buddies?"

"You know about them?"

"He told me he belongs to a militia but I don't know any more than that."

"I don't know whether to call them militia, or survivalists, or what. Let's put it this way, if Denise wants to stock her cellar for the apocalypse, Ray and his buddies are the ones to see."

"Do you think he's dangerous?"

"I haven't seen it first hand but people tell me they've got a bunch of illegal military gear, including a machine gun or two and maybe a bazooka or a grenade launcher. The sounds that come from their firing range out the other side of K-25 are made by more than handguns and hunting rifles. Anyone with an attitude and that kind of hardware could be dangerous."

"The guy's weird," Denise said.

"Take some advice from me, Lee. Don't be talking to Crazy Ray. He's like a tar baby. He takes a liking to you, you can't get free of him."

There was a knock at the front door. Henrietta ran to the door and barked happily. Lee clapped her hands and Henrietta jumped into her arms. It was Buddy. He was with Barbara Hamrick.

"Hey, Buddy. Glad you decided to come by. Mrs. Hamrick."

"Hope we didn't come at a bad time, Lee."

"Of course not. Come on in."

Lee put Henrietta on the floor and Henrietta immediately ran sniffing around under the edge of the sofa and came running and dancing back, holding her ball in her mouth.

"Isn't that the little dog Alex...?" Mrs. Hamrick trailed off.

"Yes," Lee said, "That's Henrietta. Little ball of energy. I've fallen in love with her."

"I'm glad she's found a good home."

Lee took them back to the kitchen and introduced Barbara Hamrick to Butch and Denise. They already knew Buddy. Lee discretely put her finger to her lips to indicate to Butch and Denise to be quiet about Hamrick's computer files.

"You guys want some pizza?" Lee asked. "Get you a drink?"

"Just coffee," Barbara said, indicating a pot perking on the coffee maker. She looked at Buddy.

"Me too," he said. "Coffee would be great."

"Grab a seat," Lee said.

"Could we talk just a minute, Lee?" Buddy said. "Barb had some things come up that I don't have the answers to. I thought maybe you might be able to help."

"Sure, have a seat in the living room. I'll bring the coffee."

"Let me get my computer junk out of the way," Denise said. "I can work at the kitchen table. Closer to the pizza."

"Did we interrupt something?" Barbara asked.

"No, no," Lee said. "Butch and Denise are helping me with a computer software problem. I'm supplying the pizza and beer. They're supplying the brains."

The three of them–Lee, Buddy, and Barbara Hamrick–sat in the living room out of earshot of the kitchen.

"What can I help you with?" Lee asked.

"It's the problem I mentioned before," Barbara said. "The problem concerning Alex's death certificate and the insurance companies. I know you said laboratory results are not back, and I can appreciate the procedures you have to go through. I just would like to tell you my situation, just in case there is anything you can do now or later."

"I told Barb the case has been pretty much taken out of our control," Buddy said.

"I've tried to contact federal authorities." Barbara Hamrick sounded near the end of her ability to understand and bear the situation. "I'm just not getting any answers."

"What is it you think I may be able to do?" Lee asked.

"I have my son to care for," Barbara said. "I had a regular income from Alex's pension and his Social Security. Now that he is gone, that income will be cut by more than half. We had the insurance policies to protect us in case anything should happen to Alex while Doug was still a dependent. Alex's insurance was supposed to take care of Doug and me and Doug's education." Barbara stopped to gain her composure. Buddy took up the explanation.

"Barb went to Lonnie Chapman about the insurance and Lonnie tells her that just about all the insurance money is gone–borrowed against to finance Dr. Hamrick's research operation."

"How much was it?" Lee asked.

Barbara Hamrick took a folded envelope from her purse, opened it and handed several papers to Lee. The insurance policies were dated some twenty years prior and signed by Alexander Hamrick and Walter Chapman, Lonnie Chapman's father, for Chapman Insurance as the representative for American Prudential Life Insurance Company.

"The main policy was for one million dollars, according to Mr. Chapman," Barbara said. "It had a cash value of $200,000 but Alex somehow got $750,000 from it."

"What is the value of the insurance now?" Lee asked.

"It's more complicated than I can understand," Barbara said. "Mr. Chapman says it depends on the cause of death. If the death was natural, like from a heart attack, the policy is worth nothing."

"Your husband borrowed $750,000 from the policy and invested that much in his business?" Lee asked.

"That's what Mr. Chapman says, and he showed me the papers. I've never seen the money and I don't know what happened to it.

"So you're left with nothing?"

"There is a second insurance policy for $1,000,000 in the event of accidental death." Barbara indicated an old faded policy in front of Lee. "He also used a lot of other terms I don't understand, like *misadventure*."

"The whole thing," Buddy said, "seems to hinge on whether the death could be ruled accidental."

All this took Lee by surprise. She had to organize her thoughts. Accidental? It hadn't really seriously occurred to her that the cause could be accidental under the circumstances. But why not? Hamrick could have been accidentally killed by his own research or by an accident stemming from Judy Vining's research project.

The figure of $750,000 bothered her. She simply did not see $750,000 worth of anything at Hamrick's laboratory. Could he have an operation somewhere else? Had he paid for something that cost that much? Could the money still be in an account unspent or invested someplace?

"Everything may eventually come down to the toxicology and forensics analysis by the TBI," Lee said. "I have worked with Tom Davis at the TBI before, and he and I are on good terms. I'll also make a determined effort to get results from the federal investigation."

"That's something I'm thoroughly confused about," Barbara said. "What kind of investigation was Alex mixed up in? What do they suspect him of?"

"I don't have any reliable information about that, Mrs. Hamrick."

"They've come around asking all kinds of insulting questions. They've made us all feel terrible and given the impression that Alex was some kind of criminal."

"Do you know Edward Wilkinson, Mrs. Hamrick?"

"Ed? Dr. Ed Wilkinson? Yes. He and Alex worked together and have been . . . were friends for years. The FBI asked me questions about him too. Ed is a person of high personal standards. I can't believe he would be involved in the theft of anything. He's my son's godfather. Since Alex has been gone from home, Ed has been almost like a favorite uncle to my son."

Lee noticed Buddy flinch at Barbara's mention of her son.

"Do you have any idea what your husband and Wilkinson might have worked on at Desert Flats?"

"Oh, no. Almost everything there is secret, even things Alex said shouldn't be. It's all part of the military-industrial mind set, he said."

"Did either of them ever talk about anything that was going on at Desert Flats? Anything about changes in the organization, for example?"

"Well, in the period leading up to Alex's retirement and after, he complained a lot about management. He said everything was being run by corporate management types and there was a big generational shift with lots of young inexperienced MBAs coming in straight out of business schools. He was very bitter about the way he had been treated. But he never talked about his actual work. From the things he did say, I know management at Desert Flats regarded him has an old man who had outlived his usefulness. It was terrible for me to think about it."

"I can understand that it would be," Lee said.

"I was glad when he decided to retire. But after that, things between us just seemed to go downhill. He wanted to come back here and start over. But we had too many connections in Los Verdes for me to just pick up and leave. And our life there is so different. I could not imagine moving back here into that old house on a dirt road way out in the middle of nowhere. Anyway, that's more than you wanted to hear, I'm sorry."

"No, not at all. It's very helpful."

"I know most of what I have said is no concern of yours, but if there is anything you can do to help work all this out . . ."

"I'll do everything I can to see that the right determination is made," Lee said. "There are good, competent people working on the investigation here and at the state level."

"Buddy has every confidence in you, and that's good enough for me," Barbara said, smiling at Buddy.

"You guys sure you won't have some pizza? More coffee?" Lee asked.

Barbara got up from her seat and Buddy followed.

"Thank you, but I think I had better get back to my motel, if Buddy doesn't mind driving me."

Lee watched as Buddy and Barbara drove away. She was worried about Buddy, hoping he wasn't getting involved in an emotional entanglement that would leave him hurt.

Who am I to be worried about someone else's entanglements? She thought to herself. *I can't even tend to my own.*

There was something else she hadn't told Barbara Hamrick. Lee wasn't sure it would be possible to make a positive determination that the body was that of Alexander Hamrick. The acid vat may have destroyed all means of determination. She would have to talk with Tom Davis.

She heard Butch and Denise coming from the kitchen.

"That was truly weird," Denise said. "Secretly working on a dead man's computer files while his widow is sitting in the next room."

Lee smiled. "It was the kindest thing for her not to know."

"I know it was." Denise looked as if she had a bad taste in her mouth. "It's just that it felt kind of conspiratorial, like being unfaithful or something. Very weird."

"Mrs. Hamrick wouldn't disapprove of our efforts. I think she wants to get to the bottom of whatever is going on just as much as we do. Have you been able to make any headway with the files?"

Denise brightened. "I think so. The biggest problem with them is that Hamrick was using some old piece of crap software designed for the government lab where he used to work. Nobody in the real world uses it. Your software can't read his files."

"Can you convert the files or do you have something that will read them?"

"Yep, I think so. What I'm going to have to do is put the converted files on a new USB drive for you. It may take me a little while to do it."

The phone rang. The caller ID said it was Helen's Diner.

"Go ahead, please." Lee told Denise, as she picked up the phone. "Whatever it takes."

"Lee?" The voice on the phone was Jack Sheridan.

"What do you want?"

"I want to talk with you."

"I don't have anything to say to you right now."

"I'm coming over there."

"No. I don't want you to."

"Please, Lee. I have to talk to you."

"Do it on the phone."

"No, I can't do that. Please. Just to talk."

Lee was quiet for a moment. She was filled with anger that she wanted to spew out at him, but not in front of Butch and Denise.

"I'll be there in ten minutes. Please."

She hung up the phone. Her hand was shaking already. How was she going to handle this?

"You want us to get out of your way?" Butch asked.

"No, please, continue with what you're doing."

Lee went to the kitchen to look for something to help her calm down. Milk? She didn't want to be calm. She wanted to be violent, mean. She wanted to take control.

She didn't know how to be mean. But she could quit being scared. Her hands were still shaking. Blood sugar. She had to do something about her blood sugar. It must be sinking fast. She took a tall glass, filled it with beer from the keg and drank as much as she could without stopping. Half a glass. She drank the rest of it and filled a second glass. *Is this how alcoholism starts?* She wondered. *To hell with it. Worry about rehabilitation later.* Right now she needed all the fortitude she could gather.

She had finished two and a half glasses by the time she heard Jack pull into her drive. She walked to the front door, a little tipsy now, but she was definitely calmer and not as shaky.

Jack was getting out of his Jeep. She walked to the passenger side and got in. He got back in and closed the door. She couldn't look at him.

"OK," she said, "what is it?"

Jack reached out a hand to touch her shoulder. "Lee," he said.

"Don't touch me!" She snapped. "Just say whatever it is."

"I love you. I've been worried sick about you."

"No you don't. Don't say that to me. You've used me and lied to me."

"I never lied to you."

"Shit. You never told me the truth."

"Everything I told you was true. I just couldn't tell you everything."

"Couldn't? You couldn't tell me you work for the FBI?"

"No, I couldn't."

"Couldn't tell me you're working on the Hamrick case?"

"No."

"You told me you didn't know Hamrick. Wasn't that a lie?"

"I said I never met him. I didn't."

"Your fingerprints are all over his house."

"I was in his house. I didn't meet him. I never saw the man before he died."

"Did you see him after he died?"

"I never saw him alive or dead. Never talked with him."

"What about the nonsense about being a Carters Mill faculty member?"

"I am a temporary faculty member, just as I told you."

"Your whole life as I know it is a lie."

"No, it's not. There are just things I couldn't tell."

"I can't be trusted enough for you to tell me what's going on?"

"I trust you completely. I would tell you everything if I could."

She turned to him. "You tell me *something* or I'm getting out of the car," she said, and she waited, her hand on the door.

"Hamrick was involved in something illegal connected with his prior work at Oak Ridge and Desert Flats. He was involved with other people. Something valuable and dangerous was taken. We don't know for sure where it is, but we know some of the people involved. My job was to come here to identify all the people involved and recover the missing items."

"Why did you involve me?"

"Your job brought you into the picture when Hamrick died. Your investigation brought you closer to the heart of things. I didn't intend to involve you in any way. We tried to remove the investigation from your jurisdiction. When that failed I wanted to follow your investigation because you were uncovering things that might help the federal investigation. I was also concerned that your investigative activities might carry you into danger. I didn't intend to use you. I didn't intend to fall in love with you, but I did."

"And just when did you intend to let me in on the whole charade?"

"I will tell you everything as soon as the case is concluded and the danger has passed."

"You sound too much like Ray Durbin to suit me."

Jack didn't respond.

"Oh, shit," Lee said, "Crazy Ray Durbin *is* involved. I thought he was a lunatic."

"He is a lunatic, but he's also dangerous. You were right, he is paranoid."

"When did you hear me say he's paranoid?"

Jack hesitated. "His conversation with you at Luther Morris's was monitored."

"Monitored? You mean you had us bugged. That crazy Ray Durbin told me but I didn't believe him . . . Is my phone tapped?"

Jack hesitated again. "Yes."

Lee slammed the ball of her fist against the dashboard.

"Why? Why?" Lee shouted at him.

"Because of who may call you," Jack said. "You are not the subject of the investigation."

"All my calls are being listened to? Recorded?"

Jack did not respond.

"Our calls–yours and mine–have been recorded and listened to?"

He still did not respond.

"Do you know what an invasion that is, Jack? Do you know how that makes me feel?"

"Do you know how it makes me feel?" he asked.

"No. Why don't you tell me?"

"It makes me feel like a traitor to you. It makes me feel dirty. It makes me ashamed. But it had to be done. The stakes are very high."

"Is my house bugged?"

"No."

"Well, thank goodness. At least there is no recording of us screwing." She was furious. "Why are you telling me this now?"

"Because I could not let you put yourself in danger. Because I couldn't go on with the deception. Because I love you."

"I wanted that to be true, Jack. I've been ill over this. I've been hating you."

"I don't blame you. I want you to promise me something."

"Promise you? All I can promise you right now is that I may never speak to you again."

"I hope that when this business is finished we can put it

behind us and start again."

"I can never forget it."

"No one outside of you, the sheriff, and the TBI know who I am and why I'm here. It's important to my safety and to the safety of others that it remain secret."

"So you've come here out of a concern for yourself and your own investigation?"

"I came to tell you everything I can about the situation that exists here, and to ask you to keep what I've told you confidential so that this case can be concluded without harm coming to anyone. But most importantly, I came to confess to you and to ask you to please stay from harm's way."

"What do you want me to do?" Lee asked.

"I want you to stop digging into the Hamrick matter."

"What about Judy Vining and the Morris case?"

"I'll help you with those."

"How?"

"If we learn anything, I'll share it with you."

"Are their deaths connected to Hamrick's?"

"They must be. There's too much coincidence, but we don't yet know the connection."

"They all had contact with Hamrick."

"Don't pursue that, please," Jack said.

"What?"

"Anything involving Hamrick or Hamrick's work."

"Do you have Hamrick's research journal?"

"No. It's missing," Jack said, "But I'm asking you, please stay away from the Hamrick matter."

"All right, but under one condition."

"What condition?"

"That you share with me, as soon as you have it, any information relating directly to Hamrick's cause of death."

Jack started to protest but Lee interrupted.

"I don't want to know any germ warfare secrets. I need to determine if Hamrick's death was natural, accidental, or otherwise, and I need a positive identification of the body. There are innocent people involved whose future welfare depends on that determination."

"OK, I agree, but I can tell you that it is not about germ warfare."

"What is it about?"

"I can't tell you that now."

"So, what am I to do now?" Lee asked.

"Follow your doctor's orders. Stay home and rest."

"How do you know my doctor's orders?"

"I asked him about you."

"Where were you when I was in the hospital, Jack? I was scared. Why didn't you come to see about me or call?"

"I did call. I would have been there but I was on a plane to Los Verdes when you became ill, and I didn't know anything about it until I got back."

Jack reached into his glove compartment and retrieved a cell phone. He punched some numbers into the touch pad.

"I want to give you this. If you need to call me, call me on this phone. I've programed my cell phone number into the first button. It won't be monitored."

Lee took the phone and placed it in her pocket.

"When will all this be over?" She said.

"Two weeks or so, I hope."

"When it is all over, come to see me–without your badge."

"OK."

"I'm going to kick your ass."

Lee got out of the Jeep and went back inside her house.

"That didn't take too long," Denise said.

"What?" Lee asked, confused.

"Converting the files. It didn't take as long as I thought. I've copied the new files to this USB," she said, holding up a memory stick. Denise looked concerned. "I think you probably need some rest. Butch and I will get on out and leave you alone. Anything you need before we leave?"

Denise was right.

"Thanks to both of you," Lee said. "I do need rest. I'll take a look at the files tomorrow when I'm rested and my mind is clear." Though she didn't know now if she would ever look at the files. She had a lot to think about.

Chapter 20
Mr. Terry

LEE HAD GONE to bed worrying over the Hamrick case, Judy Vining, and the Morrises, and upset about Jack Sheridan. She was distraught at having let herself get into such a mess with him. Fortunately, medication prescribed for her by Peter Raymond resolved all that worry and anxiety into a night of uninterrupted sleep.

Sleep is a wonderful thing. Lee awakened refreshed and her head was clear. She had to admit, two days away from the office had been good for her. She looked in her refrigerator and her cupboard. Not much there that appealed to her. She dressed and drove to Helen's Diner for breakfast.

Business at Helen's looked pretty normal. There were greetings and how-are-you's from a number of people as she walked to a back table where she found Buddy already settled in. Helen gave her a hug and a kiss on the cheek.

"You look a lot better than the last time I saw you," she said. "It's good to see you looking so good."

"You ought to have some of these flapjacks of Helen's, Lee. Nothing better."

"No, she's not," Helen said. "You can't eat pancakes without syrup, and I'm not going to be the one to ruin her blood sugar this early in the morning. I'll bring her something good that she can eat."

As if Lee had no say-so about it, Helen went off to the kitchen without taking Lee's order.

"You back on the job this morning?" Buddy asked.

"The doctor says no. Is there anything going on?"

"Have you seen the paper?"

He handed Lee the morning edition of the *Bartram County Echo*. The headline read "Bartram Deaths Raise Panic." Lee read excerpts from the article.

"The rash of five unexplained deaths of Bartram County citizens and a Carters Mill University student has residents demanding an investigation by the Centers for Disease Control. Tennessee Bureau of Investigation crime labs and the state health department have yet to identify the cause of death in any of the cases. The atmosphere at recent meetings of county residents has risen to near panic levels, with citizens demanding action by county and state officials. The county commission has scheduled a special closed session with the mayors of Carters Mill and Oak Ridge and other officials to discuss the situation this afternoon at the Bartram County courthouse in Carters Mill at 2:00 p.m. Some citizens have expressed outrage that the special meeting will not be open to the public."

"I wouldn't be surprised if they mob the courthouse," Buddy said, "with that kind of publicity."

"Is it really this bad?" Lee asked.

"Pretty bad. It's good to have you back up and around. I don't think there's anyone but you could handle this situation."

"Then we may be in trouble," Lee said.

"You eat every bite of this and you'll be able to handle anything," Helen said, setting on the table a serving tray filled with omelet, bacon, grilled ham slices, sausage links, biscuits and gravy, grits with margarine, sliced tomato, fried apples, golden wedges of ripe cantaloupe, milk, orange juice, decaffeinated coffee, and a glass of iced water.

"Good God," Lee said. But by the time she finished her breakfast there was little left on the tray.

"Did you see this?" Buddy said, indicating another article on the front page of the paper. "UT-Battelle to Build Lab at Chernobyl," the headline read.

"Big change since the days of the Cold War," Buddy said. "It's hard to believe sometimes."

Lee read the article.

"How you reckon they're going to run that research project," Buddy said. "Volunteers? I'll bet their children will glow in the dark."

"I hope they know what they're doing," Lee said.

"Oak Ridge Labs is sure involved in some high-powered stuff. Is this the kind of thing Hamrick was doing? I mean, scary stuff like this?" Buddy asked.

"He worked for Oak Ridge Labs and Desert Flats, and I'm sure they have had many projects scarier than that."

Helen came to their table. She had a look of genuine shock on her face.

"You're not going to believe this," she said. "Mr. Terry just dropped dead of a heart attack."

Lee felt a sudden involuntary intake of breath.

"Mr. Terry? Where? When?"

"Just now, not thirty minutes ago. I just got a call from Margy. It happened at the courthouse."

Lee and Buddy drove straight to the courthouse. An EMT rescue unit and several sheriff's patrol cruisers were in the driveway. An ambulance was just pulling out into the street, accelerating at a normal speed. Its lights and siren were not on.

Lee parked and she and Buddy went in through the back door. There were a dozen or so people in the lobby and in the adjoining offices. Cybil, the county clerk, stepped out of the bathroom just as Lee past. Her eyes were red and she had a tissue to her nose.

"Oh, Lee," she said, "I guess you heard?"

"Yes. What happened?"

"He was standing in the lobby talking to some folks, getting ready for the meeting this afternoon, and he just dropped dead. One minute he was talking just like anyone else, and the next minute he was dead."

"I can't believe it," Lee said. "Did he seem ill?"

"Well, yes, to tell you the truth. You know how he gets all red faced? We used to say when he got mad it looked like his eyes would bulge out? Well, this morning his complexion was just the opposite. It was pale white. And he seemed a little short of breath–not enough to alarm anyone, but enough that some of us noticed later when we thought about it."

Lee thought with regret that the last encounters she had with Mr. Terry were not pleasant. She was sorry she had not been more generous and tolerant toward him. "It's so sad," she said.

"It is sad, and you know the saddest part?" Cybil said. "His little dog that he always carried with him died last night. I think that's what had him upset this morning. He was grieving over that little dog."

"It had to be a shock to all of you who witnessed it."

"I've never seen anyone die before. I hope I never do again." Cybil turned and went back into the bathroom.

Around the corner in the hallway the county commissioner was talking with a small group of people. He saw Lee approaching.

"Hello, Lee. A sad thing about Mr. Terry. He was as much a fixture around here as the courthouse itself. You know, he was seventy-eight years old. Too old to still be working, but he was one of those people that his work was all he had and he didn't want to stop."

"Maybe he died doing what he wanted to do," Lee said.

"I hate to talk business at a time like this Lee, but you know the situation we have coming up this afternoon. With Mr. Terry gone I'm going to ask you to serve as acting coroner. I want you to represent the coroner's office in all official matters."

"Yes, of course."

"We all recognize that you know more about what's going on with these deaths than anyone. I need you at the meeting this afternoon."

"Yes, I'll be there."

"Is there anything you can tell me now that might prepare me for the meeting?"

"I'm waiting on lab results from the TBI right now. I'll check with them before the meeting to see if they have anything."

"I hope they do. We certainly could use some answers. Come by my office a little before 2:00 if you can, please."

Mr. Terry's death knocked her off balance just when she thought she was about to get her thoughts and emotions back under control. She found Buddy and pulled him aside.

"I've got to make some preparations for the meeting this afternoon. I'm going by the office for a few minutes and then back home. That's where all my notes and records are. Stay where I can reach you if anything comes up, OK?"

"Call me if you need me."

It felt strange, almost like trespass to be in Mr. Terry's office going through the items on his desk. But it was necessary to sort through the recent mail and faxes to see if any information had come in regarding their pending cases. There was nothing from the TBI, the state toxicologist, or anything that seemed related to the ongoing investigations.

Lee checked her own in-box, her telephone voicemail, and her office e-mail. There were lots of voicemail messages for the time she had been out, but nothing that contributed to the investigation, except one item. Lee smiled at the rumbling bass voice.

"Dr. Turner, this is Frank Hayes at Rocky Mountain Bonding in Los Verdes, New Mexico. I called to let you know that your lead paid off. We found Mr. Wilkinson. If you will call me, I'll give you the details."

Lee wondered what Frank Hayes looked like. If he looked anything like his voice suggested, he must be a big man. She didn't want him looking for her, unless she wanted to be found. She didn't have time to call him back right now. It didn't seem to matter much anyway. The FBI surely had found Wilkinson also.

When she arrived back at home her mind was churning. There was a lot to think about. There were things she had to sort out and things she needed to know, both for the investigation and for her own peace of mind.

Judy Vining, for one thing. Lee needed the autopsy and forensic reports on Judy. Fortunately she was on good terms with Joe Gaines, the medical examiner who performed Judy's autopsy. That's also where Mr. Terry's body was taken.

She called Joe Gaines' office.

"Hey, Lee. Sorry to see Mr. Terry come in here."

"It was a shock to us here. Can you tell me anything about the body?"

"It looks like a straightforward heart attack profile. He was under a doctor's care, he had a history of heart disease, his arteries were blocked tighter than a tick, he had high blood pressure, and he died in the presence of witnesses who report that he was displaying classic symptoms of a heart attack. You want an autopsy? I'm not planning one unless I get a request."

"I don't have any grounds for one. My nerves are on edge because of the other things going on out here, but I don't see anything about this death that doesn't look like natural causes. It is strange about the dog, though."

"I heard about that. I've seen it before. Old people can become as attached to a pet as to a child. When the pet dies it can be a traumatic experience. They tell me the dog was almost twenty years old."

"The two of them were never apart."

"Kind of sad. I think the dog and Mr. Terry were in a contest to see who could grow the oldest. Mr. Terry was walking in the shadow of death for years. In our business we grow too suspicious sometimes. But I could autopsy the dog if you like." He laughed.

"You're sick, Joe."

Joe laughed again, then asked, "What's the latest on the Morris family?"

"Still waiting for toxicology from the TBI."

"Yeah, I was talking to Tom Davis this morning. He was asking what we found with the Vining girl."

"I think she's connected somehow with the Hamrick death. What did you find?"

"She died from ingestion of a neurotoxin called Diethyl nitrophenyl phosphorothioate, or DNPT for short. Ever heard of it?"

"No, what is it?"

"It's one of a family of very nasty chemical pesticides. Parathion is probably the most commonly known name for it. It's used on a variety of agricultural crops. But there are a bunch of other forms of it. Horrifying stuff in its pure form. Deadly even when diluted one part per million. It's almost certainly what killed her."

"No idea where it came from, I guess?" Lee asked.

"None. That will have to be up to somebody else to track down. I can tell you that it was eaten or drunk. It started in the digestive system, but by the time she died it was in every organ of the body."

"What are the symptoms?"

"Early on it can look like a case of the flu. Headaches, muscle aches, mucus discharge and the accompanying coughing and sneezing. It's a cholinesterase-inhibitor of the nervous system, so you get vision and balance problems, deterioration of the motor functions, spasms and convulsions. If you live long enough, you can develop nose bleeds, blood in the stool and urine, abdominal pain, diarrhea. You get inflammation and breakdown of major organ tissue. The brain becomes involved with inflammation and build-up of fluid. The victim lapses into unconsciousness followed by coma and death, usually from heart block, muscle paralysis and respiratory failure."

"What's the length of time from exposure until death?"

"Depends on the amount of exposure, of course, the age and condition of the victim. A single drop on the skin can kill a healthy man within fifteen minutes. Very small doses can take anywhere from twelve to thirty-six hours. With young children and the elderly it's faster."

"Nasty stuff."

"I read about a south Georgia farm hand two or three years ago. Dropped his wristwatch into a tank of liquid pesticide he was using to treat soy beans or something. He reached his bare arm into the tank to get his watch. The DNPT permeated his skin and killed him within thirty minutes."

"Can you estimate how long after exposure Judy Vining's death occurred?" Lee thought about the last time she saw Judy Vining, in Hamrick's office.

"From the limited amount of tissue degeneration, I'd say she died within thirty-six hours after ingestion. There was nothing in the digestive tract to indicate the source, but it had been pretty well cleaned out by vomiting and diarrhea. Plus, her condition may have been masked by a case of the flu."

"Do you have any information on the form in which DNPT might be found, other than pesticides?"

"It's used in some industrial processes, so it can be bought in pure form. It can occur as a liquid, solid or gas. It's honey colored in its pure liquid form. It takes such small amounts to be toxic that it can appear to be odorless and tasteless, but in doses large enough to detect with the bare senses it has the aroma of honeysuckle. If you get enough in your mouth to taste, you're dead anyway and the taste doesn't matter. If it's heated, mixed with water or steam, it forms a deadly poisonous gas. It can be easily processed into Sarin, the terrorist chemical of choice that you've heard so much about in Japan and elsewhere in recent years."

"Is there an antidote for it?"

"Yes, one. Abstinence. Just don't do it. If you catch it right away, a ten times maximum dose of atropine for forty-eight hours works sometimes, but the damage may be too great to heal."

"Did Tom indicate whether they found anything conclusive in the Morris case?"

"No, but he seemed very interested in DNPT as a possibility. He's probably running tests for it even as we speak."

"How did you come upon it?"

"Technology, my dear. We sent blood samples to the Poison Control Center and they had their technological wizardry sniff it out. They sent me a full profile on the compound. How do you think I know so much about it?"

"I thought you just had it all stored and indexed in that wonderful brain. Can you send me a copy?"

"Be happy to," Joe said. "You can also find it on the web at the PCC web site. Do you think DNPT is a possibility in your recent cases?"

"Hamrick is certainly a possibility."

"He was in agriculture, wasn't he? Keep me informed, will you?"

"Yes, I will. Joe, have the FBI or other federal investigators been in contact with you on this?"

"No."

"I need to ask you to do something for me."

"Sure. Shoot."

"Judy Vining's office on campus needs to be sealed until I can make arrangements to have it checked for poison residue. Maybe we can find some leads as to where the poison came from. You know the situation here. I won't be able to do a thing before tomorrow. I don't want that office disturbed or someone else moving into it."

"I'll send a request right now to University police. That should lock it up until you can get to it."

"Thanks, Joe. You're a prince among medical examiners."

Poison. Judy Vining died from an agricultural pesticide. Did it come from her research work? Her contact with Hamrick? Or some other source? None of Judy's colleagues showed signs of exposure, no other students in her department or her dorm.

She called Buddy on the cell phone Jack had given her.

"Buddy, it's Lee. I need you to do something for me. Where are you now?"

"I'm at the sheriff's department."

"OK. Go to my office and find that list of students who worked with Judy Vining and who were reported to be ill. Find out their current condition. If any of them are seriously ill, I want the details. Get that information to me before the 2:00 o'clock meeting this afternoon."

"I'll let you know as soon as I make the calls."

Another thought came into Lee's head, one that she didn't like. In Ray Durbin's paranoid scenario, poison was the method of assassination. The connection between DNPT and Sarin gas could certainly explain the level of concern being shown by the FBI. She wondered if Ray Durbin and the Sons of Freedom might really be involved in development of a Sarin chemical weapon. She called Tom Davis.

"Tom, it's Lee."

"Hey, Lee. I was just about to examine a body. I'd rather talk to you. What's happening?"

"Joe Gaines told me about the DNPT in Judy Vining. Have you found it in either the Morris case or the Hamrick case?"

"We lost the Hamrick body, what was left of it, to the feds. I was not able to have any analysis of the tissue and bone fragments before we had to turn it over to them."

"Damn."

"Yeah, I know. We put up a good fight. I sent a request for our labs to test for DNPT in the Morris remains. I also sent tissue and blood samples to the Poison Control Center and asked them to see what they can find. Their capability in that area is a lot fancier than ours. Haven't heard anything back. I only sent the request this morning after I talked with Joe."

"Did you hear about Mr. Terry?"

"No, what?"

"He dropped dead of an apparent heart attack this morning."

"Whew. You think there's a connection?"

"What? With the other deaths? As far as I know, he had no direct contact with any of the cases. Joe says it's classic heart attack profile."

"I guess an old man can't die around here anymore without me thinking it's something sinister. I need to do something inspirational and uplifting for a change. But right now I guess I'll just examine this headless body. It's beginning to smell. I'll put a rush on the toxicology and call you as soon as I get any results."

"Thanks, Tom, and think pleasant thoughts."

Buddy called while she was gathering her things, getting ready to go. None of the other students who worked with Judy Vining had become seriously ill. Even the student in Terre Haute had been diagnosed as anemic, had recovered and returned to campus. Judy Vining was the only student showing signs of poisoning. It had to be connected to Hamrick.

Chapter 21
Myra Johnson

OUTSIDE THE COURTHOUSE the parking places were all taken and vehicles were parked on sidewalks and lawns when Lee arrived. Three TV news vans with their satellite dishes were already set up, and another news crew was trying to find a place to park their van. The hallways inside were crowded with officials, business people, and ordinary citizens. Some gathered into clusters talking, others stood and waited expectantly. Many of the faces were familiar to Lee, and those looked to her. Some nodded, some spoke, all of them seemed to expect something from her. There were others whom she did not recognize and who did not look like local people. Their clothes had a slight unfamiliarity about them, and some of them had an expensive manicured look.

Inside the commissioner's office was standing room only. A third of the council members were already present, others came in behind Lee. Impatient and scared voices were raised almost as soon as she was inside.

"What's this about a contagious disease, Dr. Turner?"

Before Lee could attempt an answer, someone else was saying, "What has the sheriff got to say about all these deaths? Is it murder?"

The commissioner's voice, which everyone recognized and yielded to, penetrated through the confused voices with a tone of calm authority.

"Let's have some order, please. We're here to be briefed by Dr. Turner and others on what has happened. I'm sure she will address your concerns."

The door opened and more council members tried to

come in the already cramped office. The commissioner moved the expanding crowd to the council chambers. The door was closed behind them and everyone seated themselves, with the commissioner standing at the front.

"Perhaps all of you know by now," the commissioner began, "of the death this morning here at the courthouse of Mr. Oscar Terry, our county coroner. Mr. Terry died suddenly of an apparent heart attack. He had served as coroner of this county for 39 years. He was a friend of mine and of many of you. We will miss him.

"In view of the crisis situation we're in, I consider it no disrespect to Mr. Terry's memory for us to continue his work on this day. I have appointed Dr. Lee Turner to serve as acting coroner. Dr. Turner knows more perhaps about the current situation than anyone else. We also have members of the county and state health departments here as consultants. Dr. Turner, I'm going to turn this over to you and let you get right to the business at hand."

"I know that all of you," she began, "have read the newspaper stories about the unusual events that have occurred in and around Bartram County during the past two weeks. I am here to clarify for you, to the best of my knowledge, the chain of events that have occurred and to tell you the most recent information we have to date."

There was some minor squirming of people in their seats and a whisper or two.

"You all have heard of the discovery on September 15th of the body of a man at the home of Dr. Alexander Hamrick on Paradise Road. We believe the body to be that of Dr. Hamrick, a former Carters Mill University faculty member. Dr. Hamrick returned here in retirement from Los Verdes, New Mexico. A colleague of his in Los Verdes is being sought for questioning in Dr. Hamrick's death."

"Was it murder?" someone asked.

"We don't yet know the manner or the cause of death," Lee said. "Both our own TBI and the FBI are working on that right now. You may have read in the newspaper that Dr. Hamrick was involved in a federal investigation. That is correct. The FBI has informed us that Dr. Hamrick and the associate being sought for questioning were both objects of a federal investigation. The nature of that investigation has not been made known to us.

"On October 2nd a CMU student named Judy Vining was found unconscious in her dormitory room and taken to Carters Mill General Hospital where she subsequently died. Miss Vining was a student in Dr. Hamrick's department at CMU and shared an office with Dr. Hamrick on campus. Miss Vining died of exposure to a toxic substance called DNPT. DNPT is an agricultural pesticide. You may know it as Parathion. We don't yet know how she came in contact with it."

This last bit of information brought a round of questions even before Lee could continue. As the commissioner was trying to restore order, Lee's cell phone rang. She put her hand over her other ear so she could hear above the noise in the meeting chambers.

"Lee, it's Tom Davis."

"Couldn't have called at a better time, Tom. Hold on just one minute."

Lee asked the commissioner to have Sheriff Eberhard report on the deaths of the Morris family and the surrounding circumstances. She stepped out of the meeting chamber into a side alcove where it was quiet.

"Do you have anything?"

"I have a negative result," Tom said. "The Morris samples I sent to the Poison Control Center turned up negative for DNPT. Whatever it was that killed the Morris family was something else. Of course, it'll be another twenty-four hours, at least, before we have any results from the Communicable Disease Center."

"So, one possibility has been eliminated in the Morris deaths," Lee said.

"I wish I had something more helpful to tell you, but that's all we have at the moment."

"Thanks, Tom."

Different causes of death, Lee thought to herself. Are the Morris deaths connected with Judy Vining or coincidental? She walked back into the meeting chamber. The sheriff was being asked questions for which he had no answer. Everyone seemed to turn almost in unison to Lee.

"The Poison Control Center has eliminated DNPT — Parathion — as the cause of death for the Morris family. We're still waiting to hear results from the CDC on a battery of tests they're running. We can't expect to hear anything from them for at least another twenty-four hours."

"So it might be something contagious?" a frightened sounding council member asked.

"We don't have enough information to draw any conclusions at this time," Lee tried to explain.

"How many more do you want dead before you take action?"

The chamber erupted into a cacophony of loud voices. The commissioner was trying to gavel them to order, but general chaos had temporarily taken control of the meeting.

Then, just as suddenly, a hush fell over the chamber and

the chairman was left with his gavel hanging in mid-air. Lee turned around to look behind her in the direction to which all eyes were fixed.

In the open doorway to the council chamber stood a small woman of no more than thirty-five years of age. She was wearing a simple flowered cotton dress, her face was tear stained, her eyes were sunken and dark. The limp, prone body of a child hung from her arms. She searched the faces in the chamber until she saw Lee. She tried to talk but all that came out was, "My baby is dead."

It was obvious to Lee, even without examining the child that he was dead, but she rushed to the woman and checked the child's eyes and felt for a pulse to confirm it. There were blood stains in the corners of the child's mouth. As Lee bent over him she detected a pungent metallic odor about him.

The woman was in shock. Without revealing to her the obvious conclusion, Lee lifted the weight of the child gently from the woman's arms. When she first appeared in the doorway she had held tightly to the small body, but she released him into Lee's care. Lee handed the child over carefully to a deputy.

"Can you tell us what happen?" Lee asked, taking the woman gently by the arms, trying to focus her attention. "Can you tell us your name?"

"My name is Myra Johnson. My children are dead. Both my babies are dead."

"Where are you from, Myra?"

"We live on Buttermilk Road. Why are my children dead?"

"You need to go to the hospital, Myra," Lee said in a quiet and comforting voice. "This man will take you and your son there. Do you understand me?"

The woman looked at Lee and then looked around the room and said in an eerie pleading tone to the council members who were standing in silence, "My babies are dead. Can someone save my babies, please?"

The woman was shivering from shock. Billy Longtree came through the doorway carrying a blanket. Lee said to the woman, "Deputy Longtree will take you to the hospital. You will be safe with him."

Billy wrapped the blanket around the woman and gently picked her up in his arms and said, "You come with us, ma'am. We'll take care of you and your children."

When the woman and child had been taken out and the door was closed again, everyone was silent except for the quiet sobbing of some of the men. Lee had an overwhelming need to get out of the meeting. She had to talk to Joe Gaines and to Tom Davis. She had to get to Myra Johnson's home, to try and find out what had happened to the children. But she could see in the faces of the council members the beginnings of the same desperation they had all just seen in the face of Myra Johnson.

"I know all of you are just as shocked as I am by the tragedy we just witnessed," she said. "I know you want answers. As of this hour and this minute, we don't have those answers. The only way I can get to the bottom of this is to get out of here and do my job."

In the circular driveway outside the courthouse Myra Johnson's van sat, its doors open. EMT technicians had placed the body of the second child on a stretcher. Lee's examination of the boy revealed the same symptoms as the first child. She pronounced them both dead and signed the

EMT's response form as acting coroner.

Chapter 22
The Death of Innocence

"WE'RE ON A runaway train." Lee said to Buddy as they left the courthouse square and pulled into the street. "We've got to stop it."

"That's about as close to public panic as I've seen in this county. Is it disease, Lee? Some kind of plague?"

"I don't know what it is."

Lee called Joe Gaines, the Medical Examiner.

"I'm waiting for the arrival of the bodies now," Joe said. "The medical transport should be arriving here any minute."

"I only performed a brief examination of the bodies. I estimate time since death on both of them to be less than one hour. They both had blood on their lips and a pungent metallic smell about them."

"That's consistent with the Vining body. Is there a connection?"

"The mother is in shock and could not be questioned. I'm on my way to their home now. Give me a call as soon as you have any results, will you?"

"You know it."

Buddy had been listening to one side of Lee's conversation.

"What does the blood and the metallic odor mean?" He asked.

"They're symptoms consistent with death from toxicity."

"Toxicity? You mean poison?"

"Yes."

"So, it's something different from what killed the Morrises?" Buddy asked.

"It looks that way, from the lab results we have right now."

"Is it deliberate poisoning, like murder?" Buddy asked.

"I don't know if it's the result of the actions of an individual, or something in the environment, or something in the food or water."

"What connection do you think the Johnson children could have to a university student?"

"That's what you and I are going to devote ourselves to finding out," Lee said. "I want to get to Myra Johnson's home before anything is disturbed more than it may already have been. I want to find out if anyone else in the neighborhood has been ill. I want to look for a cause and a connection with any of the other deaths."

When they reached the Johnson house on Buttermilk Road near Woodlawn Church, cars were parked along the roadway out front. The house was a small white wood frame structure common in rural areas. There were construction materials and equipment in the yard and signs of renovation and addition being made to the house. A new well-made treehouse had recently been constructed in the fork of a large oak tree. Two shiny bicycles stood on the front porch. The house was very quiet. Lee knocked lightly on the front door. The door opened and a forty-something woman who showed a family resemblance to Myra looked out.

"I'm Dr. Turner from the coroner's office. This is my assistant, Buddy Ruff."

The woman opened the door and Lee walked in. At the sound of her entry the several mourners who were sitting and standing in the modest living room grew quiet. Not knowing who to address her questions to, Lee spoke to the woman who had answered the door.

"I'm terribly sorry to have come at a time like this, but it is very urgent that I talk with anyone who may live in the house with Myra and the children."

"I'm Myra's cousin Edith," the woman said. "I live next door. You want to talk with Myra's father, Mr. Duncan. He lives here with her and the kids. He's back in the den. I'll show you."

Lee placed a hand gently on Edith's arm.

"Could I speak with you in the kitchen first?"

Edith appeared a little shaken but led Lee and Buddy to the kitchen. Three other women were working in the kitchen preparing food. One was just taking an iron skillet of fresh baked cornbread from the oven.

"Edith, can you tell me when the children first became ill?"

"When Myra called me to tell me something was wrong, it was yesterday evening. Both the kids were feeling sick and Myra thought it was the flu. They both complained that their heads hurt, and Myra said they had a fever and wouldn't eat anything.

"She called the doctor and made an appointment for this afternoon. She let them sleep a little late this morning because they were going to the doctor later.

"About eleven-thirty this morning Jeff, the youngest one, wouldn't wake up. By the time she got him dressed and got David up and dressed, David started having convulsions. We tried to get her to call the ambulance but she wouldn't wait. She loaded both of them into the van, and her and my husband started off to the hospital emergency room with them. My husband called and told us they both died before they got fifteen minutes down the road. They pulled over to check them in Carters Mill, and when Myra saw them both dead, he said she just went into shock right there. She picked up Jeffrey, the smallest one, and carried him into the courthouse for help. But it was too late."

Edith recited her story as if she were reading it written into the back of her mind, seen through vacant eyes, tears streaming down both cheeks.

"It has to be a terrible thing for all of you," Lee said.

"What are all these deaths about?" Edith said. "Jeff was in Bonnie Morris' class at school. You think Jeff and David died of the same thing as Bonnie?"

"We just don't know yet."

"You don't think they all got sick from the food at school, do you? Are there any other children sick?"

"We don't know what caused the death of Myra's children. We haven't had time to get any lab results yet, and we haven't heard of any other children. But we have to take precautions to be safe. I need you to gather up all the ingredients used in the making of any food that was eaten yesterday or the day before. Give them all to Buddy and we'll have tests run on them to see if any of them contain the source of the children's illness."

"You mean you think the Morris family and Myra's children might have all got food poisoning or something from bad food?"

"Oh, goodness," one of the women exclaimed, "I just made this cornbread with Myra's milk and eggs. We might have all been poisoned."

"Please, I don't want you to jump to any conclusions. We just have to check everything they've been eating and hope we can either rule them out or find a connection with other deaths in the county."

"What should we do about our own food at home? Should we throw it out?"

"You really don't need to do anything unless something turns up in Myra's food."

Unfortunately, Lee's information frightened the mourners to the point that husbands and wives were immediately sent home to clean out pantries and refrigerators.

"Edith," Lee said, "are there any food leftovers or scraps from food the children may have eaten?"

"I can look in the refrigerator for leftovers, but I know that table scraps are fed out back to the kids' dog."

"Is the dog outside now?"

Edith went to the kitchen door and called the dog's name, and within a few seconds the little beagle was at the screen door wagging its tail.

"Seems all right," Edith said.

Lee left Buddy to oversee the collection of the food items and she went to the den to talk with the grandfather of the dead children. When she reached the door there was a minister kneeling, saying a prayer beside a man in his sixties leaning forward in his seat, his forehead resting in the palms of his open hands. She waited until the prayer was finished before entering the room.

Edith introduced Lee to Mr. Duncan and to the minister who made small talk for a few moments before leaving Lee and the grandfather alone.

"Mr. Duncan, I'm truly sorry for the loss of your grandsons."

"I won't live long enough to get over it," he said. "I'm dying of cancer, you know."

"No, I didn't. I'm sorry."

"My daughter and those boys are all I had to live for. I hoped to live long enough to see them become grown men, to take care of their mother after I'm gone. Then when I was diagnosed with cancer, I just hoped to see them one more year at a time. Now they're gone and I'm still here, dying, without them, and a burden on my daughter. That's not the way it was supposed to be. I just don't think I can face it. I don't think I can get through it."

"Mr. Duncan, there is nothing I can do to ease your pain, I know."

"You can find out what killed them."

"I promise you, I will do that."

"That could give me some peace, and their mother too."

"I'm working right now, looking for anything that might connect your grandsons' deaths with others in the county. Would you mind looking at a picture for me, to tell me if you know the person in the picture?"

Mr. Duncan nodded. Lee took a picture of Hamrick from her briefcase and showed it to him.

"That's the old man that died two or three weeks ago, isn't it? I saw his picture in the newspaper."

"Yes, it is. Do you know him or have you ever seen him?"

"No, I don't know him. Never heard of him or saw him except for the newspaper. How do you think he could be connected to my grandsons?"

"I'm just looking for any possible connection. My next

question may sound strange, but it could be important. Do you know if your grandsons ever collected animals for anyone? Dead animals or live animals?"

Mr. Duncan sat in silence for several moments and Lee was not sure if he was going to respond to the question.

"No, ma'am," he said. "Not that I ever knew about."

"Did you know any of the Morris family who died? Luther, his mother, his wife, or the little girl Bonnie?"

"I know who Luther was. I think just about everybody in the county who's lived here for any length of time has probably run across Luther Morris at one time or another. I didn't know Luther or his family personally. Never heard anybody say anything against him or his family. My grandsons and the Morris girl went to the same school, but I don't know that I ever saw her or heard her name spoke by my grandsons."

"Do you have a garden in the summer?"

"Yes, we always have a little vegetable garden. Myra's been the one to tend it the past couple of years. I've been pretty worthless for anything like that."

"Do you have any chemicals stored that might have been used in the garden? Pesticides or fertilizer?"

"There's a shed out back that might have some leftover from last summer. You're welcome to have a look. I don't think they would have got into that. Of course, you never can tell what kids will get into, especially boys."

"I'll have Edith show me. Have you or Myra used any rat poison or mouse poison recently, or any other type of poison?"

"Nothing that I know about, and I know Myra would

have told me."

"Are any other children or adults in the neighborhood sick, that you know about?"

"No one has mentioned any. I think somebody would have told us if anyone else was sick."

Lee gave Mr. Duncan one of her business cards. "If you think of anything that you think might be important, or if you need to call me for any reason, here are my numbers."

"God bless you, child. You let me know when you find out what killed them."

Lee walked into the Johnson's back yard and called Margy at the sheriff's office on her cell phone to get the number of the superintendent of schools for Bartram County. Superintendent Jim Williams picked up the phone.

"Jim, it's Lee Turner with the coroner's office. I guess you heard about the Johnson boys."

"Yes, everyone here is in shock. That's three of our children who have died within the month. Do you know yet if the deaths are connected?"

"We've got everyone from here to Atlanta working on it right now, Jim. I need to ask a favor of you."

"Whatever I can do, Lee."

"I need your office to compile a list of the names of every child absent from any of the county schools today, and I need someone to call and check on the health of those children."

"I'll get started on that right away. It may be tomorrow before I can get the complete list checked out."

"Thanks, Jim. Let me know immediately if you discover any serious illness. When you talk to the parents, ask if anyone else in the household is seriously ill." Lee gave him her cell phone number.

Lee searched through the Johnson garden shed. The arrangement of items in the shed and the amount of dust and spider webs seemed to indicate that nothing had been disturbed recently. The family beagle followed her every step. There seemed to be nothing whatsoever wrong with him. In fact, he formed a very amorous attachment to Lee's leg. At the moment she was trying to detach the dog, Buddy showed up, shaking his head and grinning.

"Don't just stand there, Buddy. Do something with this dog."

"Like what?"

"Put him on your leg."

Buddy picked up the dog.

"He don't want just any leg, Lee. I think it's yours in particular he likes."

"It's good to see him healthy."

They headed back along Buttermilk Road the way they had come. Buddy looked over at Lee and motioned toward her dashboard.

"I don't want to worry you, Lee, but you've got a red light blinking."

"Yes, I see it," she said. "I'm running low on gas."

At the next intersection Lee took a left and headed west toward a gas station and truck stop about a mile and a half down the road just the other side of I-40. She pulled into the service center and stopped next to one of the many sets of gas pumps.

"While I fill up my tank, Buddy, why don't you take this picture of Hamrick into the store. Find out if anyone in there has seen him around here."

"You think Hamrick has been way out here? You think the Johnson children's deaths are related to Hamrick in some way?"

"I don't know, Buddy. We just have to check everything out."

Buddy went inside and Lee called Jack. She told him about the Johnson boys. He had already gotten an alert about them. He told her the FBI lab report had just come back on Judy Vining and that it confirmed DNPT as the cause of her death. Buddy came back to the truck and opened the door.

"We got something on Hamrick. I think you better come inside."

Inside the store was a teenage boy, perhaps seventeen years old. He was dressed in camouflage hunting garb.

"You askin' about the man in the picture?" he said. "Yeah, I know him. I sold him some possums and rabbits and stuff. I ain't seen him in about a month though. Used to come to Buck's Bait Shop on Saturdays and pick 'em up."

"Where's the bait shop?" Lee asked.

"Back up the road toward the river," he said, pointing back in the direction they had come. "It'll be on your right."

"Thank you," Lee said.

"I think they got some collected down there now, waitin' on him to pick 'em up."

A shiver went through Lee as she closed the door of the Land Cruiser behind her.

They found Buck's Bait Shop where the young man said it would be.

"You're not here to buy bait, are you?" Buck said. "You don't look like fishermen."

Lee laid the picture of Alexander Hamrick on the counter.

"Roadkill Man," Buck said. "That's what the kids call him. That's what everybody calls him. You know him?"

Lee nodded her head. She showed Buck her coroner's badge.

"He buys dead animals. Pays good money. He claims to be some kind of scientist. Says he's studying parasites in their guts. That's what he says anyway. I don't know whether he is or he ain't. Drives an old yellow Buick. Keeps a big styrofoam box with dry ice in the trunk. He makes the boys bring their animals in a plastic bag and he puts a tag on it. He won't pay unless they can show him on a map right where they found the animal. They're not all roadkills, of course. Some of the fellows don't have nothin' much to do, so they been puttin' out traps to catch animals and bring 'em in to sell to him. He used to come about twice a month and pick them up. Saturday afternoon there might be half a dozen men and boys waitin' here to collect from him. He ain't been by here in maybe six weeks. I had a bunch of stuff saved for him that the boys brought in. I kept them in an old fish freezer out back. I thought he probably wasn't coming anymore, so I threw the lot of 'em in the river a week ago. Let the catfish eat 'em."

Lee thanked him and started for the front door. Buddy touched her on the arm and winked. He walked over to a counter filled with fishing lures and equipment.

"You got a Hula Popper?" Buddy asked.

"Why, sure," Buck said. "What color and what size do you want?"

"Gimme a green one," Buddy said, "One of them that

looks like a frog with a yellow skirt. The little size. That's it. How much is that?"

Lee grinned at the goings on and walked out to the Land Cruiser. Buddy came out in a minute carrying a paper bag with his Hula Popper, a new pocket knife, two colas and two Moon Pies inside.

"You got to buy something if you want their help next time you come by," he said.

"Then I guess you're planning on writing the Moon Pies off as business expense," Lee said.

"Can I do that?" he said. "Just kidding. How do you think Hamrick ties into these kids' deaths? Is it the dead animals?"

"I'll have health department investigators interview the Buttermilk Road households. They can find out how many people in this community have had contact with Hamrick, and they can verify if there is any further illness in the community. Maybe we can find a connection. Right now nothing makes a lot of sense."

"You're not eating your Moon Pie?" Buddy asked.

"Sugar is my enemy. I have to stay away from it. I think we better stop and have some dinner."

"Well, that's a switch. I'm usually the one who wants to stop, and you're the one who wants to keep going."

They had finished dinner at Helen's Diner and were sitting drinking coffee, going over the events of the day when Medical Examiner Joe Gaines called.

"Thought you would like to know right away, Lee. The Johnson children died from ingesting DNPT. It's very unusual for deaths from toxicity to occur so concurrently. I would say they were each exposed to a concentrated dose at the same time."

"I collected suspect food items from their home. I'll send them tonight so you'll have them first thing tomorrow."

Lee told Buddy the news. "I want you to take the food items to Joe Gaines' office tonight. He'll run the tests tomorrow."

Lee lay in bed that evening trying to make sense of the pattern of deaths and their causes. It didn't make any sense. In the morning she and Buddy would go back to the Morris farm.

Chapter 23
Looking for a Vector

"WHAT ARE WE looking for at the Morris place?" Buddy asked as he and Lee drove along the two-lane blacktop.

"We're looking for a vector."

"A what?"

"The thing that connects the Morris deaths with any of the others. Whatever killed them had to travel along a path through a series of points in order to finally end up at the Morrises. If we can discover anything that connects the Morrises with any of the other deaths, then we have at least two points along the vector's path. Then perhaps we can learn the how, the why, and the who that are responsible for their deaths."

"Are you thinking it might somehow be deliberate?"

"Not yet. It might not even be the same vector. It could turn out to be a coincidence that the Morris deaths occurred at about the same time as the others."

"Are we looking for something like contaminated food?"

"Might be. Might be from some other source. There are a lot of possibilities around a farm. We'll just have to look and hope we find some answers."

The Morris farm had been sealed as a crime scene, and Lee had expected to find it dark and deserted. It was dark, but it wasn't deserted. She stopped the Land Cruiser in the narrow road leading up to the barnyard.

"Holy shit," Buddy said. "The buzzards are back. What do you reckon?"

"There's something else dead."

"Lots of somethings, judging from the number of buzzards. I thought everything here that could die had already died."

Lee pulled slowly into the barnyard. Clusters of vultures rose to the air from points around the barnyard and extending into the adjoining field and woods.

Buddy and Lee sat on the rear bumper of the Land Cruiser putting on their rubber boots, their masks and gloves.

"I'm thinking seriously about a career change, Lee. The working conditions in this job have definitely deteriorated."

"Nonsense. What else could you do that would give you the enriching experiences you get from this job, not to mention the deep satisfaction derived from working with me?"

"Well, actually, you hit it right on the head. I was thinking I might just go up to Chicago with you. You're going to need somebody to look after you and give you a hand when you get into trouble."

"What do you mean by that?"

"I mean, you need a partner to look after you. You have a real knack for getting yourself into dangerous situations. It's not all your fault, of course."

"Thanks a lot."

"No, I mean, this has gotten to be a dangerous occupation lately. You know, I'll bet if we didn't have the county's group health insurance we couldn't find a company that would insure us. What do you call those tables where they figure your chances of dying?"

"Actuarial tables?"

"Yeah. You know, they got categories on those tables like low risk, medium risk, and high risk. You and me would be way out on one end of the table in the category called 'Do Not Insure Under Any Circumstances'. Most people's life expectancy is measured in years. Ours would be measured in months."

"One thing about it," Lee said. "Our life expectancy is a lot better than the people we investigate."

"You got a point there." Buddy looked up at the circling vultures overhead. "Unless they know something we don't."

"Let's find out what they've been eating."

On the ground in the barnyard where the vultures had been was the carcass of what appeared to be a medium sized dog.

"What is it?" Lee asked.

"A possum," Buddy said.

"What do possums eat?"

"Anything whatsoever. Vegetable or animal, raw or cooked."

"That doesn't narrow it down much."

Behind the house at the edge of the yard was an old wooden outbuilding, weathered and tumbledown. A small flock of the scavengers behind the structure flapped and rose suddenly just in front of them. Among the thick weeds and grasses around the building were dark clumps of rotting flesh and hair.

"Jesus. Is it squirrels?" Buddy asked.

"Rats."

"No, they're too big for rats."

"They're wharf rats," Lee said, "*Rattus norvegicus*. Look at the round hairless tails and feet. Squirrels have hair on theirs."

"Wharf rats?"

"They originally came in on ships from Europe and first showed up around docks in this country. That's where they got their common name. Now you can find them most any-where, often near some kind of water. These came up from the river and formed a colony under this old building. They've been feeding on some kind of grain here on the farm."

"How do you know that?"

"It's normal habit for these animals."

"I've never seen this many rats of any kind."

"Normally you don't see them except at night or if they're driven out of their nest. I've seen dozens of them in vacant lots and people's yards in the city after poison was put out for them."

"You think these were poisoned?"

"It's a good possibility. Let's take a look in the barn."

A large number of vultures were circling overhead. Several had returned to the compound and were sitting in groups in trees. For the most part they were motionless, but occasionally one or two would give a push, spread their wings and glide to the ground out of sight among the trees and brush. As Lee and Buddy walked toward the barn, the black sentinels in the trees abandoned their posts and rose to the air with a flapping of massive wings, preferring their solitude or the nearness of their kin to the company of humans.

The main corridor of the barn was dark and foreboding. Bits of hay hung suspended from the hay loft by dusty spider webs. The large outside wooden doors dragged on the bare ground as Buddy opened them to let the light in. The stench from inside was overwhelming. More rat carcasses lay on the floor.

Just inside the barn to one side, Lee opened a rough wooden door. Inside was a feed room. The floor of the small room was littered with kernels of corn. Fifty pound bags shredded from animal activity had corn spilling from them. Lee picked up the remnants of one of the bags and held it for Buddy to see. A label on the bag said Seed Corn, along with other identifying information. Clearly visible on one corner of the paper bag was a small skull and crossbones along with the words 'DANGER! Not for human or animal consumption'.

"I never heard of poison corn," Buddy said.

"If we're to believe the message on the bag, and if the animals ate this, it may be what killed them."

"Do you think Luther and his family might have eat it?" Buddy asked.

"Let's take a look in the kitchen."

They approached the house from the rear. An open porch with a tin roof ran along the back side of the kitchen. On the porch sat an old chest type freezer similar to but older than the one at Hamrick's lab. A padlock secured the lid of the freezer.

"Do you think you can get that lock open?" Lee asked.

Buddy bent over and inspected the old lock and turned it over in his hand. "I don't know. Maybe."

He put a hand on the side of the freezer and left it there for several seconds.

"I don't think it's running, Lee."

He opened the back door to the kitchen, reached in and flipped a light switch. "The electricity is turned off. Whatever is in that freezer, we probably don't want to know."

"Go ahead and open it."

"Jesus, Lee, there's no telling what's in there."

"Yes, I know. It could contain whatever killed the Morrises. We don't know when the electricity was turned off, but these things will stay cold for days. There's a good chance the contents are still frozen. Go ahead and open it."

"I thought it was the corn in the barn."

"It may have been the corn, and it may not. We need to know what's in this freezer."

Buddy tried various keys on his key ring, but nothing would work in the lock. "How bad do you want it open?" he asked. "I may have to break it."

"Go ahead."

Luther Morris' axe was standing in the corner of the porch opposite a stack of split firewood. Buddy pointed to the axe.

"Go ahead," Lee said, "Break it."

The first blow from the butt of the axe did more damage to the freezer than to the lock. The next couple of hits scarred and dented the lock. Buddy stopped and inspected the damage.

"Why would he padlock an old freezer like this?" He asked.

"Could be to keep the kids out. Could be it contains something valuable."

The sixth or seventh blow broke the lock open. Buddy pushed upward on the lid without success.

"It's stuck tight," he said.

"Pry it open with the axe blade."

Buddy stuck the sharp edge of the axe blade in the corner between the base and the lid of the chest. At first the rubber gasket did not want to release its hold, but the leverage of the axe succeeded in breaking the adhesive grip. They forced the lid up as smoothly as they could on the stiff hinges and looked inside.

"Jesus Christ, Lee, let's close this back up!"

Inside the chest, sealed plastic bags were blown up like balloons ready to burst. Inside some of the swollen clear plastic bags were amorphous masses of yellowish, mossy-looking matter. Others contained a dark, dangerous looking liquid excretion from the rotting flesh inside. Lee pulled down on the lid. It did not want to close. Buddy pulled down with both arms.

"Easy. We don't want to shake it or jolt it. Some of those bags look ready to burst," Lee said.

The persistent pulling down of Buddy's weight on the lid finally forced the cover back in place.

"This is bad business," Lee said.

"Bad business? This is worse than vulture vomit. What is that stuff?"

"It looked like animal carcasses. We better try and seal it back up."

"You can say the hell that again," Buddy said.

He pulled the damaged lock hasp closed and put the old lock back in place and tied the affair with a piece of wire. They sealed the edge of the lid with duct tape from a roll they found in Luther's tool shed and wrapped a piece of crime scene tape across the lid.

"I draw the line here, Lee. I am not going to touch whatever is in that freezer. If you want my advice, we'll just dig a big, deep hole, drag that freezer in and bury it. Let some archaeologist dig it up someday and wonder what in the hell they have found."

"Whatever it is, I pity any poor soul who may be called on to examine it."

"Well, just to let you know," Buddy said. "If the call comes to me, I'm not answering my phone."

"Let's check the kitchen."

Lee had already surmised a scenario before they entered the house, and her surmise was supported by what they found. On the floor next to the cupboard was a five gallon metal container. Lee removed the lid. Inside the container was corn.

"We'll have it tested to be certain, but it's better than an even bet that this is the same corn we just found in the barn."

They heard the sound of a vehicle approaching as they prepared to leave the house with a sample of the corn bagged and labeled. The vehicle was the truck of Itch Morris, Luther's brother.

"Somebody called me and told me they saw a truck come in here," Itch said. "I thought I better drive over here and see who it was."

"We're looking for anything that might help to explain how they died," Lee said. "There's a locked freezer on the back porch. Do you know what Luther kept in it?"

"Oh, yeah. I don't guess it hurts to tell now," Itch said, scraping the toe of his shoe on the ground. "Luther done a lot of hunting to help feed his family. He wasn't always careful about when he done it. Sometimes he kept game in there that he might have killed out of season. But it was food, you understand."

Lee showed Itch a sample bag of seed corn she had taken from the barn.

"Do you know how Luther might have come by this corn?" She asked. "We found about a dozen fifty-pound bags of it in the barn."

"Yes, I do know about it. Me and Luther do a little hauling work for the University farms, like I told you before. Well, last time we was over there, they was moving things all around, bringing things in and putting things out. There was a big pile of stuff they had piled outside, like to be throwed away. Luther saw them bags of corn mixed in with it and he asked what they was going to do with it. They told him they was going to bury it. Luther asked them what was wrong with it. Nothing was wrong with it they said. It was an experiment corn they had been testing, and they was through testing it. Experimentin' how? I asked them, and they said, trying to grow better corn.

"It's not the first time they've throwed away valuable stuff, you know. That's one of the reasons we like to haul over there. You never know what you might pick up for free."

"So, they gave it to Luther?"

Itch rubbed his short beard with his fingers as if he were considering how to answer that.

"Didn't give it, exactly. They said it was being throwed away. They said there was nothing wrong with it, they had just used all they needed and was throwing away the rest. Anything that is throwed away is free to whoever can use it. Me and Luther loaded it on his truck and brought it back here."

"Do you think there is any chance Luther was feeding this corn to his pigs and chickens, or that he might have been eating it himself?"

"I guess he might have. Why? You don't think the corn

killed them, do you?" Itch said, not believing that it could be true.

Lee showed him the skull and crossbones and the warning printed on the bag.

"It's seed corn," she said. "It's been specially treated with chemicals."

"Oh, Good Lord, no." The shock of the revelation showed in his face. "I never paid no attention to the warning on the bags. Everything's got warnings on it these days. Even toothpaste has got warnings on it. I didn't even read it."

"We don't know for sure what happened," Lee said. "The warning says the corn is not for human consumption and is not to be used as an animal feed."

"Oh, no, no," Itch said, shaking his head. "Poor Luther killed himself and his family. He never would have known, even if he looked at the bag. Luther couldn't read much of anything but his own name."

* * *

"Luther couldn't read. Killed by ignorance," Buddy said as they left the Morris farm. "Are you satisfied that's what happened?"

"It looks like what may have happened was, he brought the corn from University farms, and he took a tin of it to the kitchen where his wife cooked with it. It was used to make cornbread and hush puppies, and it killed all of them who ate it. Before they became ill, they fed table scraps to the family dog, and the dog was poisoned. Luther used the raw corn as feed for the livestock and chickens, and the livestock and chickens died. Laboratory comparison of the samples will tell."

"You know," Buddy said, "that's the thing about poison. You got to be real careful with it. You put it out for one thing, but you never know what else is liable to get into it. The University had to know better than to dump that poisoned corn out where something or somebody could get into it."

They were both quiet for several moments, trying to absorb the full implications of what they had just discovered. Lee called Joe Gaines' number.

"We'll know for sure by tomorrow, Lee, when we get the toxicology report back from the Center for Poison Control, but the Johnson children's symptoms are consistent with exposure to DNPT."

She told Joe about their discovery at the Morris farm.

"We have a few cases of that kind of thing happening across the country every year," he said. "Lot's of people just don't understand about treated seeds. It's a shock when it happens in your own back yard. If the Morrises did die from an isolated cause like that, at least you can separate them out from the others."

When they arrived back in Carters Mill, the clock on the courthouse tower said it was less than an hour until time for lunch. Lee was making an effort to keep her eating on a schedule. They beat the crowd to Helen's.

"There's one thing I don't understand," Buddy said.

"Only one?" Lee joked.

"I know that Luther's little girl went to the same school with the Johnson boys, but that's a mighty slim connection when you're talking about a means of death. I just don't understand how the death of Luther's family can be connected to any of the others if him and his family died from eating a batch of leftover poison corn from the University farm. How could anybody else outside of Luther's farm have got hold of it? And I don't see any connection whatsoever between the Morrises, the Johnson boys and the Vining girl."

"The only thing I can see that connects any of them is Hamrick and the University farm," Lee said.

"How's that?"

"We don't know what Hamrick died of, but we know that Judy Vining died from DNPT. Judy was his officemate. Judy's research involved the University farm. The map on Hamrick's wall showed that he was tracking Judy's work, and he was also doing something in the area of the University farm. We know that Luther Morris did some work for the University farm and had some contact with Hamrick. So, Hamrick was connected to Judy Vining, Hamrick was connected to the University farm, Judy was connected to the University farm, and Luther was connected to the University farm and to Hamrick."

"Wait a minute, Lee. You've got my head swimming. What is the bottom line?"

"The bottom line is that the key elements in this puzzle are Hamrick, DNPT, and the University farms."

"What about the Johnson children? How do they fit in?"

"I haven't found any connection for them, except possibly for the cause of death. If it turns out they did die from DNPT, that's the only connection we have found with the others. They are not connected to Hamrick, or to the University farms, or to Judy Vining."

"The Johnson boys do have one connection to Hamrick,"

Buddy said. "Hamrick had been coming to their neighborhood collecting roadkill."

"That's right. I need to know what Hamrick was doing. I still find it difficult to believe he sank $750,000 into that research operation since he came back to Bartram County. But if he did, I would sure like to know what he spent it on. I think I'll pay the bank and his insurance company a little visit this afternoon."

"You want me along?" Buddy asked.

"No, but I would like you to do something for me. Can you ask Barbara Hamrick to call Emmett at the bank and Lonnie Chapman and authorize me to look at Hamrick's bank accounts and insurance records?"

"Sure. I don't think that would be any problem."

"Do it right away if you will. I want to see them right after lunch."

Chapter 24
Venture Capital

LEE'S FIRST STOP was the Commercial Bank of Carters Mill. Barbara Hamrick had already talked with Emmett Caldwell the bank manager. Emmett showed Lee right into his office and had all of Dr. Hamrick's bank records brought in for her inspection.

"Didn't really know him that well," Emmett said. "He began doing business here at the bank about two years ago when he first moved back to the county from out west. He seemed a nice enough sort of fellow."

Hamrick's accounts showed an initial deposit of $10,000 in checking, and $75,000 in certificates of deposit. Gradually over the past year he had converted most of his CDs to cash to go into his checking account. The current balance for all his funds was just under $15,000. Copies of his checks showed no unusual expenditures, just household expenses and a number of payments to chemical and industrial suppliers.

"He had a mortgage on the house and property," Emmett said. "The old place was in pretty bad shape when he moved into it, and he had to make repairs to the house and the well. Luckily he had credit life that will pay the balance of that mortgage off for his widow. That is, if his death is confirmed. Right now everything is on hold because of lack of a death certificate bearing his name."

"Did Dr. Hamrick ever come to you for a business loan?"

"Why, yes, he did. He brought a proposal to us asking to borrow quite a large amount for an agricultural research business he was trying to start. But considering his age, the doubtful nature of the business he was proposing, and lack of collateral, the loan committee did not feel it would be a good risk for the bank."

"How much was he asking to borrow?"

"I have the loan application here somewhere." Emmet sorted through the file folder, retrieved a document and handed it to Lee. "Here it is. As you can see, Dr. Hamrick requested a business loan from us in the amount of $350,000."

"I understand he had a life insurance policy. Couldn't that have been used as collateral?"

"Yes, he did have quite a sizable life insurance policy with a cash value in the neighborhood of $200,000. But the committee did not feel it would be ethical for the bank to use the man's life insurance policy on a loan they thought was a bad risk. If he had equity in a piece of real estate, or another business to use as collateral, that would be one thing. But if his new business venture were to go bad, we would not want to be in the position of having to take the life insurance he had paid into all those years that was meant for his wife and child."

"What was the nature of the business he was proposing?" Lee asked.

"That was part of the problem. He was proposing a technical and esoteric kind of research operation that our loan committee members simply did not feel qualified to evaluate. He really needed to be talking to a venture capitalist in the scientific research area."

"Mrs. Hamrick is under the impression her husband was eventually successful in borrowing a large amount of money, but there is no indication in these records of any large sum ever being deposited to his bank accounts."

"That's true as far as it goes. But if he were successful in borrowing the money elsewhere, it might be managed through some other type of financial institution."

"Of course. Thanks for your help, Emmett."

"Always a pleasure, Lee."

Her second stop didn't go quite so easily. Lonnie Chapman was not in the office and his secretary didn't know anything about the arrangements. The secretary rang his cell phone and located him on the 14th green of the Anderson County golf course.

"Mr. Chapman says he can meet you here at the office this evening after dinner if that would be convenient for you, Dr. Turner."

Lee agreed to come back at 7:00 p.m. She left Chapman Insurance and drove to her office. She sifted once again through Mr. Terry's records to assure herself she had everything that had come into the office on the outstanding cases.

On her own desk she found the copy of the UNESCO report by D'Ambrosio, Hamrick and Wilkinson entitled *World Food Supply and the Promise of Science: Some Cautionary Notes*, that Madeleine Brown had gotten for her through the University library. She opened the report and began to read.

In the 225 page report she learned more than she had ever hoped to know about the scientific efforts directed at increasing and stabilizing the global food supply. The focus of this report was on the high tech methods of biotechnology applied to agriculture.

There was detailed discussion of genetically modified organisms, or GMOs as they are called. She read about crops genetically modified to have a resistance to herbicides and pesticides, about DNA promoters, gene silencing, toxin genes, ribosome inhibitor protein, recombinase enzymes, repressor protein coding sequence, the use of tetracycline to activate recombinase, the practice of inserting genetically altered material by use of viruses and bacteria, and the recent patent for a terminator technology that produces a plant that kills its own seeds to prevent replanting.

Most of the discussion she understood. Some of it was familiar to her and some of it was new. None of it was exactly pleasure reading. The authors concluded with a list of warnings in plain English.

- Biotech is being used to ignore underlying problems that confront humanity.

- The unpredictability of genetic engineering leads to food safety risks.

- Genetically altered food has many documented and unpredictable allergic, toxic and antibiotic resistance effects.

- The escape of herbicide resistant genes results in disruption of the ecosystem.

- Through mutation or accident, a microorganism can develop that would kill terrestrial plants and animals.

- Genetic engineering can damage beneficial insects and cause genetic pollution.

Their major suggestion was to concentrate on reducing the amount of loss to well-adapted successful crops already being grown. Specifically, they proposed that efforts be focused on methods of controlling the artificially large populations of pests that damage and destroy harvested crops and seeds in storage.

Their major caution was to go slow, grow genetically altered plants and animals long enough in the laboratory to know their manifestations at least ten generations down the road.

No wonder he was forced into retirement, Lee thought to herself, his arguments probably ran counter to the majority of projects and all the time tables at Oak Ridge and Desert Flats.

Seeds in storage, she thought. *The seed corn at Luther's farm.*

There was a welcome interruption to her reading by a call from superintendent of schools Jim Williams.

"We've talked with all the children who were absent yesterday or with their parents. Other than the usual kinds of things for this time of year, we didn't discover any unusual or severe illness. In fact, all the children absent yesterday, except for a handful, are back in school today."

"Did you ask about other family members being suddenly ill?"

"Yes, we did, and that didn't turn up anything suspicious. We've already followed up on all absent children today. Again, thank goodness, nothing to be alarmed about. We have a dozen or so cases of what appear to be hysterical illness. The children are frightened by the deaths of their three classmates. But that is understandable. We've spent the past couple of days trying to help everyone deal with it."

"Thank you, Jim. Please keep a close watch and alert me immediately if anything should show up that concerns you."

"Thank you, Lee. Perhaps this will all be over soon."

That was the first bit of good news in this whole catastrophe. No new cases among school children or their families in the county.

* * *

When she arrived at Chapman Insurance for her 7:00 P.M. meeting with Lonnie, Lee realized she had just broken her new rule. She had failed to stop for dinner. She could feel the effects of high adrenalin and low blood sugar. She would have to get something to eat soon.

Lonnie met her with his usual big smile and firm handshake. The outer office of Chapman Insurance was nice but no frills.

"Come on back to my office," he said. "It's more comfortable and I want to show you my trophies."

For a moment Lee had visions of deer heads and stuffed fish, but then she remembered golf. You couldn't think of Lonnie without thinking golf. Just to say *trophies* was an understatement. One entire wall of Lonnie's spacious office was a display case containing at least two hundred different golf trophies.

"You won all these?" Lee asked in amazement.

Lonnie laughed a little self-consciously, like a shy kid. "Yeah. I just like golf, so I play whenever I get the chance. I got pretty good at it. I won this one last month down in Florida." He indicated a two-foot high gold trophy containing a winner's cup and miniature gold clubs.

She was afraid for a minute he would tell her about every one of them, but he had too much of the salesman's judgement for that. He knew when to talk and when to listen and what to talk about.

"I guess you've been pretty busy with all that's been happening lately," he said, motioning for Lee to take a seat in a very inviting looking leather chair.

He sat down behind his desk and leaned back in his chair, his feet propped up. Lee couldn't help but admire his relaxed, healthy appearance, his golf course tan, his boyish smile and his sun bleached hair.

"Folks in the county are really upset by all the deaths. It's all people want to talk about. I'd like to help out if I can, whatever I can do."

"I need to discuss Hamrick's insurance with you."

Lonnie nodded. "Mrs. Hamrick called earlier and said you would be coming. I've pulled all my records on him. What would you like to know?"

"I saw the original policies on Hamrick that were written by your father."

"Yes, there were two. A whole-life policy with a payoff value of one million dollars, and an accidental death policy, also for one million dollars."

"Mrs. Hamrick said her husband borrowed heavily against his insurance to invest in his business. Can you tell me anything about that?"

"Technically, he sold his insurance policy to a company called Millennium Viatical."

That company name rang a bell somewhere in Lee's mind. Lonnie saw her expression.

"You've probably received a mailer from them. The whole region has been flooded lately with their brochures."

"No." Lee remembered. "I got a request from them to certify Dr. Hamrick's death. Their form is in my office now."

"You'll hear from then again soon, I'm sure. They have a big investment in Dr. Hamrick."

"Can you explain to me what their arrangement is and how it came about?" Lee asked.

"Dr. Hamrick came to me last spring looking for a way to borrow against his insurance policy in order to generate money for his startup business. He had a whole-life policy he took out about twenty years ago when he and Mrs. Hamrick first got married. It had about $200,000 in equity value."

"Mrs. Hamrick said he borrowed a much larger sum than that."

"Well, there's more to the story. Dr. Hamrick said he needed $350,000 for his business, but I told him the policy had a cash value of only $200,000. Of course that's a lot of money, but it wasn't as much as he wanted. He said he would take what he could get and find the rest somewhere else. He was entitled to borrow against the policy. It belonged to him. Emmett had already called me from the bank inquiring about the policy. He told me Hamrick had been to the bank asking for a loan, offering the policy as collateral. I knew Emmett had turned him down. I told Dr. Hamrick I thought he was making a big mistake, risking his family's security on a startup business venture."

"So you didn't lend him the money?"

"It wasn't up to me. As I said, he was entitled to the money. What I told him was I didn't feel right cashing in a policy of that size without consultation with his wife, because she was its legal beneficiary. I asked him if he would mind if I discussed the matter with Mrs. Hamrick."

"What did he say?"

"I can't repeat what he said, but let me characterize it by saying he flew into a rage and stormed out of here trailing a chain of threats and insults behind him that would embarrass a Hell's Angel. He had a right to get mad. As I said, it was his money. I just wanted him to think about it some more, and I did want to speak with Mrs. Hamrick about it. I had to make sure Dr. Hamrick was in full possession of his capacities and that he was converting the policy of his own free will. I had the legal and ethical obligation to do that."

"How did Millennium Viatical come into the picture?"

"It wasn't four weeks later that I received this copy of a contract from the Millennium Viatical Insurance Benefits Company."

Lonnie took a stapled packet of paper from a file folder and handed it to Lee.

"To cut through all the legal gobbledygook, Dr. Hamrick sold his whole-life policy to them, naming them as legal beneficiary, in return for the sum of $750,000."

"Jesus." Lee muttered.

"My thoughts exactly," Lonnie said.

"How does a viatical work? I mean, is it a legal business? How could they pay him $750,000 for a policy that had a cash value of $200,000?"

"Legal, perhaps," Lonnie said, "but not always ethical. A viatical company is betting on a short term investment. They look at a man like Hamrick and the odds of his death in the coming years. They look at the full payoff value of his policy and calculate the potential return on their investment, considering how long he's likely to live."

"Their investment being the amount they paid him for the policy?"

"That's right. The viatical business is kind of the reverse of the life insurance business. The life insurance business is based on the probability that the policyholder will live a long time and pay premiums over a period of many years. The life insurance company takes those premiums and invests the money so when the policyholder dies the total value of the policy is a lot more than what the policyholder paid in. If the policyholder should happen to die earlier than expected, then the life insurance company loses money, but that's a calculated risk they take."

"That's what the actuarial tables are used for, to calculate that risk," Lee said.

"That's right. The viatical company looks at the same actuarial tables I look at, but they look at them from the other end, you might say. The viatical company comes in when the policyholder is nearing the upper end of the actuarial table, when life expectancy is short. They pay what seems like a large amount of cash for the insurance policy. But they're betting the policyholder will die within a relatively short period, leaving the viatical company to collect the full payoff value of the policy from the life insurance company. The quicker the policyholder dies, the quicker the viatical company collects its profit on their loan."

"So, in Dr. Hamrick's case, Millennium Viatical is due to collect one million dollars from his life insurance policy after paying him $750,000 for it just six months ago?"

"That's correct. They stand to earn a return of $250,000 after just six months. That's a return of 33 1/3%."

"Mrs. Hamrick said Dr. Hamrick's policy would pay more if the death were accidental?"

"Yes, Dr. Hamrick's whole-life policy pays double for accidental death. If his death were to be ruled accidental, Millennium Viatical would collect $2,000,000."

"A two million dollar return on a $750,000 six-month investment?" Lee was not sure she understood correctly.

"Doesn't sound like it should be legal, does it? A payoff of $2,000,000 on the policy would give them a profit of $1,250,000. That's a return of, let me see," Lonnie punched some numbers into his desk calculator. "A return of 167% in six months. Beats just about any other investment you could name."

"Who is this Millennium Viatical?" Lee asked. "Are they a legitimate company?"

"They're kind of the pariahs of the insurance business. Really not insurance at all. They're headquartered in New Jersey or Delaware, or some place in the northeast. As far as being legal, as I said, it may be legal but it's not always ethical."

"Is there much of that kind of business going on?"

"There's getting to be more of it. They target older citizens and terminally ill patients who have any kind of life insurance policy, because they're the ones with short life expectancies. It's kind of heart breaking to think about."

"It makes me sick to think about," Lee said.

"You know, there's good and bad in every kind of business," Lonnie said. "In every part of life, as far as that goes."

Lonnie had a fishbowl filled with chocolate kisses on his desk, and as they talked he had eaten several. Lee's eyes fell almost involuntarily on the candies.

"Here," Lonnie said, picking up the fishbowl, "help yourself to as many of these as you want. I have them here for my visitors. People seem to like them."

"I love chocolate but I'm trying to stay away from sugar."

"What, with your figure? I believe you could eat this whole bowlful and wouldn't show any effects whatsoever. You're like me, you have one of those metabolisms that burns everything up."

"I'm hypoglycemic."

"Are you? So is my mother. You know, she has those

spells where her blood sugar drops way down and she gets the shakes."

"It happens to me, too," Lee said.

"Mother always keeps a little candy close by just for emergencies, so when that happens really bad, she can eat a piece or two to bring her blood sugar back up."

"It's a thought," Lee said. "But I'm going to have some supper as soon as I leave here. Thanks anyway."

"How is the Hamrick investigation going, if you don't mind me asking? And what about all these other deaths? Do you have a lead on what's going on?"

"We know the cause of some of the deaths. We haven't been able to pinpoint the source, but I think we will eventually be able to. Even in the Hamrick case I think I've figured out how to find the cause of his death."

"I hear his body was dissolved in a vat of acid or something?"

"That's been the problem with identification. We didn't have anything to identify. But it just occurred to me a little while ago that there is a way."

"Well, that will be good news for Millennium Viatical. I wish it were better for Mrs. Hamrick."

"I'm not giving up," Lee said. "I think there is a way to get to the bottom of everything that's going on. I'm also looking into what happened to the money Millennium Viatical paid to Dr. Hamrick for his insurance policy."

"I certainly wish you every good luck," Lonnie said. "If there is anything else I can do, my door is always open to you."

"Where would the money from Millennium Viatical have

been deposited? Dr. Hamrick's bank account at the Commercial Bank has never reflected the influx of that kind of money."

"It could have been put on deposit anywhere, a check might have been drafted directly to him, or a line of credit might have been set up through Millennium Viatical."

"I suppose I can get that information from Millennium Viatical." Lee got up to leave.

"Here, let me give you something," Lonnie said, opening the door to a mahogany cabinet behind his desk. He took from the shelf a prettily decorated box of candy. "I always keep some of these for my mother," he said, and handed it to her.

"Why, thank you, Lonnie."

"Keep these close by and if you get caught out somewhere and have a low blood sugar attack, eat a couple of them and I guarantee you'll feel better. But don't go giving those away. I paid a king's ransom for them. If you want to give some away, take some of these in the fishbowl, they're cheap."

Lee laughed. "Thanks, Lonnie."

"Anytime."

Lee had waited almost too late to eat. She was definitely developing the shakes. She was tempted to eat the whole box of chocolates but she managed to resist long enough to get to Helen's. Baby steps, she said to herself, baby steps.

Chapter 25
Eddie's Story

As SOON THE next morning as Lee thought Tom Davis would be in, she put in a call to the TBI office.

"Tom, whose fingerprints did you find on the keyboard in Hamrick's house?"

"Hamrick's," Tom said.

"Would you say from the fingerprint evidence that Hamrick was the last person to use the computer before we arrived?"

"I can say almost certainly that he was the only person to use the computer for quite some time. There were no other prints on the keyboard, and only his prints were on the backup tapes."

"Did you find blood on or around the chair where we found the body?"

"There were tiny aspirated droplets on the chair, on the computer desk, and on the keyboard."

"How about the rug around the chair?" Lee asked.

"Blood, tissue, and other body fluids from the decaying body."

"Is there enough for a DNA match?"

"If you have something to match it against, I can get a DNA profile."

"I need a profile on the samples from the chair, the keyboard, the desk, and the rug," Lee said. "We want to be sure we're dealing with only one individual. Were there clothes in the dirty clothes hamper?"

"Yes, there were," Tom said. "Where are we headed?"

"I'm going to identify the body and the cause of death. Were the trash cans checked?"

"Has a chicken got feathers?" Tom asked.

"No, what I meant to ask was, did you find any blood residue in the trash cans, such as on tissue?"

"Only kidding. I know what you mean. Yes, we did find blood residue on tissues in the trash cans in the living room, the bathroom and the bedroom."

"OK, I'll need a DNA profile from those blood samples also."

"How many times do you need to identify this fellow?"

Lee laughed. "I need to verify that there was no one else in the house whose body could have been in that chair."

"This whole thing could be settled if the feds can get a DNA profile on the remains we took from the vat."

"True, but I'm also going for cause of death. By the time the body was removed from the vat, the cause of death may have been obliterated."

"I see what you mean. So you will also want the blood and fluid stains tested for DNPT, won't you?"

"You guessed it."

"You know, if this works, Lee, I'll nominate you for the Sherlock Holmes award for impossible to solve body identification puzzles."

"Was there a hair brush and toothbrush in Hamrick's bathroom?"

"Yep."

"Did you take them as evidence?"

"Nope, they're probably still in the house if the feds didn't take them."

"I'll get back out there and check. If Hamrick died from DNPT, his blood residue containing DNPT might very well be on his toothbrush."

"You want me to send someone out, Lee? Now that I see the direction you're going, there are a number of possibilities we could check."

"OK, Tom, that would probably be best. Your guys will do a lot better job than I can in collecting the evidence."

"I'll send someone out this morning. We have some crackerjack technicians who would just love this assignment. I would sure like to beat the feds to the identification."

Lee's next call was to Barbara Hamrick's hotel to arrange for Mrs. Hamrick to meet her. After she hung up, Lee turned on her computer, inserted the Hamrick memory stick, called up her word processor and asked it to search the files for DNPT. The little hour glass turned over and over so long Lee thought her computer must have crashed. Then suddenly the screen cleared and a list of files scrolled down and off the screen. If the number of hits she scored had been fireworks, it would have been the Fourth of July. No doubt about it, Hamrick was working in some capacity with DNPT, or reading and writing a hell of a lot about it.

For the next half hour Lee read and cross referenced computer files, trying to understand the technical language and processes Hamrick described. The detail and completeness of his records showed he was a meticulous scientist and researcher. But his subject matter was highly specialized. It would take a microbiologist or perhaps a team of microbiologists to decipher exactly what he was doing in his research lab.

The best she could tell, DNPT was one of many compounds he was working with. In a document titled *Strategies for Limiting Post-Harvest Storage Loss in Food Grains* she found a discussion that was almost understandable. It was about methods for controlling the damage to food grains in storage caused by agricultural pests such as mice and beetles. One whole section of the article dealt with the use of pesticides. Among the active ingredients discussed was DNPT.

What Lee needed most was a non-technical, plain English discussion of Hamrick's research processes. What she needed to do was talk with someone who knew and understood what Hamrick was doing. She needed to talk to Dr. Edward Wilkinson. That cemented in her mind what she must do. She put on traveling clothes, packed an overnight bag, and drove to her office.

She got there before time for her meeting with Barbara Hamrick. She took the opportunity to call Cybil at the courthouse to ask her to make a reservation on the next available flight from Knoxville to Los Verdes, New Mexico.

It was only a few minutes until Barbara Hamrick arrived accompanied by Buddy. Lee invited Mrs. Hamrick into the office and turned to Buddy.

"Buddy, I hate to ask this, but I have not had time for breakfast. Could I ask you to run over to Helen's and get me a sausage and biscuit?"

"Sure, Lee, glad to."

"Take my Land Cruiser, and bring me some orange juice and coffee too, please. Bring Mrs. Hamrick whatever she would like and get yourself something."

When Buddy left, Lee told Barbara Hamrick, "I didn't want Buddy here when I ask you some things, Mrs. Hamrick."

"I think you know me more than well enough to call me Barbara. I would feel more comfortable."

"Of course. Barbara, I think I have devised a way to make a positive identification of Dr. Hamrick's remains. But it depends on my ability to locate some of his DNA to compare with what we found at the scene of death."

"You're asking if I know where any of Alex's DNA might be found? Like what?"

"Some people have units of their own blood kept in a blood bank for use in transfusions, for example."

Barbara Hamrick's face blushed.

"There is one thing. Alex was advancing in years, you know. We didn't know if we would ever want to have another child, and if . . . well, if Alex would be capable. So, several years ago, it must be ten years or more, we had some of Alex's sperm frozen."

"Would you give me permission to take a sample of that sperm for DNA comparison with the blood samples we collected following his death?"

"I guess that would give positive identification, wouldn't it?"

"Yes, it would. If the samples match I'll be able to put his name on the certificate of death."

Barbara had begun to cry.

"I know it's difficult, Barbara. I'll try to make the whole process as quick and painless as I can."

"No, it's not that," she said. "I was just thinking, those sperm are the only thing left of him still alive. And I had forgotten about them."

"They may be our only hope of preventing even more loss to you and your son. Can you give me the name and address of the medical facility where the sperm are stored?"

"I don't know the exact street address. It's in Los Verdes."

Lee handed her a notepad. Barbara wrote the name of the clinic on the pad. Lee sat down at her computer and typed out a brief permission for her to retrieve a sample of Hamrick's sperm, printed out the note on office letterhead, and had Barbara sign it.

"Do you have a picture of Dr. Hamrick I could borrow?" Lee asked.

"Certainly." Barbara Hamrick took a small photo album from her purse and unsnapped its latch. Inside were more than a dozen pictures of the late Dr. Hamrick and her. But mostly there were pictures of her son, from infancy to high school graduation. "Would you like to see a picture of my son Douglas?" she said, taking several of the photos from her purse.

"He's a very handsome and happy looking boy," Lee said.

"He was always a happy child," Barbara said, "until about the time the trouble started for Alex at the laboratories. That worried Douglas. He's had a difficult time with our separation, and now with Alex's death. He's a sophomore at the university now."

Cybil called with news on the airline reservation just as Buddy arrived back with the breakfast takeout.

"Can you be at the Knoxville airport Delta terminal by 1:20?" Cybil said.

"I'll try my best."

"If not, the next available is 4:12. I had to tell them it was urgent police business in order to get you a seat. It'll have to be first class."

"I'll cry a tear," Lee said.

"I thought you would like that. They may even give you something to eat."

"Thanks, Cybil."

Lee hung up the receiver and looked at her watch.

"They're two hours behind us in New Mexico. I can be in Los Verdes in time for an interview with Wilkinson tonight or first thing in the morning."

"Los Verdes?" Buddy said. "Damn, Lee, don't do anything sudden-like."

Then Lee called Frank Hayes.

"Rocky Mountain Bonding," the big voice said. "Where it's always spring time."

Lee could not help but laugh.

"Mr. Hayes, this is Lee Turner in Tennessee."

"Yes, ma'am, I recognize your voice. You have a lovely light Tennessee accent peppered with a little California."

How does he know about California? Lee wondered.

"Mr. Hayes, I'm on my way to Los Verdes. I need to talk with Dr. Edward Wilkinson. The federal authorities would not approve a request for an interview if I were to ask them. Do you think there is any way an interview can be arranged?"

"I think so. When will you be arriving?"

Lee was sure she heard the sound of delight in his voice.

"I'll call you when I know for sure which flight I'm on. I expect to be arriving in Los Verdes sometime this evening."

"This evening would be good," he said. "I'll meet you at the airport."

Lee grabbed the bag of breakfast from Helen's and started for the door.

"Take care of Henrietta for me, will you please, Buddy?"

"Are you gone? Just like that?"

"Just like that," Lee said.

"Let me drive you to the airport," he said. "You don't need to be eating and driving at the same time."

* * *

The first leg of the air trip was a commuter flight from the Knoxville airport to Hartsfield International Airport in Atlanta. The roads, automobiles, houses and farms below passed so slowly that it was difficult to believe the plane was traveling at the high speed it was. The cabin was quiet, just the hum of the two engines. The other passengers were not the talkative type, which suited Lee. She passed the time trying to sort out in her mind the parts of a puzzle that didn't seem to want to take shape.

The little plane arrived over Hartsfield airport in plenty of time to catch the Delta flight out but they were kept in a holding pattern until she thought she would miss her connection. The pilot pulled every string he could to get them on the ground, including "urgent police business." Apparently it worked, because the small plane was directed to the Delta terminal area for docking.

Once the big Delta jet was off the ground, Lee closed her eyes and tried to sleep. But she had too much of a buzz. She took out a notepad and began to draw diagrams of people, places, causes of death, and timelines. After an hour she had pages filled with lists of events, circles, squares and triangles connected by arrows, but no solutions. She had a drink and gave her mind a rest.

There was a connection in Dallas-Fort Worth that seemed much too complicated. Once back in the air she dozed off and the next thing she knew the attendant was telling her to prepare to descend to the Los Verdes airport.

The thought had been in her mind that she should have asked Frank Hayes for a description of himself or she should have given him one of her. *God*, she thought to herself, *a bail bondsman. I hope he's not a sleaze.*

She needn't have worried about being able to find Frank Hayes. A blind man could have found him. When she stepped out of the connecting walkway into the terminal she heard his unmistakable melodious deep voice. Frank had caught one of the flight attendants, or she had caught him, it was impossible to tell which. The attendant pointed Lee out and he came to meet her.

Frank Hayes was every bit of six feet-four inches, but his two hundred and thirty pounds or so were all business. He moved more like a race horse or a wild animal than a large man. His brown leather jacket and boots and his jeans and Navaho Indian shirt had a decidedly southwestern flavor but were low key and definitely expensive. His smile was disarmingly unpretentious and sincere in a face that showed so much history.

"Dr. Turner," he said, extending a well-manicured hand that looked as if it could crush Lee's.

Hell, it could crush my entire body, she thought.

"I'm Frank Hayes."

"Thank you for meeting me."

"I had to meet a woman with a voice as charming as yours. Of course you could have been big and ugly like me, but you're not. You're a beautiful woman."

Not only was he a physical presence to be reckoned with, Frank Hayes also had the gift to talk himself into or out of trouble. Lee liked him. She had liked the voice and now she liked the man. They picked up Frank's Jaguar sedan from the curbside and drove through the unfamiliar streets of Los Verdes.

"Do you have a hotel room?" Frank asked.

"No, I don't."

"I'll get you a room at the Courtyard. It's a nice place and not far from the hospital. I've arranged for you to see Wilkinson in about two hours."

"The hospital?" Lee asked.

"The veterans hospital."

"Why is Wilkinson in the hospital?" Not the result of his apprehension by Frank Hayes, she hoped.

"His nurses tell me it's acute toxicity from something deadly called Parathion. I followed your tip and that's where I found him. That's why I'm covering your hotel. You saved me a hundred thousand dollars."

There goes that illusion, Lee said to herself. *I thought it was because of my good looks.*

"I could really use something to eat," she said.

"Of course, what kind of food would you like?"

"Protein. Something good. A steak maybe."

Frank took her to a restaurant where the valet who parked the car knew him by name, and addressed him deferentially as "Mr. Hayes." The *maître d'* seemed well acquainted with Mr. Hayes, and the waiter was very pleased to see Mr. Hayes again. There was no menu.

"Bring the lady something succulent in a charcoal steak with a light mesquite. Let's start with some of those fresh shrimp in a cocktail, and that peach colored wine I had last time that I liked so much."

"And for you, Mr. Hayes?" The waiter asked.

"I'll have the same as the lady."

Lee sipped the cool wine perhaps a little to quickly but the atmosphere of the whole place seemed to encourage it. It relaxed her and increased her appetite.

"The wine, the shrimp, the salad – everything is delicious, Frank."

"That's why I come here." He smiled. "I'm pleased that you like it."

Lee felt warm and cheerful. She felt happy. It seemed more like an adventure than business.

"Frank, I don't mean to be personal, or to pry into your business."

"Be as personal as you like."

"Your lifestyle, Frank. This is not the lifestyle I pictured for a bail bondsman."

A pleasant, cheerful rumble came from deep within his throat, and his eyes reflected a glint of amusement.

"My company bonds many things, anything that needs assurance."

"Why kind of things?" Lee asked.

"Oh, let's say you're a contractor, for example, and have been hired to install a computer system for a chain of banks. Your contract might be for a million dollars. The bank would want you bonded to assure that the job is completed and the system you install is what they are paying for and works as advertised. So I would investigate you and, assuming you appear to be a good risk, I would provide the bond for you, to guarantee your fulfillment of the contract.

It's a kind of performance insurance."

"I'm embarrassed," Lee said. "That's not the kind of business I thought you are in."

"Bonding of criminal defendants to assure their appearance in court is a very small part of the business. But in many ways, the bail bonding, the criminal apprehension, and the private investigations are the part of the business I like the most. There is something personally rewarding to me in helping the little person who needs help, and in tracking down those who are fleeing justice."

"How large a business do you run?"

"In employees, about twenty on average. In dollars, about five million."

Lee almost choked on her wine.

"Five million dollars a year?"

"Income, not profit. Most of that comes from the bonding of construction contracts."

"And you answer your own phone?"

"Sometimes," he said. "I never let the business run itself. I was just lucky to be there when you called."

The restaurant chef himself accompanied the serving of the food to their table, overseeing its presentation and describing each of the dishes in detail. Lee decided it had to be one of the most delicious meals of the past ten years.

They stayed and talked until time to go to the appointment with Edward Wilkinson. Frank signed for the bill. Lee didn't see the amount but she knew it was more than eating at Helen's. When the valet brought the car he told Frank, "I put a case of the wine in your trunk, Mr. Hayes."

Frank thanked him and tipped him with a bill that looked suspiciously like a fifty.

"It's all part of the image," Frank said as they drove away.

"Do you know a Major Harold Cates connected with the national research laboratories?" Lee asked.

"Wild Harry? Yes, I know him. How do you know him?"

"He and I had a little run in, back in Tennessee. He tried to take my crime scene away from me."

"Did he now?" Frank asked, with a laugh. "Did you let him?"

"No, I didn't. He was pretty upset about it."

"I would love to have seen that. If Wild Harry personally directed an operation in Tennessee, there must be some pretty heavy stuff involved."

"It's all been a big federal secret. I've got whole families dying, and the feds have kept me shut out of whatever they know about it. And whatever they know seems to be at the center of it."

"What is Wilkinson's connection?"

"Edward Wilkinson is involved with a former colleague named Dr. Alexander Hamrick who was the first in a string of deaths to occur in our county. I learned from an FBI agent that Hamrick and Wilkinson have been the objects of an ongoing investigation involving the theft of something important from the national laboratories at Oak Ridge and Desert Flats. Something dangerous involving their work, as it was described to me. That's really all I've been able to learn. I think Carters Mill University may be connected with it."

The hospital was located on the grounds of the massive Desert Flats National Laboratories complex. They passed through two security checkpoints after registering their names on a log. Inside the entranceway to the hospital they were logged in again.

"Do you have a weapon to check?" The security officer asked.

From somewhere under his coat, Frank produced a 9mm Smith and Wesson automatic.

"You, ma'am?" The guard asked.

"No." Lee shook her head. She almost laughed.

From the patient information center they were given directions to the ward where Wilkinson's room was located. The head nurse on duty knew Frank Hayes from his last visit there.

"This is Dr. Lee Turner, from Carters Mill, Tennessee," Frank said. "She's an expert I have flown in to consult on Edward Wilkinson's condition. Is he in his room?"

"Yes, he is, Mr. Hayes. I wasn't told to expect anyone. Is there anything you need from the staff, Dr. Turner?"

"I just need to see the patient's record and be shown to his room, please."

The nurse pulled Wilkinson's folder from the patient records and gave it to Lee. Wilkinson appeared to be sleeping when they opened the door to his room.

"I can hardly believe it's the same man," Lee said, almost to herself.

The man lying in the hospital bed might have been young or he might have been old. His appearance was so distorted by his illness that Lee was unsure at first if it really was Wilkinson. The once robust and towering young man whose strength had overwhelmed her and Buddy at Hamrick's house was now a gaunt, sunken-chested, white skinned distortion of his former self. His hair was thin and limp, his eyes dark and set deep within his face.

He wavered as he opened his eyes and tried to raise his head to look toward them. His movements were unsure and shaky.

Lee tried to speak calmly and evenly. "Dr. Wilkinson, my name is Dr. Lee Turner. I'm here representing the Bartram County, Tennessee coroner's office."

The voice that answered was weak but more lucid than his appearance would lead one to expect.

"Yes, I remember you . . . at Alex's house. You and a man. I'm sorry what happened. I never meant to harm you. The truck I hit . . . the family . . . I sent a note . . . to apologize, offered to pay for damages . . . never heard back."

There was hesitation, and a look more of resignation than anything else showed in Wilkinson's face.

"Do you feel well enough to talk with me for a few minutes?"

He nodded.

Lee took a small digital recorder from her pocketbook and turned it on. "Dr. Wilkinson, I need to record our conversation. Is that OK with you?"

"Yes," he said.

Lee had looked at Wilkinson's chart. He was diagnosed as suffering from Parathion toxicity. He was being treated with mega-doses of atropine. His condition was critical.

"Do you know how you became exposed to Parathion?"

"In Alex's lab."

"His lab in Bartram County, Tennessee?"

"Yes. He used it. Containers were sitting open . . . They should not have been."

"Is that what happened to Dr. Hamrick? Did he accidentally contaminate himself?"

"Don't know. Must be what happened."

"Please tell me what you do know."

"I got a message that Alex called. I tried three days to call him back. Got no answer. I was worried and flew to Tennessee to see about him. He was dead when I got there. Had been for days. His body was . . . You saw it."

Eddie's face was flushed and his breathing was becoming irregular and labored.

"Are you able to continue?" Lee asked.

Wilkinson nodded his head.

"Why were you destroying the body?" She asked.

"I thought he was contagious. I had to stop the contagion."

"Contagion from what?" Lee asked.

"Bacteria. Alex worked with bacteria . . . same as we did here."

"Here at Desert Flats?" Lee asked.

Wilkinson nodded. "Yes."

"He was collecting and processing animal carcasses. What was that about?" Lee said.

"Desert Flats and Oak Ridge labs are field testing in Tennessee. Alex was looking for signs in the animals."

"What signs?"

"Changes in bacteria."

"In the wild population?" Lee asked. "What bacteria?"

"*Yersinia pestis*. You know what that is?"

"Yes, I do. What are the labs doing with *Yersinia*?"

"Altered it. Made it deadly to rodents."

"Genetically altered *Yersinia pestis*?"

"Yes. They developed a spore producer. . . will survive in the spore forever. . . very dangerous. Alex tried to stop them."

"Are they using coated seed grain to deliver the *Yersinia* to the rodent population?"

"Yes . . . you know about it?"

"We found some of the grain. How was Dr. Hamrick using Parathion?"

"It. . . activates recombinase."

Eddie's voice had become less strong as he talked. At points he coughed and seemed to try to get his breath.

"What does the FBI think you and Dr. Hamrick took from Desert Flats or Oak Ridge?"

"Colonies of the altered *Yersinia pestis*."

"Did you take them?"

"No . . . only information. Should have been given to Alex anyway. He knew more than anyone."

"Why were you helping him?"

"He was good to me. He was my mentor. He was alone. It was our work."

Eddie was visibly weakened. He now made no unnecessary movement beyond speaking. His voice had become less coherent. His eyes stared toward Lee with a particular focused intensity.

"He told Oak Ridge they . . . were going too fast, taking chances. He warned them . . . they persecuted him."

Eddie had a violent spasm of a deep rattling cough, covering his mouth with a white cloth. When he finally stopped coughing and laid his hands back at his sides, the cloth was stained with blood.

"I found him dead . . . thought he was infected. I had to dispose of the body. I . . . was not thinking straight . . . exhausted . . . panicked. I hope you never have to . . . destroy the body of . . . of a friend."

Wilkinson laid his head back on his pillow, his eyes closed. He had told Lee all she needed to know, and he was in no condition to continue the interview.

"Can you hear me, Dr. Wilkinson?"

There was no response.

"Thank you, Dr. Wilkinson. You did the right thing."

Frank Hayes drove them out of the gates of the Desert Flats National Laboratory grounds back to the Courtyard Hotel.

"Did that help clarify your situation?" He asked Lee.

"Yes. He gave me answers to several pieces of the larger puzzle. I understand a lot of what has happened now."

"What's this *Yersinia* you two were talking about?"

"*Yersinia pestis* is the bacterium that causes the plague."

"The plague? What have they been doing in your little county? Is that what killed all your folks?"

Lee shook her head. "Not all of them. All rodents carry *Yersinia* in their digestive systems, but it's normally not lethal to them. From what Wilkinson said, Desert Flats and Oak Ridge have developed a version of *Yersinia* that is lethal to rodents. I think he said they have modified it to reproduce by spore, which makes it virtually indestructible. Putting together what he told me with what I have seen, I think the new *Yersinia* is deadly to a whole lot more than just rodents. I think that's how one family died, but three other people have died of exposure to the toxin DNPT, which is one of the forms of Parathion."

"The same thing that's killing Wilkinson?"

"The same thing, yes. It looks as if Hamrick died either from the *Yersinia* or DNPT, but I don't know which. What I still haven't figured out is how all the deaths in the county are connected." Lee looked at her watch. It was too late to call Joe Gaines and alert him to the *Yersinia*. The CDC labs might have figured it out by now anyway.

"When are you going back to Tennessee?"

"I have a return ticket for tomorrow noon. There's something I have to do here in the morning."

The hotel was a beautifully landscaped new structure designed for travelers of means. All the vehicles in the parking lot were new and expensive.

"Would you care to stop for a drink before you go to your room?"

"I could use a drink. But I can't stay up too late. My clock is two hours ahead of yours and I'm dead on my feet already. A drink might put me right to sleep."

Lee didn't go to sleep right away. She didn't go to sleep in Los Verdes. As she sat in the Courtyard lounge relaxing, trying to get the images of Edward Wilkinson out of her mind, she looked across the room to a TV set hanging above the bar. On the screen of the TV was a blurred series of images of police cars, ambulances, faces of people she knew and the words *Bartram County, Tennessee.*

"What the hell?" she said.

Chapter 26
Rolling Hills

THE LOUNGE WAS too crowded for Lee to run between the tables to get to the TV over the bar, but she would if she could have. By the time she reached the bartender to ask him to turn up the volume, the news article about Bartram County was finished. She turned to go back to explain to Frank, but he was right behind her.

"What was that about?" he asked.

She told him about the images she had seen on the TV.

"Wouldn't they have called you if something was wrong?" Frank said.

Lee found Jack's cellphone in her purse.

"They couldn't have," she said, looking at the phone. "I turned it off before I got on the plane, and I forgot to turn it back on."

They sat back down at their table and Lee called the sheriff's office. Margy was still on duty.

"Margy, it's Lee. What's happening?"

"Oh, Lee, honey, I've tried to call you. There's some kind of epidemic out at Rolling Hills."

"The nursing home? What can you tell me about it?"

"Not much. Dr. Raymond and his hospital staff are there with some doctors from the State Health Department. Nobody knows what's going on. We hear that people are dying. When are you coming back?"

"The next plane out of here. I'll try to be back by morning."

Lee laid the phone on the table. She had to think. This

was not making any sense.

"What is it?" Frank asked.

"Can you get me to the airport, Frank? I've got to get back home. Something terrible is going on."

On the way to the airport Lee told Frank what she knew. She called ahead to Delta. There were no return Delta flights or any others departing to Atlanta until 5:00 a.m.

Frank used his phone and called military security at Desert Flats. He got the number of the flight control center at the local Army airfield. A couple more phone calls and he located an Army jet leaving for Dallas-Fort Worth in forty-five minutes. He turned his car around and drove her to the Army airfield with time to spare. After an explanation of the urgency of the situation and a couple of phone calls to Desert Flats, the officer in charge arranged for a seat for Lee on the Army jet.

As Lee was taking her things from Frank's car she remembered the letter in her briefcase from Barbara Hamrick.

"Frank," she said, "I need to hire you to do a job for me."

"No hiring necessary. What can I do for you?"

"It's a job that takes a real man," she said, with a teasing smile. "I need a sperm sample."

"My pleasure," he said. "Do you want it right now?"

She told him about the need for Hamrick's DNA and about the frozen sperm she was to pick up in the morning.

"That wasn't exactly the picture I had painted in my mind," he said, "but I'll see that it's taken care of."

He took Lee's hand and kissed it before she boarded the plane. "You are the most mysterious woman," he said. "I understand duty, but come back sometime when you can stay longer."

"Thank you, Frank, for everything."

"Call me and tell me how everything turns out."

On a sudden impulse, Lee put her arms around his neck and kissed his lips.

"I guess that means you want it done for free?" Frank said.

"Think of me when you pick up that sample tomorrow," she said.

Frank laughed, then kissed her again. "I'll think of you before then."

She waved to him as the door to the plane closed.

The return trip to Dallas-Fort Worth and on to Knoxville was a mirror image of her trip out to Los Verdes except for the military jet on the first leg back. At Dallas-Fort Worth she was put on standby but caught a flight out with little delay. In Atlanta she had to hurry across the airport in time to catch a seat on the first commuter flight back to Knoxville.

The little Lear Jet sat down on the Knoxville runway at 5:40 a.m. in pouring rain. Lee had called ahead and Buddy was waiting for her. It was the kind of cold, dark, overcast morning that made the raindrops blown by the strong wind feel like tiny ice needles hitting the skin. She got in the passenger side of her Land Cruiser, closed the door, pulled her arms close to herself and leaned back in the seat with her eyes shut.

"Bad trip?" Buddy asked.

Lee opened her eyes and smiled at Buddy.

"No, it was a good trip. I'm just tired and cold."

"Did you get any sleep?"

"About two hours on the jet," she said.

"You lean back and go to sleep. It'll take about forty-five minutes to get back to Carters Mill." Buddy headed west into the steady driving rain.

"What's going on at Rolling Hills?" Lee asked.

"I can't tell you a whole lot. The best I've been able to learn, a handful of residents got real ill yesterday sometime right after lunch. At first they thought it was food poisoning. By the time anyone knew what was happening and they got a doctor out there, three of them were dead, just like that." Buddy snapped his fingers.

"The first doctor on the scene quarantined the place right away and called the CDC. By dark yesterday the place was swarming with medical people, police, relatives of the patients, TV news people from everywhere. It's like a disaster area. Nobody can get in or out and nobody is talking."

"I wish I were ten years younger and twice as strong," Lee said.

Buddy chuckled. "Don't we all. Did you go shopping in Los Verdes?"

"Shopping?" Lee looked over at him like he was crazy.

"You smell good. I thought maybe you bought some new perfume."

"It's not me. I haven't even had a shower since night before last. I thought it was you. Have you been driving women around in my truck while I was gone?"

"I wish," Buddy said. "Did you find out what you went out to Los Verdes for?"

"I talked with Wilkinson. I understand a lot more than I did before I went out there. I'll tell you about it later."

"All right, you get some sleep."

* * *

Buddy drove by Lee's office to pick up her forensics bag, gowns and gloves. The message light on her telephone was blinking but they hurried on with their preparations, leaving the light blinking behind them as they closed the door to the office.

"A lot of people have got family and friends at Rolling Hills," Buddy said. "This is going to hit home hard in this little county."

As they drove toward the cove in Poplar Valley where Rolling Hills nursing home stood, the sky had become dark with blue-black clouds. Lightning lighted up the thunderheads from within like strobe lights, and drops of rain as large as quarters hit the windshield of the Land Cruiser and thumped in rapid fire on the roof.

They crossed the bridge spanning Poplar Creek and they could see the flashing lights of ambulances and sheriff's department vehicles outside the nursing home. A large number of automobiles were in the parking lot. And there were clusters of people, many of them with their arms around each other's shoulders, many with their faces covered by their hands, most of them with their heads lowered and their shoulders sagging. Other people sat in their automobiles waiting. Sheriff's deputies in yellow rain suits were directing the flow of traffic, trying to keep the driveway open. A deputy waved Lee to a space next to the emergency entrance. As she and Buddy stood under the entrance awning putting on their white lab coats, they could hear the crying of people in mourning.

Inside the emergency receiving room a ward nurse sat, pale-faced and motionless. In the room with her were three stretchers, each one holding a zipped black plastic body bag covered by a white sheet. Lee uncovered the first of the body bags. Attached to its zipper was a tag listing the name and Social Security Number of the deceased.

Lee zipped open the bag. Her first reaction was of repulsion. Out of the bag rose the same pungent metallic odor that had come from the Johnson children. She made a brief examination of the body. There was sign of bleeding from the nose, the mouth, and ears. Lee looked over at the young nurse. She appeared to be in a state of exhaustion.

"Can you give me a positive identification of this patient?" Lee said.

The nurse looked up slowly out of her vacant stare.

"That's Mrs. Moore," she said.

"You'll have to come and look at her and give me a positive ID," Lee said.

The young woman got up from her chair, came to the stretcher and looked down at the woman's face. A shudder went through her body.

"Do you know this woman positively?" Lee asked.

"Yes. That's Mrs. Iris Moore. She was one of the patients on my ward. She died at approximately 3:00 a.m. this morning. I was on duty at the time and checked on her just thirty minutes before I found her dead."

Lee filled out a preliminary certificate of death for the woman, leaving the cause of death blank, and had the nurse, with shaking hand, sign the death certificate as a witness. Lee wrote the time on the tag on the woman's wrist, added her own signature to the tag and zipped the bag closed.

Lee went through the same procedure with each of the other two bodies. All three had the same superficial symptoms. When she finished, the ambulance crews were waiting to transport the bodies for post mortem examinations.

The young nurse had sat back down, her face in her hands. Lee took off and disposed of her gloves, went over to the nurse and sat down beside her.

"I know you must be tired and very upset," Lee said. She took the nurse's hand in hers. "Have you been here since yesterday?"

The nurse nodded almost imperceptibly. "They won't let me leave."

"Perhaps it will all be over soon."

The nurse just looked at Lee through dark, vacant eyes.

Lee walked down the hallway to the administrator's office. She opened the door and saw Murray Gordon standing next to the window, looking out into the rain. He asked Lee to come in and close the door.

"I just got in from out of town, Murray. What's the situation here?"

"We have eight dead, another six critical the last report I had forty-five minutes ago."

"Have they identified positively what caused the deaths?"

"We're waiting for a CDC team to get here. Perhaps they can tell us for sure. We're quarantined until we know if it's a danger to the community. Can't take a chance of it spreading."

"They think it's contagious?"

"They think it may be some, what do you call it? A hot virus or bacteria?"

It was possible, Lee thought, but the symptoms were too similar to Judy Vining and the Johnson children not to suspect DNPT poisoning. She didn't say it to Murray Gordon.

"The doctors don't know what it is. And after the other recent deaths in the county we can't take any chances," he said.

"Who is the physician in charge here?"

"Peter Raymond. He's one of the physicians on call to us."

"I know him," Lee said.

"His mother is one of the patients stricken ill."

"My God," Lee said. "It must be rough on him. I had better find him and see if there is anything I can do to help."

She put on gloves and filtration mask. In the first room she passed there was one empty bed and one patient connected to an IV in an apparent state of coma. In the next room two medical personnel were bending over a bed, one of them supporting a half conscious patient who was moaning and saying something unintelligible. In the third room were two beds, each one containing a closed body bag just visible from under sheets.

Walking down the hallway past a line of rooms with curtained off beds and patients connected to intravenous feeds and oxygen masks, she encountered Peter Raymond coming out of a patient room, putting on a fresh pair of latex gloves. Even though he was looking out from behind a surgical mask and was dressed in a nondescript surgeon's gown and cap, there was no mistaking him.

Lee could see he was tired and worried, but he had a look of purpose about him and an intensity in his eyes that reflected his dedication to his responsibilities. Even from behind his hospital garb and his mask Lee could see the crow's feet form at the corners of his eyes by his unseen smile as he looked up and saw her.

"How is your mother, Peter?" she asked.

"Holding her own right now. If she can hold on for another twenty-four hours I hope we will see some progress."

"Do you know yet what you're dealing with?"

"Have you seen the patients?" he asked.

Lee nodded that she had.

"Then you see the similarity of symptoms?"

"DNPT?"

"That would be my best guess, and that's the assumption underlying our treatment of the patients. But as you know, if it is DNPT then the fate of the patients is not something we have a lot of control over. We're taking counter measures but if the dose of DNPT was large enough, our efforts will be of little consequence. We had to set up a quarantine until we know for sure that it is not something contagious."

Lee stayed at Rolling Hills to help until more medical personnel could arrive. She was not able to leave by noon to attend a special meeting of the mayor and council that had been called. She was still there at 5:00 p.m. when personnel from the state department of health relieved her. The last death certificate she filled out was for Mary Ann Raymond, Dr. Peter Raymond's mother.

When she walked out the emergency entrance it was almost dark and still raining. The red and yellow flashing lights from emergency vehicles swirled past in a random pulsating chaotic rhythm and reflected off wet surfaces. When she got to her Land Cruiser, Jack Sheridan was sitting in it waiting for her. She had been strong all day, but when she saw Jack her bravery dissolved with each step she took. He stepped out of the vehicle and came toward her. She held out a hand to motion for him to stop, and she bent over, her back to him, and her arm on the front of the Land Cruiser for support, and she vomited. When finally she stood up weakly, Jack lifted her in his arms and put her in the passenger side of her truck.

"I've worried about you all day," he said.

She wept all the way home and was still weeping while Jack prepared a warm shower for her, undressed her and carried her into it. Sometime during the shower she stopped crying. She hadn't eaten anything but vending machine snacks since Los Verdes. She was shaking when she sat down at the kitchen table in front of a glass of warm milk Jack had made for her.

"You've got to eat or you'll be back in the hospital," he said.

He made her the only meal, Lee suspected, he knew how to make–peanut butter and jelly on toast. But then he surprised her with a bowl of warm oatmeal fresh from the microwave. She tried to make a joke about it but what she said didn't make any particular sense. Jack put her to bed and lay himself down on her sofa for the night.

Her dreams were filled with frightening things and sad things. She cried in her sleep and she was lost. Somehow Hamrick's body had returned to the chair in his house and Wilkinson was there again, threatening her and Buddy with a rattlesnake in a sack. She could hear its rattlers buzzing. Then she was transported to a rural farming village where all the people were very poor. Small children in tattered clothes were lying dead in the field, and before Lee could get to them their bodies were covered over by dirt from a tractor plowing the field.

In her dream she awoke and Jack Sheridan was holding her cradled against his strong chest. He was telling her it was all a dream. They were in the restaurant having another wonderful meal. For desert she had a fragrant smelling hot liqueur with melted chocolate drops in it. She looked at her feet and her shoes were covered in mud from the plowed field. She went to the bathroom to clean her shoes but when she went through the door, she was back in Hamrick's laboratory. Only this time it was filled with the dead and decaying bodies of the Morris family and the Johnson children all piled together with the patients from the nursing home.

Lee awakened with a jerk. Her heart was pounding. She was in a near blind panic. She made her way to the kitchen and opened the refrigerator. She drank a glass of milk and waited, hoping her anxiety attack would subside. It was daylight. The clock said the time was 7:30. It must be 7:30 in the morning.

She heard the sound of Jack's voice talking to Henrietta, and the sound of the two of them coming through the front door. He found her in the kitchen.

"Are you feeling better, I hope?" He asked.

Henrietta ran over to her and jumped up, wanting to be petted. Lee picked her up and held her close, talking baby talk into her ear and kissing her on the head. Somehow it helped Lee to feel better and Henrietta enjoyed it. Jack had put a pot of coffee on to perk and the coughing and wheezing sounds of the coffee maker signaled that it was ready.

"It smells absolutely delicious," Lee said. "But coffee always smells better than it is."

"Would you like something in it?" Jack asked. "How about some chocolate or a little cappuccino mix? That should make it taste as good as it smells."

"That would be good."

"Wait right there," he said. "I've got just the thing." He walked into the living room and out the front door. She heard car doors opening and closing and he came back with a small green box of chocolate candies.

"I found this in your Land Cruiser last night," he said. He opened the lid of the box and smelled the aroma from the candy. "They smell so good my mouth waters just getting close to them. Did you get these in Los Verdes?"

Lee watched with fascination as Jack opened the box of candies, took out a foil wrapped piece and placed it next to her coffee cup. For a moment she was afraid she might be dreaming again. It was just like in her dream. A hot fragrant liquid with melted chocolate drops in it. Her heart was racing so fast that her head was swimming.

"I know how it was done and why it was done," she said.

"What?" Jack had no idea what she was talking about.

"The murders."

Chapter 27
The Devil in the Details

"WHICH MURDERS?" Jack asked.

"The deaths. They're all murders except the Morris family."

"The nursing home patients were murdered? How did you reach that conclusion?"

"Well, Mr. FBI, if I have figured it out, surely you and your colleagues have it figured out."

"No, we don't. Tell me what you're talking about."

Lee put the piece of chocolate back in the box and sipped her cup of coffee as a plan formulated in her mind.

"Did you ever find Hamrick's daily journal?"

"No, it hasn't turned up. How is that connected?" Jack asked.

"Is it true you suspect Ray Durbin of being involved with illegal weapons and conspiracy to commit a terrorist act?"

"What do you know about that?" Jack asked.

"Oh, Jack, get off it. Just answer my question."

"Yes. The militia group Ray Durbin belongs to has ties to a loose national network of paramilitary fanatics who are collecting weapons and planning terrorist attacks. Hamrick purchased a quantity of high quality concentrated DNPT that is now missing," Jack said.

"Yes, it's missing. But you don't know who took it, do you?"

"We suspect it fell into the hands of Ray Durbin and his group."

"You think they're trying to make Sarin gas, don't you?"

"Yes, but how do you . . ."

"Well, you're wrong about the motives of Ray Durbin. He thinks he and his friends are stopping a terrorist attack already in progress against the citizens of Bartram County."

"An attack by whom?"

"By the National Research Laboratories at Oak Ridge."

"Lee, how do you know this?"

"It doesn't take a rocket scientist, Jack. I talked with Edward Wilkinson. He gave me a deathbed statement. He was involved in an honorable quest trying to help his aging friend. They were not plotting a conspiracy. Hamrick and Wilkinson took nothing of value from Oak Ridge or Desert Flats. They didn't need to. They already had it. In fact, Hamrick tried to give them a lesson in good judgment, free of charge. They returned the favor by defaming him to the FBI."

"The Sons of Freedom are no fabrication," Jack said.

"No. But The Sons of Freedom are not the motivating force. They came into the picture after Ray Durbin alerted them that something suspicious was happening here. Ray Durbin stumbled across Hamrick at a concerned citizens meeting about the landfill project in the county. They struck up some kind of weird friendship based on their mutual opposition to the landfill."

"Durbin gained Hamrick's help," Jack said, "either of Hamrick's own free will or through deception. But either way, Hamrick aided Durbin."

"It's not conspiracy if it was against his will, Jack. Hamrick was a bitter old man who talked too much to the wrong people. He complained about incompetent administrators at NRL who he said stole his research. He told Durbin that Oak Ridge and Desert Flats are right now field testing products of that research here in Bartram County, despite his warnings. These were hot button issues to Durbin. He got on the Internet and told his Sons of Freedom buddies what Hamrick had told him. That information confirmed their very worst paranoid fears about the national research labs' secret weapons development. In pursuit of their own brand of proof of what is going on, the Sons of Freedom took Hamrick's research journal, either before or after his death, I don't know which, but I'm virtually certain they don't have the DNPT."

"Do you know they have his journal?"

"Who else? You heard Durbin. He said he was going to show me absolute proof of what NRL has been up to. He was talking about Hamrick's journal and the things it would point to. When you do find Hamrick's journal, it won't contain any information about poison gas. What it will contain is details about the production and testing of a genetically altered *Yersinia pestis*, the plague bacterium."

"How long have you known all this and how did you find out?" Jack said.

"I've had all the pieces but I couldn't make them fit together into anything that made sense. I just figured it all out in my sleep last night. That's the way the human mind works, you know. It mulls things over and tries all the little bits and pieces of a puzzle until it gets them to fit together into a picture that makes sense. Or it keeps you frustrated until you get the information you need. That's why I had to go to Los Verdes, to get information I needed. And the last piece just fell into place."

"What?"

"I'll tell you later. Right now we need to find a way to get that journal out of the hands of Ray Durbin before something happens to it. Can't you arrest him and his militia friends on a federal weapons charge before they get out to the University farms and do something really stupid? I think they're probably ready to make some kind of move."

"How are you deducing all this?"

"Listen to his own words. You have him on tape. Read the Hamrick UNESCO report. The Sons of Freedom did. I did. Look, Jack, rumors are flying all over that some mysterious deadly illness is striking the citizens of Bartram County. Put that rumor in the twisted mind of Durbin after he has talked to Hamrick and read Hamrick's UNESCO report and the information on the Internet about biological weapons development at NRL, mix that in with a whole family dying at once, and what do you have? Boom. Waco. Ruby Ridge."

"You could be right," Jack said. "One of Durbin's associates is a deputy inside the sheriff's department. He has access to everything the sheriff's department knows about all the deaths in the county."

"It's not Billy Longtree?"

"No. Billy's a good man," Jack said. "It's Deputy Faust."

"Thank goodness it's not Billy."

"Do you have some suggestion as to how we might get Durbin to turn over the journal if he does have it? We could arrest him, but if we do there's a good chance the journal will never be seen again."

"He won't destroy the journal. It's their trump card. He wants me to see it. He wants me to reveal its contents to the press. I think we can use that to get him to bring it to me, or me to it."

"I can't let you go to them." Jack protested. "There's too much danger in that."

"OK, we can use the deputy. I can't contact Durbin directly, but we'll have the deputy carry a message to him. Here's the plan."

Jack listened to her proposition. After some negotiating over the details, he agreed to it.

"You should have been a military strategist," he said. "What are you going to be doing?"

"I have a murderer to catch."

"What murderer?"

"I need for you to do something, Jack. I want to know every person in this county who has any dealings whatsoever with a company called Millennium Viatical. You find that out and you'll uncover the murderer and the victims. I know who it is but I need the detailed proof."

"I don't know if I can do that."

"Then you are not worth your salt. I can do it but by the time I get through all the red tape the murderer may be gone or more people may be dead."

Lee was at her office by 10:00 a.m. She wasn't sure Jack had believed what she told him but it would be up to him to decide that. She called Joe Gaines on the phone.

"Joe, are you swamped with work from the nursing home deaths?"

"No, Lee. Those bodies didn't come to me. They were turned directly over to the CDC people. Have you heard the latest news on them?"

"No, what?"

"It was DNPT."

"What's the death count now, do you know?" Lee said.

"It stands at nine. They still don't know the source of the poison. Peter Raymond's mother was one of the victims, I guess you heard."

Lee knew only too well. The images of the nursing home filled her mind again. She tried to clear her thoughts.

"I've discovered some things, Joe. Did you take any blood or tissue samples from Mr. Terry's body?"

"Mr. Terry? If I didn't, what are we going to do?"

"We're going to dig him up."

"What's going on Lee?"

"I think he was poisoned also."

"Do you mean accidental or deliberate?"

"Deliberate," Lee said.

"Who would poison Mr. Terry?"

"I think I'll be able to tell you the answer to that by this time tomorrow. If I'm right, it's the same person responsible for all the deaths except the Morrises. And on the exhumation, Joe, there will be more than one."

"Holy cow, Lee. Does Tom Davis know about this?"

"I'll be talking with him shortly. Listen, Joe, there's something else too. Remember I asked about having Judy Vining's office sealed?"

"Yes, and I did. It's under padlock."

"I believe there is something there that will help us tie these deaths together. Would it be asking too much to have someone from your office go there and collect some evidence for you to analyze?"

"There is no way I could refuse a request like that. What is it you want me to get?"

Lee told Joe what she had seen there.

"Be sure to collect it in separate evidence bags and be very careful in handling it."

"You don't have to warn me," Joe said. "I've seen the gory details of what that stuff can do. I'll get right on it."

Lee dialed Tom Davis at the TBI office and gave him the same information she had given Joe Gaines.

"We'll need to know exactly who at the nursing home came in contact with it," Lee said.

"Could it be that cold blooded?" Tom said.

"It's a crime of greed and fear, Tom."

"Is there enough evidence for an arrest? The killings could go on."

"By the end of the day when all the lab results come back I think we can make an arrest. Will you be available?"

"You bet your life. I wouldn't be anywhere else."

Lee started out the door and met Buddy. He was getting out of Lonnie Chapman's car.

"How about going with me, Buddy."

"Sure thing," Buddy said.

Lonnie rolled down his window, smiled and spoke.

"Hey, Lee. You're looking great. I was thinking of going in to Knoxville for dinner this evening. Would you be interested in joining me?"

"I'm sorry, Lonnie. I have a date with the devil this evening."

Lonnie whistled. "That sounds hot. Did you enjoy the candy I gave you?"

"I'm saving it for a special occasion," Lee said.

"You can have all you want. I have plenty more." He waved and backed his Cadillac out into the street.

"What are we doing?" Buddy asked as Lee headed the Land Cruiser in the direction of the sheriff's office.

"First thing, I've got to pay a brief visit to Sheriff Eberhard."

The sheriff showed Lee into his private office and shut the door.

"I just got off the phone with Jack Sheridan, Lee, and I want you to know I think you meeting with Durbin and that bunch is too dangerous."

"We should have all the options covered, Sheriff. I don't think there is any risk to me. The FBI will handle the arrest."

"If anything were to happen to you," he said, "I couldn't forgive myself for letting you do it."

"There is something else just as urgent that I need you to know about," Lee said. She told him of her suspicions regarding the source of the poison behind the numerous deaths, and the collection of evidence now going on that would make or break the case.

"My God," the sheriff said, "I can't believe it."

"Can you maintain surveillance until we're prepared for an arrest? It'll have to be very discreet."

"I'll ask Anderson County to lend us a plainclothes detective and request an unmarked cruiser. Those will be less recognizable than using our own personnel. Is Buddy with you?"

"Yes."

The sheriff opened a locked metal cabinet and removed

a Glock 9mm automatic.

"Keep this with you until this is over," he said.

She hesitated, then took the pistol and put it in her waistband under her coat.

Lee was torn over the question of how much of her suspicions she should tell Buddy. There were things he should know if they were true, but there was also harm that could come from premature conclusions and speculation. She decided to wait a little while until she had definite proof one way or the other.

"So, where to now?" Buddy asked.

"To Myra Johnson's. I have to get the answers to some questions from her and her father."

"It's a shame about the old man having cancer. It just doesn't seem right that his young grandchildren should die like that. It's enough to kill a healthy person."

"Think about Myra," Lee said. "She lost both her sons and now is about to lose her father. Two of the greatest tragedies in any person's life."

Buddy shifted a little in his seat. After some hesitation he finally found voice to his concern.

"Has Lonnie been coming on to you?" He said.

"Just the usual. Why do you ask?"

"I see the way he looks at you."

"He's a womanizer, Buddy. He looks at lots of women that way. I don't think he knows any other way. Is that all that's bothering you? Why have you been hanging around with him, anyway?"

"Oh, he's been after me for months, trying to get me to put money in some investment scheme of his."

"Do you have money to invest?"

"You mean besides my coin collection?" Buddy joked. "Nah, I get a little military pension, you know. Lonnie wants me to invest that. Claims he can double my money in a year."

"What kind of pension do you get?"

"Disability. I got shot in the ass. Lost the use of one leg for a while."

"In the Middle East?"

"Yeah, Afghanistan."

"How did it happen?"

"I was in a foxhole. They told us to keep our heads down. They didn't say anything about our asses. They said later it was the only thing sticking up."

Lee was smiling to herself.

"It's OK, you can laugh," he said. "It's pretty funny to me too when I think about it now."

Myra's new green van, the same one she had carried her dying children in, was sitting in her driveway when they got to her house. An old faded blue and grey station wagon with the paint chipped and peeling sat next to the house.

Lee sat in her Land Cruiser writing out a list of items on a notepad before going to Myra Johnson's door.

"They told me it was poison," Myra said. "But I just don't understand it. I don't understand where my boys could have got into poison."

"Other people have been exposed to it too, Myra. We're trying to track it down."

"Is it in the food? My sister Edith told me you thought it might have been my cornbread. I just about died when she told me that. I just couldn't live if I knew I poisoned my own babies."

Lee put an arm around Myra's shoulders.

"No, it's nothing you did. Wherever it's coming from, it's managed to poison people as far away as Popular Creek. It was not in your food."

Myra wiped her eyes. "Oh, thank God it wasn't me."

"Is your father home?" Lee asked.

"He's sleeping now. Poor thing. Do you want me to wake him up?"

"No, don't wake him," Lee said. "How is he doing?"

"It's just about killed him. I tell you the truth, he has aged more over the past week than he did over the past year. And that's saying a lot, because he has incurable cancer, you know, and he's been going down real fast over the past couple of years."

"It's got to be terrible for you," Lee said.

"I'll live on, one way or another. I've got my church and my Christian beliefs. But he's dying. He knows he's dying. The doctors have told him. But every day of his life since he found out, he's tried to do something for me and the boys. All this renovation of the house, he had done, and he bought me a new car, and bicycles and toys for the boys."

Myra reached out her hands as if she would like to touch the things and hold them to her.

"It's not that Daddy is a wealthy man. He's not. He worked all his life at sawmills and textile plants–hard work that's killing him now. He gets his Social Security and Disability, but that's just enough to get by on. I don't know where he's getting the money. He's the kind of man that won't tell anybody his business. When I ask him he just tells me his union insurance is paying for it."

"He obviously wants to see you happy and cared for," Lee said.

"He loved my boys. I know that. We all did."

"What we're looking for now is a list of items we've found that could possibly be connected with the other deaths. Would you look at this list and tell me if any of these items have been in your house lately, or did your boys have them, to your knowledge?"

Myra read down the list. Somehow, taking part in the investigation, even a little bit, seemed to give her purpose. She went over the list two or three times.

"You know, I think I have seen this one here." Myra pointed to one of the items on the list. "Daddy has always spoiled the boys. You know how grandfathers can be. He was always bringing things into the house. Some of it he would hide from them. Of course, boys being boys, you couldn't really hide anything from them. When he wasn't looking, they'd sneak around and find what he'd hid. He always knew when they did, and he'd play this little game with them about having something for them but that somebody had stole it. I think he might have had this one."

"Could you look and see if you can find any of it still here? The poison smells like honeysuckle, but you might or might not be able smell it."

Myra searched through bags and boxes in the den near her father's chair, but came back empty handed.

"Could the empty package have been thrown in the trash?"

"I don't know," Myra said. "I don't think the garbage for this week has been picked up yet. It's in bags in the garbage cans out back if you want to look."

Lee looked at Buddy.

"I'll get the gloves," he said.

They began emptying the contents of the thirty-gallon plastic garbage bags onto the ground.

"I think I see why you brought me along," Buddy said.

There were five bags. They made a terrible mess in the yard and Lee had about given up hope of finding what she was looking for. Then a small square green box fell out of the last bag.

"Get an evidence bag, Buddy."

"What did you find?"

"The murder weapon," Lee said.

They shoveled up the mess and put it back in Myra's garbage cans and headed back to Lee's office. On the way back to town Buddy had waited as long as he could.

"OK, Lee, are you going to tell me what's going on? I'm beginning to feel like that mushroom again." He held up the evidence bag and looked at the now empty box of imported chocolate candy.

"I expect the lab will find the inside of that candy box to contain residue of DNPT. The candy was poisoned. That's what the Johnson children ate that killed them."

"How do you come by that?" Buddy asked.

"The first time we went to the Johnson house after the children died we both saw the renovations to the house and the new bicycles on the front porch. And we saw the new van Myra was driving when she came to the courthouse with her dead children."

"Wait a minute. Are you saying the children were killed for money?"

"No," Lee said. "The children were killed by mistake. Mr. Duncan, the children's grandfather, was the intended victim."

"I'm lost, Lee. Have I missed something important? I feel like I fell asleep in the middle of a movie and woke up right at the end. Who would want to kill Mr. Duncan? And what has money got to do with it? You talking about a murder for hire?"

"Money has everything to do with it. No, it wasn't a murder for hire. Open my glove compartment."

Buddy opened the glove compartment. He didn't have to be told what he was looking for when he saw what was inside. He retrieved a clear evidence bag containing a small green box of imported chocolate candies identical to the one they had just taken from Myra Johnson's garbage.

"Where did this come from?" He asked.

"Smell it. Don't open the box. Just take a small whiff of it."

Buddy raised the bag near his nose, partially opened it and took a cautious sniff.

"Smells like flowers."

"Honeysuckle," Lee said. "It smells like honeysuckle. I should have picked up on it the other night when you brought me back from the Knoxville airport. You told me I smelled good. I thought it was you."

"Yeah, I remember. What's the deal about honeysuckle?" Buddy asked.

"DNPT has the aroma of honeysuckle."

"Damn, Lee," Buddy said, holding the bag away from him with two fingers. What do you want me to do with it?"

"Just reseal the evidence bag."

"So that's the source of the poison? Imported chocolate? When did you figure this out?"

"This morning at breakfast. Jack Sheridan offered me a piece of it."

"Jack tried to poison you?"

"No. Jack didn't know it was poisoned."

"Where did it come from?" Buddy read the label through the evidence bag. "Austria? Where did you get it?"

"It was given to me by the murderer."

"Who?"

"The same person who killed Dr. Hamrick, and Judy Vining, the Johnson boys, and all the poor souls at the nursing home."

"Who?"

"Lonnie Chapman."

"Lonnie Chapman? Come on, Lee. Lonnie Chapman? I've known Lonnie all my life. Why would Lonnie kill half the county, and try to kill you?"

"It's all about money."

They arrived back at Lee's office. The office was dark and quiet.

"As contrary as the old man was, the place is not the same without Mr. Terry huffing and puffing and grumping around," Buddy said.

Lee took the Glock 9mm out from her waistband and laid it on top of the desk in front of her.

"Damn, Lee, when did you start carrying?"

"Today," she said.

She opened the desk drawer and took out the form from Millennium Viatical requesting certification of Hamrick's death. She pushed the form across the desk toward Buddy.

"This is what's at the bottom of all the murders," she said.

"Millennium Viatical? Where have I heard that before?" Buddy asked.

"You called me at home right after I got out of the hospital. You told me the things that were in my mail. One of them was a brochure from Millennium Viatical."

"Your memory is better than mine." Buddy shook his head. "So, what is this Millennium Viatical?"

"It's a social vulture. It preys on the dead and dying. If you are old and sick, they want your business. They'll pay you fifty to seventy-five cents on the dollar for your life insurance policy and hope you die soon so they can make a quick profit when they cash in your policy for its full value. The sooner you die, the more they make."

"So this Millennium Viatical company is buying people's insurance and then murdering them?"

"It's not quite that simple, but that's what it's all about."

"Why do you think Lonnie is the one behind it?"

Lee picked up the phone and called the TBI office.

"Tom," she said, "it's Lee. Have you been able to do anything with those blood samples from Hamrick's house? Not the DNA, I know that will take longer, but what about the toxicity?"

"I can't tell you for sure who the blood came from," Tom said, "but I can tell you that whoever it was, he died from DNPT poisoning."

"That's what I thought. Any word on the forensics from the nursing home victims?"

"The same thing. DNPT," Tom said.

"Has Sheriff Eberhard talked with you in the last couple of hours?"

"Yes," Tom said. "We have everything in place, ready to move whenever the arrest warrant is issued."

"Let me talk with Joe Gaines. If he found what I expect he did, I'll go to Judge Glover immediately."

Buddy was listening with undivided attention to Lee's side of the phone conversation. Lee hung up and then dialed Joe Gaines.

"Yes, Lee, you were right. The items in both Miss Vining's desk and Dr. Hamrick's desk were contaminated with DNPT. And I've ordered the exhumation of Mr. Terry's body. You said there would be another one?"

"Mrs. Jamie Anderson. Died two weeks ago here in the county. She was one of Peter Raymond's patients. He should be notified. Thanks, Joe."

"I wish these were happier times," he said.

Lee stood up, took the pistol from her desk and put it back in her waistband.

"Let's walk over to the courthouse, Buddy. I need to have Judge Glover issue an arrest warrant. I'll explain everything on the way over."

Chapter 28
Making the Case

JUDGE GLOVER WAS in his chambers when they arrived at the courthouse. Buddy was still saying, "I just can't believe it," when Cybil showed them into the judge's office.

"Sheriff Eberhard told me to expect you," Judge Glover said. "Cybil, you stay and record this. OK, Lee, give me your formal request."

"I am requesting a warrant for the arrest of Leonard Chapman and the search and seizure of all his personal and business financial records on charges of suspicion of murder in the deaths of the fourteen residents of Bartram County named on this list."

Lee gave Judge Glover a written list containing the names:

John Doe (Alexander Hamrick) 1201 Paradise Rd.
Jeffrey Johnson
David Johnson
Jamie Anderson
Oscar Terry
Nine residents of the Rolling Hills nursing home

"Evidence will show Lonnie is also responsible for the deaths of Judy Vining, a student at Carters Mill University, and of Edward Wilkinson who died in Los Verdes, New Mexico. Pending the results of toxicology testing, I will add to those charges the attempted murder of Lee Turner, Acting Coroner of Bartram County.

"I am also requesting a warrant to search his property for the presence of a quantity of a toxic substance known as DNPT, which is the cause of death of these citizens."

Lee laid out for Judge Glover the accumulation of evidence pointing to Lonnie Chapman, from his fingerprints at Hamrick's, to the interview with Edward Wilkinson, to the mysterious disappearance of $750,000 from Dr. Hamrick's insurance policy held by Chapman Insurance, to the presence of DNPT in the wrappers from boxes of candy given away by Lonnie.

The judge issued the arrest warrant for Chapman and the search and seizure warrants for his office, home, and automobile, as Lee requested.

"You be careful in dealing with Mr. Chapman until he can be apprehended, Lee. If your accusations are correct, he is a very dangerous man," Judge Glover said.

The warrants were delivered to Sheriff Eberhard for execution according to plan.

On their way back to the Coroner's Office, Buddy was still turning the events over in his mind.

"There's something I don't understand, Lee," he said. "With $750,000 or more already in his pocket, why would Lonnie commit all the other murders for more money and run the risk of getting caught?"

"I've wonder that myself," Lee said. "I don't know if it was greed or desperation. It's pretty obvious Lonnie needed a lot of money to support his lifestyle."

"I always wondered how he can drive new Cadillacs and buy expensive clothes when he spends most of every day playing golf and loafing around," Buddy said. "He always was interested in making a fast buck with double your money type schemes and that sort of thing. For a while him and Hardy Cook and the other fellows in the investment club were involved in day-trading stocks over in Knoxville. Lonnie tried to get me involved in that, but I don't know anything about trading stocks. Turns out, they didn't either. They made a lot of money for a few weeks, then they lost their shirts and gave that up."

"You told me about the 31% annual return the investment club was supposed to have made on some mutual fund," Lee said. "And how Lonnie has been trying to persuade you to turn your VA pension over to him, claiming he can double your money. That sent up red flags in my mind. It sounded an awful lot like some kind of Ponzi scheme. If that's what it was, then he needed more and more money to keep his schemes going."

"Robbing Peter to pay Paul," Buddy said.

Their conversation was interrupted by the sound of helicopters flying in their direction. They watched as two military choppers flew in a straight path overhead, headed west. Lee looked at her watch.

"Time for us to move," she said.

"Where are we going?"

"I want you to go to Helen's Diner and the courthouse and make sure people know that the FBI and federal marshals have taken control of the research facility at University farms. Let it be known that the sheriff got a call directly from the FBI informing him. I want you to make sure it's the talk of the county. Have somebody call the radio station and alert them."

"How about that cute little reporter?" Buddy wiggled his eyebrows.

"You get the *Bartram Echo* involved. I'll contact Katie Horne," Lee said. "I'll tell her Buddy Ruff is the key contact in Bartram County."

"Now don't go embarrassing me, Lee."

Lee went back to her office while Buddy went about his public awareness campaign. She had another task that needed to be handled. She called Gerald Campbell, the Agri-Sciences department head, on the phone.

"I have linked the death of the Morris family back to its source at the University farm, Gerald."

"I resent your continuing efforts to hang this epidemic in the county on the door of the University," Campbell sputtered on the other end of the phone line.

"We have the bags of seed corn, Gerald, and we have eyewitness testimony that the fatal corn came from the University farm. I'm waiting on CDC analysis to confirm that it was *Yersinia pestis*. I'm not blaming the department or the University, I'm just pursuing the truth."

"The truth?" Campbell said sarcastically.

"I called to ask for your help. You have an obligation to do the right thing."

"The right thing from your perspective, I suppose," Campbell spat back.

"I want full disclosure on this, Gerald, and I want it by tomorrow. I'm not screwing around. My people are dying out here and you have to own up to the role the Agri-Sciences department played in it. I'll be completely fair about it, but you will come clean or I'll have your ass. And I don't mean next week."

"File an open records request."

"No bureaucratic bullshit, Gerald. Be a hero or be a villain. I'm coming tomorrow morning at ten o'clock to pick up all documents and records on the research at the University farm and the connection with the National Research Laboratories at Oak Ridge. And I want a letter from you stating the Department's involvement. You better have it ready when I get there."

Lee slammed the receiver down on the phone. The confrontation left her upset. She had said a particularly nasty explicative somewhere upwards of a dozen times when the telephone rang about twenty minutes later. It was Clifton Caldwell, president of Carters Mill University.

"I spoke with Dr. Campbell," he said. "He was somewhat overwrought. Judging from what I understood from the conversation I wonder if it might be productive if you and I were to meet?"

"I think that's a fine idea," Lee said.

"I can come to your office in, say, about thirty minutes?"

Lee phoned county attorney Gary Goodman and asked him to join her for the meeting. When Gary arrived, Lee briefed him on the nature of the coming meeting with president Caldwell.

"What do you want my role to be?" Gary asked.

"Look as serious and intimidating as you can."

There was really no time to plan a strategy. Caldwell's limousine arrived within minutes after Gary Goodman. Caldwell was a tall, well-groomed, conservatively dressed man with a definite presidential air about him. His introduction of himself and his administrative assistant was polite and respectful.

"After the news of the serious situation in Bartram County came to my attention," he said, "I had my staff prepare a briefing for me on the ways in which the University might be able to use its considerable resources to provide aid and assistance to the good citizens of this county. The University understandably has close economic ties with Bartram County. Many of our faculty and staff are residents of Bartram County, and we have a long history of mutual support and cooperation through our research and service programs. I've come here to ask you what you think the University might be able to do in terms of resources to be a good and responsive neighbor and partner in this current crisis."

His tone and sincerity were almost reassuring. He didn't get to be president of a major university by being a klutz.

"President Caldwell, Luther Morris, a poor hard working but illiterate man was performing services at the University farms when he came in contact with a fatally poisonous substance that subsequently killed him, his wife, his elderly mother and his five-year-old daughter. That substance was part of a research experiment sponsored by the National Research Laboratories at Oak Ridge and performed under the direction of the University."

"It was a terribly unfortunate accident," Caldwell said. "And we all grieve for the family and for the community. It's the kind of thing that no one could anticipate but everyone takes steps to avoid."

"The University research personnel were well acquainted with the dangerous nature of the materials. There are standard safe procedures for handling and disposing of those materials. Those procedures were not followed. The deaths of the Morris family were the result of an act of negligence."

Caldwell moved to respond, but Lee stopped him.

"I am not speculating. I have deathbed testimony from one of the key researchers at the national lab. I have all of Dr. Hamrick's files and notes on the research. I have Dr. Hamrick's detailed research journal. I have correspondence from him warning NRL and officials at CMU of the dangerous and reckless course they were pursuing. As of right now, the FBI and other federal personnel are at the University farm and are prepared to seize all records there unless they are turned over voluntarily. If they are forced to that action, all University records relating to its involvement with NRL will follow."

Caldwell's exterior appeared unshaken. His assistant was beginning to look a little panicky.

"What would you suggest to be an appropriate course of action?" Caldwell said.

"Luther and his family died as a result of an accident during the course of his service to the University. An accident that it was the University's responsibility to prevent. His only surviving baby daughter is entitled to compensation for the loss of her father, her mother, her sister and her grandmother. I would suggest that, as a minimum, the University has the moral obligation to set aside the resources to see that baby Elizabeth Morris will be cared for and educated at the same level you would provide for your own children. I suggest an investment trust fund be set up with an initial investment of one million dollars to provide for Elizabeth Morris in her old age, or at such time as she might become unable to care for herself and be in need of the support that a family would be able to provide her were they alive to do it."

Caldwell was quiet for several moments.

"That's a considerable sum of money," he said. "You have been a faculty member yourself, and perhaps might be again. You are aware of the restrictions under which we operate."

"I accepted your offer to help as coming from a man of honor," Lee said. "I know very well the way the University operates. Every year there are over a hundred fully funded positions within the University that go unfilled. The money budgeted for those vacant positions is redirected and spent wherever the University decides it needs to be spent. The salary from just one of those positions invested and multiplied could provide for baby Elizabeth's continuing needs until she is an adult, including funding of her college education.

"May I suggest that Gerald Campbell is in large part responsible for putting the University in this difficult situation. If his position were vacant and were to be held vacant for just one year, that one position, including benefits, would provide an unspent item in the University budget of more than $300,000. Put just one other vacant associate professor position with it, like the one now held by Jack Sheridan, and you have $500,000 in unspent dollars. Hold the positions unfilled for just two years and you have a budget surplus of one million dollars. We know from published figures that the University Foundation earns regular annual returns of over 17% on its investments. That amount of money put in trust for baby Elizabeth and earning that rate of interest would cast a very positive light on the University as a responsible neighbor. Doesn't that sound reasonable to you?"

President Caldwell smiled and looked very appreciatively into Lee's eyes.

"I had something very much like that in mind," he said. "I'll personally oversee the matter."

He got up to leave and shook hands with Lee and Gary Goodman. "I look forward to many years of continued friendship and cooperation between the University and Bartram County." He turned just before he walked through the door and said, "The community should be very proud of you."

When they had left, Gary Goodman said, "Lee, I'm undecided whether I just witnessed a negotiated settlement or an extortion."

"It was just good neighbors talking over the back fence," she said. "Just discussing the best way to control some worms in the vegetable garden."

She hadn't told the whole truth to president Caldwell about Hamrick's journal, or what the FBI was really doing at the University farms, or about which records she had in her possession and which she didn't, but it was close enough for government work. It was all negotiating tactics to reach an agreement.

The next phase of her strategy to actually get her hands on Hamrick's journal would involve some slight of hand. Without that journal her bluff could be called. But with it in a safe place, the wolves would be held at bay.

Chapter 29
Beating the Bushes

KATIE HORNE WAS thrilled to get the big scoop before any of the other reporters in town. She promised to be on site within the hour. Katie was a good kid but she wasn't CNN. Lee put in a call to the AP office in Knoxville to put out the alert to the news community about the federal takeover of the University farm. That should guarantee credibility to the plan.

She called Buddy and arranged to pick him up.

"Where are we going now?" he asked when he got in the Land Cruiser.

"We're going to rescue Hamrick's research journal."

Lee drove to Jack Sheridan's apartment. Jack was waiting inside for them.

"The helicopters and troops are on the ground at the University farm now," Jack said.

Jack took a small round black dot less than the diameter of a dime and taped it under the collar of Lee's khaki shirt, then picked up what looked like a cell phone.

"That little device will transmit a voice signal up to about three-quarters of a mile to this receiver," he said. "And GPS can locate it just about anywhere. If we should get out of touch, we can always find you."

"That's some little trick," Buddy said.

"If you get Durbin to bite," Jack said, "We'll be listening and monitoring your location. Major Cates has a receiver just like this."

"Cates?" Buddy said.

"He and his men are in place. They'll move in as soon as

we have the cover of darkness."

"Ain't that kind of like being saved by the devil?" Buddy said.

"He's a trained military leader," Jack said. "When you're threatened with deadly force you'll be glad to have him standing between you and danger."

"We've had enough deadlies around here lately to last me a lifetime. I put in my time dealing with deadly force a long time ago. I want all this craziness to be over with so I can talk to some normal people again. This ain't no damn war zone. People live mostly normal lives here. I don't need help from somebody who has to be told whether I'm the friend or the enemy."

"We've met Major Cates face to face already," Lee said. "Buddy didn't much like looking down Cates' gun barrel, and I can't say I did either."

"He's a pompous son of a bitch who shouldn't be allowed to handle a loaded gun," Buddy said. "He's liable to hurt somebody."

Jack looked at a loss for words. He just shrugged. "If everything goes well, he and his troops will be out of here tonight."

"It can't be soon enough to suit me," Buddy said.

"You're not sympathetic to Durbin, are you?" Jack asked.

"Hell no. I'm not sympathetic to him or Cates. They're two different versions of the same military pretend game. Ray Durbin is the amateur version and Cates is the pro version. They're both dangerous. I got drafted into that nonsense already and got my ass shot off. And I got out lucky.

Everybody else I knew got killed or hurt a lot worse than me. And now here I am just trying to grow old and be happy and they bring it here to the last place on earth I would ever expect it. This ain't Korea, or Vietnam, or Northern Ireland, or the Middle East, or Yugoslavia. This is Bartram County, Tennessee, USA. This is where peaceful, God-fearing good folks live. I wouldn't care if Cates and his men and Ray Durbin and his buddies got together on some make-believe battlefield in a desert somewhere and killed each other, but I don't want any of them here."

Buddy had worked himself into such a state of agitation by the time he quit talking that his face was red and he was breathing hard. He looked exasperated for a moment, shook his head once, opened the door and went outside.

"What was that all about?" Jack asked.

"Buddy is pushed right to the edge of a post traumatic episode by all that's going on. Every time the military helicopters get close it seems to set him off. It's not his fault."

"Do you think you can trust him? If things go according to plan this should be a routine apprehension. But if something should go wrong, things could get a little delicate. Everyone has to be thinking straight and keep a cool head. I know you will, but I don't know about Buddy."

"Listen, Jack. If everyone were thinking straight, we wouldn't be here in this situation now. I trust Buddy with my life. He's earned that trust."

"But what about the things he was saying?"

"He's angry. He has wounds in him that have never healed, but that doesn't make him some kind of reject. It makes him an honorable man."

"I'm only concerned about his judgment in a potentially

dangerous situation."

"If we get in a dangerous situation, I would have more confidence in Buddy than in you and Cates put together."

As soon as the words were out of her mouth Lee was sorry she had said them because she had no desire to hurt Jack. But she realized almost as quickly that they were the truth and she had to rely on the truth to guide her decisions.

"Damn," Jack said, "You have more *esprit de corps* than the Marines."

"Yes. Yes, I do."

Lee went out to the Land Cruiser where Buddy was sitting waiting for her. She got in and closed the door but did not start the engine. Buddy was fidgeting nervously with his hands.

"Do you have to have Hamrick's journal, Lee? Is it really that important? Couldn't we just let Jack and Cates round up Durbin and his militia?"

"We need that journal, Buddy. We need to make sure this whole thing is done properly."

"I don't understand," Buddy said, looking at Lee.

"Hamrick wrote everything of importance relating to his work in that journal. He would have recorded in it if he was working with DNPT and what he was doing with it just before he became ill. Without that evidence we will never know whether he died by accident of his own hand or if he died at the hands of someone else."

"Why are you telling me this?"

"Because you need to know the importance of getting the journal back. I know you have feelings for Barbara Hamrick. She and her son's financial future depend on the determination of exactly how Hamrick died. You and I need to keep our hands in it to be sure the right determination is made. Hamrick told Ray Durbin and others that NRL and CMU stole his patents worth millions of dollars. Just suppose he was right and his journal contains proof of that claim. It could mean the difference between day and night for Barbara and her son."

"Why do you want it back?" Buddy asked.

"I want to see justice done."

Buddy's breathing had slowed and calmed. He had quit fidgeting.

"Are you trying to shame me into doing this?" he said.

Lee was sure she detected a smile half-hidden behind Buddy's hand.

"No, I'm just telling you why I'm doing it, trying to get you to help me. I told you before, I can't do it alone."

"I'm sure you could part the Red Sea if you set your mind to it, or talk God into doing it for you. OK, what do you want me to do?"

Lee told Buddy about deputy Faust being involved with Durbin's militia group, and about her plan to use Faust as a messenger.

"You just play along and back me up," she said. "And remember, it has to be convincing."

She drove the two of them to the sheriff's office where they found deputy Faust on duty with the sheriff as planned. The sheriff did his part right on cue.

"Lee," he said, "what in the hell's going on out at the University farm? Nobody will tell me anything and my phone is ringing off the hook from reporters calling."

"That's what I've come to tell you, Sheriff. The FBI is out there with Major Cates and his men, and they're stripping the place clean of any evidence of what the feds have been up to out there. It's all related to this outbreak of deaths we're having in the county."

"What's the University farms got to do with it?" The sheriff asked.

"They've got everything to do with it. You know I just got back from a trip to Los Verdes, New Mexico. I went out there to interview Dr. Edward Wilkinson, who the feds are holding supposedly on a federal conspiracy charge. With the help of a private investigator I found Wilkinson being held in a military hospital. When I finally got to him he was dying of the same thing that killed the Morris family and all the other folks in Bartram County over the past month."

"I thought that was all some kind of agricultural pesticide," the sheriff said.

"No, that's not the cause. Dr. Wilkinson worked with Dr. Hamrick at the National Research Labs at Oak Ridge and later at Desert Flats on research with genetically modified bacteria for use with agricultural crops. Wilkinson had firsthand knowledge as a researcher on the project, and so did Dr. Hamrick. Dr. Wilkinson died before my eyes during my interview with him. I know he was telling the truth."

"What did he say is going on?" Deputy Faust asked.

"Wilkinson said NRL has been working for several years on a way to destroy the mouse and rat population that eats the seed grains for crops like corn and oats. He said what NRL is testing at the University farm are seeds that are coated with a bacterium that lives in the guts of mice and rats. The bacterium is normally harmless to rodents and to humans and other animals, but NRL genetically modified it to be deadly to rats and mice. What they did not realize before they field tested it is that when the modified bacteria come in contact with the common pesticide Parathion, the Parathion changes the bacteria in such a way that they are deadly not only to rats and mice but to just about any warm blooded creature that comes in contact with it. It's the same bacteria that causes the plague in humans, only it's genetically mutated and unstoppable by any known treatments. Contact with it means death within twenty-four to thirty-six hours."

"God all mighty," the sheriff said. "What are the feds doing about it?"

"They're trying to wipe their hands clean of it. They took every scrap of evidence they could find from Hamrick's place, and now they're out at the University farm doing the same thing. But there's one thing they need that they have not been able to find, and that's Hamrick's personal research journal. Wilkinson told me Hamrick kept details of everything they knew in that journal in a kind of code that he told me how to decipher. That journal is the only hope we have for saving ourselves and letting the rest of the country know what is happening to us here. The FBI has already been to my office and my house searching for it. They have my phones tapped and they've had an FBI agent on my tail for weeks."

"Is that Jack Sheridan?"

Lee looked hurt, as if she might cry.

"Yes, it is," she said.

"What do you want me to do?" The sheriff asked.

"I'm going back to Hamrick's house. Wilkinson told me Hamrick kept his valuables in a safe hidden under the fireplace hearth. I think the journal may still be there. I want you to keep Jack Sheridan off my trail long enough for me to get there and get the journal."

"What do you want me to do with Sheridan?"

"Lock him up. Do whatever you have to do. Then send someone out to the University farm and let it slip to the feds that I said I know where the journal is and I'm going back to Hamrick's office on campus to get it. That'll keep them away from Hamrick's house long enough for me to get the journal."

"All right. Can you get Sheridan over here?"

Lee punched Jack's number into her phone.

"Jack, it's Lee. I'm at the sheriff's office. Can you come over here at once? There's something here that you will want to handle. Please hurry."

Preparations were made to take Jack into custody. Deputies Faust and Longtree waited just inside near the door.

"Do you want an escort to Hamrick's place?" The sheriff asked.

"No. I want no attention whatsoever drawn to me. Buddy and I will do what needs to be done."

Within five minutes Jack walked through the front door of the sheriff's office. Before he had a chance to say anything, Billy had handcuffs on him.

"Sheriff," Lee said, "I want you to lock this man up on suspicion of the murder of Alexander Hamrick."

"This is crazy, Lee," Jack said. "What are you trying to pull?"

"His fingerprints were found all over Hamrick's house, yet he denies any knowledge of Hamrick prior to his death."

"I explained that to you," Jack protested.

"I found Hamrick's briefcase in his office on campus. He has been interfering with my investigation, lying to me in an attempt to hamper my investigation, and withholding evidence from me."

"Sheriff, you know who I am," Jack said, his face red with anger.

"No, I don't know who you are, Mr. Sheridan. You are a stranger to this county. I do know Dr. Turner and her authority in the Hamrick investigation. I am placing you under arrest."

Despite Jack's protests and threats, they locked him in a cell and closed the door to the cell block.

"Faust," the sheriff said, "You go on out to the University farm and tell the feds the story that Lee is on her way to Hamrick's office on campus to get the journal."

Deputy Faust practically jumped at the opportunity.

"Yes, sir," he said, "I'll be glad to do it."

"Give her plenty of time to get where she's going," Sheriff Eberhard said.

Deputy Faust headed west toward the University farm. Lee and Buddy headed south toward Hamrick's house and the trap laid for Ray Durbin.

"I didn't know you were such an actress," Buddy said.

"Who was acting? I believed at least half of what I said."

"Which half was that?"

"Let's hope deputy Faust couldn't tell either."

"How long are we going to wait for Ray Durbin to show up with the journal?"

Lee reached under the flap of her shirt and pulled the tiny transmitter loose. She pulled the Land Cruiser to a stop on side of the road, got out and taped the transmitter to the back of a road sign and got back in the truck.

"Jesus, Lee. What are you doing?"

"I'm changing the plan." Lee pulled back onto the roadway and accelerated rapidly.

"Why did you leave the bug back there? What if we need help?"

"I left it there because I don't want the feds to know where we are."

"Why not?"

"Think about it. There we are at Hamrick's surrounded by twenty or so armed federal troops led by Major Cates. If Durbin were to show up with that journal, who do you think would walk away with it?"

"Not us, I guess."

"You bet, not us. Cates would have the journal and we would never see it again, just like the rest of the evidence they took from Hamrick's place. Has it bothered you that the FBI and NRL have been completely unwilling to share the evidence from Hamrick's house and office, but at the same time we had unrestricted access to the actual research going on at the University farm? In fact, we have samples of their experimental grain being analyzed by the CDC, without a word of complaint from NRL. But I lay out this elaborate plan to get the journal, and the feds are suddenly ready and willing to send in more federal troops than this county has seen since the Civil War."

"I don't get it," Buddy said.

"They are not concerned that we would find out what they've been doing at the University farm. What they really wanted all along was Hamrick's records because they know his records could prove his claim that their discoveries and products are the rightful property of Alexander Hamrick. They also know that Durbin doesn't have the journal in his possession or they would have seized it already."

"Well, I'll be damned. If Ray Durbin doesn't have the journal, where is it? I know you just made up that story about the safe underneath his fireplace hearth."

"Carters Mill University has it. But they don't know they have it."

"I'm glad you're driving, Lee, because I'm lost."

"Judy Vining said Hamrick always carried his journal in his old leather briefcase, and she had seen the briefcase recently in his office. I found that briefcase in Jack Sheridan's office, but the journal had been removed. Jack doesn't have the journal. As far as we know, Ray Durbin never went to Hamrick's office on campus, so what happened to the journal?"

"It beats the hell out of me. What happened to it?"

"I'm betting Hamrick put his most precious document in the hallowed place he stored all the important documents of his long academic career. He deposited it in the archives of the University library where it would be preserved and cared for for decades, perhaps centuries to come."

"Well, naturally, no one would ever think to look in the library. How silly a thought," Buddy said. "Are you absolutely certain Ray Durbin doesn't have it?"

"Ray Durbin would have called me as soon as the Morris family members died if he had it. There would be no reason for him to sit on it. He believes there is a conspiracy. From his viewpoint, the longer he waits, the greater the risk the conspirators will find a way to destroy all the evidence before he can unmask them. No, I don't believe Ray Durbin has anything of substance. He only has odds and ends of loosely related information he's collected to feed his conspiracy theories and his fears."

"So, what is our plan now? It's not going to take long for Jack and Cates to figure out you're not going to show up at Hamrick's house."

"I'm hoping they'll take the bait from Deputy Faust and go looking for me on campus. I want them to think I have the journal so they'll focus on getting it from me and not think of other alternatives."

"The old harry hand trick. So how do we make them think you have it?"

"We're going to leave a false trail."

Lee drove to her office where she made copies of a number of documents and papers relating to the Hamrick investigation and placed them in an envelope along with a copy of one of her favorite mystery novels from her bookshelf. She showed the book to Buddy.

"Appropriate title, don't you think?"

"Questionable Remains?"

"Fits the situation and the evidence bag perfectly. Now we need a copy of a journal." She slipped a copy of the *Journal of Forensic Science* in the envelope and sealed the envelope and its contents inside the evidence bag and wrote a phony case number on the outside.

"I think I owe the sheriff an explanation. He put himself on the line for me."

The look on the sheriff's face when Lee and Buddy walked into his office was one of surprise and confusion. Lee told him how it had been necessary to mislead the FBI in order to keep Hamrick's journal in local custody. She told him the journal was in a safe place and she gave him the evidence bag she had prepared. She didn't tell him what was in the envelope, or more correctly, what wasn't in it.

"I want this logged in, just as you would any evidence from an ongoing investigation. I don't want the FBI or anyone else to say you have concealed evidence," Lee said. "But I would ask that you lock it in your safe where no one but you can get to it."

"Then I guess it's best I don't ask you what's in the evidence bag," the sheriff said. He made the entry on the evidence log, opened his safe, deposited the bag and locked the safe back.

"You have every right to be angry with me for misleading you," she told him. "I just did what I thought I had to do to protect the case and to protect you from charges of conspiracy to obstruct."

"I wouldn't be angry with you, Lee. I've seen you work. I don't question your actions. You've never questioned mine."

Lee took the Glock 9mm from her belt and handed it to the sheriff.

"I don't think I'll be needing this."

"You're going to need it when a certain FBI agent finds out what you've been up to," Buddy said.

"I hope they've all learned a little respect," the sheriff said. "Do you think we're any closer now to the end of this investigation, Lee?"

"Yes, I do. When all the lab results come in and we get Lonnie Chapman into custody I think we'll have all the parts of the puzzle. What is the status of his apprehension?"

"I went to pick him up today but his secretary says he

left for Knoxville this morning and isn't expected back until sometime this evening. All the surrounding counties and the state patrol have lookouts for him. I've got somebody watching his house. He doesn't have any reason to suspect we're looking for him. His car is easy to spot. We'll get him when he gets back here, if not before."

That was when they heard Billy radio in from Hamrick's that a firefight had broken out between Cates' forces and Ray Durbin's militia.

"It was all over in a minute," Billy said, his voice reflecting a flow of adrenalin.

"You need ambulance?" The sheriff radioed back.

"Negative. The helicopters are transporting the wounded."

"Who got hurt?"

"Ray Durbin and a couple of the other militia. One of Cates' men got hit in the leg. Nothing critical that I can see."

"10-4. Stay there. I'll be there in a minute."

"I guess your plan worked better than you thought, Lee," the sheriff said. "The feds may never know the truth. I better get on down there."

While the sheriff called for someone to man the dispatch phone, Buddy whispered to Lee.

"Do you think maybe Durbin had the journal after all?"

"I don't know," was all Lee could say truthfully. "Why don't you go with the sheriff and find out what happened? Call me later when you know something."

Lee left Buddy and the sheriff preparing to go to Hamrick's and she headed home. She had been tempted to go with them but this was one instance where she thought she should leave well enough alone.

Driving back along the highway through town she noticed a car parked just off the main street alongside Chapman Insurance. It wasn't Lonnie's car. It was an old automobile she had the uneasy feeling she had seen somewhere before. She drove her vehicle around the block and pulled down the side street.

It was the old chipped and faded blue and gray station wagon she had seen at Myra Johnson's house. There was no one inside the vehicle. It hadn't been sitting there long because there was a small mist of steam rising from the front of the car.

Lee parked her Land Cruiser and turned off the lights. She thought at first it must be Myra Johnson who had driven to the insurance office. Mr. Duncan was too feeble to be out by himself this far from home this late at night. She couldn't call the sheriff. He was on his way to important business at Hamrick's. She didn't want to call the sheriff anyway and cause a problem for Myra or Mr. Duncan if there was a simple explanation. She got out of her vehicle and walked around to the front door of the office.

The front of the building was illuminated by a nearby street light but the office inside was pitch black. She took a couple of steps closer and tapped on the glass pane of the wooden door. There was no response from inside. She looked around to see if anyone was standing in the shadows along the street. She saw no one.

"Hello," she said. "This is Dr. Turner from the coroner's office. Is anyone inside?"

There was no response. She tried the door knob gently. It turned but the door was locked.

She decided that she was too suspicious. The car had steam coming from under the hood. It had probably overheated and been parked there hours ago. She walked back to her vehicle and was about to get in, but she decided to check the back of the building.

There was light from a single lightbulb in back. In that dim shadowed light she could see a crack in the wood frame of the back door. Someone was inside. She was fairly certain she knew who and why. She knocked on the door and called out.

"Mr. Duncan, this is Lee Turner. I know you're inside. I'm coming in to talk with you. I mean you no harm. I'm alone and unarmed."

She pushed the door firmly and it slide open, dragging on the broken door jam.

She continued to talk as she walked through the dark back room of the office, repeating the same message, hoping the person she was talking to was rational enough not to kill her.

"I wish you hadn't come here," the tired, sad old man's voice said from the dark.

"Mr. Duncan, you don't need to do this. We already have the arrest warrants for Lonnie Chapman. He'll be in jail before morning. We have all the evidence we need to convict him. He'll go to the electric chair. Please don't put yourself in danger by being here. It's all going to be over very soon."

The raspy voice came from the side of the room where Lee remembered that a leather chair sat.

"If he goes to court I won't live long enough to see justice done. It'll drag on for ten or fifteen years. I'll die not knowing for certain if he was electrocuted or if his lawyers found some way to get him off."

"He won't get off, Mr. Duncan. I promise you he won't."

"I know you mean to do good, child," he said. "But he

took my life from me already. Myra told me about the chocolate box. I knew right then what he did."

"It was your insurance, wasn't it?" Lee said. "He did it to other people. He thought he was being smart, but we found a trail that leads right to him. Please, let the sheriff and the judge handle him."

"You think you have proof that will hold up in court. I've been around too many years to believe in true justice unless I see it come to pass with my own eyes. There are always loopholes for the devil to pass through. I know I'm about to go against God's word. But God didn't save my grandchildren from the devil. Now, the last thing in this world I am able to do is sit here in this chair in the dark and wait. If God chooses to let the devil's disciple walk through that door, then my hand and my eyes will see that justice is served. My soul may burn in hell for it, but my heart will not ache as bad as it does now."

"You know that when I leave here I'll have to try and prevent this from happening."

"If what you told me is true, there won't be anything to prevent. I'll still be sitting here when the sun comes up in the morning and Lonnie Chapman will be behind bars in the county jail. If you believe what you told me, leave me alone here for God and the devil to deal with. I mean harm to no one but Lonnie Chapman."

He had her on logic. She didn't even know if he was armed. She didn't know if he would last until morning. By then Lonnie should be under arrest and behind bars.

"All right. I know you have been hurt more than any person should ever be hurt. I know you are suffering. I'm going to leave you alone and go on home. I hope you can find peace."

"God bless you, child."

Lee walked out the back door the way she had come in and left the dying old man sitting in the dark. She drove onto Main Street and headed toward the sheriff's office, but she turned her vehicle around and drove home. It was up to the authorities to take care of Lonnie Chapman. Mr. Duncan was right. God and the devil would have to deal with him.

Chapter 30
Justice and the Law

THERE WERE MANY suspects in the death of Lonnie Chapman but no arrest. His body was found at 7:45 A.M. when his secretary came to open the office. He lay inside his trophy case, a shotgun blast through his heart. He had died instantly, but not before he knew why.

Lee told herself she had done the right thing that night. She believed she had. She also told herself that when all the evidence was in, if Lonnie Chapman was not clearly implicated in the many murders in the county, she would go to the sheriff with what she knew about Mr. Duncan's whereabouts that night. But it never came to that.

TBI analysis of the chocolate candies in Lonnie's cabinet tested positive for DNPT. A search of his house turned up the vial he took from Hamrick's laboratory. When the audit of his business and personal records was complete it was found that Lonnie Chapman had defrauded hundreds of his customers over a period of more than ten years.

FBI investigation of the Millennium Viatical company's connections to Bartram County revealed that the company was originally incorporated by a group of investors who were all elderly clients of Chapman Insurance who were un- aware that they were investors. Millennium Viatical was in fact a business owned and run by Lonnie Chapman.

Ten days after the death of Lonnie Chapman, Lee, Bud- dy and Sheriff Eberhard sat down to breakfast for the last time with Jack Sheridan. Jack was explaining how Lonnie had operated his fraudulent business.

"Chapman sold shares in Millennium Viatical to get enough operating capital in the beginning to purchase a group of life insurance policies from some of the elderly clients of Chapman Insurance."

"So Lonnie himself was responsible for the flyers showing up from Millennium Viatical in mailboxes all over the county," the sheriff said.

"Yes," Jack said. "Millennium Viatical was his left hand and Chapman Insurance was his right hand. He took operating capital from Millennium Viatical and bought life insurance policies of long-time policyholders of Chapman Insurance for a fraction of the value of the policies. The sales were fraudulent from the beginning. Most of the policyholders knew nothing about the sale of their policies. Lonnie took the money from the sale of the policies and deposited it to various of his accounts. Then Millennium Viatical sold the discounted insurance policies in the investment market so that their ownership transferred to some third party. If the sale went quickly, Millennium Viatical quickly regained the money it had used to purchase the policy."

"What happened when someone died and their life insurance suddenly didn't pay off?" Buddy asked.

"That's where the real juggling came in," Jack said. "Lonnie used a fraudulent paper trail to cover up what had really happened. If relatives of the deceased policyholder didn't know anything about the life insurance policy, Lonnie would just sit tight and say nothing. On some policies he never had to make a payout. On others he forged papers to show that the elderly policyholder had borrowed against their life insurance many years before and never paid back the loan, thus making the final payoff value of the insurance a very small fraction of what the heirs expected. He was smart enough to arrange for some fraction of the value of the policy to be paid in order to support the credibility of his story and partially placate the heirs."

"Everybody trusted and respected old man Chapman," Sheriff Eberhard said. "It's hard to understand how his son turned out so bad."

"Fraud is almost always based on trust," Jack said. "The policyholders' trust of Lonnie's father made it possible for Lonnie to carry out his scheme. Lonnie looked and talked and acted like a clean cut, honest, responsible business man. He had an innocent boyish manner about him. I'm sure it was impossible without the most direct proof for almost anyone in the community to believe Lonnie could be a racketeer and a murderer."

"Nobody but Lee," Buddy said.

"I didn't want to see it either. That's why I didn't figure it out sooner. In fact, I was so blind to it that I almost became one of his victims."

"What happened to all the money he stole?" Buddy said.

"The auditors say over two million dollars of it was spent on his houses, his automobiles, his trips around the world, and his high priced lifestyle." Jack said. "The rest went to propping up his failing business and funding his investment schemes."

"Is there nothing that can be done to get some of that money back?" The sheriff asked.

"Gary Goodman is representing a group of defrauded customers to the state insurance commissioner," Lee said. "He thinks most of the sales of the insurance policies will be declared null and void because of Lonnie's intent to deceive and defraud his clients. If Gary is successful, some of the victims' families may get the insurance money that is right-fully theirs."

"As in all cases where fraud has been perpetrated over a long period of time," Jack said, "some of the victims will be able to recover their loss. Others will never get what was stolen from them. Most of the money is simply gone."

"What happened that made Lonnie turn to murder?" Buddy asked. "It looks like after all those years of theft and fraud he might have just kept doing what he was doing."

"Just as Lee suspected. He was constantly shifting money," Jack said, "and always in need of larger sums of cash. He got to playing with larger amounts of money than he could juggle. When Hamrick walked into Lonnie's office asking to borrow money against his million dollar life insurance policy, the temptation to Lonnie was too great. Like all schemers and con artists, Lonnie was always looking for that one big deal that would get his creditors off his back and set everything straight for him."

"In Bartram County you don't get much bigger than a million dollar insurance policy," the sheriff said.

"I'm sure Hamrick talked to Lonnie just as he talked to Ray Durbin," Jack said, "about what he claimed were his stolen patents and about the dangerous chemicals and such that he worked with. It didn't take much temptation for Lonnie to see a way to get a fast turnaround from Hamrick's life insurance."

"Why did he think he could get away with so many murders?" Sheriff Eberhard asked. "He had to know he would get caught sooner or later."

"He picked policyholders who were old and infirm

enough there would be no suspicion when they died sudden deaths," Lee said. "When ninety-year-olds like Mrs. Anderson, elderly patients in nursing homes, and policyholders with terminal illness like Mr. Duncan die there is usually no reason to suspect anything but a natural death. If it hadn't been for Edward Wilkinson, Lonnie's scheme might have gone on for a lot longer."

"When Wilkinson destroyed the body in acid," Jack said, "Lee couldn't make a positive identification, and Hamrick's life insurance company refused to pay. That left Lonnie needing a quick three-quarters of a million dollars."

"So he went looking for other quick victims." Buddy shook his head. "It's still hard to believe he was so cold blooded."

"He started with Mrs. Jamie Anderson," Lee said. "The ninety-year-old retired school teacher had two life insurance policies paid in full and drawing interest for over thirty years. She was very vulnerable. The poison killed her so quickly that no visible symptoms developed. Her doctor missed it and I missed it."

"There's no way you could have known or suspected," Jack said.

"And he picked out Mr. Duncan," Lee said. "A man with terminal cancer who told no one his business, not even his daughter. No one would have suspected any foul play in his death either. But that's the second major misstep in his dirty plan. He broke the rule you told me, Buddy."

"What rule did I tell you?" Buddy said.

"You've got to be real careful when you put poison out because you never know what's liable to get into it."

"So, he left it for the old man, but the children got into it."

"The children got into it," Lee said. "The same thing happened with Judy Vining. She accidentally got into some of the poisoned candy left for Hamrick. Suddenly we had four suspicious deaths on our hands—the last thing Lonnie Chapman wanted. Things went from bad to worse but he didn't give up on collecting Hamrick's insurance. Mr. Terry refused to certify Hamrick's death without a means of identification of the body, and he pulled me off the case. So Lonnie eliminated Mr. Terry, betting on me to come up with a way to make the identification."

"When the Morris deaths happened," Jack said, "Lonnie took advantage of the confusion they created and struck for his really big kill at Rolling Hills nursing home. Among the nine deaths there, five were clients of Chapman Insurance whose policies Lonnie had sold to Millennium Viatical. The other four were innocent casualties like the children."

"All those old folks, and those poor children," Buddy said.

"It seems like a terrible coincidence that Luther Morris stumbled on to that poisoned corn right in the middle of the murder spree by Lonnie Chapman," the sheriff said.

"It wasn't a coincidence," Lee said. "It seems that way when we look at it from Lonnie's point of view. But you have to remember, everything leads back to Hamrick. Hamrick needed money for his research business and went to Lonnie, looking to borrow against his million dollar insurance policy. Hamrick had the DNPT in his lab and without knowing the consequences of his words, he told Lonnie how deadly it was. Without realizing it, Hamrick provided the parts Lonnie needed to put together his murder scheme."

"I still don't see how Luther finding the poisoned seed was anything but a coincidence." Buddy said.

"Hamrick, more than anyone else, was responsible for the research that was being field tested at the University farm," Lee said. "It was his work that resulted in the development of the poisoned seeds that Luther found. It was Hamrick's warnings that stopped the field test. Because the test was stopped early, there were bags of treated seeds left, which Luther Morris found and took home with him. Hamrick was back here in Bartram County because he wanted to monitor NRL's field tests of spore-producing bacteria at the farm. That's what his collecting of dead animals was about. He was looking for tell-tale spores inside the animals that would be produced if they consumed the experimental seeds."

"The old man had no idea what he was setting in motion," Sheriff Eberhard said.

"No, he didn't," Lee said. "Even Ray Durbin and the Sons of Freedom were put in motion by Hamrick. None of it was intentional by Hamrick, but he was the center of influence around which all of it revolved."

"When you think about it, Hamrick was a very influential man, in a perverse sort of way," the sheriff said.

"In many respects," Lee said, "Hamrick was a great man. He discovered things, he invented things, he built a research empire, he made a lot of people a lot of money, and he left a legacy."

"All that, and for him to die like that, and the only thing most people will remember about him is that he was Roadkill Man," Buddy said.

"He outlived his reputation, I guess," the sheriff said.

"It's more that he had it stolen from him," Lee said. "Dr. Hamrick was the victim of another kind of fraud. He was betrayed by time and age and defrauded by younger men who took from him by force what they themselves lacked the knowledge and the intellect to produce."

"Damn, Lee," Buddy said, "You're going to have to talk at a level I can understand." He winked at her. "But listen, I still don't understand how in the hell those damn roaches tie into all this."

"At this point, no one does," said Lee. "We don't know what caused the surge in the roach population or why it happened in the two places it did."

"It's got to be more than a coincidence, with everything else that's been going on," Buddy said. "What's that I remember you said about a vector?"

"Yes, you're right," Lee said. "The substances being tested at the University farms had some harmful side effect consequences that were never envisioned by the scientists who developed them. It may be a long time before we know the full extent of those consequences and where they will lead. History is full of this kind of thing."

"Yeah," said the sheriff. "Experiments gone wrong . . . the Frankenstein effect."

Everyone laughed again. Buddy looked at the sheriff and chuckled. "I never knew you were such a film buff," he said. "First it was Natasha Romanoff, and now it's Frankenstein."

Lee continued, "We don't yet know if some predator of the cockroach was changed or killed in those locations, or if the vitality of the roaches was somehow increased. It may come down to a simple genetic alteration derived from the altered *Yersinia pestis*. One roach outbreak was on campus, and we know Hamrick and Judy Vining worked on campus and Judy lived in a dorm. And we know that many CMU faculty and students frequent the Blue Eagle. It's possible that it's something as simple as a DNA alteration being carried from campus to the Blue Eagle on people's shoes. Who knows at this point? If the ecology people on campus dig long enough and hard enough, perhaps they can discover the mechanism that links all the locations."

"What's going to happen about Ray Durbin's militia, Jack?" The sheriff asked.

"They're facing federal charges for possession of illegal firearms, conspiracy, attempted murder, and assault upon federal officers."

"Did you ever find Hamrick's research journal?" The sheriff asked.

"No. Durbin's story is he never had the journal. He claims he and his militia were coming to Hamrick's house to offer protection to Lee."

"Protection from who?" The sheriff asked.

"From the FBI and the federal security forces sent there to protect her," Jack said.

Buddy squirmed in his chair but Lee bumped him gently with her foot and shook her head.

"Well," the sheriff said, "I'd love to stay here and drink coffee and talk all day, but I'm sure there's something waiting for me at the office. So I'll just say goodbye to you, Jack. Let us know if we can be of help to you. And come back and see us."

"Thank you, sheriff. The same for me. It's been a pleasure."

Jack got up to leave also.

"Lee," he said, "Could I speak with you before I go?"

Buddy winked at her again and she kicked him under the table again.

"Ouch, Lee," Buddy said. "That's my bad ankle."

She followed Jack out to his Jeep in the parking lot.

"It's not going to be the same without you," he said. "I never intended for things to end this way."

"I guess that makes all of us," Lee said.

"You know," Jack said, "you could have told me more about what you were doing. I could have helped. It hurts me that you couldn't trust me, for whatever reasons."

"I think you're saying my lines, Jack. I didn't know who I could trust. Ray Durbin knew about Hamrick and NRL. He knew you had my phones tapped. I didn't know who was passing him that information. I had to keep my plans to myself."

"But you could have trusted me," Jack said.

"Tell me something, Jack. When you and Cates and his men were at Hamrick's that night waiting for Durbin and the militia, if I had been there with you, and Durbin had brought Hamrick's journal, who would have left there with it?"

Jack's face showed his answer even though he didn't speak it.

"I love you, Lee. I wish this hadn't happened to us. I wish we were both someone else, somewhere else."

"You can be anyone or anywhere you want to be. You came here and you found me here. If you love me, you have to love me as you found me, not someone else somewhere else. I think you love the thought of me, but not me. And I'm not trying to be hurtful, but I was in love with the thought of you, not you as I see you. You could be wonderful for someone, but it has to be the right match."

"I guess we just have two different lives and two different ways of seeing things," he said.

"Yes."

Buddy came up beside Lee as Jack's Jeep disappeared down the highway.

"You'll get over him in no time," Buddy said.

"I'm already over him."

"See? I was right. Did you get by the University library yesterday?"

"Yep."

"Well?"

"All of his personal journals for the past forty-seven years. Every scientific observation, experiment and discovery, down to the day and minute. Every major entry was notarized."

"What did it say?"

"It will take a firm of patent attorney's to figure that out, but I think the University will be willing to pursue the answers. Most of the work of his career was done here. If Hamrick is the rightful owner of valuable patented products and processes, the University stands to gain a standard seven percent share as their royalty."

"What are you going to do about the journals?"

"I'm going to tell president Caldwell where they are and what the University has at stake."

"Do you think you can trust him?"

"I think he's an honorable man. But as a precautionary

measure, in case he should be replaced by someone I feel less comfortable trusting, I took out a little insurance."

"I don't even like the sound of the word *insurance* anymore. What kind of insurance?"

"I removed four key volumes of the journals to a place for safe keeping."

"Where did you put them?"

"I'm giving them to Judge Glover."

"What interest does Judge Glover have in Hamrick's journals?"

"Hamrick had no relatives living in Bartram County, so Judge Glover is acting as the executor of his estate."

"Yeah, Barbara told me she has to see Judge Glover this morning."

"I'm due at his chambers in about ten minutes. I'll catch up with you a little later."

Barbara Hamrick was already in Judge Glover's chambers when Lee arrived. Without revealing to Judge Glover how she came by the volumes of Hamrick's journal, she gave him two of the volumes and explained to him and to Barbara Hamrick about the entire collection stored in Carters Mill University archives and of their potential value.

"I'm turning these two volumes over to you, Judge Glover, as executor of Dr. Hamrick's estate," Lee said, "so that his estate will have bargaining power in seeing that the question of the rightful ownership of his discoveries and inventions is established. I feel sure the University will be interested in protecting their interests. I want to be sure Mrs. Hamrick's and her son's interests are also protected."

"I see your point," Judge Glover said. "I duly receive and enter the two volumes into Dr. Hamrick's estate and will see that the question of ownership of patents is diligently pursued with the University. On the matter of Dr. Hamrick's life insurance policies, I have spoken with American Prudential Life Insurance Company and they inform me that payment of the one million dollars in death benefit from the whole-life policy will be paid to the beneficiary named on the insurance policy, namely you, Mrs. Hamrick. The transfer of the ownership of the policy to Millennium Viatical having been declared null and void. That settlement is to be made immediately in one lump payment."

"Thank goodness," Barbara said.

"I believe you owe most of the thanks to Dr. Turner," Judge Glover said.

"As to the matter of the property in Bartram County held jointly by Dr. and Mrs. Hamrick, title to that property is transferred automatically to you, free and clear, Mrs. Hamrick. If you will excuse me for a few minutes, I'll have all necessary papers and orders drawn up and witnessed."

Judge Glover left Lee and Barbara alone in his chambers. Then Lee did something her better judgment would never have allowed her to do, but her heart made her do it.

"Barbara," she said, "I love Buddy like a brother. He hasn't said anything directly to me but I know he has been tortured over something. I have absolutely no right to ask you this and beg your forgiveness even before I ask it. I'm asking only for Buddy's sake. Is there any chance your son could be Buddy's child?"

Barbara Hamrick didn't get angry. She didn't look shocked. She was suddenly very calm and looked straight into Lee's eyes.

"Yes, he is," she said. "Buddy doesn't know, Douglas doesn't know, and Alex didn't know."

"Buddy doesn't know it, but he feels it," Lee said.

"I thought it would never come up, never be an issue," Barbara said. "I don't know how to tell Buddy or Doug, or even if I should. Doug has only ever known one father, and that was Alex."

"How old is he now?"

"Nineteen."

"In the pictures of Douglas you showed me I could see Buddy in his face."

"So can I," Barbara said. "I can see Buddy in everything about him. But Buddy and I have grown so different over the past twenty years. I don't know that it would be fair to either one of them to tell them."

"I don't pretend to know anything about what Buddy was like or what you were like twenty years ago, but I know Buddy today. He is a trustworthy man. If you decide to tell him, he would handle the information like a trustworthy man. I can't tell you what to do. I don't even know what I would do. I just thought I should speak what Buddy is unable to speak for himself."

"I don't know. Douglas is in mourning over Alex. I don't know that I can spring something like this on him. I don't know what it would do to him."

"Now is probably not a good time," Lee said. "And a good time may not come anytime soon. But in life things happen. There may be a need in the future, for medical reasons or personal reasons or some reason we can't anticipate, that Douglas and Buddy will need to know their biological relationship. I'm not trying to force you to do anything. As I said, I care about Buddy and I felt as if I should represent him in some way."

"I understand," Barbara said. "We both care about Buddy."

Judge Glover came back with a packet of papers he gave to Barbara and she left, on her way back to Los Verdes.

"I have a related matter I need to discuss with you," Lee said to Judge Glover.

She took the two remaining volumes of Hamrick's journals from her briefcase.

"These look familiar," he said, leafing through their pages. "What am I to make of this?"

"It's my understanding that you are the chair of the trust set up by Carters Mill University for baby Elizabeth Morris."

"Yes, I am."

"I know President Caldwell has every intention that the trust will be fulfilled for its entire term, throughout the life of Elizabeth Morris. But I also know that to be a very long time, longer than Clifton Caldwell will be president of the University."

"And longer than I will be alive to be a trustee," Judge Glover said.

"These two volumes came into my possession as evidence during the investigation of the death of Luther Morris and his family. I want to turn them over to the trust for Elizabeth Morris, to be used by her trustees to her benefit." Lee offered them to Judge Glover.

"I'm going to ask you to hold on to those," he said. "I think the trust needs young, energetic blood to help it meet its obligations. I think you are just the person with the proper resources to take on that responsibility."

"You want me to be a trustee?" Lee asked.

"If you will accept."

"Yes, of course I will."

He gave her a folder.

"Here is a copy of the trust agreement. You will want that for reference. I'll have your name added to the list of trustees. You will receive notice of the time and place of the next meeting of the board. It should be interesting."

When Lee returned to her office there were two phone calls she needed to make. The first was to Ira Aaron in Chicago.

"Dr. Turner, very nice to hear from you. Do you have good news for us, I hope?"

"Your offer is very appealing, Ira. I've given it much consideration, but I'm going to have to say no."

"I'm very disappointed, of course, Lee. Is it the money? If it is, perhaps we can find a way."

"No, Ira. Your offer is very good. But I have longterm interests and obligations that require me to remain here. So I must say no. I thank you and the University for your consideration."

"I had hoped you were the one for us, Lee."

"It's best that we both know now rather than later. I'm sure there are well qualified candidates who will be a very good match for you."

"If you ever change your mind and want to leave Tennessee, please give me a call."

Her second call was more pleasant. The voice on the other end had a melodious roll to it.

"Rocky Mountain Bonding, where it's always spring time."

"Hello, Frank. It's Lee Turner. Thank you for the DNA sample and all the work you did on my behalf."

"As I said, it was my pleasure. You got away so quickly, I never had a chance to tell you, but I am originally a Southern boy myself."

"Are you?" Lee said. "I had pictured you as a gun-for-hire from the Old West."

Frank laughed a gentle and friendly laugh. "I may have come to resemble that in these later years. But I spent quite a few years of my innocent youth in and around Birmingham where I was born, and I lived for a while in Macon, Georgia during some interesting times."

"I never would have guessed. So do you get back to this area often?"

"From time to time. I inherited a little property, and I still have some family connections and a few old friends there."

There was a pause.

"I find myself in need of a vacation, Frank. Do you have a favorite place?"

Frank's voice began to sound like a big cat purring with delight. "This time of year I get to yearning for sunshine, warm breezes and the sounds of birds singing. The Barrier Islands off the coast of Georgia are nice. It's peaceful and quiet, eighty-two degrees, a pleasant breeze in the air, clear blue water, pure white sand, some wonderful little restaurants."

"About a week's restful bask in the sun would do wonders for me. Does that sound appealing to you?"

"It sounds like paradise to me."

"Can you recommend a hotel?"

"I have a condominium there. Why don't you use it?"

"Is it available, say day after tomorrow?"

"Funny thing, I was planning on going down there for a few days myself. I could show you the local attractions."

"Why don't you fax me directions?"

"I'll meet you at the airport."

Author Note

The authors lived in Oak Ridge, Tennessee during the period in which this novel is set. Many of the fictionalized locations portrayed in *The Poplar Creek Murders* were based loosely on real locations, but places were moved about and changed to suit the needs of the story. In no case are the portrayals of people, events or places in this novel to be taken as factual. This is a work of fiction. Names, characters, places, and incidents either are the product of the authors' imaginations or are used fictitiously. This novel, like all good fiction, was designed to be read purely for purposes of entertainment.

About the Authors

Charles Connor

Charles Connor grew up in Alabama in and around the little communities of Caffee Junction, Green Pond, and McCalla just outside Birmingham. He received B.A. and Masters degrees from the University of Alabama, attended graduate school at Vanderbilt and received a doctorate from the University of Georgia. He taught at several state universities in the southeast before joining the faculty at the University of Georgia where he founded the Harriette Austin Writing Program and the HAWC writing conference and directed them for twelve years before retiring from university life. He and his wife, novelist Beverly Connor, now live in Oak Ridge, Tennessee, The Secret City, home of the atomic bomb, 3D printers, and the world's fastest computer (or second fastest, it's a race). He is co-author of *The Poplar Creek Murders* and *Murder In Macon* with his wife Beverly.

Beverly Connor

Beverly Connor is the author of the Diane Fallon Forensic Investigation series, the Lindsay Chamberlain archaeology mystery series, and co-authored *Murder In Macon*, and *The Poplar Creek Murders* with her husband Charles. She holds undergraduate and graduate degrees in archaeology, anthropology, sociology, and geology. Before she began her writing career, Beverly worked as an archaeologist in the southeastern United States, specializing in bone identification and analysis of stone tool debitage. Originally from Oak Ridge, Tennessee, she weaves her professional experiences from archaeology and her knowledge of the South into interlinked stories of the past and present. Beverly's books have been translated into German, Dutch, and Czech and are available in standard and large print in the UK, and in ebook format worldwide. More information about Beverly Connor and her work can be found on her website at beverlyconnor.net. (You can visit Charles there, too).

Made in the USA
Lexington, KY
30 March 2018